# KATE KNIGHT'S
# ILLUSIO TEMPORIS

# THE ILLUSION OF TIME

All rights reserved, no part of this publication may be reproduced or transmitted by any means whatsoever without the prior permission of the publisher.
Text © Kate Knight

Cover image from the public domain modified by Veneficia Publications
Edited by
Veneficia Publications and Fi Woods
Additional editing Holly Knight

April 2023

ISBN: 978-1-914071-97-3

VENEFICIA PUBLICATIONS UK
veneficiapublications.com

*This book is dedicated to those who
I chose to be family*

CONTENTS

INTRODUCTION................................. ...i
THIS LIFE ........................................ III
EARLY TIMES ..................................... 1
LIVIA ................................................ 14
MY TWO DADS.................................38
JUNGLE LIFE....................................66
THE CURSE OF FAME ......................81
UNREQUITED LOVE ........................100
THE SIMPLEST LIFE .......................137
GHOSTS........................................... 166
THIRD EYE ......................................199
EGYPT..............................................226
THE OLD SOUL................................258
SILENT HELL ...................................264
MINI HARVEY ..................................312
BLOOD OF THE INNOCENT ...............374
SCARLET .........................................402
SEEKING JOY ..................................448

# INTRODUCTION

I have lived through many different lives and suffered a variety of deaths. I've lived to see several millennia go by, as a man, woman, and everything in between. I've lived in every country on planet Earth, from the arid deserts to the humid jungles, from crowded cities to isolated villages, and even lived a short life at sea. With *this* life, in particular, I am female and enjoying an adulthood of solitude and isolation. I just hope that it lasts for many more years, as this is by far one of my more favoured lives.

So far, since my adulthood began, this life has been uneventful, because not many lessons have been thrown my way, I'm enjoying the peace and quiet. Most of my time is taken up by doing what I love the most: reading books. It's the one hobby that always has something new to offer.

I have no need for history books as I have lived through most eras, so I only question their accuracy, which can be irritating at times. I love nothing more than delving into the unknown: into a mind filled with imagination and adventure. Often fairy tales have wonderful endings: love conquering all or battles won, which always warms my heart.

Some stories are written about discovering new worlds, which fascinates me, as the diversity of these worlds is as broad as the individual's imagination will allow.

My story is one that I cannot fit into a single book, or even a dozen. I have come to the conclusion that it is unique because, despite searching the globe, I have not yet found another person like me.

This is not to say that I smugly look down on others, puffing out my egotistical chest; on the contrary, I would love this life to eventually end in my death, and to have no memories when I wake in my next life. It would be even better to remain in what others describe as 'heaven'. I have seen glimpses of that paradise but not yet been able to get there. I expect that that road only flows one way, and my time has not yet ended. Perhaps it never will; it certainly feels that way.

From the beginning of what's known of human history, detailed memories have been cemented in my mind. Every sound and smell, every word I have ever spoken, and every word spoken to me. My eyes have seen several sights that I wish to forget, and some that warm my heart and still make me smile. I remember the roar of the ocean a thousand years ago, and the ever-changing echoes of the jungles as evolution worked its magic.

# THIS LIFE

Throughout my existence I have revealed my secret to only a few others, but so far, I've yet to find someone who can remember every life as I can. On the one hand, I hope I am alone with this curse, as I wouldn't wish it upon my worst enemy. Other times, I yearn for a companion who could jump from life to life with me, because there are times when I feel so alone. Leaving behind so many good friends, family, and partners is hard, especially when strong bonds have been created.

Sometimes I feel honoured to be able to fill my mind with so much information without my brain exploding, but mostly I wish for a way into that place beyond the darkness. I say 'darkness' but it is not quite so dark as I describe. I do have *some* choice, some of the time.

In my earlier lives I had no choice as to what my life would hold. I had trouble understanding what was occurring and thought that I was like everyone else. However, I am the one with a photographic memory, who is denied the ability to disregard the nightmares like my fellow man. I had to accept fairly quickly that I was alone with this curse, and pretty soon, I settled into the never-ending cycle of life and death. I began experimenting, just a little, between lives.

While waiting for my next life to begin, I tried to imagine myself as a man or a woman, tall or short, thin, or chubby. As far as my body is concerned it can be a personal choice, as long as my life can still accommodate what my mind pictures. For example, if my life lessons were to be found living amongst a pygmy tribe, I couldn't turn up and grow to seven foot tall. The rest is a little trickier, as my personality will come from my parents. In the life to come I may need to be confident or timid, laid back or angry. I may need to have an addictive personality or have some physical abnormalities. As to who foretells my coming lives, to me this is and always has been a mystery. All I know is that whatever they are doing, they are making sure I live every experience a human being possibly can.

I have lived in most eras, seen wars and famine, but I've also seen the golden age that brought greatness and prosperity to all human beings. These stories are only a sample of the lives I have lived. With every one, the age of my death varies but I have not yet reached the age of one hundred. Some of my lives I was far too eager to leave behind, only to be thrust straight back into them. Some lives didn't even begin. I can only assume those lives were given to me in error, or that my demise was part of someone else's lesson. I can only make assumptions, as I don't know for sure.

I've been known by many names, but those names that are remembered throughout history are because of my urge to change the way the world is. I have tried in the past to let my secret be known, but it usually ends in my death. I have been hung upside down by my leg and had wolves eat me from the head up. I've been burned as a witch, crucified, drowned, hung, drawn, and quartered. I have been beheaded and shot. I have been labelled a vampire, a prophet, a god, and even a monster, but we will come to that later in this book, or maybe those that follow.

One thing I can tell you now, is that time is an illusion. My life will begin at any era in the history of Earth and in any location. There is no order at all. I am here for a reason, whether I like it or not. Sometimes I must suffer to the point of breaking and learn to crawl back up on my hands and knees. My soul must live and experience every trauma and every emotion; you get the picture, I'm sure. I had conversed only once in the darkness, which gave me the reason for my everlasting journey; a reason that, to this day, I still have trouble coming to terms with.

At this very moment in time and in this specific life, which I am pretty sure will not be my last, I sit here in front of this laptop and explain what I know. This world has its own cycle of good and bad. It's something that has occurred for millions of years and will continue for millions more to come. I have lived thousands of lives and if I were to put them all in order, it all becomes clear. There are ages where everyone treats each other kindly and with respect, and there are times when those who wish to control do so in the most horrific ways, causing pain and suffering to those they view as undeserving.

This world has sheep and wolves, and it just depends on who has the loudest voice, who is the most convincing preacher, and who has the most treasure. All in all, most humans need to follow a leader, and sometimes that leader will supply their followers, with the rose-tinted glasses needed for their domination. The human mind is far more fragile than we all think.

I am now living my life in a house in a small town. As to where, I will not say for reasons of privacy. Outside my window I can see a man sitting on the path across the road. This man is cross-legged upon a blanket, in front of an empty shop that used to be Woolworths. It is raining, so he has moved his few belongings into the doorway to keep them dry. He looks to be around thirty-five, yet his hair is already turning grey. He is dressed in a torn puffer jacket, and tracksuit bottoms, which are badly stained and frayed in places. His shoes are held together with brown tape, and he has his hands wrapped around a cup of lukewarm coffee that the local cafe passed him ten minutes ago. As he sips the beverage, I know that the steam is not from the drink, but from his breath. It's cold outside, so cold that the clouds threaten a snow flurry. I can see by the way he has tucked his knees into his body and covered them with a thin woollen blanket that the chill air already threatens his well-being. His feet still tap furiously on the ground to keep the circulation flowing; the tips of his bare fingers are blue, even as they grasp the paper cup.

Men with long coats over designer suits, gripping briefcases, rush by wearing their leather gloves. It's almost like they are rubbing their wealth in this homeless man's face. They pretend not to notice him, as they hold their top of the range phones to their ears, muttering about deadlines and employees who need to work harder. The man in the doorway is a ghost to them, he is simply not their problem. What they will find out one day, is that everyone is everyone's problem. Whenever a powerful man falls, it is because of his cruelty. It's the cogs that turn the big clock: if the cogs are not looked after and treated fairly, they will cease to work properly.

What the rich men don't know is that the man in the doorway was once the manager of the shop behind him. Every day, he woke at the crack of dawn and opened the shop. He took care in his appearance and pride in his work. He began the job as a shelf stacker at the age of sixteen and worked his way quickly through the ranks.

His homelife was tough, having to care for his grandmother after his own parents abandoned him with her as a toddler. When she grew ill, he was the one who looked after his ageing grandmother, and he was proud to do so. His grandmother eventually died, but the man kept turning up to work although he was no longer so keen and eager to start the day. Eventually, the store closed, and the man could not keep up with the payments on his grandmother's house, so the bank came in and repossessed the property. The man tried to get help, but there is little help in this country for a young, single man.

Whether you are rich or poor, a lesson can come at any time and throw you off the pedestal that others place you on. Perhaps one day, the richest man on earth may be found in such a place, cold and alone, wondering what on earth happened to his empire. Warming his hands up on a lukewarm cup of tea, wishing he had treated people better.

This time, I had the choice of what gender I wanted to be, and so, in this life I am a woman. I feel that they are stronger in spirit. Apologies to all of the guys out there, but it tends to be true. I refuse to have children or a partner, because I have lived through motherhood many times already, and being a wife can be too tiring; the men I tend to attract are generally needy and unappreciative. I have no more love to give to a partner, even if someone were to pursue me.

My home has only two other occupants: my cats, who chose me. They were strays who came to my meadow to catch mice. We quickly became friends, and in time they followed me home. When they realised that my home was warm and I was generous with my food, they decided to move in. It's as simple as that. They are good company and I feel they somehow know me. Maybe from one of my previous lives, as I have been graced with the company of more than my fair share of cats over the years.

In one of my more recent lives, I used my knowledge to become wealthy on the stock market and then I started a business. This was one of many attempts, as I always hope that things will be different from the last time. I gave my wealth to people who deserved it, making a lot of them rich. I dragged those like that man outside Woolworths off the street and set them up with a home and a job, but they were soon begging for more.

I paid my workers handsomely, and they left my employment and started businesses of their own. I was happy for them, but they soon attacked me and my business. My wife left me after numerous affairs, and even my children turned out to be fathered by other men. Life was spiralling out of my control, and I became very unhappy. I left what remained of my wealth for another one of my lives to find, 'Just in case' I called it. I was eager to start again, so I took my own life. I'm not proud of that fact but, as I said before, I never learned some of the lessons put before me. No one knows of my wealth; in fact, no one knows I exist except for my utility providers, bank managers, the tax man and the woman who leaves my shopping on the doorstep on Friday. I do not leave the confines of my home because, even after all these years, there are still some things I'm afraid of.

My existence has left me with so much trauma that I am in desperate need of a rest. I'll call it 'A mental health holiday'. I think I've lived through just about everything, except for solitude and that is my life of choice this time: solitude. I just pray that this life will not burn off my skin like Nagasaki or drown me in lava like Pompeii. I feel safe from the world in my little house, but one can never tell if nature will decide that it wants to have a little party of its own, or, indeed, whether mankind will decide that it fancies throwing a few bombs around. The walls in this old house are thick, but not indestructible.

In this life, all I ask for is a holiday from fear and hatred, evil and murder, rape, and betrayal. In this one I just want peace. The one demon I face is boredom, so I'm writing a book, if only to pass the time. Maybe I will publish it, I haven't decided yet. Maybe I will just hide it somewhere, so I can pick it up again in another life. I'm swayed more into letting it loose, just out of interest, as I have no need for fame and fortune. I will find out, maybe in my next life, if the name I used is lit-up brightly on the internet. I very much doubt it will be, as there are so many wonderful books out there. I'm not sure what I will call myself, because every name has been taken from one of my lives. Maybe I will use my cat's names: Spike and Buster. Hmm ... Spike Buster ... Buster Spike. Maybe not. I'll think of something, I'm sure. In this life I have a name that has been given to me twelve times already, maybe this will be lucky thirteen.

My home is just big enough for me and my cats. It has a well-stocked kitchen, a bathroom with shower, and a comfortable living-room. My bedroom overlooks my garden, which is my only extravagance. My garden stretches far and at the bottom is a meadow, which I own. I let it grow wild to accommodate my thirteen beehives. I plant flowers and shrubs, fruits, and vegetables, which I spend my days caring for.

There's a small plum tree at the end of the garden, which I planted when I first arrived. The fruits are so juicy and sweet that I make enough jam to last me through the winter. The excess I leave on my front garden wall for passers-by to take for free. They knock sometimes to thank me, but I never reply. They do yell sometimes, through the letterbox, that my jams are the best. Of course, they are; I learned how to make jam properly in around 107 BC, from a lady named Malanya.

I have no need for plumbers or electricians, painters, or decorators. I have mastered every skill life has to offer, even those lost to time and denied to those living in this era. Sadly, sharing this knowledge may get me into trouble so, in fear of my peace being shattered, I will have to keep them to myself. Well ... who knows ... I may throw in a few hints. If there is something new that I have not yet learned then my old friend, the internet, will show me how.

At birth, I was blessed with a loving, single mother and being her only child, she nurtured me for as long as she could, before cancer took her at an early age. Since then, my only human company has been my reflection.

I don't know how long this life will last, but I only hope that the end will be peaceful, even if it does end with my bones being discovered years later, my flesh having been eaten by my hungry felines. I have fitted a cat flap just in case.

I suppose by now you may have guessed I have a lot to talk about. My mother used to say that I rambled on so much that she went to bed every night with my voice ringing in her ears. Being alone for 30 years, I have far too many memories to catch up on, so I'd better get going with my story and stop rambling.

# EARLY TIMES

I remember my very first life: the endless thudding of my mother's heart; the whooshing as the blood raced through her veins; the feeling of the warm, viscous fluid surrounding my small body; and the touch of the leathery, twisted cord that I used to pinch with my tiny fingers. My soul joined my small body in my mother's womb when I had already formed my spindly limbs. All at once my brain began taking note of every small detail, even those that had little significance. I had no idea of what was to come next, things simply were what they were. As my hearing developed, the faint murmurs of voices scared me at first, especially when they became louder, but I soon learned that with a quick kick of a foot or a stretch of my spine the voices slowed and became quieter. The end of my stay in that watery kingdom came with the shrill sound of my mother's screams and the racing beats of her heart. My surroundings tensed and the waters escaped in one swift rush below my head. The walls of my space compressed my body to the point that I could feel the blood gathering in my head; the pressure behind my eyes made it feel as though they were about to explode.

I remember those cold, bony hands that hooked themselves under my chin. They pulled me from the darkness and rested me upon a bed of fur. Suddenly my small world expanded infinitely. I drew in my first gasp of air, but coldness took my breath away and made me scream. Hearing that deafening noise escaping my body frightened me even more. I wanted to return to the warmth of my sanctuary, but my body was helpless. I will never forget the blurred face of that old woman as she wrapped my naked body in the soft pelt; all except for my left foot, which hung from the bottom and captured the chill of my surroundings. I can still clearly picture being brought to my first bare breast and the feeling of the engorged nipple tickling my lips. The urge to open my mouth and draw out the warm, comforting milk that filled my mouth and belly seemed only natural. The sweetness felt like liquid energy on my tongue, quickly overwhelming any thoughts of fear and lulling me into a calmer place. I remember wanting more whilst young and it was usually available. All I needed to do was make a noise and turn my head towards the person that smelt of warm milk. This person was my whole world. My mother.

The feeling of being sleepy and safe, snuggled into my mother's arms and being gently rocked, was the greatest feeling of all. The sensation of her lips as they kissed my head and her gentle touch as she stroked my soft face. The tune she hummed to get me to sleep and the way she tenderly tapped my back in time with her song. I can picture her now: her brown eyes, matted hair, and heavy brow; her arms embracing me tightly. I felt truly and unconditionally loved—a feeling that became addictive, and as I grew older, I stayed close to her. We lived in a small round room, built with wood, mud, and stone. The entrance was covered with animal skin that flapped when the wind blew. My mother covered the floor with fresh leaves every day. The room was bare, but there was little we needed: a meal every so often, and a pile of leaves and fur to sleep upon. I recall the grinding pain in my knees as I pulled myself to my feet, using my mother's leg as she knelt on the floor. The joy in her expression when I clapped my hands together for the first time or had the courage to take my first steps. The ache in my gums as teeth pushed through the flesh and the agony in my right heel when a rodent bit me. Other people came to our round room to watch me take my first wobbly steps; their teeth showing as they smiled. They pinched my cheeks and scooped me up as they spoke words I could not understand. I was not interested in them; they were intruders invading that invisible bond that I had created with my mother and *only* my mother.

I remember the yellow and orange skies filled with birds, and the trees that reached so high into the clouds. Most of the day I was resting on my mother's hip, sometimes other people would carry me. Every time we went out of the home, I'd point at animals and objects in search of an explanation as to what they were or why they existed. A tiny bug with a hundred legs or a flying insect with bright green wings: what was the point of them? Why did they look so strange? Great beasts that pulled foliage from the ground mostly ignored us. I remember hearing the sounds from within the trees, the deep groaning that echoed for miles around. I remember the open fire and the smell of cooking, the sounds of laughter and, sometimes, heated discussions.

I remember the shouts of men as they ran to the trees with spears in their hands. My mother scooped me into her arms, cradled my head and ran back to the safety of the hut. From over her shoulder, I saw a man flying through the air, slamming his back on a tree trunk. He fell to the floor in a heap, screaming in pain.

That life did not last much longer. My last memory was the terrified screams of others, outside our little round room. The frightened look etched on my mother's face as she pulled me closer and closed her eyes. The scared feeling as the curved structures of the roof of our room cracked and collapsed on us both. The last sounds I heard were the roaring of a large animal and spears hitting the ground. That's when my world went black for the first time.

It was dark, yet I could feel a rushing sensation, as if I was being pushed and pulled through space and time. The fuzziness that tingled like electricity engulfed my soul, but my body no longer existed. I had been torn away from my flesh and from the life that I had been living. I heard no sound and had no control over my movements. My soul was floating in what I can only describe as a space of nothing, just pure energy. I could feel other souls rushing past me, and sometimes we collided, while other times my soul passed straight through them. Our lack of control prevented it from being a race; we were all literally *energy*. When we arrived at our destination, we waited. Some travelled on, some travelled back, and some just hovered like a dandelion seed on a still day. In an instant it felt as though I was falling, and fast, but fear didn't overwhelm me. Some of the others fell alongside me, only for us to part ways soon after. The end was approaching, and with a bright flash of light everything stopped.

I was back in that familiar dark space again: that warm, viscous liquid with those echoing sounds that soon became hypnotic. I waited, clinging to my cord, for that space to become tighter and that liquid to escape before me, once again. As I waited, I wondered if this womb belonged to the same mother; were we starting again? Was this to be a rerun of my last existence? I was confused and filled with questions, which ultimately took lifetimes to answer. Some I still ask today.

Most of my earlier lives did not last long. Sickness, disease, and birth complications took me far too soon. Sometimes my life ended along with those who carried me, before I even ventured outside of the womb. But every so often, my life would go on long enough for a story to be told.

It was strange that in one life I grew up in a world where the land was dark, the clouds covering the sunlight in a thick, grey blanket. On the odd occasion when the sun *did* emerge, it was a time for celebration. The reality was that the climate was so very different in those early years. Volcanic activity was more frequent and harder to escape from. If the wind blew the wrong way, the smoke clouds blotted out the sun for months at a time. Our crops would fail, leaving the hunting of animals as our only option for survival. When the animals died of starvation, we followed shortly afterwards. Our demise mostly came from the predators, as we were not fast runners. Our only advantage was our weapons, which required skill as well as speed and strength. Speed and strength are quickly taken away when you're starving—so is the will to survive. We discovered that there was safety in numbers, which helped, and we travelled far and wide to avoid the dark skies. We followed the animals who migrated towards more forgiving climates; we figured that they knew something that we didn't, and this usually paid off.

My first hunt was when I was a boy of around four years old. I stood by my father's side, clutching a small bow steadily in my hand. My two fingers pulled back the string, as I looked down the shaft of my home-made arrow tipped with a flint head. I watched quietly, as the small rabbit-like creature carelessly nibbled on the undergrowth. The air was still, so it had no idea I was pointing this deadly weapon at its soft fur. The animal's long ears twitched, but we remained still and silent, camouflaged in the brush. I held my breath as my father gave me the cue to shoot. My fingers released and the arrow shot out towards the creature. It was as if time slowed down, almost to a stop, as I watched that arrow pierce the air. My thoughts began to race. What if ... What if the animal had a nest filled with tiny babies, reliant on the return of their mother? What if we were taking a meal away from the next creature who was starving to death? What if it had a belly filled with young? The arrow continued its flight, and regret filled my thoughts as I released my breath. My eyes widened as the arrow punctured the creature's skin. It spun on the spot and leaped into the air in shock, but it was too late. I gasped as the flint head pierced through its spine and exited through the left side of its neck. I felt like screaming as the guilt filled my body. I wished to take back the last few moments—but I couldn't.

Time caught up with itself as the creature fell to the floor. Its back leg was still kicking and twitching, its mouth widening as it gasped for breath.

"Well done, boy," said my father.

His heavy, calloused hand rested upon my shoulder as he spoke. He strolled over to the animal and grabbed it by the ears. It squealed one last time, so my father held the head and twisted it. I remember hearing the crack as its neck snapped in two, then the animal fell limp and lifeless to the ground.

"Gotta put the poor thing out of its misery."

My father always said very little, but the few words he *did* say explained everything that a young boy needed to know. Like me, he had compassion for the poor creature, but its flesh would feed our family that evening, and its pelt would be used to keep us warm. He tied a leather strap around its ears and attached it to his belt. By the time we arrived home, that small animal was accompanied by three more; they swung like pendulums with every step he took.

My mother and two sisters awaited our return, in our small dwelling built from branches and clay. She had built a small fire in the clearing and was eager to greet us. Her expression lifted when she saw my father and I return, nodding with satisfaction on seeing our bounty. My father untied the carcasses from his belt and handed them over to her. Mother kissed him on the cheek and carried our kills at arm's length into the house. A while later she re-appeared with four red, skinless carcasses, which she hung over the fire to cook.

As I watched them change from red to brown, I thought of that sweet, little, fluffy creature and wondered if we had the right to take its life. I imagined what it would be like to live in a burrow and never be hungry, having an abundance of foliage covering the forest floor. I was reluctant to eat into its flesh, yet the grumbles of my empty stomach easily persuaded me. One day I asked my father why we had to kill just to eat, and his answer was simplistic, as expected:

"We eat because if we do not, we will die. Man cannot live on greens alone, my son. Meat will make us strong."

He may have been a simple man, but I know that he loved us all. He was one of the better fathers that I had in my time.

It was during a fishing trip that my father met his end. As we patiently waited with our spears for a large fish to swim by, a hungry bear appeared from the trees. The bear did not hesitate and leapt on my father, knocking him into the water. He quickly scrambled to the bank as the bear approached me, and he stood tall waving his arms high above his head, roaring his loudest. His method failed him this time. I raised my spear and aimed the tip at the bear's head and tossed it with all my strength. My father watched as the spear passed him by, but the flint only penetrated the flesh and bounced off of the bear's thick skull. The beast grew angry and lunged for my father's throat with its teeth bared and claws extended. I tried to help, but the bear was far too strong. My father's last words were muted by the animal's ferocious growls. It was only afterwards that I realised what he was trying to say. The words that left his lips were easy to read, yet my brain chose to ignore them:

"Run, my boy! Run!"

I didn't run, instead I stood by helplessly as my father was mauled to death. Unbeknown to me, the bear was a mother of two almost fully-grown cubs that were watching and learning hunting skills. I was to be the cubs' first victim and their efficiency was second to none—my life was over almost instantly. I do not know what happened to my mother and sisters; I wasn't there to see.

Those times were unforgiving, and we held no hierarchy over the creatures that roamed the earth. We were on the menu for many creatures, and only those with skill and a great deal of luck lived to reach an old age. Even raising a child past the age of five was an accomplishment. Human children are weak and powerless for the first few years of their lives and could burden those who cared for them. I'm sad to say that sacrifices of the weaker children were often made to give the stronger children a better chance of survival. Back then, life was only gifted to the strong, but looking back, that's all part of evolution: survival of the fittest.

My greatest achievement in those early lives happened during a time when I was a woman. My dominance attracted many strong men who offered me protection whilst I raised my children. I birthed seventeen in that life, fathered by whoever I chose, and raised the five boys and three girls who survived infancy. We lived high in the mountains where most predators could not reach us; our home was within the caves where we built fires to keep out the cold. We were blessed with the conditions suitable to sustain life. I lived until my children grew old enough to live their own lives and died at around the age of forty with a child still in my womb. I'm unsure how. I just went to sleep feeling a little tired and woke up in the darkness. Love did not come into it back then. We coupled to create life, usually with the strongest to ensure good, healthy babies. Sometimes it worked in our favour, sometimes it did not. The men were the ones who protected the young, because the infants were so incapable of defending themselves. The women were the caregivers, not only raising the children but also giving aid to the injured and preparing the kills for the fire.

These days, men and women play an equal role in society, but times have changed a great deal. Our only predator is disease, which we cure with medicine, and even the weakest of children have a fair shot at life. The struggles of the early years of human life made us who we are today. Humans still cling to a lot of the traits of the past, but now they have a choice. A woman has a choice about being a mother, and most still choose to have children. Some take other roads, though, and pursue different goals. Some men still feel that they need to protect and hunt, but some prefer to pursue other avenues. Ultimately, we find our place in society and these days the doors are open wide. Every trait a human owns comes from a time where choice was not an option. We had to do what we did just to survive. Our brains weren't capable of much else. The cave drawings you see today are just the beginning of humans' creative spark and look how far we have come. All we need to do is look around at the beauty mankind has created. We must still survive in this life, but in different ways to before: finding an income and keeping a certain level of sanity, for example. Some struggle more than others, but those people usually find themselves alone. It's easier to survive in larger groups, and to live in a place where the conditions are favourable. It's so much harder when you are alone. We are pack animals and work better together.

      Sadly, there are those in this life that regard themselves as predators. Those people are the ones who think nothing of causing physical or emotional pain. It is because of people like this that the weaker among us feel the need to hide away in solitude. They fear pain and don't understand that not everyone wants to cause harm, but trust is broken so easily and can take a lifetime to heal.

# LIVIA

The first time I fell in love was when I was only fifteen years old. I was born a girl in a city built of granite, where ornate columns held up buildings with curled knuckles, and every floor was decorated with intricate mosaics. The structures gleamed, with the pale stone that could almost blind you on a sunny day if you were outside for too long. The streets were decorated with statues of beautiful Gods and Goddesses, adorned in simple togas. Some of the wealthier people lived in houses that had been built with great slabs included in the exteriors. These slabs flaunted carved scenes, showing men and women in their naked form. The penis was a sign of strength, whereas the breasts were usually seen as a sign of innocence and purity, but also motherhood. The naked form was something that was rarely hidden in this era. Sex wasn't only a way to produce the next generation, but it also offered pleasure, fun, and sometimes sport.

Ancient olive trees bore fruits that tasted anything from bitter to earthy, depending on their colour, which ranged from green to the deepest black. The dry leaves rustled with every passing breeze, like a flock of birds taking flight all at once. The flagged streets were lined with gutters which carried the rain into storage, to ensure that we never felt the pain of thirst. The weather was usually sunny and warm, but the heat could become overpowering at certain times of the year. We dressed in loose, linen togas and mostly wore our hair tied up neatly off our shoulders. We wore sandals made from hide, and sometimes we decorated our hair and clothing with foliage, depending on the trends of the time. The city seemed to be reasonably civilised, but we did have a substantial rich/poor divide.

In the centre of our city was a great stone colosseum; it was surrounded with arches, and each housed a grand marble statue. They were carved with so much detail that if it wasn't for their brilliant white complexion, one would think they were real. Every so often, the people of the city were called to gather there. Men, women, and children filled the stands, chanting and cheering as gladiators murdered slaves, and each other, spilling the blood of innocence on the yellow sands. I thought back to hunting with my gentler father in a past life, and how I became comfortable with killing in order to eat. Now, I was watching men murder, and being murdered, for sport and blood lust. The rise and fall of mankind in only a few dozen lifetimes. I had my first epiphany: it seemed clear that when surrounded by riches, mankind compromised their more basic emotions. The one that suffered the most was empathy: it seemed absent in this city. There were a few exceptions among the population who *didn't* enjoy watching death occur yards from where they sat, but they were seen as strange and unusual. They were the outcasts; the ones who prayed silently over the log pyres that they had painstakingly built in order to send the slayed victims to the gods.

Being a woman in those times was hard, and with so little nobility in our household I was viewed as a disappointment for not being born with testicles. I sat in the audience of the colosseum many times with my father. It wasn't by choice, but choices were not made by eight-year-old girls. My father was a mean and strict man, and always appeared to see joy in my tears. He found pleasure in shouting along with the chanting crowd whenever one man, dressed in the finest leather armour, thrust a sword through the stomach of another. The fight was never fair: the opponent was usually unarmed and wearing nothing more than a loin cloth. He stood no chance as the gladiator sliced open his abdomen with his oversized, sharpened sword. The slave's intestines spilled onto the sands, his head was brutally detached from his body and rolled a few yards away. His face still twitching, his eyes flitting to and fro, while his blood and sweat was soaked up by the sand. Huge carnivorous birds circled the skies and waited patiently for the stands to empty so they could pick up a free meal. The smaller birds did not wait, risking their own lives to pluck out the eyes of the victims with their dagger-like beaks. In the beginning, I turned my head away when a sword struck, but my father grew angry and insisted I watch. He physically held my face towards the carnage, squeezing my cheeks between his fingers and thumb and yelling at me to open my eyes. He claimed that it toughened me up to the world. I was afraid of him: he had strength in his arms and a temper that had killed before. He was very dominant and bloodthirsty, staying alive in his household was a challenge in itself. I saw him once, opening up the throat of a slave-boy who was only ten. He had stolen a piece of fruit from father's leftovers without asking permission. My stepmother feared him just as much. She spent her days running around with her head bowed, honouring his every whim no matter how difficult she found the task. She was only a little older than me and had already suffered years of torture from her own father. She was mute—mostly.

My father made no secret of going out in the evenings to the baths, to 'play' with his male companions. He'd return with wine-stained clothing, marks on his neck after being sucked on, and blood stains down the back of his legs. Sometimes he'd drag my stepmother upstairs and have sex with her immediately afterwards, giving her infections which caused her so much pain for days after. I would always hear her scream in agony during sex and find her weeping while washing her intimate parts afterwards.

He saw me as a weakling and a disappointment because I was born a girl, and not the son he always wanted to carry his name. His new wife was expected to give him his son but, despite my father's persistence, he had no other children besides me. My only use as a woman was as a bargaining chip, to be sold as a wife to a man of greater standing, in the hope that father would gain greater notoriety.

"Women are here to have children. I have no other interest in their existence" was one of his favourite sayings.

I was sold to an older, wealthy man a week before I turned fourteen. The news spread around town quickly that only a week before, he had slit his last wife's throat for giving birth to a stillborn baby. She was classed as unworthy and being that the child was a son, she had committed the greatest insult to a man of such stature. I did not know of my place in the home until I arrived, accompanied by my father. Without explanation, he gripped my wrist and dragged me through the streets to a huge ornate door, beautifully carved with fruit and leaves. He banged on the door and stood impatiently on the step. A tiny waif of a woman, who wore a loose-fitting, saffron toga opened the heavy door. Her breasts sagged down to her waistline and her scraggly white hair hung over her bony shoulders. She looked like she should have shaken hands with death long ago, but here she was, wrinkled like a ripened prune and smelling of dust and urine. Her lips had all but disappeared and her eyes had sunk deeply into her skull. She was quick to inform me that I was to take the place of her son's murdered wife. Her ashes were still warm on the pyre and the stain of her blood still visible on the mosaic flooring. He was keen to move on and felt no remorse for what he had done.

      The woman placed a small bag of coins into my father's open hand, and they exchanged a few unwritten promises before he left. I thought that maybe father might have said goodbye, showing me a spark of tenderness or regret, but he simply walked away, satisfied with the price this woman paid for me. My first job was to get down on my hands and knees and scrub the blood from the tiny tiles as a lesson not to repeat the previous wife's errors. My second was to get busy producing a male heir, but I was not yet a woman. This displeased both my husband and my mother-in-law, but they had been assured by my father that I would flower at any time because my breast buds were beginning to develop.

I was taught how to cook and clean by my mother-in-law, even though I already possessed the skill to a much greater level than her. She made unrealistic demands, which required treating her precious son like a king, with foot rubs and massages using scented oils and powders. I had to remind him of how extraordinary and handsome he was, despite him slouching over the table looking like a balding bullfrog. Most of the time he was gnawing on the leg of a goat, drool seeping from the corner of his mouth, whilst his mother fussed over him. I knew from my past lives that a woman had just the same rights to live on this earth as a man, but sadly not in this life. The voice of one woman, in a land overrun by dominant men with knives tucked in their pockets, would only end one way: my death. Knowing these humans, it would be horrific, and no doubt require an audience. I knew straight away that women were not his preference either. Like my father, he would look away whenever I entered the room and make excuses when it was time to lay with me. His mother demanded that I expose my breasts and fondle his manhood whenever we were together, which was strange to say the least. Fearing that my own throat would be sliced like the last wife, I did pursue him on one occasion, if only to shut her up for a while.

He lay asleep in his bed, twitching as he dreamt. I entered the room carrying a fresh linen toga for the morning and saw his engorged penis laying across his belly. I had lain with men many times in previous lives, so I well knew that the first time in a new body hurt. It would be especially painful as I was still so young; although I had the figure of a girl, I was expected to be a woman.

The room was lit by the full moon and the cotton curtains billowed in the cool evening breeze. He was not attractive to me in the slightest, so I did my best to avoid looking at his pitted, rounded face. My fingers touched the spidery vein that wrapped his fair-sized penis. It startled me as it twitched, but I wrapped my hand around it to feel the stiffness in my palm. It felt so solid that I thought it was made of stone. He woke up as soon as I moved my hand; he pushed me away and yelled obscenities at me.

"Get out you little whore. I will not lay with another poisonous wretch, especially not the likes of you."

He struck me across the face, and I fell to the floor.

He threw himself out of bed, got dressed, and left shortly afterwards, stomping out of the house in a rage. I hid myself away the following day, in fear of my blood being spilt by either my husband or my mother-in-law. The bruise across my face was clearly visible but was never mentioned by anyone. My husband and I never spoke of this incident. In fact, we did not speak again at all, which was perfectly fine by me.

Love *did* find me in that lifetime, and it hit me like a speeding train. It was certainly not with him, but with the beautiful and graceful Livia. She was his daughter from the first of many wives. Her mother had died in a more natural way, while giving birth to her. Livia was a little older than me and the kindest, gentlest woman I had ever met. I instantly fell in love with her; her deep brown eyes showed me kindness with every glance, and she had a warm smile which gently wrinkled the corners of her eyes and made little indents in her rosy cheeks. Her sweet face made my heart pound whenever she looked my way, and she knew it. She teased me all the time, taking my hand in hers and leading me to her room, laying me on her bed like I was the companion she always wanted. She was wise in the world of sex and taught me how to lie with a man and give him pleasure in more ways than just orally. I was already a graduate in the art of sex, but I let her teach me anyway, if only because I enjoyed her company.

Her room overlooked the home of an amorous couple, and she liked to watch them make love to each other and with strangers. Sometimes they held parties that ended in group orgies where anything was possible. The sight of Livia's soft, pale nipple cheekily and purposefully peeking out from the side of her toga sent my erotic thoughts into a frenzy. She explained that if I touched certain parts of my body I would flower and discover feelings that I didn't know existed. I sat and listened like I was clueless and learning lessons from the great sex therapist, Livia, and she seemed to enjoy teaching and touching me. When I had my first bleed, I was fifteen and our relationship had bloomed into romance. We lay together most nights, as my husband was occupied entertaining his gentlemen friends in our marital bed. We embraced from sunset till sunrise, her naked body alongside my own. Her soft lips kissed the nape of my neck even when she was dreaming. She liked to lie behind me and cup my blossoming breasts in her bare hands. The first time she said she loved me it made me feel as if I were floating on a cloud to the realm of the Gods. I loved her too and had told her many times that I had loved her since I first saw her angelic smile. I was content with this life and despite its complications, I was happier than I had ever been.

  My husband blamed me for his lack of interest, for not being attractive and not having the experience he required from a wife. To his friends and colleagues, he claimed to bed me at least three times a week. It was my job to keep up with the masquerade and appear to the outside world to be a doting wife. When the doors were closed, we were strangers; this life suited us all. My love affair with Livia was uninterrupted; my mother-in-law knew about us, but as we couldn't possibly conceive children, she had no need to break up our romance. I was seen as Livia's distraction, as she was a rare beauty sought after by many men. Several suitors from our town alone fought for her affections, but the only love that she wanted was mine. She adored me and I adored her even more.

One humid evening, Livia and I were enjoying some time together in her room and began a conversation about our futures, and what we would do with our lives if men did not dominate our world. She fancied herself in the world of an artist: painting the walls of the rich with scenes of nature and sunny coastlines, fair maidens, and laughing children. I loved her ideas; her plans would have really suited her personality. She loved to paint and was extremely talented. My thoughts took me back to a previous life when I loved nothing more than planting my gardens. When it was my turn, I made the mistake of saying a sentence which she didn't understand, and it triggered unwanted questions. It started with 'In my last life,'; a slip of the tongue, but one that she sternly asked me to explain. My trust in her was great, so I thought that she would accept the truth as it was, and cautiously I told her what my existence entailed. She sat silently, listening to what I had to say. When I had finished her response was not good:

"It's not right. When you die you go to the underworld and that is that. Any other person would have assumed that you are evil or insane. I love you but I fear that you have been touched by great evil as I know that you are far from mad."

She glared at me with an expression that I could not have imagined possible; her face was usually of love and admiration for me. She shook her head, with tears cascading down her porcelain skin, and demanded that I leave her room and never return. I was utterly heartbroken and begged her to let me stay, but she threw herself face-down onto her bed.

"Just go!"

Her yell was muffled, but clear enough. I left with a promise that I'd return when she'd had time to calm down.

With my face buried in my pillow, sobbing profusely as my heart broke, I heard a commotion coming from the direction of her room. It seemed that her father had brought a man from his workplace home. I wiped away my tears, rushed to my door, and pressed my ear against the wood.

"Well?"

"Oh yes. She is very beautiful, very beautiful indeed."

"May I try her out before I make a decision?"

"Of course, go ahead. Shall I leave you to it?"

"Oh, come now. We are friends, are we not? Stay, enjoy."

A few moments later I heard Livia squeal and her bed creak as the man lay with her. The sounds of grunting and the cries of her discomfort filled me with rage, as the stranger sampled his potential new bride.

I was powerless: I wanted to rush out and pull him off her, but I could never win against two full-sized men. Livia was being raped and crying out for me, but there was nothing I could do to help her. I would be killed in an instant, and my death would do nothing to stop what was happening to her.

That night, my Livia was taken away from me, without a chance to even say goodbye or ask if she was okay. The man in question exchanged promises of good fortune to my husband and left, dragging my beautiful Livia behind him by her wrists. I ran to the window and watched the man stumble down the path. Livia's head was bowed, and her spirit broken.

When morning came, my mother-in-law informed me of Livia's fate. My husband had been at the baths as usual the previous night;

his boss had accompanied him and spoke of his intentions to claim a new wife. His old one had vanished; I expect she had run away, and he was eager to replace her. My husband saw his opportunity to increase his status and offered up his daughter, Livia.

Within a year her first pregnancy was clearly visible: her swollen belly protruding from her flowing toga. She never spoke to me again, despite my efforts. I saw her in the market on several occasions, tapping the back of a loaf of bread and delicately placing it in her basket. Her golden head-dress sat buried in her auburn hair, as she smiled and made small talk with the baker's wife. She was married to one of the richest men in our city and blessed him with sons as well as daughters. I always watched her from afar; I never stopped loving her. I was afraid, though, that she might tell my secret. I feared that my life would end just as she had said: in the jaws of those lions. I have seen what they can do to a *man* in only a few short minutes, let alone someone like *me*.

One day, after a difficult pregnancy, Livia was gone from this life, along with a twin baby girl who did not draw breath. A grand pyre was built in their honour. Her surviving twin boy and six other children were motherless, and her husband was searching for a new wife and mother to his children. I remember looking up to the sky as the smoke swept past our roof, that familiar cork-like smell had the scent of honeysuckle. I whispered to her spirit as it hovered in the air above me:

"Goodbye my sweet goddess. We will meet again, one day."

Livia's children were all beautiful, like their mother, and after her death they began to visit our home for supper. I felt myself becoming attached to them and began to imagine that they were mine and Livia's. I felt blessed that at least I had a little part of my love to comfort me in my grief.

I dream of Livia sometimes, even today. Her glowing smile and soft, pale cheeks still appear in my thoughts from time to time. When the evening sun is warm and the skies are blue, I like to take a walk into my meadow and lie in the long grass. I kick off my shoes, feel the foliage between my toes, and think of my Livia. I imagine her lying beside me, as she used to. We'd tell stories, complement each other, and just enjoy being ourselves. She'd make me laugh with her silly ways and terrible jokes and we'd sing together as the sun began to set. We first confessed our love whilst lying in the long grass in the fields surrounding our great white city. That field was also where we had our first kiss, which was beautiful. Although I have fallen in love many times over many lives, I am not ashamed to say that she is the one I am most fond of. My Livia who awaits me in the place beyond; her long auburn hair resting on her milky white breasts, lying in that summer field waiting for me to lie beside her. I'm afraid that I will never see her again, and she will grow tired of my absence. People say that you never forget your first love; it's certainly true for me. She was in my life over seven hundred lifetimes ago, but I still remember her like it was only yesterday.

    I did not bear a child in that life and, once again, I looked death in the face before old age crept up on me. At only twenty-four, my husband grew tired of the mutters and stares from his suspicious fellow bath-mates and co-workers. He was always the passive recipient at this point, and let's just say the equipment was a little flaccid, probably due to his age.

    He sent me on an errand accompanied by my haggard mother-in-law who hobbled alongside me, still refusing to die, to the home of a gladiator who had earned his freedom. After successfully battling in the arena for five years he had earned his Rudis, which was a wooden sword. Rudis were awarded for greatness, and they also signified freedom. This man had earned his by slaying twenty men in one fight. His victims were armed with weapons of their choosing; he, on the other hand, held only a four-foot-long plank of wood. He was the prized bull as far as breeding was concerned and had probably fathered half of the city's children under the age of two.

The home we arrived at was built to accommodate someone such as he, with oversized doors and steep steps. I had heard whispers that he was a giant: the product of a mating between an earthly woman and a God, but I knew how mutterings could be exaggerated. As I stood in the doorway with the half-dead woman, I felt the hand of fear rest upon my shoulder. My head told me to run and never stop running, but I stayed, frozen to the spot. The latch clicked and the door swung open to reveal a goliath of a man, the size of four grown men, standing on two giant bare feet. He was covered from head to toe in scars. One of them still showed signs of healing, probably from a more recent brawl. It stretched from his right temple down his cheekbone and seeped with yellow pus. His facial features were hidden by a mouth filled with rotting teeth and a disfigured nose, which had clearly been broken in several places. His left eye had been blinded, showing only a ghostly white glaze that seemed to chew up your soul and spit it onto the dusty floor. His menacing smile extended outwards, yet his eyes showed nothing, but evil intent and it terrified me.

My mother-in-law led me into his home and purposefully hovered her walking stick in my path causing me to stumble. I fell onto the floor close to the enormous gladiator. She handed him some silver coins and demanded the job be done by noon when she would be back to collect me. The man nodded silently and slammed the door shut in her face. He ignored me at first and sat at his table on a wooden bench that creaked under his weight. He picked up a wooden goblet of water and quickly drank what remained. I shuffled my way into the corner of the room and gripped my bent knees in fear. I had never been penetrated by a man that size before. I was terrified because he was so much bigger than I was. The room had an odour that I can only describe as the smell of death: a stench that most likely clung to his skin from years of murder and rape. Dark stains still covered his clothing, which had stiffened in places as the blood dried.

    The liquid from his goblet flowed down his throat in deep gulps until it was empty. He belched loudly and slammed it down so violently that a small dust cloud wafted up from beneath the table legs. He leant back on his wooden bench, stretched out his back, and released a stentorian roar. He slowly turned to look at me, with his giant hands resting on his hips. I tried in vain to wish myself invisible, melting away into the corner with the spider webs, but his one good eye glared at my weeping face without compassion. I could not help but pray for him not to hurt me, I was so much smaller than he was; his great stature towered over me like a mountain, and I had nowhere to run, no way that I could escape. He had the strength to snap my body like a twig if I even attempted freedom. He grinned with his rancid teeth and groaned deeply like a dragon's growl, while his singular white eye grasped hold of my bravery and ripped it away like it didn't exist. I had no choice; I had to accept my fate and hope that I would survive.

    The next few moments seemed like they happened in a single blink of an eye. He lunged my way and grabbed the hair on the back of my head; he yanked me up from the ground, effortlessly lifted my small frame like I was made of air and threw me headfirst onto the table. I shrieked loudly as my world blurred before my eyes. When he slammed me down, my head collided with the goblet, shattering the wood into a thousand shards. Splinters pierced into the skin of my cheeks and temple and a sharp unforgiving pain followed. My vision faded into a haze and the room began to spin, but I willed myself to remain conscious, scared that I'd miss an opportunity to escape. He lifted my toga and hit my bare buttock with his giant hand, slamming my upper thighs against the wood of the table. The pain grew in intensity all over my body as adrenaline raced through my veins. My head pumped out fresh blood with every rapid beat of my heart, augmenting the crimson pool around my cheek and between my fingertips. It filled the cracks of his filthy table and cascaded over the edge, gathering in puddles on the floor. My hands were slipping and sliding in my blood as I tried to push my body upwards, but my breasts crushed into the hard wooden table as he slammed me back down. I tried to use my hand to stop the bleeding but to no avail, as the wounds were too many. Covering one only accentuated the others.

The real agony came in one sharp blast from behind me. He had entered my vagina with his huge penis, thrusting it fiercely into a space that was far too inexperienced to manage his size. It felt like I had split open on the inside and hot lava was burning me, while every thrust forced a scream from my lungs. He didn't care that I was bleeding; he just kept pushing it inside and pulling it out, pushing and pulling, stabbing deeper and deeper. I closed my eyes and screamed as loud as I could, in the hope that someone might hear me. Screams from that house must have been heard before, because I was certain that I wasn't the first to suffer at his hands, and probably wouldn't be the last. I felt my insides ripping, as his penis burst through the skin at the end my vagina. I kept clawing at the bloodied table, trying to grasp something that would help me, but the shattered remains of the goblet had fallen to the floor. His grunts grew silent in my ears as did my cries, and my vision blurred, allowing me to focus only on my hand. My world became numb as I swirled my fingers in my own blood. I studied the liquid: the colour, the viscosity. My thoughts teleported me to my Livia, her smile and calming nature, and I began to smile through the tears. The gladiator grabbed my hair and thrust himself harder and faster. I began to scream again as her sweet face vanished, overpowered by sheer agony. My insides were like a furnace, burning me with every movement, yet he kept going. My feet scrambled for a foothold. I could feel blood dripping down my leg and seeping between my toes but still he pounded into my vagina until he had finally filled my shredded insides. He stood still for a moment, remaining inside of me. His penis pulsated several times, while he grunted like a wild hog. Tears rolled down my nose, mixing with the blood, as he finally pulled himself away, throwing my wasted body onto the reddened dirt floor. My head felt strange, and my body numb, which gave me some relief.

  I lay unmoving, gazing at the ceiling which rocked back and forth. I tried to fix my stare upon a small spider hanging from a wall-mounted torch, in an effort to steady my eyes. The man knelt down and wiped my blood from his penis with my toga before tucking it back inside his clothing. He looked at me as I lay on the floor, my life draining away. I did wonder, for a fleeting moment, if he might have had an ounce of compassion hidden in his stone heart, but if he did it was buried deep. His heart was as cold as ice after a life filled with death. One small, insignificant, and worthless girl would not have stirred a single compassionate thought in him. He pulled my bloodied toga down over my private parts and headed for the door. My sight faded to a whitened haze as I heard the hinges creak and the door slam shut behind him.

The bleeding did not stop but it did slow, taking my energy along with it. I could hardly breathe. My heart, which previously raced, now whispered as it pushed forth the last remnants of what blood remained in my veins. My eyes closed for the final time in that life, and the last sound I heard was my mother-in-law entering the room in a frenzy.

"What have you done, you incompetent fool?"

Then silence, as I slipped away into the safety of the darkness once more.

I often wondered what became of Livia's children. I would most likely have been quickly replaced by another poor young girl. I just hope that she didn't end her days as I did, and that a lesson was learned by my demise. Livia's boys were already being groomed for great things while I was alive, and her girls? I expect they were sent to homes where they were treated like broodmares by middle-aged men who thought themselves more important than the young girls they were raping.

Male dominance has reared its ugly head many times throughout history and still abundantly exists today. I will let you into a secret now: in my experience, when the nurturers take the upper hand, the world is a much better, safer, and organised place, where humans and animals thrive. An inflated ego is a trait that some possess more than others, but it predominantly exists in those who hold physical strength and have been raised with the belief that they are God-like. Those people can be very dangerous when they also have wealth and power. They can possess an overwhelming need or desire for more, despite those who may get trampled along the way. They care only about themselves and the profits they gain, not about those who work hard for them and receive only a menial wage in return.

A nurturing mind is also not exclusively owned by women. A man can raise a child just as well as a woman, indeed some families today choose to have the father stay at home to raise the children. As time continues, I see for myself that the sexes are becoming more equal. We still have a very long way to go, but maybe one day we will *all* truly be seen just as people, rather than what some people believe to be a different species. Men may eventually find a way to bear children and women will stand by when labour commences, watching them scream in agony. She will stand at his bedside, her hands on her hips, a smirk on her face, and say:

"See. I told you it hurts more than a kick in the balls."

## MY TWO DADS

In this story, I became the murderer of two of the kindest, most loving men who ever raised me. The story starts in a beautiful small town in Canada, overlooked by the snow-capped mountains of the Canadian Rockies. My town was embraced by lakes filled with life, and forests that looked like they were hosting a fairy-tale. The air was clean, the people were friendly, and I was a happy little girl doted on by my two wonderful fathers.

I was born in the 1970s, to a surrogate mother who offered her services in secret to my fathers. She was a close friend of theirs and remained actively involved in our family. Most of the time though, it was just myself and my two dads: David and George. They lived their lives as a gay couple unbeknown to the neighbourhood, because being homosexual was still frowned upon. To everyone else, I was George's daughter, but I actually shared my genes with David. Born two weeks late, I entered the world with a mass of brown hair and weighed nearly ten pounds. My fathers were in love and had me to complete their family, despite the disapproving comments of close family members.

We lived in a self-built log cabin, close to a great lake. It had oversized white stone fireplaces and expensive furnishings. My room was decorated to accommodate a princess, with soft pinks and purples, satin, and velvet fabrics everywhere.

The small town was mostly used by people who rented the properties for holidays, but my fathers both owned successful businesses, so were able to work from home. This meant that during the winter months, the town's population halved, which was the way we liked it. David and George gave me all the attention and love that I could ever ask for. I was a precious gift, and I felt wholeheartedly that this life was going to be a great one.

I always found it quite hard doing the baby part. As a new-born, my brain is already filled to capacity with information, but it is kept locked away until around one year of age. That is when the floodgates begin to open; slowly at first, but that little trickle soon becomes a raging river. I can speak 242 different languages, but for the first year I only spoke the one that my parents taught me, so as not to cause alarm. David and George were full of encouragement and were eager for me to achieve greatness. They began teaching me French and, lo and behold, by the age of three I was fluent. They said I was a genius: a child prodigy and they took the credit, which helped to hush the homophobic whispers of our community. I remember, when I was six, one old woman ranting at my two dads when we left a shop one time:

"It's not natural to live with two men, a child needs a mother. Where's the child's mother?" she yelled out.

The woman approached like a concerned citizen and asked if they had hurt me in any way. I held on to both of my dads' hands and looked up at the woman sweetly.

"I'm sorry. Both my dads told me not to talk to strange people. Especially stupid ones."

I confidently strolled past her, dragging my dumbfounded dads behind me. They were impressed by my sassiness and treated me to a hot chocolate with extra cream, and a chocolate-chip cookie. That evening, we had a visit from the police; it was our usual local officer, who also went by the name of 'Uncle Bob.' He was David's older brother and he looked out for us. The woman in question had later filed a report, accusing my dads of abuse.

"Well, it's a good excuse to see my favourite niece and to have a coffee break."

Uncle Bob was a good guy.

David was an architect by trade and had designed many buildings around Canada as well as our home. George was an author, editor, and owned his own publishing company. He didn't tell me what genre he wrote, but I assumed they were above my age range at the time.

One night, when I was still six, we sat around the open fire as David read a story about a time-travelling man. It sounded similar to my situation so, that evening, I decided to tell them about my life before and the ones previous to that. I thought that coming from a small child, there would be no consequences, and I was curious as to how they would react.

I sat on the miniature pink armchair and told them only a fraction of what I had lived through. David and George sat in silence while I explained what it was like to feel your feet rot while awaiting orders in the trenches, kicking rats away from your boots as they nibbled at the leather. I spoke of the time when I helped build giant monuments to honour the Gods in Egypt, and rode on horseback through a field of buffalo, with eagle feathers decorating my headdress. I spoke about the time I hid from the Germans in a haystack, along with other children from my village. Hearing my mother scream as they set the hay ablaze. They made the parents watch as we ran out, one by one, screaming. Our bodies engulfed with fire, only to be shot dead.

They both listened in silence as their little princess, the tiny girl with pigtails and dimpled cheeks, told them about the times she had died and the horror of what she had seen. Obviously, I didn't tell them about every life, otherwise I may still be there now, speaking to corpses who had died of old age. When I finished speaking, I expected to be called a liar again, but I was pleasantly surprised. Both of my fathers dropped to their knees in front of me and embraced my tiny body. They cried to the point that they shook, and I cried too. I'm not sure if it was guilt, because I had made my wonderful fathers cry, or relief that, for once, someone I loved actually believed me. It was probably both, if I'm honest.

For weeks they both asked me questions, and I answered each one with honesty. They wanted to know everything: every life and every story that accompanied it, but that was not possible. All the knowledge I possessed was too much for any human to handle. It was a burden that only I could carry. They asked me how I was still able to function with so much information, which I could not answer. Even *they* tried to find the answers but settled in the end with the knowledge that some things, just are as they are—beyond any reasonable explanation.

Around the dinner table, David asked me a question that he had been itching to ask.

"How were the huge rocks that built the great monuments like Stonehenge, or the pyramids transported? Even with the technology of today, it's impossible to carry such heavy loads."

This was one of the biggest secrets of my existence. It's a technology that has been hidden from the human race for fear that in the wrong hands, people can do so much harm. But stupidly and naively, I told him in detail. I even drew the plans for building such a device, on the condition that he kept the secret to himself. It was a mistake that I will never repeat again. I believed I could trust him, and that promise he made to me.

David immediately made plans to build his own device and began ordering in the parts to bring it to life. Through the summer months, he spent the majority of his time tinkering in the garage, much to George's annoyance. He kept the door locked and claimed that he was working on a little surprise. Only a few months later, the device was built and as expected, it worked like a dream. It lifted heavy boulders like they were pebbles, defying gravity, and the laws of physics. David kept it hidden away for months, but the temptation to make even more money than he already had eventually became too much to bear, and he broke his promise to me.

When he decided to release it to the world, he didn't tell either George or me beforehand. When I discovered what he was planning, I protested, warning him of the damage it could do. This was not the time for it to be used again. What if it fell into the hands of someone wanting to start a war? What if? What if? What if?

David was blinded by dollar signs, though, and began looking into the marketing of his amazing invention. George could see my point, but just told David to be wary of whom he sold it to. George was not a man who enjoyed conflict, especially with his David. This was a time where the internet did not exist, so marketing was an exceptionally long and drawn-out process. Thankfully, none of the larger companies believed his far-fetched story, and it seemed that David had given up trying to sell the plans. His excitement died down and life continued as it was before. The device was covered up with a dust sheet and locked away in the garage.

When I was nine years of age, my dad George and I went on our usual trip to town for groceries, nothing out of the ordinary. On the way home, we stopped at a cafe for some lunch and a warm drink, as a cold snap was in the air. It was freezing; ice was already forming in puddles left by the rain the day before. As we drove home, a snowstorm curled over the mountains. Thick brown clouds blanketed the skies, and with them came snow. It fell so thickly that we could barely see the road ahead. We were lucky that George knew the way like the back of his hand and the truck navigated the treacherous roads with ease. When we arrived at our home George noticed that the door was open wide, which was unlike David who always did his best to keep the house warm and welcoming. George looked at me with a frown of concern.

"Stay here, let me go check it out. I won't be long," he smiled reassuringly.

I watched worriedly as George trudged through the snow. I had a sinking feeling in my gut that something was amiss: maybe David had fallen ill, or we could have had intruders. As George approached the door, he stopped and looked around him. He grabbed the wood axe from the railing and cautiously headed inside, calling out for David as he disappeared from my view. I watched and waited, wondering if I should join him.

As I sat alone in the truck, I didn't notice a man appear beside my window. He flung open my door and I jumped with fright and screamed as loudly as I could, but he covered my mouth with his hand to silence me. I remember the smell of oil on his fingers, and the taste of dirt, as I tried to bite at them. I fought with all I had, scratching, and kicking him, but he was like a machine: impervious to any damage I inflicted. He sprinted through the trees with me in his arms, like I was weightless, leaping over fallen logs and ditches, and ducking under low snow-covered branches. On a narrow dirt road within the woods, a dirty white van waited with its engine purring. The back doors were open wide, waiting for me. The timber-lined space within was empty, apart from a single dim light. The man threw me in, without any regard for my safety, like I was rubbish I landed with a thud on the cold steel flooring, my back cracking on a ring that protruded from the wheel arch, which sent a pain shooting down my leg. He took one last look at me as I quickly scrambled to my feet. I lunged at him in a last attempt to free myself, but he smiled menacingly and slammed the doors shut before I could reach him.

The driver was unreachable and invisible on the other side of a slab of wood screwed to a steel cage. All I could do was scream for help, in the hope that someone would hear. The front doors of the van opened, and I heard two men climb aboard whilst whispering something that I couldn't quite hear. The engine roared, the tires skidded on the dirt and snow, and we drove away at speed. I would not give up the fight. I screamed louder, and thumped the sides of the van, by throwing my body back and forth, to alert passers-by. The snow kept people away from these roads though, as in this weather, they were treacherous. By the way the van turned, I knew it was a road I knew well: it was the route that headed up into the mountains; David often took me fishing at a lake on this road. It should have been impossible to navigate in that weather, but the driver seemed to know the way. As we drove on the asphalt sheltered by the trees, I could hear the rattle of the chains that surrounded the wheels. I stopped screaming: the cold and fear had drained my body.

We drove for hours, before the van finally stopped. One man got out, and I listened silently to his boots flattening the fresh snow and the sound of the piss hitting the leaves as he relieved himself. Soon enough we were driving again, and for another hour I sat in the back of that van, my coat doing its best to keep out the cold. Inevitably, the frigid chill got to my skin, and I sank to the floor shivering.

Finally, the van stopped, and I heard a variety of voices talking. They all spoke of a 'mission,' their walkie-talkies buzzing on and off, with mechanical voices giving them orders that I couldn't make out, all ending with "Over."

These people gathered around the doors and cautiously opened them wide. By now I was lying in a tight ball, struggling to keep warm. My fighting had worn me out, and my body shook in a final bid to keep warm and awake. Two men jumped in the back and hooked their arms under mine and dragged me out onto the snow. A male voice gave the order down the walkie talkies:

"Bring her to me."

A white concrete building stood camouflaged in the snow; it seemed only small, but it was surrounded by a dozen men, all carrying guns. They were dressed in white boiler suits and wore what appeared to be white balaclavas to cover their faces. Every one of them watched as I was taken into the bunker-like structure by the two men. They marched like soldiers as my feet dragged along, churning the fresh snow up behind me.

It was dark inside the bunker; a few torches swung from the roof but gave little light, just enough to see that the space inside was sparsely furnished. A few metal trunks, with strange red symbols stamped on the lids, sat along the wall of the entrance. We went through a steel door into a tiny room and turned around. We could hardly fit inside, yet the door closed, and the room dropped slowly. The lift took us deep into the ground and, as it descended, the corroded structure began to speed up. It made me feel uneasy for a moment, as I have a small fear of lifts and confined spaces. I was concerned that the ground might suddenly appear, and we'd crash, but it eventually slowed and stopped with a thud. The doors swung open, filling the lift with warmth in one rapid wave. For just a moment I closed my eyes, embraced the heat, and imagined I was back home by the open fire, but sadly this wasn't the case.

The corridor inside was too bright for my eyes after being in the back of the van, and I winced while my vision adjusted. Several strip lights swung from chains and dozens of numbered doors stood equally spaced on both sides. They frogmarched me along the polished white floor to the first door to the left. It was labelled 'Room Two.' One man knocked on the door.

"Enter" said a voice from within.

The man opened the door and revealed an office more dimly lit than the corridor. The walls were lined with bookshelves and filing cabinets, maps with red pins pushed in at various points, and a portrait of a person that I recognised. I had seen that face before, but I had trouble remembering, which is a rare thing for me. I had a memory that clearly pictured the time, twenty lives ago, when I watched two bees fight, yet I had forgotten that face. Then quite suddenly it hit me like the fist of a heavyweight champion. That face so familiar to me: it was back in a time when I owned very little, and the only time I saw my reflection was when I gazed into the still water on the bank of the Nile. It was me from a past life that was a time of war. I had the task of collecting the bodies to send them back to their loved ones. My beard had grown long and straggly, and my eyes were red and sore.

The man behind the large oak desk watched me as I studied the room, his elbows resting on the green leather surface. His hands were clasped together, and his thumbs fidgeted restlessly. He was dressed in a white shirt and black tie, which had a small button pinned to it. The symbol on the button appeared to be the same as the one on the trunks in the entrance: a pentagram, but I couldn't make out the details. The men sat me on a chair in front of the desk and took a few steps back.

"What is your name, girl?"

I remained silent; I had been through these interrogations before, so I knew the drill. They would ask questions and torture me for a while; eventually they would get frustrated, and either let me go in a remote location or kill me. I was hoping that the first would occur, due to my age, but these things never go the way I hoped.

"Girl! What is your name?" he asked again, in a fierce tone.

Three more times he repeated the question, but I remained silent. He slammed his hands down on the desk, to intimidate me, but I held my tongue and didn't flinch. I had the mind of an adult and a memory far greater than his. He stood up from his desk and walked around it, towards me. He perched on the edge of the desk, leaning his buttocks on the wood. I looked down at his polished, black shoes. The man swung back his hand and struck my face. I fell from the chair and hit the floor; my cheek stung like hell, but I didn't show it. I stared at him, pulled myself up from the floor, and took my seat smugly.

"One last time, girl. What is your name?"

I gave him nothing. He lunged forward and grasped my thick braid and pulled my head back. He put his foot on the corner of my chair and brought his face close to mine. I could smell the peppermint on his breath, an attempt to disguise the smell of his halitosis breath, which smelt like rotting fish. I looked straight into his eyes, and I don't know why I did it, but I smiled. This sent the man into a rage and using his grip on my hair, he threw me across the room, slamming my small body into a bookcase. A dozen or so books fell onto my head and scattered onto the floor around me. I picked one of the books up, opened it, and pretended to read. I had no idea what it was about: this was simply just for show.

The man kicked the book from my hands and grabbed hold of my arms, lifting me from the floor. He squeezed tightly but I didn't flinch. He slammed me against the wall and held me a foot from the ground by my throat.

"I know your name, girl, and I know who you were before. Your face may have changed, but we know. We have been searching for you for years: we knew you would show up eventually. It was a mistake, telling your daddy about the device, because it led us straight to you. Now, I am going to get my friends to come in and hurt you. We want to know why you are like this and we *will* find answers. So, keep your silence; we have our ways of getting you to talk. Mark my words as true, you will suffer, and I will smile with every scream."

He released me, and I fell to my feet, and stood with my head held tall. I don't know what came over me in that room, maybe I had just had enough. Maybe my entire existence had just reached a point where I simply didn't care anymore. One thing was for sure: I was not going to give him the satisfaction of hearing me scream. I had been through far worse than anything that he could throw at me. Pain is just a feeling and with training, feelings can be ignored—and I was a master at *that*.

The two men grabbed my arms and marched me out of the room. I was dragged down the corridor and tossed into a cell with a single dim light. They demanded that I strip down to my skin, but I refused, naturally.

After several unsuccessful attempts to get me to comply, one of the men took a hose from the wall and aimed it at my body. The freezing cold pressurised water blasted out and stung my exposed skin. I pulled my coat tighter around me, to shield myself. A group of women trudged into the room and started to tug at my clothing, ripping my coat away and tearing off my sweater and jeans. I was on the floor and kicking anyone who came close enough, but they were stronger than me and did not hold back.

As they stripped me down to my underwear, soaking wet, I stood back up once again with my head unbowed. One of the men who stood in the doorway looked at my immature nine-year-old body with bulging eyes. My white undergarments had become transparent with the water and had left me exposed. He made a suggestive grab at his hardened penis and smiled; his tongue licked around his lips. I looked at the repugnant pig in disgust. Paedophiles are a race of human beings that I could never entertain. They are the lowest form of degenerates and do not deserve to breathe our planet's precious oxygen. One of the other men spotted him and seemed to share my views. He promptly removed the paedophile from the area, dragging him out of the room. As the door slammed behind him, an argument ensued that ended in gunfire and the sound of a body collapsing on the cold concrete floor. The other man re-entered the room, tucking his gun back into its holster. He didn't look at me, but I knew by the expression on his face that he had wanted to do that for a very long time and was willing to suffer the consequences.

I was thrown a white boilersuit to wear, and taken to another room, with a single bed and neatly folded thin blanket, a toilet, and a sink with running water. The door slammed shut and was locked with a key and two bolts. I sat on the bed contemplating my situation. They were treating me with aggression, but at the first sign of a paedophilic attack, the man was shot dead. Was I being protected?

The room had no windows as it was deep within the earth. The vent in the ceiling had been welded shut and the door was solid steel. I had no way out. Sometime later, my door opened, and a foot nudged a bowl filled with porridge over the threshold, followed by an empty cup, an apple, and a small bar of chocolate. Not a word was spoken to me. I did eat the food, and I filled the cup with water to drink. I even had the audacity to call out for a coffee, which was rudely ignored. After my meal I thought about asking for a book to read, but after such an eventful day, I curled up on the thin mattress, wrapped myself in the blanket, and promptly went to sleep.

A loud siren blasted through my eardrums, awakening me from a pleasant dream. The light in my room brightened to a brilliant white, making it hard to open my eyes. For the first time since I was taken from my father's truck, my body felt relatively warm. A moment later, the steel door was unlocked and screeched open on the rusting hinges. Two men in white boilersuits moved apart, revealing a tall, slender woman. She wore a white lab coat, with a light blue turtleneck top underneath. Around her neck I noticed a pendant with the same star symbol that the man with the black tie wore. Her blonde hair was tied tightly into a ponytail that pulled on her temples. She wore gaudy plastic-framed glasses balanced on the tip of her nose, which she peered over to look at me. In her hand was a wooden clipboard which she scribbled notes upon. Her name badge said 'DR C.P. HUNTER', with an accompanying, unflattering photograph of herself.

She looked at me and smiled falsely, like she knew that I was going to be troublesome.

"We have a busy schedule today. You have ten minutes to sort yourself out, and then my men will fetch you and bring you to the lab. Am I clear?" she said, in a very condescending manner.

The door was pulled shut and I was left alone again. I slipped on the boilersuit and sat on the edge of my bed with my hands placed on my thighs, staring directly at the wall ahead of me. After exactly ten minutes, the two men burst in. I stood without a fuss and walked between them. They led me into a laboratory and positioned me on a fully adjustable medical chair, then they took their places either side of me like statues, without even blinking. The room was filled with machinery: some I recognised from my medical teachings and others I did not.

There were heart monitors, bypass machines, dialysis units, ventilators, anaesthesia machines, and even an MRI scanner in a side room. It was equipped like a fully functional hospital; the only thing missing was the patients. A room at the far end of the lab had a glass wall, and the two men inside, wearing blue overalls and facemasks, were surrounded by test tubes, Bunsen burners, microscopes, scales, and fridges filled with vials of solution. They glared in my direction, as if waiting for me to give them something to do.

As I took in all that I could see, the woman appeared. She perched herself on a stool with swivel wheels and wrote on her clipboard. I stared at her, awaiting some sort of instruction that I would stubbornly refuse, and she noticed. She let out a sigh and clipped her gold pen into her top pocket and placed the clipboard on the counter.

"Name?" I remained silent.

The woman took off her glasses and allowed them to swing on a chain around her neck.

"Name?" she repeated, with vexation.

Again, I stayed silent and glared into her eyes.

She pulled her glasses back onto her face and reached for her clipboard and pen.

"In this facility, you will be referred to as 'Patient Ultra.' When we call for you, we will ask for 'Patient Ultra'. When we refer to you in any way, we will do so as 'Patient Ultra'. Do you understand?"

She was throwing me that false smile again and fluttering her eyelashes. I looked away, locking eyes with one of the lab men; he averted his gaze, obviously feeling uncomfortable.

I sat quietly whilst they took blood samples from my arm, snipped off locks of my hair, and swabbed saliva from my mouth. The doctor shone lights in my eyes and sent me through the MRI scanner. I did as she asked and lay completely still during the scan. When it was over, I sat back in the chair and stared once more at the men in the lab. They were busy with my samples: dripping my blood onto slides and placing my hair into test tubes. When they gave me food I ate, and when I needed the toilet, I asked and was led to the facilities. I became robotic because I knew that they had very little on me, apart from my knowledge of that device. Every time I found myself alone, I searched for an escape route, but sadly this facility was inescapable. The only way out was via the lift, and it wasn't just locked it was also guarded by men with rifles, day, and night.

The last job on the list that day involved looking at a handful of pictures. They depicted ancient scriptures that explained technologies long lost to the modern world: harnessing an abundance of energy from the sky without the use of harmful chemicals or even much effort, medical knowledge that made modern medicine look mediocre, lasers that used the sun's rays to slice through solid rock like butter, which allowed us to build cliff-side temples in next to no time. The text on the pictures explained everything, but whether they had trouble deciphering them or were merely testing my knowledge was a mystery to me.

That night I lay in my bed and thought to myself. My only worry was my two fathers. They were good men, despite David's betrayal, and my careless actions had put them in danger, so I decided that the next day I would be more compliant.

"I will tell you what you want to know, if you can assure me that my fathers won't come to any harm."

The woman smiled, not the fake smile that she had presented me with so many times before, but the smile of a satisfied woman who thought that she had finally got her own way.

"Follow me."

She grabbed her clipboard and walked towards a door that I had yet to see behind. I followed closely. In the room were two small sofas and a coffee table, with a glass vase containing fake red peonies. The stone walls were painted powder-blue, and a free-standing heater filled the room with warmth. I sat upon one of the sofas and the woman sat on the other, facing me. She looked up at the camera, which peered down into the room, and leant towards me.

"What I can tell you is that both men are being held at another facility. If you help us and answer every question and do as we ask, then I can assure you that they will be released unharmed."

"How do I know you are telling the truth?" I asked.

"You will just have to trust me, I'm afraid."

Naturally, I didn't believe a word that she said, but I no longer had anything to lose. If there was a chance that my request might be honoured, then I was willing to take that chance.

Firstly, I had a question of my own:

"Why hide the technology from the modern world?" I knew the answer; I suppose I just wanted to hear it from her.

"That's a simple answer. Profit. If we used your lasers to build houses in a day, we couldn't justify selling them for such a huge profit. Think of the people that would be out of work if such things existed. Now tell me, am I talking to a little nine-year-old girl or a person who remembers every life she ever lived?"

She leant back, with her legs crossed, twirling her pen around her fingers. Her drawn-on eyebrows raised over the rim of her glasses as she tensed, waiting for my answer.

"Both are correct. My body is nine, but my mind is several thousand years old. I know things that would make you question your existence." I said casually, yet boastfully.

She leant back in her chair and thought for a moment. Her eyes lit up as a million questions exploded in her mind. She began to fire question after question: the history of the Mayans, ancient Egypt, Romans, Pompeii, Columbus; so many questions they made my head spin. I told her everything she wanted to know and more. Soon others joined us in the room, and they too began firing questions at me. Some shrieked with excitement as their theories were proven right, others argued until they were satisfied that I had explained the truth.

For several weeks I answered a thousand questions and told countless stories until I was exhausted. I started to feel like a circus act from the days of the freak shows, paraded around like an exhibit. I never left the complex, not even for a moment, because I was seen as far too valuable to risk losing. Every day new people would arrive: experts on this, doctors of that ... people who simply paid money to gawk at the girl with an endless mind. It was Doctor Hunter that finally put a halt to the visits; she could see that the interrogation was taking its toll on my health.

"We can help you. We can end the cycle of life and death by pinpointing the piece of energy in your brain that causes it and exploding it. You will cease to exist. Would that be something you would be interested in?" queried one of the professors.

If I ever had a chance to escape this endless cycle of life and death, I would take that chance. As they explained the procedure to me, the theory seemed legitimate. In my previous lives, we had never managed to harness the soul; it was always a concept beyond our capabilities. If this professor had achieved such a thing, then my life would indeed be over.

"We will help you if you cooperate with us fully—first, we want to crack open that mind of yours and see what makes you who you are. Do I have your agreement?"

I was fed up with living and prayed for eternity in whatever lay beyond that darkness. If I ceased to exist, I wouldn't know anything about it anyway, so against all my better instincts, I agreed. Dr Hunter passed me a form to sign, which handed over my body and my rights to it. I took hold of her gold pen and hovered it over the form.

"Can I have your reassurance that my fathers will be unharmed?"

Deep down, I already knew what had become of my fathers, but I clung to the hope that they had survived.

"Of course."

Half of me was screaming 'fucking liar' at her, whilst the other half of me was satisfied with her reply, because I so desperately wanted it to be true.

The next few days or weeks, I could not tell how much time passed, I was hooked up to every machine in the complex. Samples were taken from every orifice—even my earwax was extracted; they operated on me and took brain matter and tissue samples from my organs. Electrodes were stuck all over my body, and they electrocuted my heart until it was near to exploding. They overinflated my lungs and injected all kinds of drugs into my system. My body was subjected to experiments daily, and every day I grew weaker. My tiny girlish body had been battered and bruised: tubes protruded from my stomach, my head was shaved clean, and scars criss-crossed my head and torso.

The doctors made sure I remained relatively pain-free, so most of the time I slept in an induced coma of sorts.

The last night I spent on Earth in that life was supposed to be my final procedure: the one that would ultimately kill me, and I was promised that it would be for good. Yet I live today as a testament to their failings. I was strapped to the bed under a blazing white light and electrodes were applied to both temples. Into my vein, they pumped a massive amount of lysergic acid diethylamide, or LSD as it is known. As the drug entered my arm, I felt like my spirit had already left my body. I felt as though I could fly away into space itself. I saw objects surrounded by glowing auras, and ghosts from my past with their arms outstretched towards me. I felt happy and at peace with everything for what felt like hours but were more likely moments. I floated around that room, surrounded by love, then all at once my body was slammed by what felt like a bolt of lightning into each temple, which pierced my brain, dragging me back to my body. One by one, my eyes exploded right before I was thrown back up to that familiar dark place where my next life would be waiting.

I had suffered greatly even before my tenth birthday, and I vowed never to let humans and their mediocre technologies ever attempt to help me again. I do worry sometimes that they had unlocked my secret, being that my body was theirs to dissect. But I now know that my memories are untouchable and remain elsewhere, with my spirit. My body is merely a vehicle that I must drive to gain experience in all genres of life. I am a puppet in this never-ending journey called life.

As for the fate of my fathers? I did look up the news reports, as I usually do in these more modern times. For months, my Uncle Bob placed 'missing' posters on telegraph poles and in shop windows, but sadly the case of the two missing men and the nine-year-old girl was never solved. To this day, the file remains in a box marked 'cold case'. Some presume that we all left in a hurry, to start a new life elsewhere. Bob knew different; he knew better, but nobody would listen.

After a few years had passed, Bob took over the house in the hope of finding clues into our disappearance. I can only presume that he must have had a shock when he read my journal in my room; that's if it was still there. I have no doubt that whoever took us that day had a good look around for any evidence before leaving.

So much technology has been discovered but hidden from the world. The fear of an evil mind with a cruel nature using it for his or her own benefit is very real, especially when the technology in question has the ability to cause genocide. I can imagine that if Hitler had had access to the device in this story, he wouldn't have thought twice before using it to topple buildings or to develop flying machines which defied gravity. The war would have been lost and we may all be speaking German, raising our right hands in fear of what would happen if we didn't.

# JUNGLE LIFE

It wasn't all doom and gloom: some lives were good and filled with love, laughter, and happy memories. I can't tell you what year the life I am about to tell you about took place, and I'm not even sure of the era; all I can really do is guess. The reason for my uncertainty is simple to explain. I was born a boy when the sun was at its highest. My surroundings were a thick jungle as far as the eye could see. As my mother pushed me into the world, the monkeys that surrounded us filled the air with a chorus that echoed throughout the trees. The birds tweeted and the bullfrogs croaked, and my village rejoiced. I was the latest baby born to a hidden tribe in what I can only presume to be the Amazon rainforest. My mother was gathering fruits with the other women of the tribe when she collapsed with the pains of labour. When a birth occurs, all the women gather round to offer comfort and medical aid. The men were out hunting in the surrounding area. It worked better that way, as women tended to communicate more openly. Men spoke very little so that they could easily go unnoticed by their prey; they were also stealthier on their feet and didn't have children strapped to their bodies like the women. It wasn't that they were not trusted with the infants, it was purely a case of nourishment. The women had breasts to feed with, where men were obviously lacking in that department. It was the women who held the tribe together and set the rules, as they were the smarter, more forward-thinking members. We were all comfortable with the fact that the men held the strength, and the women had the intelligence to do what was best. They were the nurturers and had everyone's best interests at heart.

The men found life easier when they did what they had been asked, and the outcome always turned out to be more beneficial to the entire tribe. It was not a sexist way to live, as we were all classed as equals; each of us had our place, and that was that. It was also not unusual to have a woman with an overwhelming desire to join the men in the hunt, and they did so freely, as was the case with the men who preferred to stay at home and converse with the women. They were never frowned upon or laughed at. If anything, they were the ones who became the best of us all, and helped us evolve as a tribe, bringing new ideas and strategies.

We lived in simple homes, with grass roofs and walls of clay mixed with twigs and leaves. They stood on stilts to protect us from some of the more poisonous species of insects and snakes, and from the river, which tended to swell during the rainy seasons. They also gave us some protection from the wild cats that hunted around our village. We had respect for the big cats, and they kept their distance. We did lose livestock from time to time, but it was better than losing one of our people. We knew that the cats only took what they needed to survive, and never killed just for sport. We were taught from a young age that we were also animals, and part of the jungle. We held equal rights to it, along with all the other creatures who lived there. We all had a right to live, but we also had a right to eat, like any other predator.

      The women in our village wore nothing more than a flower in their hair, and maybe a garland around their necks. Men usually covered their manhood with bark. An animal's horn made a fine shield if they were lucky enough to find them. They had to protect their dangly parts from attacking animals and thorny foliage. A man's private parts were believed to be the creators of children, while women were the vessels. A wild animal who saw a man as a threat always aimed for the private parts in order to assert its dominance.

      My name cannot be traced through history, so I can reveal that it was simply Eyok. Well, that's the closest spelling I can match to the sound. We did not go to school or drive cars; we did not watch television or go shopping—we lived on what the jungle provided. Our air was pure and our lives free from additives, preservatives, chemicals, or colourings. Meals did not come on plastic dishes wrapped in cellophane, or ready-made, nor did we have a microwave to reheat our food. We grew or gathered our fruits and vegetables, caught our fish in the rivers, and hunted only what we needed. We did not produce any harmful waste and the only smoke we put into the atmosphere was from burning leaves, branches, and animal dung. Our lives were simple, and we were probably the happiest tribe you would ever meet.

We didn't believe in a god or religious texts—we worshipped the earth that fed our crops, the sun for growing them tall, the rains for watering the seeds, and our elders who gave us the wisdom to grow them successfully. We grew bananas, citrus fruits, cocoa plants, sugar palm, spices, and herbs. In the evenings we sang and danced around the fire, and we drank what can only be described as 'fermented fruit.' It was basically alcohol, and even the children drank it! Our elders thought that it would make them grow tough and that their young bodies would grow immune to disease, and, truth be told, all the adults found the staggering children amusing.

Our village did suffer casualties from time to time, usually from snake or spider bite. When I was small, our healers made special poultices to put on the bites, which were not always successful, but they could be, if applied quickly and the bite was from a less deadly species. When I grew old enough to make myself known, I gave them the knowledge and the expertise to create a more successful antivenom: a recipe that I'd kept in my memory from a previous life.

My childhood moved into adulthood at the tender age of around seven years. We didn't keep track of the years, because living close to the equator meant that every day was pretty much the same. I was made chief medicine man of my tribe, and had a home all to myself, yet my mother was never far away. I can still picture the pride on her face when she saw her little boy fly through the ranks to become the medicine man, her youngest still suckling from her breast. As stated previously, I have never taken too well to killing anything, so this job suited me down to the ground. Every day I gave my orders to my gatherers: bark from the kapok, the bottom leaves of the yellow bromeliads, cacao seeds, and skins of the banana. Hundreds of ingredients were needed for all of my recipes, and supply was never an issue. The forest grew all that I required in abundance, plus, new species were found every day. I soon mastered the art of curing most ailments, and even discovered some that I had no previous knowledge of. The jungles have often been referred to as 'the chemists of the world', which is the best way to describe them. Every cure is in those leaves—every cure for every ailment. It's a shame we're losing them so rapidly.

My people thrived, and we lived in the forest of plenty without worry or care for what lay beyond. I had no clue of the year that I arrived in this paradise. I only hoped that it was way before deforestation was becoming a problem.

Our seclusion was our biggest asset. We occasionally had peaceful visits from neighbouring villages, which usually consisted of relatives coming to catch up with family, for medical supplies, or to find a partner. These occasions were celebrations. The tribespeople arrived with baskets filled with fruits and nuts, from the forests around their villages.

The fire was built in the clearing, and the music would commence. The drums were only brought out on special occasions, but when they were, they were played continuously for three days straight. This was also the time for partnering, where the tribesmen from one village took the women of another. It was not all heterosexual either: none of us frowned on a person's sexual preference. We believed that people were born into the body they had, and that was just who they were. Women would lay with women, and men would lay with men.

Sometimes one man would choose one man and one woman. There were no rules, it was simply whatever made a person happy. Sure, fights did break out, when both sexes battled over a prized partner. It was resolved peacefully though, with the choice being made by the one being fought over. If she or he could not decide, they could choose to have neither of them, or both, as she or he so wished. They had around a year together before the next meeting when it would all begin again. Some were happy and stayed with their chosen partner, some for their entire lives, but mostly we took this opportunity for change.

We were all sure of our mothers, but most of us were never quite sure who our fathers were. They probably didn't know either, as sex for pleasure was the main goal. I have never known a race to have so much sex. Maybe that was why we were such a happy tribe!

We had one large dwelling in the centre of the village; it was the biggest of them all. That was where the children would gather every evening, including myself in my youth. We all sat cross-legged in rows, the smallest at the front and the biggest at the back, and we'd be silent. The elders of the village came in with leaves in their hair, and necklaces made from cocoa bean husks around their necks. One by one, they took turns telling us the story of our existence. They were stories that their elders had told them and we, in turn, had to tell our children and they had to tell their children. This was our story of creation ...

When the world was new, a star fell to earth and in its wake grew one, single tree. This tree grew mighty and pierced through the clouds to capture the light from the sun. The ground was solid black rock, but the tree's roots stretched deep below the surface. Every year, the rains would come and offer the tree a drink. The giant tree drew in the rain and grew thick leaves that covered the earth with shade and cooled the parched ground. When the tree grew thirsty again and the rains didn't come, it drank the moisture from its leaves to survive. They dried and fell to the ground, and the wind blew them far and wide. For many years the tree grew leaves and dropped them, eventually creating the soil that thickly covered the earth. When the tree saw that the surroundings offered sustenance, it gave birth to its young and dropped its seed onto the ground, which grew the first sapling. It was soon followed by others.

The soil held the rains, when they came, giving them an abundance of water, but the saplings soon withered and died in the shade of the great tree. No matter how hard they tried, they couldn't outgrow their mother and reach the sun. The giant tree gave birth to insects, who would carry the seeds far and wide, but the insects thrived and soon began to eat the tree. The tree gave birth to reptiles and birds to eat the insects, and carry the seeds in their dung, but the birds, having no predators, thrived. They nested in the great tree's branches and grew tired of flight, while the lizards were more content to laze in the sun.

In an effort to survive, the tree gave birth to all of the creatures you see today, until the balance of predator and prey was successful. Despite its efforts, the tree still eventually withered and died of old age leaving behind forests of trees. As it took its last breath, it gave birth to man, to watch over its children.

The trails where the roots once lay became the rivers, and the trunk became the mountains. The branches became the hills, and its children thrived. In return, the forest we see today provides man with shelter and food, and the rivers quench our thirst so we can live and care for the forest.

We understood that it was our job to care for the forest and the trees. The only trees we would ever harvest were ones fallen to insects, storms, or old age. We carried the seeds to clearings and planted new forests, and for generations we thrived. The forest provided medicine and cured our injuries, plants that helped us sleep, and leaves that would, let's just say, help us relax. Some roots helped to open our minds and allow us to observe our ancestors, who lingered in their happy place, even after death. We didn't fear them: they were people we once knew and loved; spirits who whispered in our ears when we slept, offering us warnings or just advice.

This reminds me of another of our tribe's teachings, one of my favourites, which I feel compelled to tell. This story was told once every full moon. It was about how our tribe came to be ...

The moon was full and Guaba, a young boy, was sent out into the wild to prove his worth. Armed with a knife and bow, he entered the forest and was not to return until the next full moon. He was brave and wise.

On the first day, he found shelter from the rains, fruits to eat, and water hidden in the leaves. On the second day, he walked from sunrise to sunset, and again found shelter, food, and water. For two weeks he did the same, but soon felt he did not prove his worth. On the fifteenth day he slept on the ground, ate only insects, and sucked muddy water from the earth. But the ground was damp and rotted his skin, the insects were poisonous and made him sick, and the water was dirty and did not quench his thirst. On the sixteenth day he was weak; his stomach hurt, his skin was sore, and his throat parched.

As he lay dying, he looked up at the forest with sorrow. A tree looked down upon him and took pity on the boy. His ancestors had planted the seed that grew the tree, many years ago. It asked the boy why he did not shelter in its branches, and eat the fruit that it freely offered, or take water from its leaves. Guaba explained that it was far too easy, and he wanted to prove his worth. The tree smiled and explained that life didn't need to be hard:

"We trees provide all that you need, as long as you care for us, in return." Guaba sobbed that his father was a great man and he wanted to be like him. The tree asked him what made his father great. Guaba thought for a moment, and his heart warmed. He explained to the tree that he gave love—that every day he felt the warmth of his father's love. The tree held out a branch and gave Guaba a gift, a seed. It asked him to plant the seed and call it 'home'. On the seventeenth day, the boy drank the water from the tree and ate its fruit, found shelter under its leaves, and felt his health return.

Soon he was fit and well, so on the twentieth day, he walked and walked for eight more days, till the moon was full, but he was not home. He stood in a clearing where the moon's rays hit the mud floor. He dropped to his knees and pushed the small seed into the ground. He found water in a tree to quench the seed's thirst, fruit that he squeezed over the soil for food, and a large leaf to cover the seed and hide it from animals. Guaba fell asleep in the branches of the nearby tree.

In the morning he awoke to a sweet song. The tree had grown tall and strong overnight, and sitting on the lowest branch was a beautiful woman, named Gilly. Guaba did not return home to his father, although he visited often. Guaba and Gilly stayed by the tree and had many children. But Guaba always remembered the lesson taught to him by the tree: life doesn't have to be hard—the earth will always provide. He also remembered that the best way to prove your worth is to love. Love is the most powerful force on the planet—love for a child, a partner, or an entire village—but mostly, love for a planet that provides.

I lived for many happy and wholesome years. I was old, my knees were weak, and my back bent. My entire life was happy and pure. I spent it well: saving lives with my medicine and having many children with only one woman. Her love was all I ever needed, and in return, I gave her all the love I had.

I took on my eldest as an apprentice; he was smart and listened to my instruction with fascination and eagerness. When I grew old, he took my place as village medicine man and carried on my work. He, in turn, taught his daughter, who proved even better than either my son *or* me. My family took care of my every need when my sight became milky, and my ears heard only whispers. They washed and fed me and dressed my wounds. They told me news of the family and at the very end, I even got to hold my great-great-great-granddaughter. What a joy that was. The last touches of my crinkly fingers were the soft, peachy skin of her cheeks and the fluffiness of her hair. I even heard the sound of her babbles, as I sang her a tune in my wobbly voice.

I died in that life only hours later, but I was happy and surrounded by my family. I had little in life, and I took nothing but memories and a smile. I left behind my medical knowledge, and my genes, which had already spread out around the jungle.

I am not sure if any of my tribe survive today. All I know is that we never saw any other people. I spotted no planes or other machinery. I like to think they are still out there in the rainforest, still using my medicine. Maybe my blood still flows through their veins. The harsh likelihood, that I dread, is that they were eventually discovered and became a tourist attraction until their simple existence became little more than a novelty. The precious forest would be flattened, and my people either killed from exposure to a virus, like so many others, or forced to live in towns with the 'Civilised'. They would have to sell cheap trinkets from the side of the road to survive, as they would not find employment. I *hope* it is the first option. I like to *think* it is, for my own sanity.

One of the most important lessons learnt in my existence is quite simple, and most people already know it. A person can buy the most expensive ... let us say ... mobile phone. For a month he feels like a king, but his ego loses him friends and gains him false ones. His bank is empty, but his hand feels rich, so he is happy. Then another man buys a better phone, and the first man is no longer king; his bank is empty, and he holds the second-best. He has lost all of his friends, so he becomes unhappy. Another man is wise: he needs a phone, but doesn't care if it makes him king, he simply wants to make calls and keep in touch with his friends. His bank is full, his friends are in abundance, and he is happy.

My lives have seen all sorts of horrors, but they have also seen times that I did not want to end. I have had all the wealth I could have ever dreamt of and been surrounded by those who pretended to love me, but only loved my wealth. I loved them fiercely, but they did not return the same feelings. I hoped and prayed, even bribed them with gifts, but they still left when the money was gone.

Some lives I have nothing but a banana leaf covering my danglies, and the knowledge to do good. I was treated like a god: not with wealth, but with love and joy, happiness and a family that cherished me, and I in return cherished them. This made me the happiest naked person on the planet. I was lucky with that life and lived to see many, many years.

Whenever I think back to that time I smile. Even when we had a death in the village, we celebrated their life with song and dance, and returned the body back to nature. No tears were shed; we told stories celebrating the person and the life they lived. I have no doubt that my own life was celebrated in this way; I would love to have been there.

*Things* make you happy for a few moments, but the real riches are free. A walk in the woods on a summer's day, with a short break for a picnic while you talk about things that don't matter much. A night in, with your socks on, sipping a warm drink while you watch an old film. Or something as simple as a kiss before you sleep, or a rub on the shoulders after a hard day. Those moments mean so much more than *things*. They grow love and appreciation; they are the seeds of happiness, and the recipe for joy. The greatest gift you can give is *time*, and the greatest gifts you can receive are good memories because they last an eternity.

## THE CURSE OF FAME

I have explained before that most of the time, I can pick my gender in a life, and although this is possible most of the time, the *personality* I am born with comes from the genetics of my parents. Sometimes I have the strength to withstand whatever life throws at me, other times I am weak and helpless as a kitten. This life brought me an unusual mix of frailty and ambition, but also taught me the greatest lesson about love.

This is a fact that many people know only too well: one insult can dwell in a mind that is swimming with compliments, devouring them all one by one. My insult was not one that was spoken but was one of abandonment. I was born a girl in 1926, in Los Angeles, which was also known as the City of Angels. My mother craved stardom, but instead fell pregnant with me—obviously not part of her plan. I never knew my father but was told he looked like a famous film star. At the age of only two weeks old, after trying to smother me in my crib, my mother abandoned me for the first time, claiming to have mental health problems.

America was a vastly different place back then, and I expect that society looked down upon young, single mothers as burdens on society. It seemed apparent that she hated me for ruining her dreams. I was eventually placed with a family friend and her husband for my own safety, but they could not care for me for very long. At the age of seven, I was placed into the care system. I suffered many horrors, which I will not focus on too much. Sexual abuse occurred on occasions, and I was viciously raped, at only eleven years old, by one claiming to care for me. Unfortunately, this was the story of many children at that time, and it's the same, even now. I was hoping that times would change, but not a day goes by that I don't read about such horrors in the newspapers.

My childhood ended when my boyfriend offered to marry me. It wasn't because we wanted to wed—neither of us were ready for such commitment. He was given the choice marrying me or seeing me shipped off to another orphanage. My carers could no longer provide for me, yet again; so, as soon as I turned sixteen and he twenty, we were married.

Jimmy was a lovely man, who treated me respectfully. I was fragile by this time, deeply traumatised by my upbringing. I felt abandoned and unloved by my mother, and the abuse I had suffered affected me more than I realised. I think Jimmy was relieved to be called away on duty when World War Two broke out. I was hard work, I can admit that now; I tirelessly craved love and attention from him, constantly wanting reassurance of his affections. I was left alone, like so many wives at that time, and wallowed in self-pity, feeling lost and abandoned yet again.

I was offered a job in a munitions factory, earning myself just enough to live on. It was good work, it kept me occupied and took my mind off the loneliness. I began to feel like I was surrounded by friends, like I was part of a team whose members genuinely wanted and liked me; but my heart still didn't feel full.

A man came to the factory where I worked, looking for models for a photoshoot. He was young, handsome, smartly dressed, and eager to prove himself to his company. Some of the girls who I worked with pointed in my direction. I'd been told by those who abused me that I was beautiful, but I hadn't thought it was true, and I still didn't. Whenever I looked in the mirror, all I could see was a vulnerable, scared little girl, who nobody wanted. Any beauty possessed by me only brought trouble my way. 'Plain and ordinary' was what the other children called me and believing them was easier than believing an abuser, who would say anything to get a young girl to lift her skirt. He took one look at me and flashed his pearly white teeth. He decided straight away that I was the girl he wanted.

So, there I was, with my spanner in my hand, perched on the body of a drone, with a big cheesy grin across my face. The awkwardness of the situation was clear from the photographs; he had to remind me several times to look into the camera. When the work was done and the day ended, I took myself back to our home and sat alone, wondering what Jimmy might be getting up to.

Thinking back to that photographer, his enthusiasm felt quite overpowering to someone like me. No illusions of fame or fortune from the pictures came to mind, only that extra bit of cash that sat in my pocket, and what luxuries I might spend it on. The pictures would be used to promote women playing their part in the war effort; well, that is what I was told anyway. He wanted to take more and more pictures, and eventually my employers grew annoyed and asked him to 'wrap things up'. He was a little flirtatious and, without realising, so was I. Nothing would ever come from our meetings; he knew that I was strictly out of bounds, because he was informed very quickly of my marriage. Right or wrong, I had always thought that a little flirting was harmless fun and nothing more.

So, whilst Jimmy was doing his duty, I could not help my thoughts. I wondered what it would be like to be one of those women you see in films, with their glossy hair, perfectly smooth faces, and the glitz and glamour of it all. I assumed that I had inherited the idea from my mother, but that lifestyle, with all its attention, seemed completely out of reach for someone like me. I bet those women film stars never felt abandoned and neglected, or unloved. They were surrounded by people shouting and screaming how much they loved and adored them. I could only sit back and admire such a life. As an orphaned girl from Los Angeles, a housewife at the age of sixteen, the opportunity would never come knocking at my door. I was nervous and terribly insecure, certainly not the right ingredients for a star of the silver screen, but this didn't stop me dreaming. Dreams are free, and this was one thing I could *always* afford.

    As time went by, a call came through from a gentleman asking me to model some clothing. He had seen my pictures and liked my friendly face and big smile. It was a good job, which didn't interrupt my usual employment, and the extra cash was needed at the time. I fought a battle that day: my nerves screamed at me with every step I took, but I knew that once there, I'd enjoy every second. It was like an addiction: the clothing was irrelevant, and I moved my body with every click of that camera. My makeup looked perfect, and the attention was exactly what I needed. Just for a little while, I could imagine that I was one of those women whom I dreamed of being.

    This was the first of many calls for modelling, and every one was a battle with my lack of self-confidence. I wanted to hide away, but I had an angel on my shoulder urging me to get going and ignore the devil that gnawed at my thoughts. I soon realised that the attention was becoming my addiction: I loved being an exhibitionist. What I didn't expect was for Jimmy to open up a magazine one day and find his wife in the centre-page. He was proud at first, showing the pictures of his beautiful wife to all his comrades. After a while, his pride turned to jealousy at the thought of the woman he hoped to learn to love one day being stared at by a bunch of men having indecent thoughts.

When Jimmy returned, I was well-known in the modelling world and soon after, I landed myself a part in a film, which was followed by other roles. They were small parts, but they brought in extra cash and gave me a chance to shine as brightly as I could. Acting and singing classes came with the job, even if I only had a single speaking line. It was not long before Jimmy and I decided to divorce. He had wanted the stay-at-home mother and wife all American men seem to dream of. I simply couldn't provide that for him, as that life was a road I wasn't ready to walk down at that time.

We had been growing apart for a good while, so it didn't come as a surprise, if I am honest.

Four years later, one of the biggest filmmakers around signed me up and made quite a few successful films. Without noticing, my name had become very well-known and people, complete strangers, were now calling my name. I couldn't even go to my local store without someone waving frantically. I had the glitzy life and the money to go with it, a wardrobe filled with designer brands and a driver waiting to take me wherever I wanted to go. The work was hard, and I had to make some tough decisions, all the while fighting with that nervous devil dancing in my head. It yelled into my thoughts, telling me that I wasn't good enough, pretty enough, smart enough, or glamorous enough, despite everyone else telling me otherwise.

Around 1950, I was introduced by a good friend to Joe. He was a baseball player, one of the best of his time. We got along from the very second we spoke. He told me how much he admired me and that he had been trying to meet me for a while. I couldn't say too much at our meeting, as I didn't really follow baseball, but there was something about him that caught my attention like no other man. He was caring, kind, and very generous. We began dating straight away. He spoiled me with expensive restaurants and evenings with his wealthy friends. He quickly grew very protective of my timidness and innocent demeanour. I was blind to his feelings towards me, due to my insecurities, but I know now that Joe was the one who truly and deeply loved me, despite everything. Of course, the film industry loved our partnership, calling us a 'power couple' and endlessly printed stories and took photographs of us both. Joe was one of the richest men in his field, and I was climbing the ranks to be one of the top women in mine. Behind the scenes, all Joe and I really wanted was to start a family. I was willing to give up my career and become a stay-at-home wife, and for Joe to look after me like he wanted to. It was never the riches that I craved; I only ever wanted to be loved—truly loved, beyond anything else. And he loved every inch of me, more than I realised at the time.

We dated for four years, while we both concentrated on our careers. We were still young, but vowed to settle down once we were eventually married. We figured that there was no rush. We were content in allowing each other to fly, knowing that we would both return to the nest that we had built, and the dreams that we had promised each other. That time ultimately came too soon, because when you are famous your life becomes everyone else's property. Pressure was building for a marriage, not only from the public, but more so from the film industry. We were big news, and they were about to make us even bigger.

We were pressured into marriage in 1954, very publicly, for the whole world to see.

I was already under contract, so after the wedding I had to resume filming. Joe saw less and less of me as my schedules were demanding. I would sometimes call him, crying and begging for him to come and rescue me from the madness, but he had a job to do himself as he was also bound into a legal contract. He hated seeing me work so hard, so began to fight for me. He called my bosses and tried to find ways to release me from my contracts, but this angered them. Only nine months later the newspapers printed lies, which forced us to separate and ultimately ended in divorce. The news said it was due to a scene that I played in the film I was working on, which made Joe rage with jealousy. It was a story that was totally fabricated by my bosses and the press. I'm pretty sure that money was exchanged under the proverbial table. My bosses decided that I was far too valuable to lose and my marriage to Joe was a threat, as he held power that matched their own. If I broke that contract they would ruin me, and Joe too, swiftly ending his sporting career with one cheap blow, spreading his name in the mud. I had no choice but to file for divorce for mental cruelty. I remember the press conference that they held. I wanted to scream at them that it was all a lie, but I couldn't. They held a proverbial gun to my back and were primed to shoot me and Joe down with the same bullet, all in the name of money.

So, life continued without him, and my name became bigger than I had ever imagined; yet still I could not shake that feeling of insecurity and being unworthy of the attention. My acting skills were too mediocre, evidently: being cast in roles that would depict me as stupid and pathetic. I was told that it made me look attractive to men. I was not that woman; I was smart and hated acting the imbecile, but every role I was offered was that of the 'dumb blonde with ample breasts and thin waist, dizzy personality, stupid questions, and flirtatious body language'. I yearned for a role that would push me, expose my talent, and make me work with my soul, not just my body and apparent lack of intelligence.

I had posed nude for a photographer a while back, which I felt turned out to be quite artistic and elegantly beautiful; 'beautiful' is a word I rarely use when describing myself. They showed the feminine form and all its curves and imperfections, yet others saw them as smut. Some said that being naked was a sin—I could never understand why showing the naked body, given to you by whichever god, would be a sin. We were not born clothed, after all. That was the only time that I agreed with my bosses.

The only way I would overcome this scandal would be if I owned it, and did so with a smile. I was asked shortly afterwards, in an interview, if I had anything on whilst those pictures were being taken. I replied that the radio was on. I was playing stupid, but at the same time I wanted it to be clear to everyone that I was not ashamed of those pictures. Surprisingly, my comment went down tremendously well. I was told that it empowered young women everywhere. Sales of the prints soared, and they were even shipped abroad. What a surprise that was; I had fully expected the controversy to bring my career to a swift end but, on the contrary, it launched me even higher.

Well, I had survived the nude onslaught and seemed to only gain popularity, despite the efforts of a handful of churchgoers. Unfortunately, this tactic also cemented my dumb blonde sex symbol status in stone. I had finally had enough of the stereotypical box that I had been thrust into. After being offered yet another role that fitted into that box I refused, and they suspended me on the spot for breaking my contract.

The next film I was offered was a step towards what I had yearned for, so I was satisfied that my actions had done me a good turn. It pushed me beyond my abilities, and I put my all into it. The hard work paid off, as the film was a success and threw me up to the top of the celebrity 'A-list'. I had made it, and like the idols of my teenage years, I wallowed in fame, fortune, and glory. Thousands were chanting my name. I was in all the magazines, hung on walls and billboards. I had a star on Hollywood Boulevard, and was loved by the whole country, but I felt the most alone I have ever felt.

I married again, and we tried to start a family, but our attempts only ended in miscarriage, which was the worst feeling ever. My schedule was a busy one, fuelled by alcohol and drugs prescribed by my doctor. Drugs to help me sleep, drugs to wake me up, and drugs to relax my nerves. My pregnancies probably ended due to the cocktail of chemicals entering my body. My marriage was again short-lived, and I decided to take some much-needed time out.

I booked myself into a rehab facility, not only to wean myself off the medication, but also to shut myself away from the outside world. I needed time away from the chanting and the high demands of my bosses. Fame always comes at a price, and I was paying for it with my health and my body.

I was shut away in a room with padded walls, whilst I battled with that demon that taunted me. There was still the original demon though: my shyness and my vulnerability, but now this demon was superpowered: high on drugs and piercing my brain with his pitchfork.

It was my fault that I was alone, my fault that I wasn't truly loved, and the most painful of all, my fault that my babies had died. I did not feel worthy of life; my existence was becoming unbearable. I knew that I had to find myself again. I had been kidnapped by the industry; even my body was owned by the industry. I had affairs with powerful men, just because I could. My body no longer belonged to me; it was a tool that had propelled me through life and was now the tool that was toppling me.

For a few brief months I thought that I had taken my body back, while my children were being grown, but this was all an illusion when they were evicted too soon. At the sight of each tiny, little, lifeless foetus lying between my legs, and the blood-soaked sheets surrounding it, the crippling pain paled as I felt my whole world crumble, collapsing into nothingness. By the time I had the last miscarriage, I had lost all control, all rational thinking, and was close to ending it all and joining my children. I felt that I was like my mother, therefore unworthy of motherhood. I was being punished for always being drunk, and taking tablets, and giving others control of my life.

The clinic was brutal, with the detoxification starting the instant I signed the papers. For days I sat in my cell, craving my drugs. My body had no idea when to wake and when to sleep after months of drugs making the decisions. I craved my substitute, alcohol, but that was also taken from me. I knew I needed to do this; I had to be strong, but the side-effects were a living hell. It was a journey that I had to take; I had contracts to fulfil, and feared what my employers' solicitors would do if I breached them again. I kept telling myself, "Just one more film and I'm done. I'll be free."

I had travelled through history in very many lives by this point, but this was the first time I had ever experienced fame. I'm sure that these days people are better equipped to cope with it, but I also see those who have ended their lives abruptly, unable to take the pressure. One can dream of riches and a recognisable face, but what they don't realise is that that face is taken from them. Their life is auctioned to the highest bidder, and that body has a schedule to keep, and God help anyone who stands up and says, "NO MORE".

I was rescued from the hell of that facility by none other than my Joe: we had remained friends for a long time. He said that he would always love me and no other. I had assumed that he was just giving me the kind of false love that the thousands around the world gave. I thought so little of myself at this point that I did not recognise the face of true, undeniable love. We were meant for one another, and always had been. I loved him with a passion, but feared my heart being broken again. He marched into that facility and reassured me that he would look after me, so I signed myself out, and into his care. He took me to his home, to recover in comfort. To the outside world, I had simply gone off radar, but in reality, I was with my Joe. He cared for me in every way he could. He spoon-fed me soup, and helped me wash, comforted me when I screamed, and held me tightly when I cried. We spoke for hours, and he eventually made me smile. After a while I had to return to work, and I showed up refreshed and ready to take on the world. Thanks to my Joe.

However, the old pressures slowly crept back in. Where Joe treated me gently, the industry treated me rougher than they had before. I had to meet deadlines that I found impossible. I tried my best to remember scripts, but my brain became muddled. I didn't bother Joe with my troubles because I had assured him that I would cope, and I wanted to prove to him that I could. But it takes power for a lion to roar loudly, and my batteries were running on empty. I didn't want to lose this battle, so I kept going as best I could.

Some days my mental health wouldn't allow me to get out of bed, so I didn't turn up to filming. Again and again, I was spoken to and warned about my misconduct, which would put me deeper into depression. I asked the doctor what I could do: I needed something to steady my nerves. It didn't take long before I was popping those pills again: pills to fall asleep and pills to wake up. Turning up on set drunk or so medicated that I couldn't see straight. I was falling into that spiral again, and falling so fast that the end came rushing forwards. The film was axed, and the project closed down; so much work lost, so much money wasted. A few months later, I went home alone one evening and took pills to help me sleep, but I had had too much to drink so took far too many. I read in the papers, in the following life, that my housemaid had found my body. Of course, my death was taken over by the press—it was headlining news. Despite Joe's best efforts, I didn't even get the dignity of a peaceful funeral—I had the press doing everything they could to get a shot of my body in its open casket; as distasteful as that was.

  Until his own death in 1999, my Joe laid flowers at my memorial three times a week. He never remarried, he never spoke of us, and he kept my name out of the dirt. He was the one true love of my life. Sadly, I was already in an abusive relationship with the industry, which kept me in chains and unable to reach him. I was loved by the whole nation and beyond, but only truly loved by him. That is the only life where I have felt so much love, yet none at all. I know how strange that sounds, but it's simple. They loved the actor, singer, stupid girl, sex symbol, and ditsy blonde. They loved my vulnerability, my feistiness, my glitz, and my glamour. They were in love with the manufactured image. Joe was just in love with *me*: the no makeup, slightly tubby in places, bad-tempered woman, who looked like an ogre in the morning, and had bad breath, and athlete's foot. He didn't care for any of that other stuff, and that's the truest love that anyone can ever find.

Now that I look back at that life that ended so many years ago, I am humbled that my name is still alive today, remembered by young and old. My face still hangs on walls and soft furnishings. Songs have been written, and documentaries and films made of my life. It's just a shame that the only person in this whole world who knew the real me spent so many years mourning and alone. Darling Joe ended up living the very existence that I feared the most.

I have been lucky enough to come across this kind of unconditional love a few times on my journey; some I lose too soon and some last the course. They have come with ups and downs, but we always held each other up. If you can successfully grab hold of love, where you are adored, despite your flaws and mental difficulties, and if you love them in return, even when you cannot understand why they love you so fiercely, cling to them tightly and never let go. This is the purest and truest love, that only the 'worthy' deserve. You *are* deserving of that love, despite what you see when you look in the mirror. Something inside you reached out to them and infected their soul with you, and only you. Breaking the heart of a love that fierce can be devastating and can rarely be repaired.

The worst kind of love is unrequited love: it is horrific, and burns the soul like a thousand blazing knives. I thought that my mother loved me, but simply because that is what a child expects from a mother. I never told Joe of my ability to remember my past lives. I didn't feel that it was necessary but, I'm sure that no matter what, he would have loved me anyway. How I wish that I could have spent those last years with him. I would have quit everything just to be with him, raise our children, and grow old together. Just the thought of sitting around an open fire, cocoa in hand, rocking back and forth in our wooden rocking chairs after a day worn out with visits from the grandchildren. Or a Christmas feast with a large table surrounded by family, my place next to my beloved Joe, sipping wine while we tell bad jokes. Dreams that I wish could have been but were stolen by those using me for profit. They didn't only murder me—they murdered

Joe, and any family we could have made together.

No matter how beautiful or handsome my body turns out to be in any future life, even if I am born with the acting abilities of all the greatest actors that ever lived, I will never again be a slave to an industry so cruel. I have been to Hollywood, and I'm not ashamed to say that I have spat on the graves of the worst of the men. It made no difference to them, but it made me feel better. Whilst I was there, I laid a single red rose on my Joe's grave and kissed the black granite stone. I may walk wearing a different body, but for now, my spirit is still his.

# UNREQUITED LOVE

The story I am about to tell you is from a life I lived back in the 1800s. It is a lesson that I learnt in the most difficult way; it is about unrequited love. On one side, love and passion burned like a blazing sun, whilst the other side didn't love at all, but just pretended to for his own gain.

I was born a girl in 1827, on the cold streets of Ireland. I have no recollection of my mother, as her face was blurred due to my poor eyesight. What I can tell you though, is that she was alone, young, probably unmarried, and undoubtedly scared. I remember the sounds of her screams when she pushed me into the world, and her heartfelt sobbing as she left me on the steps of a church. She wrapped me tightly in her woollen shawl and kissed my head, her tears hitting my cheeks and falling under my chin. She banged on the heavy doors three times, as loud as she could, before disappearing into the night. Only a few moments later the creaking of the old hinges caught my attention. It was a nun, who scooped me up from the step and took me into the church.

"Oh, my lord help us. Sister June, it's another. Fourth one this week."

Another nun appeared from behind and unwrapped my shawl, exposing my naked fragile body to the chill of my surroundings. The sensation frightened me, and I began to scream.

"It's a new one: still has the cord attached."

Sister June wrapped me up again and led the other sister, with me in her arms, into the musty back room. At the time, I could not understand why I had been abandoned. Later in life, I learned that an unwed mother was considered to be a sin, at that point in history. If my mother had decided to keep me, I would have been torn from her arms anyway, and placed in an orphanage. She would have earned a lifetime of punishment in one of the sisters' workhouses for unwed mothers.

I was raised in a very strict orphanage run by the sisters. They insisted on all of us saying the Lord's Prayer every hour, or so it seemed, and they could be spiteful and physically abusive if you ever questioned their teachings. I was one of forty children in the home, of various ages, and we were all constantly reminded of the burden our existence placed, not only on the nuns, but on Ireland. We were made to feel like we were rats in the sewer, but in the next breath we were called the children of god. I did not understand how children of god could be treated so cruelly by women who were supposed to serve him. If we spoke in class, or were even a second late, we faced the cane across our knuckles or, worse, our backsides. We were the lucky ones: most babies left out in the cold did not make it to the orphanages but were left to freeze to death. Ireland was poor, and there was never enough food in the average large Irish family to feed another mouth, no matter how small that mouth was. So, adoptions were rare.

With the knowledge from my past lives, I knew exactly how to act for a peaceful life. I was always on my best behaviour, and kept my head down, despite some of the other children's bullying ways. I took the beatings and foul name-calling, and never retaliated—not even when I woke up with all of my brown hair cut from my head by a girl named Anne. She held the scissors in her hands with a smug look on her face, but I did not react. I scooped up the hair and placed it in the bin. I received twenty canes around the backside for that one, because they presumed, I had cut my own hair.

Anne was a cruel girl, but she had a troubled past. A year later we found her in the garden, hanging from a tree by her neck. She had a note attached to her, accusing Father Dudley of being indecent with her. Father Dudley kept his place and Anne was labelled a liar.

"She was born with the devil's tongue. How dare she accuse a man of God of such atrocities? She will no doubt burn in HELL for that one." I heard the nuns say.

A few of the girls became pregnant in the years that followed—all of them regular visitors to Father Dudley. Their babies were shipped off to other orphanages before they could even say goodbye. Father Dudley *did* take one boy home to his wife, who could not have children of her own. He claimed that he was an orphan, and they raised him together. I heard that a few years after, his birth mother left the orphanage and tracked down Father Dudley and his wife. After a heated row, she was arrested and was never heard from again. His wife later stuck a knife in his back, before killing herself. Unfortunately, it did not fatally wound him, and he continued to raise his son, along with his new, fourteen-year-old nanny. She had been gifted to him by the orphanage; poor girl thought she was one of the lucky ones.

My breasts were always small, and my boy-like figure didn't warrant any attention from filthy-minded men. I was sixteen when my menstrual cycle arrived. I had left the orphanage a year earlier because the nuns saw me as responsible.

I took up residence in a room within a house above a bakery. It came with the position of baker's assistant to a very lovely, elderly gentleman named Patrick. It was my job to wake up at the crack of dawn, usually at four in the morning, and light the ovens. They still smouldered from the day before, so only needed the tinder and a bit of work with the bellows.

Soon after, my boss Patrick would appear, yelling and god-damning his way down the narrow staircase. He wasn't a morning person—he didn't fully awaken until around 7:30, after he'd drunk his first glass of whiskey. He was a very kind man, with a bulging stomach and bright red cheeks. He giggled at his own jokes, which made everyone else laugh, regardless of its humorous content. He was friendly and generous, and called me his 'apprentice.' Patrick loved teaching me how to bake and, having no family of his own, treated me like his daughter. I loved the smell of the fresh bread, as it baked in the ovens. The yeasty, warm scent made me feel constantly hungry, and it also attracted customers from far and wide. Patrick called the smell his 'church bell for fresh bread', announcing to everyone that it was ready. During the day, my boss disappeared for around an hour to prepare the stew for us to have in the evening. We'd use up any unsold bread to soak up the juices and wash it all down with a pint of ale.

It was a happy time; we had a remarkably close relationship. He made me laugh and provided me with enough money to live comfortably, and in return I gave him the company that he needed. It was never a sexual arrangement, as he was in his sixties. I loved him like a father, and he loved me back—to the point that he ended up telling the customers that I was his long-lost daughter. He knew my past and wanted to make me feel that I was *part* of the community, rather than a *burden*. They all believed him, saying that I looked like him. I looked nothing like him, but I expected they were just making small talk.

Tuesday mornings were the shifts I looked forward to the most, because that was when John would pick up his mother's loaves and butter. He was a year older than I was, and his smile lit up the room when he entered. When he first saw me, he was waiting in line to be served, and his gaze never left my face the entire time. Each Tuesday after that, he'd lean against the wall with his arms crossed, one foot crossed over the other, with his big brown eyes following me around the room. He called me 'Ells' and I called him 'Mr Doogan', his family name. He was usually dressed in oversized trousers and a big white shirt, because in our town, owning clothes that fitted was a privilege in itself. He was the sweetest man I had ever met. My heart would flutter every time he walked into the room, and when he left, I felt empty and longed for him to return. I was falling in love with him, and he knew it, and encouraged my flirtatious looks with a smile. My boss teased me constantly, mimicking my voice. He claimed that it rose a few octaves whenever I spoke to John. To me, he was perfect, and all I wanted to do was marry him and start a family. I wanted to have children in this life, as in my previous life I was unable to have any. I was still only sixteen at the time but, being a Catholic, marrying as young as twelve was seen as acceptable.

One day it was unusually hot when John came trudging in for his loaves. I could see his smile a mile off.

"Usual three loaves, Mr Doogan?" My smile hurt my cheeks.

"And a coupla little ones for our picnic this afternoon." he said, laying his hands on the counter close to mine.

"Going anywhere nice?" I asked, my heart fluttering like it was about to stop completely.

"I'm off to the river with a beautiful young girl with a gorgeous smile. If you can get off work." John looked over to my boss for approval. Patrick threw his towel down on the table, sending a flour cloud rushing into the air.

"About feckin time if I may say so. She's been drivin' me mad. I tell yeh. John dis 'n' John dat. Come by at two, 'n' I'll be done wid her."

John agreed, picked up three loaves of bread, butter, and two small buns and headed out of the door, giving me a quick wave and smouldering smile as he left.

My world began spinning and the room felt like it was pulsating. I couldn't catch my breath. I felt a heavy hand on my shoulder, which took me by surprise.

"You right, Ellie?" my boss sniggered.

"Would yeh like a drink 'o' water or summat stronger?"

I took a deep breath and continued to serve my customers, pretending that everything was completely normal. My smile was fixed on my face like a mad woman who'd just found the pot of gold at the end of a rainbow. Every customer commented on how cheery I looked. Patrick, of course, engaged in conversation with every one of them, spreading the joyous news of my first date with John. That was when I realised that our flirtations were no secret: it appeared that the entire village had been rooting for us—including John's mother!

"About bloody time," was the general sentiment.

At 1:45 John appeared at the door of our bakery, carrying a basket filled with bread, cheese, and homemade biscuits. Our eyes met as they always did.

"You're early." yelled Patrick.

"Ah, only by ten minutes. Surely you can let her off." he called back.

My boss looked at me and glanced back at John; one hand leant on the sideboard, while the other rested on his hip, clinging his towel.

"Ah, be off wit yeh. But don't be havin' her out too late; she's up early t' morra."

I was so excited that I gave my boss a kiss on the cheek and ran out of the shop, still covered in flour and with dough under my nails, but I didn't care. I was on my first date with the man of my dreams and life couldn't get much better. We walked to the edge of the river and sat down on a knitted rug. We spoke about life and love, and our expectations for the future. We both had simple lives, but John had a strong family who were eager to wed him off and expand the Doogan name. He made me laugh with anecdotes from his youth, and complimented me on my looks and personality, which was nice to hear. He didn't ask many questions about my childhood—I think he had an idea of where I came from, but knew I felt uncomfortable speaking about it.

A few days later, John asked me to come to his house to meet his mother and father—a trip that made me feel sick with nerves. As we walked into the small, thatched home with whitewashed walls, I couldn't believe my eyes. John was the eldest son of fifteen children, and the house was bursting with people, old and young; the youngest was still in his mother's arms. John's great-grandmother, who sat by the fire, also lived there. She had become deaf, which I thought to be a blessing in this house, because the noise of children laughing, crying, and arguing was pretty deafening. His mother was sitting on the other side of the fire, stirring a huge, black cooking pot that hung from an iron hook. The bubbling stew was filled with potatoes, vegetables, and lamb; the smell permeated the home.

Above the fireplace hung bundles of dried herbs and flowers, and a warm kettle sat at the side, ready for a cup of tea. John's mother stood up to greet me and introduced herself as Margret. She seemed really friendly and welcomed me into her home.

His father sat on the far side of the room, in a more comfortable armchair. He had a stern disapproving look on his face as I walked in. He barked his orders at Margret like she was his slave. The children played and yelled to one another, trying to make themselves heard over the number of bodies occupying the house. The noise would get to a certain volume before the father would explode in a fit of rage, reducing the children's noise back to a quieter level.

"Don't mind him, darlin. He's just not had a drink yet." Margret scowled at him.

"John will ya gowan get him a glass. Keep him quiet." John placed his hand on his mammy's shoulder, which was graciously received, and swiftly entered the back room, returning with a glass half-filled with neat whiskey.

    I never really warmed to John's father. He seemed like a cruel man, who treated his wife with disrespect, even though she would do anything to please him. She walked with a limp, an injury that she claimed was caused by the family horse kicking her shin. I later found out that she had made conversation with my boss from the bakery. He used to deliver the bread to her door. John's father, also named John, pushed Margret down the stairs in a jealous rage. She broke her leg badly, but refused treatment because there was no one to care for the children. The break healed, but her leg was not as it was before.

    She also lost the baby she was carrying in her arms at the time: she was four months old and named Gabriel. Despite Margret's best efforts, the baby was crushed under her weight. She confessed to me just before she died, that she had hated her husband from that day, and often dreamed of taking his life with poisoned broth or a knife to his heart. She loved her children and seeing her poor, innocent baby daughter die in her arms broke her soul and spirit and killed any residual love she had for her husband. She called him 'the devil' and hated him more than she could ever explain.

    The police deemed the incident an accident, and John senior was never punished for his crime. The rules on marriage were carved in stone for Catholics: once you chose a husband/wife, that was the life you settled for. There was no walking away, no divorce, and women had a moral obligation to lie with their husbands when they demanded sex. The rules also stated that affairs were strictly forbidden, but that didn't stop most of the men in unhappy marriages, which often led to yet more babies left on church steps. John junior was more like his mother: kind and caring. Watching him sitting on the floor, and playfully wrestling with his siblings, warmed my heart further. I knew at that very moment that I was totally and utterly in love with John Doogan, and nothing would ever change my mind.

We were married later that year, on my seventeenth birthday. It was a happy day, filled with song, laughter, and barrels of alcohol. The church was filled with John's family, except his father, who refused to accept me; not that I cared much. On my side, sat my customers from the shop, which mainly consisted of middle-aged ladies. Some husbands were dragged along, but only for the free food and drink that my boss provided for the reception. Naturally, I asked Patrick to give me away, which he said was an honour and a proud day for him.

"Take good care 'a' me daughter, or you'll answer to me. Yah hear me, John boy?"

He cried when he passed my hand to John and continued to cry throughout the ceremony.

We set up home close to John's parents, in a one-room cottage that used to belong to his grandparents. It was simply furnished: an open fire at one end complete with hook and bastible, a kettle and a few pieces of crockery on a dresser, a double bed, a small table that sat two, a couple of armchairs, and a hearth rug. The walls were painted white, and the door was rotting so had to be replaced. It smelled like damp and old people, so I hung sprigs of lavender and rosemary. They filled the room with pleasant odours, especially when the fire was lit.

John set to work straight away and built a new door from timber that he found at his workplace. He worked at the family farm, which was owned equally by his father and three of his brothers. The farm was poorly managed because they argued constantly about what to do with the land.

It was the same story around the entire country: with the exports to England and the growing population in Ireland, food was at an all-time low. Children were the first casualties: their small bodies began to die for lack of sustenance. Mothers cried for them daily in the streets, their echoing screams could be heard everywhere.

By this time, I was heavily pregnant with our first child, and I worried for our future. I worked at the bakery until there was no more work to do: the bakery closed down when the stock didn't arrive. Patrick died shortly afterwards, after drinking an entire bottle of whiskey to drown his sorrows. As he had no family to speak of, he left the whole building to me. So now I was jobless and pregnant. The farm brought little our way, as most of the food was being used to feed the rest of John's family. We did eat fairly well, compared to most, but I worried about how long we could go on living that way.

John came home early one autumn day, his face red and swollen.

"Michael died last night. Evie is sick. I have been offered a job that will help improve our lives. I just need money to get us there."

Michael was one of his cousins, who he was very close to, and Evie was Michael's twin.

"Money I can do: MacMurray wants to buy the bakery. He's offered me half of what it's worth, but ..."

"Sell up; take what yeh can get. I can book us a ticket for next week. There's nothin' left for us here."

John was offered a job in America, working on a farm. I sold my bakery, which raised enough money to ship most of John's family over with us. Some of the older children decided that they wanted to stay in Ireland, to manage the farm. Two weeks after the sale was complete, John, myself, John's parents, and eight of his siblings boarded a ship. The conditions were cramped, but it was comfortable, all things considered. I remember standing on the deck, and watching my country disappear over the horizon. I had a sudden fear of being in the wide, open sea and not being able to see land. At the same time, I was excited for the opportunities that lay ahead in America. For once, we would live like we deserved: no more begging for scraps, cooking up last night's potato skins, or digging in the dirt in the hope that the carrots could be harvested early. No more sickness, starvation, and death. I felt guilty in some ways: my money could have seen more people over to the promised land, but we needed to keep some by for living. I held my bulging stomach and closed my eyes, felt the cool breeze on my face and took a deep breath. This was going to be good for us; I was sure of it.

    The job promised to John was in a state called Ohio. The ship landed in New York ahead of time; we had our papers checked and were led to the awaiting trains. John's family trailed behind us wherever we were taken. After a week's journey by train, we reached Ohio and a coach took us to the outskirts of Cincinnati, to a town with few people compared to Ireland.

They did not have oversized families like we were used to. They seemed to resent us at first, but we ignored their disapproving looks: after all, they didn't know us.

John's father took up residence in a rented house, along with his family, and found employment building canals. He later fought in the civil war. The last I heard, he and his pals were seen riding on horseback in their ghostly garments, torturing men for no reason other than the colour of their skin. Margret died shortly after arriving; she had been bitten by a rat on board the ship, and the sickness coursed through her body quickly. The older family members watched over the children until they were old enough to fend for themselves. I tried to help when I could, but John senior always ordered me to leave his house. I don't know what I did to irritate the man, but his bitterness towards me didn't end.

Back to John and me: the farmer who offered John the job was true to his word. He needed someone to care for his huge herd of cows. John had only experienced small herds of around twenty but, in this job, he tended to a herd of three hundred in the pastures. I was worried for John, but he was a hard-working man and took the work on without protest. We were given a residence on the farm: a two-bedroom cottage. It was so much bigger than our last home in Ireland and, although the wages were poor, we lived better than we had ever lived.

Our child was born shortly after John's mother died, so he had mixed emotions. She was a little girl, with an extraordinary amount of copper hair and brown eyes like her father. We named her Margret, after his mother, and I called her Maggy for short. Life seemed good for a while. Raising a child in those times was hard but we soon settled into a routine. I took it upon myself to help the farm owner's wife, Elizabeth, around the house and grounds as much as I could, and we became good friends. I would watch her children when she wanted to rest, and she seemed to like having a new baby around the house and often gave me clothing once used for her own children.

By the time John arrived home from the fields, I had completed my wifely duty, as was expected: supper was prepared, and the house was cleaned. Life was almost perfect for a while, and our marriage was happy. That all changed once he found the pleasures of alcohol: for him, it was whiskey, like his father. It began with only a glass of an evening, to relax after work, but it eventually took over his evenings and days off. He never drank while working, as he needed a clear head to work around such clumsy creatures, but as soon as his day was finished, he'd have that whiskey bottle to his lips. Sober, John was the best man and husband a woman could want or wish for. Drunk, John was a monster. He did not merely get a little tipsy or even worse for wear: he rolled in at night or the early hours of the morning, unable to hold himself up to stand. He yelled at me and woke our baby by insisting on holding her. I never allowed him to touch her in the state he was in, which made him crazy.

"Give me my feckin darter, will yeh." he'd shout, with a menacing stance.

I'd block the door to her room with my body, to protect her from him, which only made him worse. I'd try to reason with him, offering him sex to take his thoughts off our daughter, which generally worked. I became flirtatious and led him to our bedroom across from her room. Most of the time he fell asleep as soon as his body fell on the bed, and he wet himself, soaking the mattress. Sometimes he took my offer, and we would have sex. If I was lucky, he'd fall asleep before finishing, but other times he did not sleep until he had filled me with his seed. The reality was that we were Catholic, and a catholic marriage never ended in divorce. Sadly, birth control was also prohibited, which inevitably led to a second pregnancy.

I was in my second trimester when the violence began. Blocking the door with promises of sex no longer worked, and he'd call me 'a fat bitch' and 'an ugly whore'. He'd accuse me of sleeping with his boss, which obviously was not true, but John's whiskey-fuelled mind said otherwise. The first violent blows came during the summer, when the full moon shone down onto our little house. It was a sticky evening and Maggy was sleeping, so I decided to sit on the porch with a cool drink. It had been a hard day, and I was enjoying a little time to myself.

It was around midnight when I spotted John's silhouette staggering up the road, swigging air from an empty whiskey bottle. He was singing an old Irish ditty, while trying not to fall into the ditches that lined the road. He was no more drunk than he was the night before, and no more drunk than he would be the day after. I stood with my hands on my hips, waiting for him to reach the front steps.

"Drunk again, John?"

John shielded his eyes from the moonlight, and attempted to focus on which one of the figures before him was the actual me. He swayed from side to side, then took a further swig from the empty bottle.

"I'm outta whiskey. D'ya have any in da house, missus?" I walked down the steps and hooked John under the arm. "Let's get you in bed, shall we?"

I tried to get the bottle from him, to dispose of, but he protested.

"Get da feck off me drink, woman."

He swung the bottle out of my reach, so I thought it best to let him carry it to bed. He stumbled up the steps whilst still singing and spoke of a woman who he'd kissed and asked me not to tell the wife. I had grown used to his cheating ways; most catholic women do. When the drink flows, all their inhibitions disappear—along with their humanity.

As I helped him up the stairs to our room, I fell, injuring my calf. For a moment I let go of John, who continued staggering up the stairs, his eyes fixated on our daughter's room.

"I'll just gowin and give her a little cuddle." He swayed, nearly toppling, as he placed his hand on her door handle.

"No John, yer in no fit state." I begged, but he swiftly entered the room.

I ignored the blood pouring from my leg and raced up after him.

"John, leave her alone will ya. She's sleepin."

He was leant over her crib with the bottle still in his hand. I rushed over and grabbed his shirt sleeve, but before I could yank him away, he swung the bottle around striking me above my right eye. He had a strong arm, and I was knocked to the floor. Adrenaline flowed, and a strong, protective, motherly instinct took over as I grabbed his ankle and tried to pull him away. By this time, Maggy was awake and screaming for me. John struck me again, swinging the bottle into my arm.

"Will ya feckin' get off me, woman." His face was screwed up with rage.

I picked myself up off the ground and faced him.

"John, you are too drunk; you can hold her in the mornin' when you're sober."

I pleaded and I begged, but he continued his mission. I watched with terror as he scooped our child from her crib; she was just a year old and screaming for me, clearly terrified. Her arms reached out in my direction, but all I could do was hold my hands under her as he swayed to and fro. The crib creaked as he leant his entire weight against the wood. Maggy clawed at my nightdress, trying desperately to escape his embrace.

"John, please. She wants her mammy." I begged him, tears cascading down my cheeks.

John looked at Maggy and grew angry at her, throwing her tiny body into her crib. Her head bounced off the wooden bars and she screamed out in pain. I barged past John to see to Maggy, but he caught hold of my hair and pulled me backwards. He dragged me out of Maggy's room, across the hall, and into our room.

"Don't ever get between me 'n' ma daughter. Ya feckin whore."

His face changed from the soft and gentle John, to what I imagine the devil looks like. His eyes looked black, and his face was reddened. Veins protruded from his forehead, and he bared his teeth as he spat in my face. I held up my hands and, for the first time in that life, I felt truly afraid that he would kill me, leaving my child alone with him. Thankfully, the bottle had disappeared from his grasp, but it was replaced by a fist. John struck me in the mouth. I remember the sound of my teeth rattling across the wooden floor, and the pain as they were ripped from my gums. My tongue tore, and blood rushed into my mouth and down my throat. The taste of the iron made me gag, and I felt the room spin. My brain wanted to shut down, to protect me from the onslaught, but I willed myself to stay awake. My Maggy needed her mother to protect her. John scooped me up from the floor, slammed me onto the bed, and began throwing punches at my face. I was scared for my unborn child, so I curled my body into a ball. The punches rained down upon my back and head until finally John had had enough, and fell back into the corner, out of breath.

The room spun, my entire body throbbed with pain, but I still managed to slide off the bed and crawl out of the door. I used the banister to haul myself up onto my feet. I hobbled into Maggy's room and grabbed the chair that stood by her crib. With all my energy, I pulled it out of her room. I slammed mine and John's bedroom door shut, tucking the chair under the door handle. I was so relieved to get to my baby. She had a large bulge on the back of her head, and was very scared, but was otherwise fine. I scooped her up into my arms and hugged her so hard; my tears fell onto her copper hair, and I cried and cried. I rocked and hugged Maggy until the sun came up over the horizon, filling the skies with pinks and yellow hues. I eventually fell asleep propped up against her bedroom door.

I was awoken a few hours later, by a knock on the door behind me. It was John, pleading for me to let him out. He sounded like he had sobered up to some degree.

"Will ya help me out? I must have murdered a man last night; I'm covered in blood. Will ya open the door?"

Maggy was still sleeping soundly, and I didn't want her to wake up, so I lifted myself to my feet and slowly opened the door. I crossed the landing and unwedged the chair, freeing John; the back of his hand was covered in dried blood, with tufts of my long, brown hair stuck to it. John's eyes met my bloodied, injured face. My nose was broken and my eyes almost swollen shut. Bruises covered my head, arms, and torso but my belly was thankfully untouched.

"Jeysus, Mary, 'n' Joseph, what the feck happened to you?"

I stared at John without responding. He looked at me with teary eyes, looked at his fist and collapsed on the floor in tears. His body shook as his hands hid his face in shame. Seeing that he was no longer a threat, I opened the door fully and sat down next to him. His hands trembled, and his tears made trails through the blood—my blood, which had splattered his face. I still loved John, I knew that, when he was sober, he was a good man and my best friend. We had shared many good times together and had created so many memories. I found it very difficult to hate him; I hated the *whiskey*, and what it had turned him into, but I couldn't hate *him*. He was my John, the love of my life; he was my reason for living, my oxygen. I hoped that on seeing the outcome of his drunken rages, he might think twice about drinking. John looked at me with the fear of God in his eyes.

"Maggy!"

"She's fine. She bumped her head, but she's fine. She's sleepin,' so keep it down."

John looked relieved for a moment, but appeared filled with regret for what he had done to me.

"Was it me? Did I do it t' ya?" He placed his hand on mine. I looked down at the floor and nodded gently.

John threw his head back and hit it repeatedly on the wall behind him. I leant over and placed my hand behind his head.

"Let's go downstairs; you can make us a cuppa."

John helped me to my feet and held me as we went down to the kitchen, where he pulled out a chair for me. As we waited for the kettle to boil over the stove, he asked me what had happened, and I told him every single detail. He looked mortified at what had occurred and promised me that he would change his ways and never touch alcohol again. He feared that he was becoming his father, and he remembered all too clearly what his mother went through. He seemed sincere and reassured me that it would never happen again. I believed him because I wanted to—so very much.

In the coming weeks, John stood by his word. As my bruises healed, he became the man I had fallen in love with. He regained Maggy's trust, and always arrived home from work shortly after he had finished. On seeing my bruised face, my friend asked me what had happened. I lied to her, explaining that I had fallen down the stairs. She looked at me in disbelief but said no more on the subject. She knew that I could never survive in the world without my husband. It was a time when women were reliant on men, and rarely made any real money by themselves. We were expected to raise the children, take care of our men, keep house, and always look like we were coping well, no matter how miserable we were.

Life became good once more, and we were blessed with our son, John junior. We called him 'John-jo.' He had my eyes and, apart from a little downy hair, he was totally bald. Maggy was walking, so both children kept me busy, but I always made time for my John. He loved his children and was a doting father, and loving husband. That terrible evening was far behind us, but always remembered. I was left with a slightly crooked nose which, as John said, was a gentle reminder to him to never touch a drop of alcohol again.

The following summer brought a wedding to John's family: his younger sister had found a husband and had invited us all to join in the celebrations. John-jo was still a babe in arms, and Maggy had become a handful, but nevertheless we attended the ceremony. It was a beautiful wedding, missed again by John senior, who had taken a dislike to his future son-in-law. It became all too clear that, in his eyes, no one was good enough for his children.

John's sister married a wealthy man; he was a big fellow, which looked strange compared to her slight frame. As she walked down the aisle in her elegant white dress, I couldn't help thinking of our wedding. It was only a small gathering in the church, the dress was handmade, and the honeymoon was a promise to each other that never materialised. There was still time, but I couldn't help feeling a little jealousy, though I didn't show it. The reception was held in a nearby bar, where the women and children all stayed together in one room. The men all gathered in the smoking room, to talk about subjects that they presumed women wouldn't understand: politics, usually, and the state of the world in general. Us ladies initially spoke of raising children and baking, but these topics eventually changed to how the women were being mistreated by their husbands, and how they yearned to become free of them. I did not mention that horrific night, and only said good things about John. The other ladies envied what John and I had together, which made me feel pretty good; I won't lie. Our children were growing strong and healthy, and we were a happy family.

As the reception drew to a close, the two children were already sleeping in the carriage. I had made a few good friends that night who lived locally. One lady had a horse and cart ready to take her home and offered me a lift with the children. I agreed, wanting to get them home and into their beds. I gave word to John to follow on when he had finished for the night, and then I headed home. The next morning, I awoke to a bang on the front door. I opened my eyes and looked over to an empty bed; his side had not been slept in. I suspected that he had spent the night at a friend's or family member's home.

I slipped on my dressing gown, headed down the stairs, and opened the door. It was John's boss. John hadn't turned up to work that morning, which was unlike him. He had never missed a single day's work since we arrived in America. I promised to send him over as soon as he arrived and closed the door. By now, the children had awoken, so I busied myself attending to their needs. As I scooped porridge into Maggy's bowl, John appeared in the doorway. He was a mess: his shirt was torn, his hair stood on end, his trousers were covered in mud, and he had small red patches on his neck. I hoped they were insect bites, and indeed they *were* bites—but not from insects. John had always been honest with me and explained what had happened.

He had been pressured by his family to have a drink, which led to another and another. He didn't want to come home after what had occurred last time, so decided to spend the night at a friend's house. In his drunken stupor, he had taken his friend's wife and had sex with her, whilst her husband watched them. Apparently they did it often, claiming that it made their marriage stronger. I was furious at him, but his honesty and regret, along with a few tears, soothed my anger. I blamed that devil drink, not John—not my John.

The weeks that passed saw the whiskey appear again. At first, only a small glass in the evenings, which swiftly changed to lonely evenings and barricading the children's door when he returned home. I tried to speak with him when he was sober, but he always said that he was in control of it, and he promised never to raise a hand to me again. But when he was drunk, he had no control over what he was doing, and he hit me on several occasions. It was only one hit at a time, and he completely denied doing it the next day. It hurt not only my body, but also my heart. Every strike chipped away at the love I had for him, until eventually I became like so many other women of that time. My love for John was replaced with acceptance that life would always be horrible—living with a man whom I no longer loved.

It was usually a punch to the arm or a kick to my shin, bruises in places I could easily hide with clothing. I knew that all I needed to do was not say a single word to him and haul him up the stairs to bed. As soon as his head was down, he'd be asleep, and the danger was eliminated. Once sleeping, he didn't stir until morning, and he'd wake up completely sober. As the children grew, he became just like his father. His chair was sat by the fire, and his dinner was presented to him, along with his first glass of whiskey. He didn't speak to the children unless it was to scream at them to shut up, and our sex life was only on his terms, never mine. I put all my love into my children and the family grew ever larger.

I had plenty of friends around me, whom I visited often and sometimes they would visit us whilst John was working. They were what kept me sane. I hated being left alone when they had gone, but that was the life I had, and nothing could change that fact.

Maggy was fourteen when she went to visit a friend's house. She stayed for tea, and her friend's father brought her home afterwards. He was a lovely chap, who doted on his daughter. He had a friendly manner and we chatted for a while on the porch, whilst Maggy introduced her friend to her siblings. We spoke of how hard it was to raise a fourteen-year-old, and how headstrong they could be. It didn't occur to me for a minute that John was watching from the field opposite the house. As we parted, the father gave me a friendly kiss on the cheek and left, taking his daughter with him. I thought nothing of it and returned to my household chores.

That evening, at around ten, I made myself some lemonade and sat on the porch for some quiet time, before John was due to arrive home. He usually came stumbling up the road between eleven and midnight, so I had at least one precious hour to myself. The moon was not out that night, but the fields were lit by fireflies. They were so beautiful as they danced carelessly in the darkness. The clouds had cleared, leaving the sky filled with billions of stars shining down upon me. For just a moment, I thought about how small this world really was. A mere speck of dust amongst trillions of other specks. I wondered where all my memories were held, because they couldn't possibly all be stored in my brain. I wondered if the sky was the darkness in which I swam between lives and, just for a second, I wished this life to be over and to start anew. Several things kept me back, and they were all sleeping in their beds.

My love for John had gone, leaving behind nothing more than the shell of what it once was. I didn't hate him; I was incapable of hate. Sometimes I wished him dead, but only at my lowest. Killing anything other than to eat would fill me with unbearable guilt. Despite his demons, John continued to work hard and provide for his family; something that I was always grateful for. I closed my eyes and took a deep breath of the cool, fresh, evening air and listened to the sounds around me. Crickets chirping in the long grass, an owl making its presence known in the old tree next to the house, and the dull grumbles of an inebriated man charging up the road towards our home.

Something was different: the usual Irish ditty had been replaced by anger and petulance. As he turned a corner, his eyes were fixed on me, and his teeth were gritted. I felt a fear greater than any fear I have ever felt before and had no idea why he was so angry. His usual staggered walk was a determined stomp, his clenched fists were stationary by his sides, and he growled with rage as he approached. I didn't have time to react, to run, hide, or scream. I placed my cup on the table and as I looked up, his fist connected with my cheek. I was knocked onto the wooden beams, and I felt the wood crack under me. His heavy boots stopped two paces away from where I lay. I looked up at the monster who had replaced my husband, and begged for his mercy, but there was no reasoning with the devil. He pulled back his leg and threw his boot into my gut.

"Don't"
He kicked me again.
"Ever"
And again: that time catching my hip.
"Let"
And again.
"Me"
Again.
"See"

Again.

"You"

After that, the buzzing in my ears grew louder, and my sight faded into darkness. I must have lost consciousness, but I still felt every kick as they shattered my pelvis and pounded my stomach. I felt a tearing sensation in my abdomen, and my body filled with a rush of liquid. As the monster knocked the wind from my lungs, my only thoughts were of my children. I willed myself to return, if only to try and gain control of the situation. I became conscious, but my eyes had been kicked and I could only see through a small slit in my left eyelid. Through my groans I could hear the children crying and begging for him to stop. Maggy rushed to my aid, resulting in her being punched in the face by his bare, bloodied fist. She fell down the steps, landing headfirst in the dirt. With all my might I gathered every ounce of strength I had left, and screamed,

"Maggy. Run. Get help."

She looked at me, with tears falling down her cheeks; her face was twisted with fear and her lip was bleeding. She mouthed the words "I love you, mum", and ran in the direction of the farm. For just a little longer I held on. I was what lay between him and my precious children and, while I was still alive, they were relatively safe. While he had something to punch and kick that was still breathing, his anger wouldn't turn to my precious babies. I curled up into a ball and tried to deflect his blows with my arms. The feeling of the bones shattering sent wave after wave of excruciating pain rippling around my body, but my eye stayed as wide open as it could.

    I watched my daughter as she ran up the path, screaming for help. Still, he kicked me, and when the strength left his leg, he dropped onto my shattered body and continued with his fists. Again and again, they hit my head and face. I watched that path, with my daughter's footsteps clearly visible in the dirt, waiting for help to arrive. Something in my brain kicked in, and the pain dulled. I no longer felt the agony; all I could do was hear my heartbeat, which had become erratic. I'm not sure if his boots had severed my nerves or if my brain was shutting down, all I know is that the last thing I saw was John's boss racing down the path, my distressed daughter following behind. In his boss's hands was a rifle, and he aimed it at John. I waited until I heard a bang before I finally let go and died.

    In a life that I lived close to that time, I looked back at the newsreels from that area, in that month and year. No news was reported that mentioned anything about the incident. I did come across a picture of a beautiful young woman with copper hair. Her name was Maggy, and I recognised her immediately. After successfully raising her siblings, she began fighting for women's rights and spreading the word of the abuse that Irish women, in particular, suffered.

She wrote a book about her life and was well-known for her courage. She was powerful and influential, and greatly respected in her community. Although she had looks that would bring all men to her feet, she took a vow to never marry. I wish I could have told her how proud I was of her achievements. I read the book she wrote about her early life merely out of curiosity; she painted a picture of a wonderful strong woman who she called 'mother', a title I felt was undeserved.

Her mother suffered for years, protecting her children, and died before her time after a fatal beating from her drunken father. It was not the boss who fired the shot, but my Maggy: she snatched the rifle from him, took aim, and fired. She hit him between the eyes, killing him instantly, and had no remorse. She took my place and protected her siblings from the devil. She took a single punch in the face from a man, but only that one, and no man dared ever touch her again. She took her father's job on the farm, with the children in tow and raised them all beautifully, giving them what I could not—a happy, loving home.

\*

The man in the bakery with that wide smile and kind manner, who gazed at me with his big brown eyes, caught hold of my love and cherished it, and I loved him fiercely in return. But soon he put that love in a cage, and labelled it as *his*, even though it already was. He was afraid that it would fly away and find someone better, but when love is caged, it either fights to gain freedom or becomes reliant on the safety of that cage. This love may sometimes be let out, but fight to get back inside, afraid of the outside world. Some cages are locked and forgotten, leaving that love empty and lost.

Forgotten love can also go two ways: it can shrivel and die and never love again, or it can grow so small that it can wriggle through the bars to freedom. Then it can find another love, one who does not own a cage, because it knows what cages can do. When love has felt the contentment of a cage, but the absence of mutual love, it might just realise that the big, open world is the best place to be. Life outside the cage was never scary at all.

The best way to love is to not rely on a cage at all. The love is shared equally, and both lovers have a life. A love that knows that if one's love leaves, they will always return safely. A love that doesn't have a hierarchy or a dominance, but equality and an understanding of the needs of the other love. A love that has faults but can be embraced by the other. An equal love brings strength, and room to grow in abundance. That love becomes powerful: more powerful than any force on Earth. If you manage to find such a love, you are the lucky one. Don't ever fuck it up or think you can do better. If you betray that love and walk away, you can never truly return, because the fractures will heal but the scars will remain.

    I have been beaten to death by a man and, as a man, I've been beaten to death by a woman. Society may think that women are the weaker sex, but you only have to look around. Some women are bigger, stronger, and more dominant than the man they choose. Love does not have gender, nor does a violent personality. A six-foot bodybuilder can be beaten to death by a five-foot woman. Men being the victims of violence is still, to this day, a subject secretly sniggered at. The reason why that should be is beyond me. I will tell you that story soon, but first I think we all need a happier story.

# THE SIMPLEST LIFE

I would like to tell you of a life I lived that was significantly easier, without too many complications or tribulations. The date or year was not known, because in this life, my village was part of a community that isolated themselves from the outside world. It was a sanctuary for those who wanted to live a simple life. We had no electricity, telephones, internet, or even a post office. We did, however, have a newspaper, which I had the honour to write. It was a job that I thoroughly enjoyed, but I'll get to that later in the story.

    I was born a boy, to a young couple in a small lantern-lit cottage, warmed with open log fires, and filled with handmade furnishings. Our village was one of a few that nestled within the rolling, grassy hills of an uncertain country. We had a woodland with a variety of trees and shrubs, and wildlife so tame that they ignored our presence. Sometimes they even approached us for a fuss.

    I spent many happy childhood evenings playing among the trees with the other village children, and during the day I helped on my grandparents' crop farm. A small temple, which could fit in only half a dozen pews and had a bell that I barely ever heard ring, was the only building taller than two stories. We were not very religious by any means; it was merely a place to hold village meetings, gatherings, weddings (which we called 'bindings'), and funerals. I expect it was built by past visitors to our village, in an attempt to convert us to some forgotten deity. The large wooden structure that they left behind had been repurposed as a post in the town square that held the oil lamps, so I can only assume they failed. We had no need to worship anything. In fact, it was a concept that not many understood. We belonged to the land, and as long as we took care of it, the land would take care of us. We had no rubbish, nor did we burn anything that polluted the air. The only thing that could have caused any harm was the methane that the animals and, indeed, ourselves emitted. All human and animal waste was fermented and spread on our fields to fertilise our crops, and money did not exist as everything was shared equally. As long as the jobs were distributed equally and fairly, it was a system that worked like a dream. We did have the occasional dispute, usually about love or lost friendships, but they were dealt with swiftly in the temple by the elders.

Our land was so fertile that we could grow anything to extraordinary sizes. The carrots that the supermarkets sell these days are mere minnows, compared to the purple carrots grown in our fields. The potatoes sometimes needed two men to pull them from the ground, and wheat grew to three times the thickness of an average modern-day crop.

We did not have cows, only pigs, chickens, a flock of sheep, and ducks. We also had huge, broad horses that we kept in the main field. They had strength and stamina that I have never again seen in an animal. Their hooves were enormous and could easily crush you under their weight, and their backs were as wide as a small car, quite impossible to ride comfortably. Thankfully, they were a docile breed who rarely made a fuss, and, unlike today's horses, they didn't scare easily. They were used to plough the fields, transport the fish from the boat to the village square, and carry other produce from village to village. Once a week, the horses were also used to turn the massive mill stones, which ground the grain to make flour. As long as they had a nosebag of hay, they did whatever you asked of them. In return, they were treated to daily grooming and as much grass as they could stomach.

Schools were never an issue: we all taught our children from home. We encouraged questions and answered them to our best knowledge. If we didn't know the answer, we would seek out those who did. Our language was one that does not exist in modern times.

We could have been on another planet if it wasn't for the familiar stars, which stretched across the night skies, and the same face of our moon gazing down upon us. The only clues I have is that a comet lingered for days on the horizon, and that the moon was much larger than it is today. Our village elders explained to the people that the comet was the sun's offspring. It was travelling through space, seeking a new world to light up. I knew from previous lives that it was actually a large body of rock and ice, caught in the sun's gravity, but their story sounded much more romantic, so I chose to keep the facts to myself.

Every night during the warmer weather, when the moon was full, we'd all gather in the cobbled square with good food and alcoholic drinks. Music rang out in the streets, with laughter, dancing, and general merriment until the early hours. I didn't like the alcohol very much, because it burnt my throat and bloated my stomach, but that didn't stop me dancing.

As I grew older, I worked longer hours on the farm. My grandparents were approaching elder status, and their time of retirement was soon to come. My own parents were to take over the farm full-time, but my future was to lead down a different path, away from the monotonous daily grind of caring for crops and handling manure.

At thirteen my voice dropped suddenly, and my village saw this as a time to celebrate my adult status, reaching the age when I was to find my place in the community. It was a chance to test the trades and see what suited me the most. Once my job was chosen, I had one year before a partner was gifted to me by my elders. That prospect concerned me the most, as I had been betrothed in previous lives, and it didn't always turn out well.

The job part proved harder than I expected. With thousands of years of knowledge locked in my mind, I had mastered pretty much every task a human needed to know. My cockiness was my undoing, as the body I was assigned to was clumsy, and came with a fragile digestive system. I tried my hand at fishing, but the rocking of the boat caused the contents of my stomach to evacuate over the side. Watching the flurry of fish picking off the pieces of my half-digested breakfast made me feel even worse. Fishing was clearly not my thing. The fisherman who accompanied me did, however, take advantage of this incident, and fished from then on by tossing porridge oats mixed with bread over the side. He waited for the fish frenzy and then cast the nets. Fishing was plentiful after that day, thanks to me, so at least I contributed in some way.

The next job assigned to me was animal farming, which I was good at, but there was always a cute little piglet that I'd have to feed and nurture into a good-sized adult. My bond with them grew as I cared for them: I loved nothing more than sitting in the field playing fetch with the cheeky little pink piggie and giving them belly rubs. The sight of me, a fourteen-year-old boy, being dragged away from the barn by his feet, yelling and crying when it was time for them to be slaughtered only made my fellow villagers tease me. I had eaten pork millions of times, but I never actually ate one that I had shared my time with. Pigs are extraordinarily smart, with unique personalities, and are far too sweet to be eaten.

I tried my hand at being a stable boy. That job included exercising the horses every day, with no saddles. The oversized equines had backs so wide that I felt as though I had to perform the splits, and my nether regions always suffered the consequences. My squeals and cries spooked the beasts, and they reared up in a panic. On more than one occasion I was left face-down in the dirt with a bruised ego. The horse then enjoyed a taste of freedom, until it was captured using a handful of sweet grass and softly spoken words. They never really warmed to me. I expect they were smart enough to know that I was a little afraid of them.

The washroom was strictly women only, as the women of the village protested at the thought of a man handling their dirty undergarments, and the grain mill was already filled with staff. I wanted to work so badly. It was important to find a place in my community, and I craved a job that didn't involve shovelling shit, slaughtering cute animals, or burying the dead.

There was one last option for me to try and that was at the paper mill. The owner was now bedbound; he was born with a bent spine and the effects on his body had taken its toll. He had no family to speak of as he had decided long ago that he did not want to pass his affliction on. The paper mill was to the back of his house, in a separate area, and the mechanics of it all fascinated me. I had to figure out how to work the manual machinery while he yelled the instructions through his wooden cone from the other room.

I had made paper before, but only out of papyrus, not wood dust. It was fairly easy to learn, but still took a while to perfect the skill. The wood dust was delivered by the sacksful from the carpenter's workhouse. I'd reduce it all to a fine powder in the grinder, soak it overnight, mix it all up with some mild glue, and dip it in the cloth frame. I put the whole frame in a press, which squeezed out any excess water, then it was left to dry laid flat upon the drying frames.

In the beginning the paper was weak and tore easily, and some pieces were uneven, but after patience and practice I got the hang of it and became very good at it. The paper was used by the villagers to write lessons and bedtime stories for their children, and some was used to keep tallies of how much grain was used on a weekly basis or how much feed the livestock had each day. I had an idea to write a newspaper of sorts, which I took to the cobbled square every other day and read in my loudest voice. I had seen its effectiveness in other lives: it brought a stop to any gossiping or tittle-tattling.

Any news that came my way, for example when Margery had her baby, or when Henry fell ill, I yelled out through the streets when the sun was at its highest. Margery had people visit with well-wishes and Henry received the best care, so the benefits were endless.

The villagers thought I was mad at first and shook their heads in disapproval as they scurried past me. After only a few weeks, though, everyone gathered to hear me speak and applauded when I had finished. I was happy that I'd finally found my place in the village, and mostly I was glad that the only things I had to kill were the suicidal insects that somehow managed to get into the wood pulp.

As expected, a year later I was to have the marriage ceremony, to a girl from the next village. She had been chosen by my parents and grandparents—all I was told was that she was kind and had a good singing voice. I wanted to trust my elders' decisions, but it was hard not to be anxious. This binding had to last me for the rest of my life. If we didn't get along, we'd both be doomed to a life of misery. The owner of the mill gave me a loan of his best clothing and tried his hardest to reassure me. He himself had taken a wife at a young age, but she had fallen ill and died shortly after. He was a kind man who thought of me as a son, but only because I supplied him with the horrid-tasting alcohol on his request. Drunk, he was lovely: the kind of man that made an entire room laugh with the stories he'd tell. He would compliment everyone and go out of his way to please. Sober, he was a short-tempered, foul-mouthed, crotchety old swine, with a tendency to throw objects at me to get my attention.

    He blamed the world for his twisted spine and his miserable life, and if the world was not to blame, it was my fault. I do feel a little bad, because on the night of my binding he asked for a full bucket of alcohol, as I wasn't expected to return that night for obvious reasons. Usually, I'd have rejected his pleas for such a large amount, but I was thankful for the lend of his clothing, so I got it for him. Although my sensible side didn't want him to over-do the drinking, I thought that one single night of being completely inebriated wouldn't do him any more harm than he was doing to himself already.

    Only a week had passed before his skin and the whites of his eyes displayed a yellow glow. His liver struggled to cope with the alcohol in his bloodstream and began the downward spiral to complete failure. He continued to drink, despite the warning signs, and a fortnight later I found him dead on the floor, by his bed. I must admit I did feel sad for his passing, feeling a pang of guilt on realising that I must have had a hand in it. On the other hand, the poor old git did lead a miserable existence, lying in bed day in and day out, with alcohol as his only distraction. He had asked me to smother him a few times, both drunk and sober. I guess that he decided to let the drink kill him, as I had refused.

The temple pews were filled to overflowing for the binding ceremony, because most of the surrounding villages gathered to witness the binding of myself and the daughter of the Harrisons. I stood by the village elders at the altar, with my brown, itchy, woollen tunic and matching itchy trousers that were tied in the middle by a length of leather. My hands were held behind my back as I studied the simple glass window. I rocked back and forth on my feet as nerves overwhelmed me. I knew when she had entered the temple from the congregation's 'oohs' and 'aahs'. I was far too scared to turn around. She was seventeen and I was only just sixteen.

I didn't really want a wife, if I'm brutally honest, but it was expected of us both to bind the two families together. At last, a figure approached me on my left. I glanced at her, quickly, and noticed she was wearing spring flowers in her hair and holding a bouquet of asters and red roses, with wild ivy trailing down the front of her dress. Her hands looked delicate and soft as she clung apprehensively to her flowers. With one final deep breath, I turned my head to face her full-on. Her long brown hair gently curled over her shoulders, her yellow embroidered dress hugged her hips and pushed up her breasts. She looked at me with her big brown eyes, awaiting my expression, unsure if I would like her. It was at that moment I realised that I had been completely selfish with my feelings. This poor girl had been thrown into this binding as I had, and terror, worry, and anxiety were written all over her sweet face. At that instant I felt a connection with her, like a bolt of lightning had struck me right at that moment. Her cheeks had a gentle glow that warmed her face. Her red lips quivered as she nervously waited for my body language to reveal how I felt. She was beautiful, and my total admiration for this precious gift made me feel like my heart was going to stop beating. I gasped, which made her frown. She turned to her parents with a look of anguish, and back to me with her eyes glistening with welling tears. I smiled at her and placed a reassuring hand on her arm.

"You are beautiful." I whispered.

She exhaled, looked down coyly, and beamed a smile that melted me on the spot. She was indeed beautiful, and it appeared that she didn't even have a clue of how delightful she was. She had all the grace of a wood nymph and the elegance of Aphrodite herself. Whatever on this good earth had I done to deserve her?

I could not take my eyes off her for the entirety of the ceremony and needed a nudge when asked to confirm my agreement to our coupling. My parents smugly looked on from the front pew; a satisfied grin and an 'I told you so' quietly whispered in my ear. When we were bound together, they asked me to seal the binding with a kiss, a task that I did not hesitate to perform. Her lips were warm and soft, and felt like they were always meant to be mine. Her name was Amelia, but to me she was my Angel. Amelia had no idea what Angel meant but when I explained that they were graceful beings with wings like doves. She was happy with my name for her.

The party went on into the night and halfway through the next morning. We didn't get to talk an awful lot, as both families smothered us with good will and praise, and the music and general cheer was deafening. Eventually, we were whisked away to her parents' home and shown to her room, with the intention of us consummating the binding ceremony.

Sex is a strange thing, performed usually with the intention of conceiving a child. Only in modern times, is it seen as something we can do for entertainment and pleasure. We now have the means to have sex without the prospect of a lifetime commitment to a child. Obviously, I had participated on several thousand occasions over several hundred lives, but this was a new body that had never had sex before. The first time is always the hardest, and I did not want to expose my experience, but at the same time I didn't want to do such a bad job that she'd be disappointed. This angel, who stood nervously before me, expected me to make love to her, and I was all too pleased to do so in the best way possible.

We talked for a while; we needed to get to know one another properly. We had only spoken briefly, as the celebrations drowned out any deep conversations. We spoke about our families and friends, our lives and our prospects for the future. I made her laugh with tales of my job-hunting, and she made me smile with anecdotes from her childhood. The room fell silent as we became lost in one another's eyes. I pushed my fingers through her hair and gently pulled her face towards mine. She reached up and held me around my waist and kissed me in return. It felt so beautiful and pure. My heartbeat raced, as did hers, and we both began to breathe faster as we embraced one another's bodies. I fumbled behind her dress for the bow and loosened the string. I hesitated for a moment, expecting her to protest, but she didn't protest at all. If anything, she curled her hand around her back and helped me loosen her dress. Before I could proceed, she had loosened my leather twine, unnoticed by me, and had begun lifting my tunic over my head. I threw it off my arms and onto the floor, releasing her lips for only a moment. Within seconds, both of us were busy pulling garments from each other until we were standing at the foot of her bed, completely naked. Our eyes met, and we sat on the end of the bed, kissing like it would be our last time. Her soft breasts rested on my chest as I stroked my hands down her spine. This seemed to turn her on further: she grasped hold of my buttocks and pulled me closer to her. I couldn't help but feel aroused. My hard penis, trapped between us, yearned to be inside of her. She took me by surprise, once again, by tentatively running her fingertips up and down the shaft of my penis a few times. One of her arms wrapped around my upper body, pulling me closer still; we both collapsed onto her bed, and my hands cupped her pert breasts. Her nipples shot out at the first touch, inviting me to gently kiss them and caress the skin surrounding them. Her skin was so soft and fresh that every inch of her sent my mind crazy with desire. She lay moaning, her hips gyrating in small circles. I moved my hand slowly down her body until I reached her pubic area. She raised her hips and moaned, inviting my fingers inside, so I obliged, placing two fingers onto her clitoris and then a single finger inside. Within moments, she was clawing at my back, trying to manoeuvre me, still fumbling with my penis. It was clear that she was ready for me to make love to her. I placed one leg over hers, my stiffened penis pressing against her thigh. We kissed again briefly, whilst I stroked her vagina, and her other hand stroked down my side. My actions seemed to send her into a frenzy, her back arched and she bit her lip. Her hands gripped my waist and she pulled at my body, signalling that it was time. I swung my hips over hers and gently inserted my engorged penis into her vagina. She expressed pain when I entered, but I continued gently, always asking if she was alright.

    Soon enough, the pain subsided, and her expression changed to one of enjoyment. Her hands swept down my back, making my body tingle, and I kissed her lips as she wrapped her legs around me. I moved my hips, slowly at first but faster as she started to climax. She moaned louder, which seemed to signal to the whole town that we had indeed achieved our goal and consummated our binding. The cheers from outside travelled far and wide. It seemed a little strange that losing our virginities would be a cause for celebration, but in that little place somewhere on planet earth, it was. Amelia was my wife and I have never felt as much passion as I did that moonlit night. I am a great believer in love at first sight, and this beautiful woman who gladly accepted me, was a love that I would never let go of. I waited for her orgasm to dissipate and released my seed inside her body. It felt magical.

The night was still young and, to my surprise, the sweet, innocent woman with angelic features was just as horny as I was, if not more so. We were a young amorous couple so, after only a short break, we began the whole ritual again and repeated it several more times that evening. Eventually, we did fall asleep, still wrapped tightly in each other's arms. We slept until after suppertime the following day. I couldn't keep my hands off her and Amelia seemed to feel the same way.

Amelia was an old soul and reminded me of my Livia; I am pretty sure that she may have been her, but in a different life. I myself am testament to the fact that souls carry on through time.

We spoke for hours every evening, about important matters, and things that had very little importance at all. She talked about her parents and friends, and I spoke of mine. As it happens, it was she who had set the wheels in motion for our coupling. Her parents had taken her to one of my news cries a while ago, and she had fallen for my "cute smile". Our parents were already acquaintances, so it took little effort to seal the deal. I was the one she wanted, and she would not rest until I was hers—she had that sort of outlook on life. She was a woman with hidden inner strength; she set goals for herself and worked hard to achieve them.

    It was not necessary for a woman to be able to read in our village, but she could read better than most men, and her mathematical skills challenged my own. She spoke freely of subjects that she found wrong and offered solutions. She was, all round, a very intelligent woman. After the funeral of the paper-mill owner, we were permitted to take residence in his home: us being the obvious choice. This pleased us both, as the dwelling was grander than most of the homes around us, with plenty of room for a family. Amelia planned on raising a large family, like her own. She loved children, and being a mother was something she craved. I worried for her because this was a time of little medical knowledge, and the birth of a child could be a dangerous business. I had plenty of experience of childbirth: I had been trained as a midwife, in a previous life in the 1890s, but I kept my secret close to my chest. If this was indeed my Livia in a new life, my secret could scare her away—like before.

A year had passed before I noticed a bulge growing from Amelia's belly. It was on one of our many nights of lovemaking. I climbed onto her and felt a hardened, rounded swelling protruding over her pelvic area. I climbed off and lay down beside Amelia, tucked both hands behind my head, and grinned smugly.

"What is it?" she asked, looking a little concerned.

"Angel, I believe we are expecting our first child."

Amelia sat upright and placed both hands on her lower belly.

"How can you tell?"

I asked her to lay flat on the bed and place her hands on her lower abdomen, right above her pelvis. The look on her face when the realisation sunk in was a picture. Right at that moment, she was the happiest woman alive. The very next day we informed our parents, who naturally began organising the next gathering. They also arranged wool to be delivered, for knitting garments and blankets, and the carpenters were asked to start work on a crib and a highchair. They seemed elated by the news, and both families planned together so that the baby would want for nothing. The pride I felt the next day, when I stood in the town square, newspaper in hand, and announced that Amelia and myself were expecting our first child, filled me with joy. As expected, the entire village cheered, and offered words of encouragement and support.

The atmosphere erupted like none other, as we danced and feasted on the finest food, and smiled until our cheeks hurt. At least several couples must have gone home and made love that night, as nine months later the population grew enormously.

It was mid-winter when my Angel felt the first pangs of labour. Her ankles had been swollen for days, and she had become weary of pregnancy. She woke me from our bed, screaming from the hearth rug by the fireplace. She was on all fours and rocking back and forth, her belly tensing with every contraction. I rushed over to help her and offer comfort. I lifted her gown to check on her progress and could see a head crowning.

"Angel, I need you to push. I can see the head."

That was the first time I heard Amelia curse. She said words that I never even knew she had knowledge of: words spoken only by drunken men who had collapsed in the street. I rubbed her back and giggled as the air turned blue. With one last push, our daughter was born. She was blue, and not breathing. Amelia's concern was clear; she looked at me with a pained expression.

"Do something. Help her." she pleaded.

I held the tiny baby upside down and gave her a firm slap on the back. Thankfully, that was all that was required. Her rattled cry echoed throughout the house—the first child that had been heard by those old walls in a long time. Amelia collapsed in a heap on the floor, glad that it was all over. She took a deep breath as we looked over our little baby: her features were squashed and chubby, and she was the cutest baby we had ever seen—and she was all ours. I tied and cut the cord and wrapped our daughter tightly in a blanket. With a beaming smile filling my face, I handed our daughter to Amelia. She held out her hands to receive our child, but her belly tensed, and she began to scream again.

"It's just the afterbirth. It will be all over after that, I promise." I explained, reassuringly.

I placed our new arrival in my wife's arms and lifted her gown. She was still pushing and pushing hard. I placed my fingers inside her and felt a tiny foot. The realisation hit me like a bolt of lightning: it was twins, and this little one was a breech. I instinctively took the situation over without a second thought. I carried the baby from Amelia's arms to our bed and wrapped her up warmly.

"Amelia, I need you to help me here: kneel as low as you can. I'll hold you up, I promise."

She waited for the contraction to pass and did as I asked without a fight. I moved behind her and hooked my arms under her armpits. She was drenched in sweat and trembling with the pain. She groaned with exhaustion, and looked at me as though she was pleading with me to relieve her pain.

"This is a big mother-fucking afterbirth." she yelled.

Her belly tensed once again, arching, and pushing down. Amelia took a deep breath, and closed her eyes; with her teeth gritted, she pushed hard, took another gasp of air and pushed again.

"I can't do it," she yelled.

"Amelia, you have more strength than any man I know. Come on my love, one last big push!"

The contraction hit hard and intensely; she gasped for air and pushed harder than she had done before. The baby fell to the floor along what remained of her waters. He was perfectly formed, but still and lifeless. The enlarged placenta fell out only a few moments later. I used my leather twine to tie off the cord, then I cut it, grabbed the baby, and held him upside down, and gave him a firm tap on his back. He did not respond, so I laid him on the bed beside my daughter, tilted back his little head, and blew small puffs of air into his lungs. His chest rose, and I pressed down on his sternum, with just the right amount of pressure, and pumped his tiny heart. I kept going and going, whilst the screams from my wife echoed around our home. After four minutes, his body lost the blue tinge and pinkness returned. I cupped his head in my hands to check for signs of life, and as he filled his lungs with air and let out an ear-piercing cry the relief was overwhelming. My wife's screams were replaced by tears of solace. He was alive and well, all thanks to his daddy.

My wife sat by the fireplace, covered with the blood of afterbirth. Her hair was matted and sweaty, her cheeks reddened with broken veins from all of the pushing. She leant up against the chair, her legs still slightly open, with a tiny baby in each arm. They both suckled on her engorged breasts, content with the world, whilst the open fire crackled behind them. My wife had a smile that I had never witnessed before: a smile of love and contentment. That scene is tattooed in my memory and, no matter how hard I try to describe it, the words do not do it justice. It was the most magical moment. My beautiful Amelia, with an expression of pure happiness mixed with utter exhaustion, while tear tracks striped her face. She was filled with love for the twins we had made together. We had done it. We were parents—and twice in one night. She looked at me that evening with so much admiration, but I admired her so much more. What an amazing, strong, courageous, and caring woman she was. I was blessed to have them all and loved them so much.

I did worry for a while that my little boy would grow up with a damaged brain, because he had been deprived of oxygen for such a long time. As we watched both twins grow, though, we knew that he had been lucky and suffered no ill effects. As the twins grew, so did our love for one another. Amelia and I ran the papermill together, whilst our little ones ran circles around our feet. In the beginning, we walked the entire route of our village in search of news sufficiently worthy to be written in our paper, but eventually the news arrived on our doorstep. If there was an announcement to be made, the people came to us. Every other day soon changed to a daily news reading, and every single morning, weather permitting, Amelia and the twins stood by my side. Granted, we did have our ups and downs like all couples; we disagreed on a lot of things but made it a firm rule to never let the sun go down on an argument. After the twins, Amelia never managed another pregnancy, but we were both content with our two little miracles.

One of my happier memories of that life is of one particular day in the summer, when the twins were around four years old. We took a rare day off from being the news-crier and papermaking, packed ourselves a picnic, and decided to head out for a walk in a direction we had never ventured. We crossed over our village field and came upon the edge of a forest filled with bird song. The weather was ideal, with the sun piercing through the tree canopy onto the mossy floor. We daren't venture too far in, because we couldn't risk becoming lost, but we didn't need to. Through the trees, the sun hit a small opening where a single, enormous oak tree grew. It was a mighty beast of a tree, old and hollow in the middle, yet still very much alive. Its branches had grown so heavy that they trailed across the ground, which gave us a place to rest. A small shallow stream cascaded over a mossy ridge, which provided a safe place for the twins to strip down to their undergarments and play in the cooling waters. The water tasted so sweet and refreshing, like the purest of water. Even today, I have never tasted water quite as luscious as that stream. I straddled a branch and leant back as it curved away along the ground, while Amelia sat between my legs and leant back into my arms. I remember watching the children play as I stroked my Angel's hand; the sound of the birds and the call from deer within the forest lingering in the air, while the sun warmed our faces. It was such a simple day, but I remember thinking that it was heaven. If I could choose one day to relive over and over, it would be that day: that moment under the oak tree with my family. My heart was full at last.

Sadly, all amazing things must eventually end, but I was blessed and lived to see six grandchildren and many more great-grandchildren born. My wife and I had made a pact years before, that wherever she went, I went. I couldn't possibly survive without her sweet smile to greet me every morning. It happened one day that we had a visitation to our village from outsiders, and along with them they brought a virus.

To most of our villagers it was just a bad cough and a fever that lasted a week or so, but, for the older members of our community, it proved deadly. It was unknowingly brought to our household during the winter, by whom we didn't know. We both caught the virus pretty much at the same time, and what began as a tickle in the back of the throat quickly knocked us both off our feet. We couldn't move from where we lay, even turning over in bed hurt every muscle in our bodies. The sound of my beautiful wife's lungs struggling for air was frightening. Our great-grandchildren attended to our needs: bringing us food, water, and medicine. It was no use; all of the best medicines in the village could not save us. We were both in our eighties and had lived a long and happy life together.

My last moments in that life were with my wife, tucked up in bed facing the open fire, in the home we had spent our lives in. We were warm and covered in thick woollen blankets. My Amelia lay on her side in front of me. I held her closely, my hand resting on her chest while her lungs rattled as her breath squeezed past the thick mucus. My breath was also struggling to keep me alive, but I refused to leave without my Angel. I felt the fragile beating of her heart as it fought to pump blood around her body: the thump, thump, thump through her collapsing veins. I kept my hand on her heart until I felt that last beat—it flickered for a second or two, then stopped forever.

    I watched in wonder as her spirit left her body. Her ghostly image stood and stared at me for a few moments. She had become the beautiful, healthy woman who I had married all those years ago. She looked confused for a time, which then transformed into a contented smile. She held out her hand to me, I took it and we left together. She arrived in the darkness with me, but had another road to take, so left me alone. As she walked into that world beyond, she was met by spirits from her past who welcomed her back with loving arms. I wanted so desperately to run in behind her and spend eternity with my Angel, but it was not meant to be. I had to go back. I have *always* had to go back.

After the birth of our twins, Amelia questioned where I had acquired my knowledge on childbirth and, indeed, about scores of other things that she'd noticed. I was desperate to share my journey through the ages with her, but it was not a time to tell such stories. People grew scared easily of things they didn't understand. They were constantly on edge and questioned *'why?'* if anything went wrong. If the rain came too soon and spoiled the harvest, it was always the fault of some poor fellow that had misbehaved and doomed us all. We had stocks in our cobbled square, where the odd drunken straggler was seen, after stumbling into the wrong home and upsetting the family who lived there. No one was ever executed because we saw life as a precious gift. We all had our role to play in the village, so a day or two of having rotten vegetables lobbed at your face was the best they could do. They looked after their elderly and even those born with disabilities—no one was ever forgotten or left behind. But if times grew tough, it was never just one of those things: it was always because someone had upset the natural flow of things. If I had blurted out my secret then, I might have been placed in those stocks for weeks, with rotting potatoes being launched at me; or worse, a bare bottom being thrust in my face, which happened more often than I cared to imagine. Worse still was the shame it would have brought to my little family. That alone was not worth the risk. We were well respected, and we had worked hard to achieve that status.

When a life like this pops up in my journey, I always see it as a respite: a holiday from the harsh lessons that I must normally battle through. Sometimes I wished I had a filing cabinet in my consciousness: a great big filing cabinet, with a key so I could securely lock away the horrors and leave the good memories out. Sadly, they run together in my thoughts, side-by-side. Sometimes it's enough to drive me mad and I wish to end that life too soon, but I know I will only be flung back into an almost identical life. Over the years I have, however, conjured up a wooden box in my mind. I've found separating good memories easier than hiding away the bad. When I feel down, I sit in a quiet place, close my eyes, and have a little search through that box. The moments my children entered the world, the loves of my lives, the adventures lived, and the friends I have made along the way. I cherish them all and have truly been blessed to have had so many to choose from. They are indeed a rest from the horrors of life, but one thing I have learned is that lives like these give me happy memories, but do not teach me any big lessons. Sure, they are lessons on how to love, and love well, and even on parenting skills, but those are easy lessons learned by most and have been learned before in previous lives. I expect the way that I will progress is to live in misery, where my lessons are tough—where I begin my life as a meek and feeble human, only to exit with the mind of a lion. To be truly unbreakable, one must be pulled through the depths of hell, and survive with the ability to accept that things are what they are, without damaging one's own soul. If this is a journey that is possible, then I have a long way to go. Even now, while I type these pages, the memories still fill my eyes with tears.

# GHOSTS

I spoke briefly about mental health in the last chapter, and now it's time to tell you how bad it can get. I have explained before about my brain's development: the memories do not enter my mind until I am a year old or more. Many religions claim that this is when the third eye opens, or the connection with the overself has successfully linked. It gives me a chance to settle into that life before the knowledge takes over. I have mostly reached the verbal communication milestone earlier than normal, depending on the development of my vocal cords. The knowledge of words and the mouth movements already exists in my memory, so that part is easy.

In one of my lives, I was born with a condition that I now know to be called 'verbal dyspraxia', where my brain sent mixed messages to my vocals. It was extremely frustrating for both me and my parents, as back then there was no diagnosis and, therefore, no treatment. I was seven years old before I could be understood by those outside of my family.

Unfortunately, I was classed as 'retarded' by my teachers and placed in separate classrooms away from the other students. I proved them all wrong when I became an adult:

I metaphorically stuck two fingers up at them when I landed a job as a lecturer at Oxford university. I even taught the son of one of those ignorant teachers; that was pretty satisfying, especially when I introduced myself to his father. I have never witnessed a face so shocked; the poor man could hardly speak. He credited his own good teaching, mind you, and I quickly corrected him on his error. A wrap around the knuckles every time I mispronounced a word was most definitely not a good teaching method.

This life was so very different from the last one that I spoke of, but I'd struggle to give you two that were similar. I have said before that my memories begin to fill my mind at around a year old, well, this next story was an exception. I was born a girl in mid-winter and, from the instant my lungs breathed the cold air, my memories poured in, all at once. It was like the floodgates opened, letting in gallons and gallons of past life memories, to the point that I felt like my brain was outgrowing my feeble skull. My screams were not because of the shock of birth, but from the pain in my head. It was thumping and expanding as the fluids gushed around, unlocking paths that should have been closed, searching for unused corners to pack the memories in tightly.

I could not move my limbs properly or see past the fuzzy shapes that danced around the room. My hearing was dull, and my voice had not yet matured so I couldn't tell anyone of the fiery pain that was engulfing my head. My poor mother was so patient and spent hours rocking me back and forth, pacing the floor and offering words of comfort. She sang songs, and cried for hours out of sheer frustration, but it was no use. What I wanted to say was, 'Put me out of my misery, mother. My brain is getting crushed,' but all that came out was noise. The screaming only stopped when a breast was put to my mouth. The sucking motion seemed to ease the pain a little, or perhaps I had become so exhausted that I slept or passed out; I can't be sure. The pain woke me several times a night, the thudding felt like a mallet to the head. It was clear that something had gone horribly wrong, and for a time I prayed for death.

    My mother left me alone sometimes, only for ten minutes or so, just to be in another room away from the din. She could have abandoned me or smothered me, but she loved me too much. She persevered longer than I thought possible, and eventually her patience paid off. As I grew older, my pain lessened while my brain sorted out the tangled mess. By the time I was eight months old, the pain had decreased to a dull ache, and my poor mother was finally able to rest. That was when I treated her to a full twelve hours of sleep. I awoke earlier, but entertained myself, any way that I could. It would have been longer, but she came rushing into my room in a blind panic. Her eyes were wide with fear and the blood had drained from her face. She thought that the silence meant that I had died in my sleep. The relief on her face when she saw me sitting contently in my crib was priceless.

    My father had left for the war a few months before I arrived and had been killed in action. He left behind my mother and my three siblings: twin boys, and a girl; and of course, me, also a girl. She named me Agnes and 'Mummy's little bean'. The two older boys went to work during the day: they both helped in the stables of the town's brewery. They were only small, and the horses were huge, which meant they could easily slip under their bellies without disturbing them and dodge the oversized hooves when clearing away the muck. They were allowed to keep some of the manure for the stove. It smelt to high heaven but burnt extremely well. It kept us warm in the winter, and my mother made a few extra shillings by selling the excess to our neighbours.

    We lived in a poorer part of town, so she didn't get much money, but it was enough to feed us all. She sometimes gave it away to those with children. My sister was not much older than I, so she stayed at home. She did visit relatives from time to time, while my mother sewed the broken seams of wealthy women's dresses. Occasionally I'd watch in wonder, as my mother dressed herself in the finery and paraded around the living room, to feel wealthy for just a moment. She was a strong woman and raised us all well. We had no real education, as this was when King Edward III ruled England; I was born in 1340.

My toddler years were difficult, as I had to hide my true self from my family. I had to wait until the usual age to talk, even though I could already speak several languages fluently. By the age of only ten months, my mother heard me talk in my sleep: an affliction which I can only guess was caused by my swollen brain. I was awoken by someone shaking my arm and as I opened my eyes, I was saw the puzzled look of my mother. My brothers were in the room with her.

"Did you boys hear her? I'm telling you now; she just asked for some rye bread and wine."

She looked into my eyes as though she was looking for a spark of magic.

"Agnes, say that again."

I so desperately wanted to tell her that it was me talking in my sleep, and that I had dreamed of enjoying a meal of rye bread and wine, but I thought it better to just smile and babble sweetly.

A full year and a half from birth I decided that it was time to thank my mother for all that she had done for me. After all, some eighteen-month-old children can talk to a certain degree. I was sitting in a wooden highchair by the open fire, eating pieces of bread and jam. My mother relaxed with a drink next to me. With no one else in the room, I took the opportunity to thank my mother, and tell her that I loved her. Her response was not what I expected.

"Oh, so *now* she talks."

She placed her cup on the table and leant towards me.

"Agnes, my little bean, you've been reciting poetry in your sleep since you were nine months old. I was wondering when you would speak up. I'm just glad no other buggers had heard, or they might have just stuck us both in the loony 'ouse."

I didn't quite know what to say after that. One thing was for sure, my mother's affection towards me ran deep; regardless of anything I threw her way, she always took it well and never asked too many questions. I can only assume that she feared the answers.

At around the age of three, I taught my family to read and write. To the outside world, it was my mother who taught us. She was illiterate, but not many people knew. Our secrets remained within the home, and we became better off with the added income that my mother gained by writing letters for people. I'd write the letters, but get my mother to copy them, for practice. I had mastered the art of toddler language for whenever we went out of the house, or had guests visit. My siblings accidentally revealed my secret a few too many times, but it was dismissed as being a slip of the tongue. They were all eager to learn and I enjoyed teaching them.

Times were tough, and the struggle to live well was always out of reach. But life had another little surprise in store, a surprise that no one saw coming.

When I was only nine, a deadly virus swept through our small town and, indeed, the continent. It travelled within the fur of rats, who swam up rivers and streams. It was the Black Death, and it pointed its bony fingers in our direction, covering each and every home with its dark shroud. The eerie sounds of mothers weeping for their children; and the crying of babies left alone, except for the mangled remains of those who had cared for them, came from every home to fill the air. Victims were only relieved of their moans of suffering and rattles of death when their soul was released, leaving behind a pus-covered corpse. My brothers arrived home from the rat-infested stables with exhaustion etched on their faces. They were pale and weak, with sweat pouring from their bodies, their eyes sunken and bloodshot. My mother tried in vain to nurse them to health, with cold towels and healthy soups, made with herbs and flowers, but it was no use. The first brother took his last breath and died at around one o'clock in the morning. My other brother screamed weakly for three and a half hours, holding the hand of his dead twin, until death returned for him. My sister and myself were not allowed to enter that room, for fear of us being infected. All I remember is my brother's hand falling from the cart as the barrow men took their bodies away—his swollen fingers were black, and the flesh rotten where his fingernails once grew.

Mother wept for days at the loss of her sons, repeating again and again that it was her fault. There was nothing my sister and I could do to console her. A few days passed by, and she locked herself in her room and refused to re-join us. We assumed that it was due to her grief and tried to persuade her to come out, but our pleas were soon met with silence. An acrid familiar smell that burnt our nostrils seeped out from under her door. It was my sister who flagged down the cart and led the black-clad men to her room. It took two men to break down the heavy oak door that she had barricaded from her surviving daughters. On the other side, our worst fears came to fruition: she had succumbed to the virus herself many days previously, and several rats were gnawing away at her corpse. In her hand was a black and white pencil drawing of my father and the twin boys in happier times, and a note to myself and my sister, which we were unable to read as her body fluids had ruined the ink. My sister and I had to fend for ourselves.

    Only a few people remained in our street, and they had gone mad with grief. Everyone was either dead, dying, or gripped in the pain of mourning for loved ones. There was no place for two orphaned girls, and the rats ran riot in our streets. We were the lucky ones, having never been bitten by the fleas. It seemed that our blood was not to their liking: death stared us square in the face, and moved swiftly to the next, leaving us alive and starving, surrounded by the stains and lingering smell of death and decay.

    I made the hasty decision to pack up any provisions that we had, and head towards the countryside, away from the smells that attracted the hordes of rats. We took with us any valuables that we could trade and set out on the long walk. All around us, piercing screams rang throughout the streets. People were begging for medical aid, but there was nothing we could do without risking our own lives. Bodies were piled up on every corner, waiting to be collected by men who were probably lying dead themselves. The barrows were left unattended, piled high with yet more corpses; the grotesque, blistered bodies were unrecognisable as humans. I tried to shield the eyes of my sister, because she began to scream at the sights she saw. She was a fragile soul, and the scenes around us became too much for her to take.

    Every so often, we stumbled upon a farmhouse and begged for food and help. Most of the people barricaded themselves inside, but some dwellings lay empty, the occupants either fled or succumbed to the virus. We stayed at one such home for a number of months. It was an old, cosy, thatched cottage at the side of an empty cattle field. The cupboards were piled high with sacks of oats and flour, cheese, butter, jars of pickled vegetables, jams, and honey; and there was a cellar stacked with firewood. We mixed oats with water as soon as we found the hoard and added a little honey for sweetness. We were too hungry to heat it, so we ate it cold. Afterwards, we built the fire to keep the chill of the night away, and I told some stories to my sister to pass the time. We had decided to stay in the cottage for as long as we could, hoping that the danger would pass in our absence. We were lucky to have found such a place. We had no idea what had happened to the occupants; we assumed they had left with the intention of returning to their well-stocked provisions but had died before they could do so.

That winter was harsh: the north wind blew ferociously into our small cottage, and around the open fire was the only place to go that kept out the icy bite. We collected as many blankets as we could, locked ourselves inside, and waited for the snow to thaw. I did all I could to keep us alive, but my dear sister grew weaker by the day.

It began with a cold that travelled to her chest. Her cough kept her awake at night and, without the means to gather herbs that I knew would help her, she grew worse. I willed the snow to thaw, so I could at least raise the alarm, but the snow grew thicker, barricading the door and windows shut. We could not leave, even if we wanted to. We were running low on wood for the fire, so I began breaking furniture. Anything I could find that would burn was tinder for the fire. As the days passed, my sister's lungs filled with mucus that was hardening and rattled with every breath that she rasped. We both huddled together around the fire, and I sang a song that mother used to sing. I hugged her frail body and swayed gently, while watching the fire engulf a pair of table legs.

"Mother is here." My sister's weak voice whispered through her cracked, dry lips.

I presumed my sister to be delusional until I saw the faint outline appear in front of us. Energy gathered to reveal a shape that I instantly recognised as my mother. She looked at me with sorrow in her eyes, and mouthed words that I couldn't hear. She leant forward towards us and held out a ghostly hand to my ailing sister. I watched, dumbfounded, as she pulled her quivering hand free from our coverings and slowly reached for our mother. In an instant, the room blurred as my eyes closed. I fell asleep, the picture of my sister's hand resting on my mother's ethereal palm still fresh in my mind.

      I awoke soon after, still clutching my sister's cold, stiffened body, warmed only by my own. She was gone, and I was left alone in the world at only ten years old. My age was not an issue though, as my knowledge stretched back many lifetimes. I was somehow unaffected by the influenza that took my sister. I sat for the next hour, clinging to her corpse, in the hope that my mother would return for me, but she didn't.

      The very next morning saw a thawing of the snow, and by the afternoon on the following day, the sun had melted enough snow to free me from the cottage. I left my sister behind, by that fireplace, as I did not have the strength to move her. Again, I gathered what provisions I could and headed out into the world, but this time alone. As I walked down the road, my bare feet sinking into partially thawed, ice-cold ground, I could see people appearing from all around me.

These people were not like those I had seen before but were the ghostly figures of those who had fallen victim to the Black Death. They still held the scars that the virus had left behind, and they were wandering aimlessly, unable to find their way into the afterlife. It appeared that my sister had been led away by the ghost of my mother, but many more had been left behind. I saw each and every one of them; I couldn't explain why. Mothers clutching their children, husbands and wives hand-in-hand. Some called out for their loved ones, while some sat patiently, like they were waiting for the heavenly carriage to pick them up.

One woman grasped my arm and tried to pull me down into a ditch, muttering that her body had not been found. She wanted me to drag it out and place it on the side of the road to be given a burial. She was convinced that it was the reason for her unrest. The body itself was a tangled mess: blackened by the icy ground and half-eaten by wild animals. Her right arm had been torn away and dragged a few feet from the body. I broke free of her grasp and ran as fast as I could; my feet were so cold that I didn't notice the flintstones cutting into the skin, leaving behind a trail of my own blood. Still, I ran, passing hundreds of ghostly figures all holding out their hands, pleading for safe passage. I had no idea who was real and who was a spectre, and I did not care to stop for either. I continued to run until I saw a church in the distance, with its tall spire reaching into the sky. As I drew closer, its bells chimed, which to me indicated life and, most of all, a place of safety.

I continued to run, though my body ached, my eyes fixated on the heavy door of the church, determined not to stop until I reached the entrance. My heart felt like it was beating out of my chest, and my legs felt like they were dragging great stones. Sweat rolled down my face, and my rapid breathing made my lungs tighten like they were lined with cement, but I continued regardless. With one last burst of energy, I had made it to the door of the church, flinging my exhausted body against the dark wood.

I lay in a heap on the floor, panting and crying for help. Figures of the dead gathered and headed in my direction; I was afraid, not of death itself but of these ghostly figures, who seemed intent on hounding me. I desperately clawed at the doors as they drew closer, yelling for the occupants to let me inside. A set of keys clattered, and the lock opened just before the apparitions reached me. A young monk with a cautious expression looked down at the heap of a girl with blood pouring from her swollen feet and a look of terror on her face, and immediately offered me sanctuary. He effortlessly scooped me off the stone floor and carried me inside, swinging the door to a close behind him.

The church was like nothing I had ever seen before. Its high vaulted ceilings and stone archways made every sound echo, yet you could hear the slightest movement of a monk's robe or a child's whimper. Rows and rows of wooden pews reached towards the white stone altar, which displayed a simple wooden cross, a statue of the Virgin Mary, and a golden chalice. Dotted around the church were some ghostly people, but they were all in prayer, and with their faces hidden by their bowed heads, they ignored my presence. The monk hurriedly carried me down the aisle, into one of the back rooms, and laid me on a wooden table.

"Wait here. I'll fetch help."

I lay on my side, shivering in the cold room, and curled up as tightly as I could. The pain in my feet spread through my aching legs. They felt like I had run the entire distance on molten lava. I couldn't help but scream and cry out in agony. Three monks burst through the door, all dressed in thick brown robes. They surrounded me and began asking questions, whilst checking my body for signs of disease. There were none to speak of: I was malnourished, but otherwise perfectly healthy, apart from my bloodied feet. Satisfied that I had not brought death to the church, they tended to my shredded feet: covering each foot with a herbal poultice and wrapping it with cloth.

They were all free from the virus, survivors like me. They gave me milk from the poppy to ease the pain and lay me on a mattress under a thick woollen blanket to sleep. The room was lit by candle-light, and I could see that some bookshelves and large tapestries lined the walls above, depicting men and women dressed in fine clothing. They held golden chalices decorated with jewels in their hands, silver halos surrounded their heads, and lambs lay at their feet. In each dark corner sat a spectre of a monk in prayer, still and silent. I tried not to look directly at them, as I feared what they might ask of me. I thought that if I alerted them to the knowledge that I could see, they might grab hold of me like the woman by the road.

I couldn't explain what was happening, but I could see everyone who had recently died from the virus, and had been able to do so since witnessing my mother's ghost. I wondered if this virus had taken so many that they had been left behind because there wasn't room in whatever kind of afterlife awaited them. Did they not enter the darkness and re-emerge as a new life, as I had done so many times? Were they trapped or, indeed, awaiting their turn? Were the dead forced to queue because their numbers were so great, or had I simply gone mad? Had the memories pouring into my brain at such a young age damaged it somehow? Had it now got to the point where my brain could no longer sustain any level of sanity? I had seen ghosts in previous lives, but never this many. I'd served in wars several times, and witnessed scores of deaths before my own, but never once had I witnessed a sight such as this.

The monks were only a few of those that lived in the monastery behind the church. They explained that they had tried their hardest to keep the plague out but hadn't suspected that the monastery's population of rats already carried the death. Despite dozens of cats roaming freely in the building and grounds, rats had always been a problem, outnumbering the felines, one hundred to one.

I had turned my back on religion a dozen lifetimes ago, but now I was only too pleased to give thanks to the god that they worshipped; if only to secure my stay in the sanctuary of the monastery. The monks were kind to me and gave me fresh clothing and nursed me back to health. They taught me lessons from the bible, and eased my fears when I was in their company. While I was with the monks, the ghosts held back, but as soon as I found myself alone they'd come racing towards me, pleading for my help.

The nights were the worst, shut away in my tiny room with the small window. The only furniture was a firm bed, a table, and a wooden cross fixed to the wall. My small candle did nothing to illuminate the space around me. I prayed for the moon to shine brightly through my little window for the whole night, if only to alert me to the ghosts' presence, but my room faced the wrong way, and the moonlight was blocked by the shadow of the church.

My candle lasted about an hour, while I tucked myself into a corner, listening to the haunting calls and pleading of the ghosts. The blackened eyes and the pale faces coming ever closer, tugging at my arms and legs and pulling at my hair. They were in the corners, under my bed, sitting on my bed in plain sight; I just could not escape their company. I remember staring at that candle, as the flame burned to the end of its wick; one elderly gentleman stared at me without saying a word. His long white beard trailed down his emaciated, naked body. His empty eyes watched me sob, as the flame shrunk down to a small, blue glow before disappearing, plunging the room into darkness. I hid my head in my hands as the old man crept closer to me. I jumped with fear when I felt his bony, pus-covered hand fall onto my upper back, and rub up and down. I heard the creaking of his elbow as it bent, and I could smell the stench of his breath as he whispered in my ear,

"Am I dead?"

"Yes, you are dead. I cannot help you, so leave me alone." I screamed the sentence again and again, in the hope that they would all leave me and seek another who *could* help them. A priest or a monk could at least say the right prayer to send them on their way, but not me. *Anyone* but me.

My screams of sheer terror woke the occupants of the rooms around mine; they were other survivors of the plague, casualties who sought refuge like myself. Some shouted for me to shut up, but some came to my aid and tried to convince me that it was all in my imagination, that I was traumatised by the death of my family. It was far more than that: I could see them, hear them, feel their touch, and smell their putrid, rotten breath as they drew closer.

The only time I slept was when I was in the garden, during the day. Surrounding myself with the living and the bright sunshine seemed to keep them away, and although I could still see them lingering in the shadows, they allowed me to sleep. One of the monks was assigned to my care and promised that I would be released from the 'night terrors', as he called them, when I agreed to be baptised. At this point I was willing to try any solution, so the very next day

I stood in the pool of holy water, and was blessed by the most senior man in the building. A prayer was said, and I was pushed back into the water. I expected a miracle to occur that day: that the waters would wash away my visions of the dead but, as I rose from the freezing cold water, I stood face-to-face with a woman in a black shroud, and in her arms was a new-born baby.

"Help my baby. He's sick."

She pushed the ghostly child towards me, and I took in a deep breath and screamed as loudly as I could. I flung my arms at the spectre, knocking the monk who had performed the baptism into the stone wall and cracking open his head, but still they came. The ghosts surrounded the pool, floated above my head, and even stood by my side in the waters. There was nowhere I could turn to avoid seeing them. I must have been hit from behind by the injured monk, as my frenzy suddenly ended with a sharp pain on the back of my head, plunging my world into darkness.

I awoke lying on a bed, with my head wound dressed, wearing fresh clothing. My hair was still wet from the pool, which captured the chill in the air. As I tried to move, I discovered that my wrists and ankles had been bound to the bed, restraining me. My monk friend sat beside me, with a look of sorrow etched across his creased face.

"I'm so sorry that we cannot help you, my child, but rest assured we are sending you somewhere that can. I have made sure it is free from plague. Good luck, and I hope to see you again."

He kissed my forehead, and his head hung low as he left the room.

When the door closed, the ghosts returned, and as I was bound so could not hide away, they had their hands all over me. My face, body, private parts, and limbs were all being pulled about. My hair was pulled from the roots, and my toes and fingers felt like they were being torn from their sockets. I closed my eyes and tried to picture a place away from this hell, but their presence brought me back to reality. A reality from which I could not escape, no matter how much I tried.

This hell lasted for what seemed like days, until the carriage arrived to pick me up. I was sleeping through sheer exhaustion at the time, in my own urine and sweat. They transferred me onto a bed with wheels and rolled me down the candle-lit corridor and into the back of the carriage. The doors were bolted tightly, which extinguished most of the light. Only a single man accompanied me on the journey. He was not of this world, but he remained silent, with his head bowed, his hat covering his eyes. He was not like the others; if anything, they seemed to fear him. He was motionless and appeared to be sleeping, so I took the opportunity to join him.

I awoke in a bright room, sitting upright on a wooden chair. I was surrounded by both the living and the dead, all watching over me. To my side was a man who claimed he had medical knowledge. He did not address me personally but did explain to his audience a procedure he was about to perform, who applauded at the end of every sentence he spoke.

"The patient seen here was admitted to Bethlam a few days ago. She came from a monastery where she had apparently lashed out in anger, injuring a monk who was trying to assist her. Her claim is that she can see the dead walking among us, and this convinced the brothers that she has been touched by evil."

The men around the room chattered to one another.

"As you can see, the scratches on her arms and face and the patches of baldness on her head appear to be self-inflicted; the tearing out of hair being a common symptom of possession. We have medicated her since arrival, which causes drowsiness but keeps the devil at bay. On witnessing one of her lunatic outbursts myself, I am in agreement with Doctor Hymes that trephination must be performed immediately. A hole will be bored into her skull, releasing the evil spirit, and setting the patient free from her delusions. We are hopeful that this young girl will be capable of re-joining society in the future, when she is fully recovered."

Men around the room commenced applauding, which echoed throughout the room.

I could not move and could barely keep my eyes open. I had been given so much milk from the poppy that my eyes rolled in my head. I knew the enormity of what was about to happen to me, but my mind simply did not care. The last thing I saw was a ghostly man, with a long, curled moustache and a bulging belly threatening the seams of his shirt. His hands were clasped behind his back as he looked at me with a menacing smile.

I was awoken by the agonising pain in my head and the shrill sound of a drill grinding through bone. A dark cloth covered my eyes, so I could not see. I heard voices speaking, but I was unsure where they were or who they were. I felt cold and began to tremble uncontrollably. A blanket was tossed over my body, but I slipped back into unconsciousness before feeling its benefits.

The next time I opened my eyes, I was in a room with grey stone walls, a bed, and a chair. Sitting in the chair was a woman in a simple black dress, with a black head covering. I was not sure at first if this woman was living or dead, all I knew was that her presence comforted me. Her eyes seemed to be alive, lacking the dullness of the dead. She passed me some water and demanded that I take a sip. The pain in my head burnt, my body felt weak, and my throat felt as if I had swallowed fine sand. I reached out my hand to grab the cup, but my arm did not respond as it should: its movements were uncontrollable, and the limb felt like it was not my own. I turned my head, but my eyes raced ahead of the movement. I tried to lift my head from the bed, but it was too heavy, as though it were made of concrete. I tried to yell,

"What have you done to me?"

But all that escaped my mouth was a long, drawn-out groan, and a little spittle that dripped from the corner of my lips.

"It will get better, child. Your brain needs time to recover. God will see to it; he will heal you."

The woman, I recognised her as being a nun, tapped me on the back of my hand and left the room. As she closed the door, the room flooded with spectres. Old and young gathered around my bed, chattering, poking, and prodding my body. Some of them became angry and marched from the room in pursuit of the nun, while others wept by my side.

As the weeks passed, my fear of the dead subsided. My body was broken, so I could not escape them, but in some strange way it gave me comfort to know that I was never truly alone. After months of willing my brain to do my bidding, I finally gained enough control to stand, and was transferred to the ward, alongside the other patients. There were fifteen at one time: all like me, shuffling around and wondering how they got there, if they'd ever get out or, indeed, get better. Some had families who visited regularly, but most of us had no family left or any that cared enough to come. My thoughts were still intact, and my wisdom still worked normally, but I was trapped inside a body that felt as though it belonged to someone else.

My days were spent wandering up and down the corridor. My doctors saw it as a sign of retardation, but in my head, I was reciting poetry, solving problems, and diagnosing my fellow patients. I spoke to my ghostly visitors in my thoughts, and they answered me back. I even witnessed a few of them pass over, finally picked up by relatives and taken to that better place. Sometimes I pleaded to be taken with them, but I always received the same response:

"You're not finished yet. You still have much to do."

What more could I do? My body was broken and my mind swimming upstream, desperately trying to escape the ocean of madness. I tried several times to take my own life, but my hands could not tie the bed sheet noose.

It was in my sixteenth year when I finally succumbed to the lunacy. Ideas in my head swirled around in a cauldron, stirred by thoughts of death. I spent my days staring out of a window at a large oak tree. I watched the seasons passing, the leaves slowly changing colour and falling to the ground. I watched as new buds formed on the tips of the branches, and the acorns changed from green to brown before being plucked off by squirrels. Every day was the same. I ate when they fed me, slept when they asked, and when I had a visit from the doctor at night, I kept my eyes closed while he did what he said was necessary. I didn't care what happened to me. I didn't care that the doctor would arrive, accompanied by others, all taking turns to 'examine' me. I just did as I was told and closed my eyes.

In my seventeenth year, my belly swelled to a point where I could no longer sleep comfortably, so they placed me in a room away from the ward. My ghostly friends had all abandoned me now; I expect it was because they knew that I couldn't help them, even if I wanted to. I was alone in the dark, and I grew to hate being alone.

A few nights later, I awoke to the pain of labour enveloping my body, and a warm damp feeling between my legs. For the first time in a long time, I opened my mouth and screamed as loud as I could. It felt good to finally release that energy, so I made the most of the moment and screamed some more. Nurses rushed in and surrounded my bed, shoving fingers up my vagina and muttering to one another. They hauled me onto a chair with wheels and wheeled me down the hallway, into a room painted white. I remember feeling the warm sunshine as it poured through the open window, and the anger I felt when the nurse closed it, while ordering me to shut up.

Foul-tasting liquid was forced down my throat, which caused me to fall into a coma of sorts. All I can remember is feeling the sharp pain on my face as an unknown hand slapped me, then being told to push. The pain was like fire within my body, but I pushed anyway; I pushed so hard because my body told me that I must. I pushed knowing that the pain would soon be over.

The final sight that my eyes saw was the doctor between my legs, holding a new baby in his blood-covered arms, the cord still attached to my insides. He held my baby up, like the proud father, whilst the child whimpered and cried for its mother. I heard a nurse mention the amount of blood that was pouring from me, and his words ring in my head to this day:

"Let the devil take her. She has no more use here."

Like so many women of that time, my life was taken in childbirth. It was a happy release; I just wish it had been sooner. Unlike my sister, no one came with their hand outstretched for me; no ghostly presence showing me paradise in the land beyond this one. I think my mind was far too damaged to even care. I kept my eyes fixed on the baby, while my eyes glazed and I fell into the darkness, and the eerie cries of my baby echoed like they were stuck in an endless loop. I'm ashamed to say that I did not fight for my life, not even for the sake of that baby. I left that place as fast as I could, and waited in the darkness, hoping, like always, that my journey was finally over.

Within the walls of that hospital was a poet who had earned his place there with his overwhelming urge to self-harm. He sat in the dayroom, where both sexes mixed under supervision. His name was Charlie. Every day he would recite poetry, waving his scarred hands like he was reading an image that his mind had somehow projected onto the filthy walls. Outside of the institute, he was the writer of poems and esoteric texts; a deep thinker, so deep that the reality of his existence had turned him to suicide. Most of the patients yelled at him or ignored him, but I sat and listened every time, immersed in the words he spoke. I remember a piece that he had recited to me: it was as though he could see deep into my soul and pluck out the words, rearranging them for us all to hear.

It summed up exactly how I felt at the time.

*My thoughts are dark and meaningless,*
*I wallow in the shade of life's nightmares.*
*Am I a prisoner in a world of tricksters and false, happy faces?*
*The stares and whispers hurt my being, clawing at my face,*
*My soul burns in the eternal fires of hatred for myself.*
*My mouth is as wide as a hurricane, my fists clenched,*
*I want to scream, yet not even the gentlest of breezes escapes me.*
*My eyes look through shattered glass, slicing my thoughts with every gaze.*
*My cold stone heart is gripped tightly in the hand of a demon,*
*An evil grin stretched across his twisted face as he squeezes tightly,*
*digging his long, blackened nails into the delicate flesh.*
*My soul is overwhelmed, unable to sustain the life it clings to so perilously.*

*Empty words from healers, they do not understand my anxiety,*
*They do not hear the tapping of death's scythe as he impatiently awaits me.*
*Tap, tap, tap ... waiting for the hour, minute and second,*
*For my name to appear on his list, announcing my impending death.*
*Someone tell him I am willing, and I'll take forth his outstretched hand.*
*Time is my greatest enemy; time will always win,*
*I'm sick of time, tired of its emptiness.*
*Set me free, death, and I will forever be in debt to you.*

It was so easy to slip into madness. In my mind the ghosts were real, and maybe they were; I cannot be sure. I can tell you that the woman who grabbed me by the side of the road and begged for me to fetch her body from the ditch, left a mark on my arm. It was a mark clearly made on my left arm by a left hand—an injury I could not have made myself. It was as though the spirit world tried to warn me, tried to steer me from danger, but I ran away. My reality was the living, and I only trusted what the living had to offer. However, I do not trust them at all now, because they have let me down so many times. I have no clue what became of that baby. I can only guess that he or she grew to do something significant, because I was not allowed to leave that life until the child's arrival.

Every now and again an angel walks amongst the living, but they are few and are outnumbered by those posing as angels. Humans are good actors and, unless you know a person completely, no one is to be trusted. This is one of the reasons I live on my own. Cats are here for their own gain but, unlike most people, they at least don't make a secret of that fact, and we just presume they love us. I feed them and give them shelter, and they return the favour by providing me with company. What more can I ask for?

Sometimes history teaches us a lesson: before that life began, I thought that I was strong and unbreakable, but even the strongest souls have a breaking point. Depression is the beginning of what may become a journey into madness. I thought that seeing spectres was a symptom of that, but what truly broke me was the hole they bored into my skull. I learned to live with the ghosts, but I could never get used to living in a body that felt like it wasn't mine. I can only describe it as feeling like my soul had stepped out of my body, and become trapped, half in and half out. They had drilled into a place where my essence was kept and assaulted it. Where my soul was once the master of my body, it became my shackles, stopping me from functioning. I was thankful that my legs could still walk, because they took me to that window where I witnessed the ever-changing seasons on that old oak tree.

So many factors can turn the mind: the death of a family member or a close friend, living through war, or simply by having too many crazy hormones racing through your body. Some people are born with a personality that is genetically destined for madness; others develop it over time or as a result of a traumatic life. We are fortunate today because, for most, medication can place a sticking plaster on the mind until such time as we are strong enough to push through. Unfortunately, some never find the strength and feel that their existence becomes intolerable. I find that sometimes people are so concerned with the little things that they don't see the bigger picture. They don't listen to others, only their own voices. A person to talk to can help, but sometimes all it takes is a friendly face, compassion, and understanding; an invite to a coffee shop, and a promise of friendship.

There are people in this world who have a lot to give but lack the confidence to bring it into the open. People who are poets and writers can see the world from a different viewpoint, and there are also the deep thinkers, who search the world for answers to every cryptic question. There are also just people like me, who have lost trust in their fellow human beings and lock themselves away in fear of being hurt, and those who yearn for someone to simply say,

"What nice weather we're having."

Or even,

"Do I know you? Your face looks familiar."

It seems silly, but simple phrases such as those begin conversations and create friendships. Sometimes, all that anyone ever needs is good friends to wash away the madness from our lives.

# THIRD EYE

Often, the lives that I struggle to live through are followed by lives with smaller, easier to handle lessons. I was born a boy, in a village named Lhasa, which resides in the hidden Himalayan country of Tibet. Back then, we were an independent country, and free to live life as we pleased. China had entered the Ming dynasty and, showing no interest in our country because we had little to offer, set us free from its grip.

I was raised in a busy household but a strict one. Like most of our village, we were raised on stories from the scripture. Prince Siddhartha Gautama, the first Buddha or enlightened one, was the first to reach Nirvana and we lived in the hope that someday in our lives we'd gain his knowledge and sit by his side. We didn't see him as a deity, but simply as the first who looked at life in a deeper way and saw beyond what most humans see.

I was blessed in this life as, unlike in so many previous lives, my memories came in as a steady trickle, beginning to seep into my mind around my third birthday. The gush of information did not arrive till I was in my fifth year, so I was mature enough to cope with the flood of past life details.

From a young age I fought with my older sister, as all siblings do. I recall my father sitting me down by the fireplace after I sent my sister to my mother, crying. I was not expecting to be hollered at like normal children, because that was not how my father worked. He was a man who taught lessons, and his children were also his students.

"Tsu, I want to give you a gift." He held out his hands, curled around an object; he nodded, signalling me to open mine. "I will give you a life to care for."

Into my tiny hand he placed a warm bird's egg, with a pale smooth shell. I held it up to my face, examining every inch of its shell eagerly.

"Tsu, this egg holds a life that began only last night. If you take care of this egg, it will grow, and grow strong. But you must understand, the egg is delicate and can break as easily as your sister. She cries tears of sadness, but this egg will cry and the life within will wash away. Keep this egg warm on your body for twenty days, and you will be rewarded with that life and a friend of your own."

I was in my fourth year, and the clumsiest boy in our village, but as I gazed at this most magnificent egg that filled my hands, I wondered what creature resided inside the egg, why was it so delicate, and why it was shaped the way it was. The smooth to touch surface was constructed from minute fragments of sand, all cemented together, to form this magnificent oval structure encasing something as precious as life. With fear that the egg may grow cold, I tucked it into my clothing. I thought that the safest place to hold the egg would be in the softest area of my body, so the egg found a home just above my navel.

Lhasa had a cold climate, being so high above sea level, so we dressed ourselves in many layers of clothing. I kept myself separated from the other children, who wrestled in the streets. I told no one of my secret for fear that they might try to crack my egg, which would deem my mission a failure. At night I slept on my back or side, still clutching my precious gift.

My sister started arguments and teased me all the time, but I remained quiet and simply removed myself from each situation. The secret of my egg was only known by myself and my father; I think my mother also knew, although she never mentioned it. Sometimes I held the egg to my ear, in the hope that I'd hear the slightest movements to reassure me that the creature inside was still alive, but I never heard a thing. On the eighteenth day I had given up hope. The egg was still warm, but I believed it was merely my body keeping it so. I took it to my father, when I found him alone, and presented it to him. He looked surprised that I still had my gift.

"Papa, I am sorry. I think the egg is dead. I do not hear any sound from within."

My father held the egg up towards the opened window and gazed at it against the blue sky.

"See the egg: see how it glows with life?"

As I stepped towards the window, I noticed the small glowing line that surrounded my egg and gasped with delight.

"I see it Papa, I see it."

My father handed me my egg with a look of pride.

"Two days and you will see life emerge from your egg; you will become responsible for that life, until it needs you no more."

I tucked the egg back inside my clothing and wrapped my coat gently around it. I couldn't help but feel proud and excited at the same time. True to his word, two days later I inspected the egg, and found a large hole and cracks along the side. I peered through the hole and saw a tiny beak, two black bulbous eyes, and two small, pale, scaled legs. Within a few hours, the soggy, feathered creature was free from the shell and lay in my hand, panting with exhaustion. A few hours passed, the feathers dried, and the bird found the strength to stand. It looked upon the small boy that had kept it alive and chirped its thanks. I presented a small fluffy chick to my father. I placed it in his hands and puffed out my chest with pride that I had achieved such a task.

What lesson did you learn here, my son?" I frowned, as I'd expected at least a pat on the back.

"For twenty days you have stayed clear of trouble, left your sister be, and took care of this precious bird. You alone, at the age of four, have dedicated twenty days of your life and I assure you that this bird is grateful for your sacrifice. Life is fragile and can be damaged so easily, not only by breaking the shell, but also by not giving it warmth. We treated you like you treated that egg: we raised you and kept you safe and warm, and in return you have learnt how to keep another safe. Every life is the same as that egg: you must treat it gently and give it safety and warmth, only then will you have the same in return."

We lived our lives thinking of others before ourselves. We ate tsampa from clay pots and drank butter tea made from yaks' milk, using the surplus only when their young had weaned. Our diets were simple, consisting of vegetables and grains, our home was basic, and we felt blessed to have a roof over our heads to shelter us from the weather.

Our home had a fireplace to keep out the chill and cook food. We sat cross-legged on mats woven from yaks' wool, which were also our beds. We had one large room with little furniture and a small back room, which we used to store our food over the winter months. We lived with what we *needed*, rather than what we *wanted*.

Our tiny home also had to accommodate a large, chatty family. It was not only my sister and myself: I lived alongside my parents, grandparents, and two other sisters; and of course, the chick, for a while. I fed and nurtured her until father said it was time for her to re-join the other chickens who ran wild in our village. I was sad to see her go, as I had grown very fond of her, but happy that she was back with her kind, and glad that I didn't have to clear up any more of her droppings.

Grandmother had grown blind with age, but this did not stop her from talking. She was a barrel of information, a library of stories, and the wisest woman I knew. She had an answer for every question, and stories to accompany them. My grandfather was a wise man also, who foretold children's future careers by the use of lucid dreams. When a child in our village reached the age of five, a dream would come to him about that child. The following day he'd ask one of us children to run over to that household, with a note summoning them to a meeting. At the age of five years and seven months, I was finally summoned to my grandfather for the news I was impatiently waiting to hear.

I sat opposite the old man, who was cross-legged with his eyes closed. He sat silent and motionless. I knew that he was in a state of meditation, and that disturbing him was not an option. As I waited for him to return, I studied his features. Grandfather had always been present in our home, but I'd never really interacted with him an awful lot. He spent many hours and often days in meditation, in the back room, or gazing into a rough crystal that had a single polished side. His crystal was his singular possession, yet he believed that it didn't belong to him—it belonged to the earth, and he was just borrowing it. I watched his wrinkled skin as it twitched beneath his long wiry beard; his head was completely bald and looked as if it had been polished to a fine shine. His paper-thin hands rested on his skeletal knees, covered only by his saffron clothing. His eyes twitched behind his lids, darting from side to side. His breathing deepened, and his spine stretched tall. His lips began to quiver, then a long gasp escaped his opened, toothless mouth.

"Tsu, do you enjoy staring at an old man as he seeks answers?"

His eyes sprung open; his gaze fixed upon me. A stern look etched across his kindly face. I shook my head and looked away.

"What did you see, boy?" I looked back at him and stuttered my words.

"Tell me, what did you see?" I shook my head again, and began spitting out words: "Your face, Grandfather, while you meditated."

The old man leant forward and reached for my hands. His face came within inches of my own.

"Not with your eyes, boy, with your mind. What did you see?" I thought quickly back to when I was studying my grandfather, and suddenly recalled a picture that popped into my thoughts. I assumed that scene was what he was speaking of.

"I saw a hill, covered in the brightest green grass, with small yellow flowers, and a single tree with green leaves. The skies were bluer than the bluest of blues, with many birds flying in all directions. One big bird was perched on the top branch of the tree, pruning its feathers with his long, crooked beak."

"Go on, go on," my grandfather demanded.

"The bird's head was covered with blood: thick, red blood." My grandfather smiled, exposing his gums, and sighed, relaxing his spine and shoulders.

"I thought as much. I have been feeling their presence calling me home. I must leave this world, Tsu, and continue to my next. You, my grandson, you will go to the monastery on the day of your sixth birthday and knock on the door seven times. When they ask you what you want, tell them who you are. Do as they ask, Tsu; you have much to achieve in life, and you have a lot of knowledge to share. Share you must—share as much as you can. Hold no secrets, as secrets poison your soul. Knowledge must be shared. Do you understand me, Tsu?"

My grandfather's hands were shaking, as he squeezed my shoulders with his bony fingers. My memories were still merely a trickle at that point, and I believed them to be thoughts of fiction. I had an imagination that surpassed any other person I knew. I never thought of them as factual.

Over the next two weeks, grandfather grew weaker and feebler than he had ever been. His pale cheeks had sunken further into his skull, leaving only a thin layer of skin covering bone. He no longer had the strength to sit in the lotus position, finding comfort laying on his back with a rolled-up blanket supporting his head. It was my job to care for him, like I had done with the egg, but I knew that I awaited no new life to emerge from his egg-like skull, only the death of his tired and worn body.

It was explained by my father that his body was failing him, but his spirit would live on without the aches and pains of the earthly bounds. I was not to be sad, as he was approaching his re-birth and his life would start anew. The day soon came when his death rattle filled our room with a numbness, as his spirit struggled for freedom. When the last breath finally left his lungs, it was my grandmother who shed the first tear. She cried not for him, but for her own heart, which would miss him. They had been together since they were young.

Grandfather's body was taken into the mountains and his skull cracked open wide, to expose the brain. The vultures circled above, eager to return his body back to the earth. That night we celebrated his life and many achievements along with all his friends, which appeared to be most of the village.

In what seemed like a blink of an eye, the family were preparing for my sixth birthday. It was to be my last day in my family home, because my place of residence would be the monastery, like my grandfather foretold. We feasted that day on vegetables and flatbread, which I dipped into my butter tea, whilst mother sang songs that she had heard her own mother sing. Before the sun set, I said farewell to my family and headed towards the monastery, wondering if I would ever see them again. My mother cried as I walked away, and my father turned his head away as he comforted my mother.

I was told by my father that it was a great honour to be a monk, and a sure way to reach enlightenment. Enlightenment was a word that I didn't fully understand at such a young age. I suspected that it meant that I was to gain the ability to glow and become the light in dark places. The monastery was a world that I had only ever heard whispers about, although I often saw the monks in our village.

One of them had even concealed himself in a cave in the mountains, to meditate in peace and quiet. My mother often took me along when she visited, offering him a bowl of tsampa. We never saw his face, only a hand that gripped the clay bowl, returning it with thanks a few minutes later. He was called a 'hermit' and was on a mission to seek Nirvana. He spent every waking hour in a meditative state, in almost complete darkness. He hummed mantras and said prayers for those in need. I expect some prayers even helped to fend off the pains of hunger until the next time a passer-by brought a bowl of oats. All he owned was a blanket and his robes, and he lived in isolation, blinded through lack of sunlight. I hoped above all that this was not to be my fate. In every life I have lived, my greatest fear is that of utter loneliness, darkness, and confinement.

The climb up the dusty path that led to the monastery was perilous at times. It had steep steps, with loose rocks, that were easy for a full-grown man. For a small boy, with bare feet and an oversized robe, passed down to me from my cousin, it was not so easy. As the sun kissed the peak of the mountain covering the snow in a golden glow, I finally reached the monastery's heavy door. I sat upon the step for a few moments, to catch my breath and take in the view. I expected that this would be the final time that I would be free in this world. A small insignificant boy, without status or destiny, in a world filled with mountains and snow, with a love of a good view, his family, and a chicken who had quickly forgotten that he existed.

    I picked up a loose stone and spun it in my hand, covering my palm and fingertips in dirt. I threw the stone into a bush and pulled myself to my feet. I looked up at the door that towered above me, like it was built for a race of giants. I could not reach the handle, so I made a fist and knocked on the wood as hard as I could, seven times as I had been instructed. I waited silently for a response: the sound of shuffling or the rattle of a lock. Nothing. I sat back down on the step and watched as the sun disappeared behind the mountain.

    The temperature dropped suddenly, plunging my surroundings to a chill that I could not bear. I wrapped my robe tightly around me and tucked the hem under my feet. The temperature dropped more rapidly, as the pink skies turned to black. My breath froze in clouds when I exhaled; my small body shivered violently, and all feeling in my fingers and toes disappeared. With my elbow, I pounded the door again, seven times, but still there was no answer. My entire body shook, and the tip of my tongue felt as though it were about to freeze. I had two options: I could try and run down the path back to my home or use all the energy I had left to make as much noise as I could.

The first option was suicide—the darkness was not lit by the light of the moon, and wild animals roamed the mountains at night. I stood up on my numb feet and screamed, hit, punched the door; I rammed it with my shoulder and kicked it with the heel of my foot. It seemed like forever before my weakened screams were finally interrupted by the sound of a wooden beam sliding across the entrance. The door creaked open, and a plain faced man appeared, wearing a saffron robe. I collapsed in a heap at his feet, my tears freezing on my cheeks. Without saying a single word to me, he scooped me up in his arms and carried me inside the monastery. As he took me down the torch-lit corridor, I could feel the heat from the flames on the side of my face. I fell asleep knowing that, at least for now, I was safe.

I awoke to the eerie sound of a never-ending hum that comforted my thoughts. I was warm and dressed in a saffron robe that fitted me well, with a thick blanket over my body. Beside me sat a monk with cropped black hair, and a smile that pushed out rounded cheeks.

"You are Ygn's grandson?" His eyebrows raised significantly when he spoke.

I nodded my head, feeling a little overwhelmed.

"He told us last night that you were coming. Please ... drink; it will warm you inside."

The monk passed me a small cup filled with lukewarm tea. It was a lot blander than I was used to, but I was thankful for it. It was enough to wash away my dry throat and melt any ice that lingered within. My grandfather had died months before, but I did not question the monk about how he knew of my arrival. I was just glad to be out of the freezing weather.

Later that day, I was accompanied by my monk, Sang, to a small room occupied by half a dozen saffron-clad monks. They sat upon folded blankets, and all turned to face me as I walked in. I gazed around, feeling like a circus exhibit: like it was the first time any of them had seen a small boy dressed as they were. One older gentleman grabbed my hand, and I turned to face him. His smile creased his ageing face, and his milky, white eyes looked as if they were about to pop out of his sunken eye sockets. His open mouth revealed a full set of yellow teeth, his thin lips disappearing the wider his smile crept across his face.

"Welcome boy ... welcome to our home. You are family now. Please, sit. Sit. You tell me everything, boy. I learn a lot from you, and hopefully reach enlightenment."

I was confused about what they spoke of; how on earth was I supposed to teach them when I barely knew anything myself? I was shown a vacant space and sat down, cross-legged like the others. One by one I was greeted warmly by everyone in the room, and more who entered afterwards. I watched and listened, whilst they chatted freely about random subjects: plants that they grew, and prayers for the villagers who were living in hard times, and babies that had entered the world, and those who had left.

One monk, who looked as though he was around thirty years of age, entered the room and stood silently in the doorway, staring at me with a cold expression. I tried to avert my gaze, but something drew me towards him, like I knew him somehow. In a second the chatting stopped, and the room fell deathly silent.

"So, here you are at last. Boy, you do not remember me yet, but we have met before, in a previous life. My name is Ang, but in that life I was called Setu, and we built monuments together." He was right, of course. At the time I had no clue who he was, but as I tried to search my mind for answers, something about him reminded me of someone I used to know. He walked over to where I sat and pulled me to my feet and knelt down to my eye level.

"Tsu, in that life you saved my life on many occasions. The last time you saved me you did not survive, but because of you, I saw my children grow into men and women, and lived to see many more years. I am truly blessed that I can again call you 'brother'."

Ang became my guide in this life, and stayed close to me until I came of age. Eventually, the memories of the life we shared previously became clear. He was indeed my brother, and we had shared many adventures.

He showed me the ways that a monk lived and gave me a few tips to gain extra comfort from what little we owned. It was Ang who was told of my imminent arrival at the monastery. I joked with him that he had not been told the precise time, otherwise I wouldn't have been half-dead from exposure when they found me at the door. Ang's answer was blunt, but true I suppose: I was being a little over-dramatic; they knew I was there the whole time.

It appeared that my secret had been let out way before the floodgates of memories opened in my mind. The monks knew that death led to another life, but they had never met anyone who had kept the memory of each life intact. I had learned every scenario, in so many bodies, yet it appeared that I still had more to come. If anything, the cycle seemed endless. The monks tried to explain my phenomenon.

Some said that I was a trapped soul, unable to step foot into the afterlife. Some said that I held a place far greater than anyone that had ever lived, which was why I had to gather as much information as I could. I had to learn every lesson that ever existed, with no exceptions. This did not explain, however, how I had managed to keep every memory intact without my brain imploding. That question was eventually answered for me, with an explanation which made sense.

Every soul that walks the earth is like a puppet of what is explained to be an overself: a puppet-master of sorts. The overself is like an endless source of memory, which is like storage for experiences. When a soul is returned into another puppet, a block between the puppet-master and puppet kicks in, clearing the mind of the new soul. The memories don't start until the child gasps its first breath, hence why no one can remember what it felt like to be in their mother's womb. As I explained before, I clearly remember every second of the womb, from around four months gestation. Every beat of my mother's heart, the blood moving in the cord, and the muffled sound of my mother's voice.

Sometimes I felt guilty that I seemed to be questioning the monks' beliefs but, on the contrary, every time I spoke freely, the monks were only too happy to give me an audience. At first, I spoke to a single monk, then a few others would join us. Eventually, I found myself in a room, telling stories to monks who had travelled hundreds of miles to hear me speak. It was an honour when I noticed our leader's face sitting within the crowd. I had no idea that our beloved Gendum Drupa, our Dalai Lama, had requested an audience with me. I was very humbled in his presence and lost my train of thought a few times, but he smiled and held no ill will.

Every morning I awoke to faces waiting for me to speak of my dreams, and I remembered every single one. I mentioned before that time was an illusion; have you ever wondered how a half hour sleep can produce a dream that lasts hours? Well, they do. On several occasions I spent the entire day telling stories of every life I had lived, but it was not until I became a teenager that I realised that they were indeed my past lives. Ang was not like me; he couldn't remember his past lives. He only knew about me because he had been taken back in time to that life, in the deep gaze of a crystal.

Crystal-gazing was a common practice for the Buddhist monks back then, and some say it is still used to this day. It was an art that came naturally to me. I had watched in wonder many times when my grandfather stared deeply into his crystal, returning with answers and ideas. I was given a crystal like my grandfather's and, like his, it did not belong to me: it was only loaned from the earth. It was roughly cut but had a single polished side and was unblemished throughout. I always kept it on my person, until it felt like it was part of me. I was not allowed to let anyone touch it, as this would interfere with my energy.

    The room was lit only by candles, and we stared deeply, almost cross-eyed, into the crystals' polished faces, transfixed on single points. Our minds are cleared of any thought or wonder, concentrating purely on the hum that continuously resounded throughout the building. The crystals grew cloudy, and our minds plunged into their mysteries, leaving our earthly bodies behind. I saw myself in lives that I had lived, and lives I were yet to experience. I saw people I had lost, and people who would betray my trust. Most importantly, I saw those I had left behind: Livia's beautiful smile, and my son from my jungle life, who took over my medicine, my children and grandchildren, partners, and lost loves.

    One discovery that I made was the impact that my lives had on those left behind. I wasn't merely flitting from one life to the next but was leaving lessons learned and teachings that had been passed down generations. I influenced the world in so many ways, so much more than I had ever imagined. I knew that my journey was far from over, as within that crystal I saw a woman, sitting at a desk. She was alone, apart from two cats, while writing her story on a laptop, with a cup of coffee to her left and a chocolate digestive (or two) to her right. She was tapping away, telling stories to whoever wanted to read, without an audience, without questions, and without obligation. Simply because she wanted to, but also because of those words that her grandfather said to her: 'Knowledge must be shared.'

Another one of my teachings was how to astral travel: a concept I had been familiar with in previous lives, so it wasn't difficult to master. This body was stubborn at first, but with a bit of persuasion I achieved my goal. It's a wonderful thing, sitting on the very tip of a mountain, gazing at the world around you, while tucked up in bed beneath the covers. The wind passing you without chilling your face, the rain pelting down without soaking you. A few moments later, I could cross the ocean and watch herds of zebras graze the savanna, or elephants throw water over their dirt-covered backs and wallow in the shallows. I was told that even time itself can be travelled whilst astral travelling, but that's a journey I was never able to master.

I did, however, on one occasion journey so far from earth that I beheld its overwhelming beauty as I looked down upon the sphere, floating in space. A spectacular sight that cannot be captured in a photograph or film, but can only be truly appreciated by being there.

Bad news for all the flat-earthers out there: our beautiful planet is very spherical. If you truly believe the earth is flat, then I think maybe you should know that it isn't. Think of it this way: if the earth was flat, that would mean earth is the only planet that *is* flat. What makes our planet able to remain flat when all around us are spheres?

Our home is merely a speck of dust, in the grand scale of things. We are just one of an infinite number of planets to have the right ingredients to maintain life. What lies beyond the known universe has always been a mystery to me, but I felt the need to hold back from travelling too far from home. I suppose to have at least *one* thing that I don't know or understand fully is a blessing. The one lesson that will always have an empty shelf in my mind.

As I grew older, I discovered the joys of meditation and the peace it gave me. I had always meditated as a child, but it was usually because I was asked to; I never really took it seriously enough to feel its benefits. When my anxiety threatened my sanity, I took myself away, sat with a rolled-up blanket to support my spine, and drifted off into my solitary world. In my mind I imagined a lotus garden, with a crystal-clear pool. Willow trees dipped their branches into the water, their delicate leaves swaying gently with the passing of koi carp. I sat on the soft, mossy banks, with the warm sun on my cheeks, listening to the comforting hum that surrounded me. It became the tune of my body, the hum of my brain as it struggled to hold everything inside. Another method I learnt was mantras: these were prayers that we repeated again and again. They were not ever for self-gain, but for those who suffered. They also reminded us of how blessed we were, to be alive, and to be living the life we had. To this day, I still use these techniques to keep the madness at bay. Madness cannot enter my lotus garden, or my flower meadow. Those places are where I go where I am happy to be alone: my sanctuary—my Nirvana.

    The Buddhists in my monastery believed that a human had thirteen lives to live before entering Samsara, a kind of heaven, where one lived for eternity. Thirteen astral planes that they must live, learning thirteen lessons. They mostly involved lessons like karma and kindness, and dealing with outside influences, like grief and mankind's evil ways. Also, we had to learn how to overcome our own darker personality traits and find solutions in a peaceful way. Buddhists were never fighters, always choosing the more practical and peaceful alternatives. Love was free, kindness was free, and forgiveness was free. Holding on to anger and malice always costs so much and can drain the soul of its good karma.

I came along, with all my lives, too many to count, and knocked their theory out of the water. One monk, who had great respect from my brothers, explained that my journey was different from the rest of mankind. I was destined for greater things in Samsara: to walk amongst the gods, as it were. It's a concept that I can't conceive of, as my ego has been evicted by the rest of my emotions. A great memory that stretches from the first existence of civilised humankind is more of a curse than a blessing. All I can hope for is eternal rest, when all of this finally ends; if, indeed, the end ever comes.

During that life, I also learned of secrets that history had forgotten, visits from the stars, and hidden places that can no longer be reached unless you know how to get there. These places are out of reach of even the satellites that take pictures, hidden under a veil of secrecy. I cannot say too much about those secrets, as I know what happens to those who reveal too much. Let's just say that we are far from alone in the universe; we are just a grain of sand on a beach of worlds that sustain life.

Some are still evolving from tiny worm-like creatures, while some have technology far beyond our own and can travel the stars in a blink of an eye. I can say that everything that we do is being closely watched, and not only by those who reside on earth. Everyone has a higher authority; everyone—without exception.

World leaders are just spokespersons for those above them.

We are approaching a time when everything will be changing for the better but, like everything, one has to fall to rise up; it just depends on who is willing to rise first. It also depends on whether we will help others to rise with us, or will step on the fallen to rise above them. Time will tell. What I can say, is that I am witnessing a day and age, where the younger generation are embracing a life without prejudice and are offering kindness. I feel that it is a time to be excited for the future. I just hope society does not poison this new generation too much as they grow.

This life was interesting, and although for most of my life I stayed in the monastery, giving lectures and telling my story, I experienced and learnt so very much. Ang became my brother once again, and one of my greatest friends. I think I have shared two lives with the same person a few times; some I was sure of, and some not so sure, but it gave me comfort to think that it was them. I must admit that on occasions I do have an instant familiarity with some people. Within moments of meeting, I'm feeling that almost spiritual connection, like our auras know one another, and are unknowingly shaking hands and catching up on past lives. Maybe they do, maybe those are the occasional true and intense friendships that last a lifetime; those that so few people are lucky enough to have. Old souls who travel through time to reconnect with those they had spent aeons grieving for. Or maybe they just collide by chance.

Ang died before me in this life. He was born with a heart condition that shortened his years: a condition that could not be cured with medicine. It was quick and relatively painless. I'm sure we will meet again someday, and when we do, I will know.

I died an old man, while deep in meditation. I expect the monks left me there for several weeks, unnoticed, as I had been known to meditate for days at a time in my old age. I expect my rotting flesh became pungent in the end, burning the nasal cavities of everyone who wandered too close. I assume that my body was fed to the vultures, not that I had much meat left on my bones. Like all monks and people of Tibet, my body was returned to the earth through the digestive system of a bird, which in turn nourished the soil and helped to feed all kinds of foliage. The foliage may have been grazed by an animal and the whole process would begin again. It all goes to show that shit is totally underrated.

Crystal-gazing and astral travelling sound like magic to some, and a far-fetched concept to others. They are activities that do not require any sort of hocus-pocus, or any strange concoctions of animal parts. They are a way of freeing your energy from its earthly bounds. The spirit remains linked via an umbilicus of sorts, a link to your fleshy body that brings the energy home at your request.

We all harness an energy in our body: it powers our brain, heart, and digestive system. It tells our organs what to do, even down to our cells fighting disease. A body is very complex and can come in a variety of sizes. An ant's heart is the size of a pinhead, whereas a human could swim through the heart of a blue whale because it's so large. They all work the same way, using energy. Energy cannot be destroyed, only transferred, which begs the question to all those who doubt the afterlife. Where does our energy go? Our energy has been shaped and moulded by the life lessons we have experienced. Our personalities grow stronger the more we suffer. Can you truly say that you are the same person that you were ten years ago? If you can pinpoint the exact moment of change, it's usually because you have lived through hardship. The key is to change for the better.

What matters in this earthly life is not how you present the physical machine. A soul does not care about make-up or a tidy hairdo, fancy labels or how fast your car is; they are just tools to get you where you need to be. What matters is the *health* of your soul. To have a truly healthy soul one must shed any prejudice, all hate and malice, any thoughts of revenge, or any wishes that a soul come to harm. Every soul has a journey to take, and each one steps on a different path.

one thing's for sure: everyone has demons—without exception. Even the purest of souls has a closet filled with skeletons and broken hearts. Treat people kindly and keep anger at bay. If someone throws abuse at you for no reason, it's more than likely that the person in question has had a rough day, and you just happened to walk past at the point of explosion. Challenging that person will only end in disaster, and a fuelled temper can grow into a raging fire. Maybe all they need to hear is:

"Who upset you? Do you want to talk about it?"

You'd be amazed at the results. Some may just throw one last obscenity and walk away, but sometimes a friend can be made.

# EGYPT

I suppose I should tell you all about my time in Egypt, and my first meeting with Setu, as he was known back then. I have lived a fair few very different lives at the edge of that Arabian desert, by the majestic river Nile. Mostly they were lacking adventure, but a few held a good story; this one in particular.

I lived in what is known now as central Egypt and was raised alongside my brother Setu. We had three mothers and only one father, who we did pity at times, because to keep one woman happy can be difficult, but to keep all three content was near impossible.

My mothers were strong- minded women, who expected more from my father, always more. He loved them all dearly, but no matter how much he tried to please them all, one was always unhappy. Despite this, he never admitted any regret for taking on so many wives, but he advised all of his children that a single partner would make life a lot simpler.

Setu and I were two of fifteen children: all fathered by the same man but shared between the three mothers. None of us knew who belonged to who, but back then such things held little importance. Setu and I were extremely close in age, so formed a bond that would last two lifetimes, and over four thousand years. Being the eldest boys, the tradition at the time was that we should follow in the footsteps of our father and learn the family trade. For six generations the art of stonemasonry had been mastered to perfection, and the specialised techniques were passed down to my father from his own. Now it was an honour held by my own father, to teach the techniques to my brother and me.

We lived in our family home, built by my great-grandfather, which still stood strong on its foundations. The blocks that built the walls were solid limestone, cut with precision, using a method I will explain later in the story. Thick, striped, palm trunks stretched across the ceiling, which held sun-dried mud bricks that were strong enough to bear our weight. This gave us access to the roof space, which we used for laundry, drying fruits, or for relaxation. It was also essential for when the river flooded, which did happen from time to time.

It was a fair-sized home, with four main rooms, a walled courtyard surrounding the front, where we kept a few goats, and a stone stairway to the side of the house leading up to the roof. My mothers had woven canopies from palm leaves, to block out the heat of the sun on the roof, so Setu and I spent a lot of time playing games up there as children. It was built not far from the banks of the great Nile, but far enough to avoid the creatures who claimed the waters as their own. The silt of the Nile had transformed our part of the yellow desert into an oasis of luscious, fertile land. It was in the time of the great pharaohs, and food was plenty, and due to my father's expertise, we never went hungry.

I remember so clearly the view from our roof, the palm tree shooting towards the skies, the luscious green leaves sprouting out of the very top, like an explosion of foliage offering its fruits to the hungry. To one side, the river expanded across the horizon, welcoming skiffs, which were boats constructed from tied reeds. They floated better than wood and could survive the jaws of a crocodile and still stay afloat. They were used by our fishermen, or those who wished to cross to the other side. The water always fascinated me, forever on the move; to where I did not know, although I often wondered.

All around us, fields were filled with wheat and green vegetables. Goats, cows, and sheep grazed in pastures penned in by walls to keep out predators. Way into the distance we could see pyramids that warped in the heat of the sun, and the far away dunes that made up the arid ocean of desert. The waters rushing past the reed beds, and the birds diving in to catch their supper, the clatter of people going about their daily business, the laughter of children, and braying animals filled the air with sounds.

I remember the sun hitting the waters, transforming the surface to look as though it were a billion diamonds tumbling together, in a race to reach an unseen destination. Some days, the wind was still, and the sun stifled us to the point where all we could do was hide away in our homes; the stone walls cooled us. Some days the wind blew hard, whisking up the sands, which turned the skies red and stung our eyes, but mostly the heat was bearable, and the deep blue sky remained unchanging.

Sometimes we caught a glimpse of a pod of hippos when they swam up-river in search of roots to eat. On occasion, their presence caused the resident crocodiles to lash out, provoking a war on territory. An onslaught of disturbances commenced in the waters, and the deep rumbling sounds of the beasts echoed across the land as they kicked up a fuss. The hippos usually won the fight, but occasionally lost one of their young to a hungry crocodile, providing a meal to most of the gathering crocs. Other times, a crocodile was discovered washed up on the bank, two deep puncture wounds in its dead body. Now and then the crocodiles came to our village looking for a meal, but out of the water they were slow and clumsy beasts that sought out our cattle, rather than humans. Satisfied with a nesting bird or young goat, they'd crawl back to the banks and sun themselves before slinking back into the waters.

When I was about four, our younger sister became a victim of a crocodile; she was two years old or so. The gate to our yard had been left open by an unknown outsider and our sister had wandered out from our home. A curious child who noticed a leathery creature approaching with a wide smile, (she was too young to know it was looking for a meal) had the natural need of all youngsters to touch something interesting. My mother screamed her name, as my sister held out her small chubby hand to touch its rounded snout. It only took a split second. One snap, and my mother collapsed on her knees, wailing with sorrow as her daughter was dragged into the murky depths of the Nile. The sound of the waters thrashing and churning as her small body was torn to pieces was undeniably harrowing. No one could do anything more than pray that the end had been quick and pain-free. It was an occurrence that happened from time to time, the price we all paid to live where we did. My mother found comfort in the belief that her daughter's spirit would return when she was ready. A year later she was blessed with another child who bore the lost daughter's name. She was seen as a precious gift from the gods. To us, she was a spoiled brat, but we loved her, nevertheless.

We villagers wore nothing more than loose cotton garments that hung from our waist and hid our dignity. Everyone had a pendant or amulet, carved from wood or stone, which dangled from a leather cord around their necks. Mostly, they were carved with their family symbols: our symbol looked like a bird holding a flame on the tip of its beak. My father carved statues in his spare time, which brought not only food to our home but material, which my mothers cut and fashioned into wearable items. We also got wool that was woven into blankets for the cooler evenings, and lotions and make-up that most of the family fought over.

As young boys who craved adventure, we wore out our clothing very quickly. Our contribution towards the home often found the pair of us scaling the palm trees to harvest the fruits. Our targets were the dates, and the occasional doum fruit, which tasted a little like gingerbread. They were mostly eaten by the men, because they had the strange idea that they came with the promise of better fertility. We'd also harvest the lower dead leaves, which were used for burning, and the greener leaves were used to weave baskets and mats. We'd deliver them to the neighbouring homes in exchange for bread, honey, and beer, and sit out in the shade achieving complete inebriation.

Beer back then was not like the beer you get in today's local pub; this was home-brewed, and the quicker your beer made people drunk, the more popular it became. This caused stiff competition among the brewing homes, which was pretty much every home at the time. The amount of times my brother and I crawled home, unable to gain stability on our two feet, was far too many to count. We were always greeted by a mother or two, yelling words that our fuzzy heads could not translate. A clip around the ear often followed, with a clay bowl tossed disapprovingly to the side of our reed beds to catch any vomit. The next morning we'd usually have to change the reeds, because both of us had been so drunk that we could not feel the strain of our bladders, or stop the flow as we slept. Our younger siblings knew to stay away from our beds on those occasions. My poor father came home to three women jabbering continuously about our antics, demanding that he speak wisely to us. To keep the ladies quiet, father asked us outside for a stern talking-to.

Father was never any good at showing dominance, he left that to my mothers, but to keep them happy he put on a show, dragging us out by our ear lobes. He was a man of stories rather than a raised voice; instead of a lecture, we'd spend an hour or two sitting under the stars, whilst he told us the stories that he had heard on his travels. My favourite was the story of life beyond death. A world that I crave still.

Every star was a past king, who had lived his life honestly and fairly, earning the approval of the Gods. Life did not end with death: death was only the beginning of life everlasting. He spoke of a paradise, a field of reeds, and a jury of gods who determined our fate. The weight of your heart was put against the weight of a feather, and the outcome determined how pure the heart was. If the weight matched the feather, it was deemed satisfactory, and the soul was allowed into paradise. If the heart sank lower than the feather, back to earth you were tossed to try again.

I remember thinking that I must have done something very wrong, at some point that I could not remember, as I had not reached that paradise described to me. I didn't see any fields of reeds, and I never saw any gods, only darkness. I wondered: how pure must a life be?

It was on a night with a clear sky, watching the stars twinkling overhead with my father, that I found myself in an unusual situation. I was around thirteen and we were on the roof, just him and I, watching the gods twinkle in the deep black night sky. As he told me the story, my mind wondered, and I plucked up the courage to ask him questions about my apparent immortality. As predicted, it didn't go down too well when I began the sentence with those four formidable words.

"In my last life ..." My father stopped me in my tracks.

"Your last life? What is this you speak of son?" His face screwed up in bewilderment.

"In my last life, I was a girl living in a land such as this, only up the river and a long time ago."

My father turned to look at my face, I'm sure he was trying to see the lie in my eyes.

"You were dreaming, boy. It must have been a dream."

I shook my head in protest.

"No papa. It was no dream. I remember my lives back many, many years. I have lived in lands that had no sand and seen people with paler skin and even darker skin than ours. I have seen creatures that do not exist here, and water so cold that the rain covered the pastures in white powder and melted back into water in the palm of your hand. I know what it feels like to give birth to a child, and I know how it feels to die."

My father rose to his feet and shook his pointed index finger at me, but although his lips were pursed, he didn't mutter a word. His head sagged towards the ground, and he paced back and forth, with both hands on his hips. Occasionally he turned his head to look at me, shaking his head, but remaining silent. Eventually, he walked away from the building, and disappeared into the night. I called out his name, but he did not answer. I felt it best that I didn't pursue him.

My mothers grew anxious after the first few hours of his absence, each woman taking turns to search for him, whilst the others watched us children.

"What were you talking about?" Ma asked angrily, as I sat on my bed. I was too frightened to tell her what I had said to him, so I simply replied that we were just chatting. On the second day, my mothers began to suspect that father had taken time out to see his brother without telling them; a sin that he'd have to pay for on his return.

On the third day, my father appeared, with a stranger. My mothers all marched out with looks of rage when they spotted him, but relaxed their glares when they noticed that he had company. The first thing I noticed was that this unknown man's well-built upper body was completely void of any hair. He wore black lines under his eyes, and a white cotton loin cloth, decorated with gold thread, held in place by a tight belt. On seeing the man, who easily stood six feet tall, my mothers retreated inside the house, with their heads bowed in respect, to the relief of my father. I was sought out amongst my siblings, and asked to join them outside, away from the rest of the family. I did so without argument, but I felt like trouble had come my way. My brother Setu called out to me, but he knew that I had to go alone. Outside, my father and the bald man sat on a carved granite block that overlooked the river. I stood before them both. My hands shook, thinking that I was to be torn away from my family, where I felt great happiness, and dragged to some far, unfamiliar destination.

"Tell him boy. Tell him what you told me the other evening." I remained silent at first; my mouth was dry, and my brain scrambled words together. My father smiled reassuringly.

"Please. It's okay."

Within what only felt like a few seconds, I had blurted out exactly what I had told my father, with a few added details. When I'd finished, I awaited their response with trembling knees and a thought in my mind to run away from the situation. The bald man leant his elbow on his arm and squeezed his pointed chin.

"What is your name, boy?"

"Mshai." I answered feebly.

"Mshai. 'The traveller.' Huh."

"He was named after my grandfather," my father said, interrupting his silence.

The man's eyes fixed on mine, making me feel uneasy.

"Mshai, I am the priest of this community, and I was visited by your father two days ago. He tells me that you are a boy who speaks the truth. Is this the truth, boy?"

His stern face frowned angrily. I was unsure if my answer was about to bring bad fortune upon our family, but I was always taught to be truthful, so before my mouth opened to speak the words, my head nodded. He sat looking out at the river, with thoughts drifting through his mind.

"Would you allow me to speak with your son alone?" he asked my father.

"Of course, of course."

As he passed me, his hand rested on my shoulder.

"I'll be on the roof. Behave yourself." he demanded. I watched as he entered the front gate and climbed the stairs, settling on the wall of the roof, with his arms crossed, watching us both.

The man smiled at me and tapped the space beside him.

"Please, sit." I anxiously obeyed.

"Please, don't worry so much. I come with no ill intentions towards you or your family. I merely want you to answer some questions, and you may ask me questions when we are done. Is that alright with you?"

The priest's demeanour had suddenly changed: his stern features softened, along with his voice. It was as though the fierceness was a facade, an act for those around him. Now that we were alone, he could be himself. As the red sun set in the distance, spilling multiple colours into the skies, the priest explained why he had come to my home.

He spoke of a sacred papyrus scroll, which was written over four hundred years ago. The author was a man who lived a life such as my own. He lived over and over again, keeping every moment he lived locked inside his memory. He became a teacher of priests and presented solutions on ways to live in a peaceful community, without war or famine, promoting empathy and equality for all its residents. He had taught them how to till the land and store grain for the months that the Nile was prone to flooding. He was a problem-solver, and preferred to live life with few possessions, yet he had acquired skills far greater than anyone of his time. He died at the age of fifty-one and, at his own request, months after he had passed, he was buried alongside a high priest in an unmarked grave. He was named Het and left this world with nothing but the knowledge he possessed.

I listened to the man tell me the story of one of my last lives without expression on my face, but I nodded intermittently. I remember writing that scroll with my left hand, having to write it backwards to stop my hand smudging the ink. The man carried on speaking as my thoughts wandered back to those times. My home was further up the river, towards the open sea. When the ocean receded, the sandbanks were vast. The whole landscape looked as though every bird in the world, had been invited to the banquet that lay beneath the damp sands. It was my favourite place to be.

"Was that you? Did you write the scroll?"

The priest placed his hand on my forearm. I smiled. I couldn't help myself—it just happened.

"I knew it was. I just knew as soon as I saw you. I felt the same way as I did when I held that scripture in my hand. You have the same soul, the same energy. An energy that you must have left behind on that scroll."

We spoke openly for the rest of the day about some of my previous lives, in Egypt and beyond, and he sat and listened to the stories I had to tell with fascination and intrigue. He did not question any of what was said, he seemed content with letting me ramble on for hours, until I became fed up with listening to my own voice.

When the day had come to an end, the priest gave me two options: it was my choice whether to go with him to teach others, or to stay with my family. I was still young and had lived that life before. I knew this life held different lessons. I decided to stay with my family, with a promise to seek him out when I was ready. He respected my wishes, on the condition that he might call upon me as he wished. I agreed and thanked him for his understanding.

I figured that in this life I had an important task to learn, and my father was itching to teach me. I was to learn the trade of the stonemasons. It was a skill that I felt I needed to acquire, and nothing on earth would stop me as I found the whole process utterly captivating. Watching my father work the kiln to fashion his tools and dry his small clay sculptures fascinated me and my brother. From a young age, we tried to defy our mothers' warnings, and get close enough to the kiln to watch as father loaded it with palm leaves and wood. We watched the way he'd use his tools to carve a simple stone into a beautiful creature, or god in only a few short days. He had skills that far surpassed any that I had ever accomplished. Something new to add to my knowledge was always an exciting prospect.

Life continued for a while, and my father began teaching Setu and I about the different kinds of rocks, their density and weight, and the tools needed to gain the desired effect. My attempts failed, because my patience ran thin, but he knew the words that were needed to calm me. I was rushing, eager to turn out as many statues as I could, sacrificing the quality. He taught me how to take my time and examine my product, adding detail and soft lines, using loose sand to rub down any imperfections. My brother perfected the skill far earlier than I, but this made me more determined, because his boasting rights surpassed my own. Eventually, as time went on, I progressed and perfected the skill. I was a long way off the skills of my father, but I was still young. Time and practice were all that I needed. Pretty soon, we were doubling our income, selling our statues to families who thought owning such a trinket brought them luck, good health, and wellbeing.

One day our father arrived back from his brother's home a little drunk, stumbling over his words and swaying on the spot. As predicted, he earned himself a yelling at by one of my mothers, and he took it on the chin, as he always did. She soon quieted down when he told her the good news.

"My brother's son has taken a wife, and she is already carrying a child; they have asked us to build them a house."

It was an opportunity to show his sons how a real stonemason cut rocks to extreme precision, with the use of his specialised instrument. We prepared to go to the quarry, to seek out the materials required to build the walls of the dwelling; they had to be strong, because they were intended to last many lifetimes. Their requirements were for three rooms and a generous courtyard area.

But before we left for the quarry, our father had to prepare the tools he needed for the job. Behind our home was the main furnace, which was bigger than the kiln in the front and used exclusively for smelting metals. As we filled it with timber and charcoal, father fetched a large, circular slab of granite that had an indent on the upper side. It was a little like a shallow bowl, smoothed to a fine polish. The furnace was used to make the saw for cutting the trees to build the timber roof beams, and the chisels to cut the joints. Tin and copper were placed in the smelting pots, and the rounded dish placed directly above the fire.

Father filled the dish with sand that had been thoroughly cleaned of any debris and patted it all down smoothly. The furnace was sealed, and the fires lit using a tiny glass lens that refracted the sun to a point of searing light. Me and my brother were given the exhausting task of working the bellows that fed the flames. This was performed in the evening, when the temperature was cooler; the furnace was so hot that the heat warmed the entire house, even though it was situated ten feet away. My brother and I pumped those bellows until sweat stung our tired eyes, our legs hurt, and our hips ached.

"That should do it, boys. Get some sleep, we have a busy day tomorrow."

We both collapsed on the floor and dramatically crawled on all fours into the house, moaning and whining about our aches and pains, all the while father laughed at our antics. Our beds were taken up by some of our siblings, who had rolled into our spaces in their sleep. Both of us decided that the bare floor was as good a place as any, and we fell asleep in the warm house, leaving father to tend the furnace.

The next morning, I was awoken by the sound of hammering on metal coming from the back of our home. My brother shook my shoulder, his whole body shaking with excitement.

"Wake up ... wake up. The furnace has cooled, and father wants to show us how to shape the tools."

I jumped to my feet, forgetting my aching bones, and nearly fell back onto one of my siblings. One of my mothers grabbed hold of my arm to steady me. I slipped my sandals over my feet and raced after my brother. It was a fresh morning; the sun still hid beneath the horizon, yet its rays lit the land with a cool blue light. Among the bushes, glowing eyes watched as my father hammered the chisels and saws into shape. He used specially made pliers to cut the teeth of the saw, which was shaped into a curve. He fixed wooden handles, tightly held in place with metal pins, at either end. The chisels were a lot easier to shape, as only one side needed to be flattened and sharpened. The hot metal, once shaped in a way my father was pleased with, was plunged into water, setting off a huge cloud of steam that evaporated swiftly in the air above us.

"This is the most important part now, boys. This task will take you two days but, in the end, it will make our job easy, and we will have that house built in no time at all."

My father wiped his hands on the cloth that hung from his belt and turned his attention back to the furnace. He lifted some bricks that hid the granite slab, and gently poured water over the top. It hissed and spat as the liquid boiled. When the steam died down, he carefully slid the slab free, his hands protected by a leather cloth. Inside was a sight neither of us were expecting: the sand had melted and transformed into a bowl of glass. With a few gentle taps of his wooden mallet, the glass freed itself from the stone and fell into father's lap. He had managed to make a lens the size of a dinner plate.

We were given strict instructions that it must always remain in the shade while we used the finest sand to polish both surfaces to a smooth finish, void of a single blemish, crack, or divot. It was a task that did not take myself and my brother two days, but three whole days to perfect. Day and night, we took turns, placing the fine sand in a cloth to protect our hands, and for three days we rubbed the cloth over both sides of the lens. In the final stages, we used clay from the riverbank to polish the glass to a smooth finish. We were both so relieved when father finally accepted that our work was complete. We were exhausted, having never really worked a job to that degree. Father told us that we should get used to it, which was the first time that I wished I had taken up the priest's proposal. We had to wait until the sun was at its highest in the clear blue sky before father showed us how it worked, and we could reap the rewards of our labour.

The lens was wrapped in a heavy linen cloth and taken into the surrounding desert in the back of a cart. We came to a ridge, where the ground suddenly dropped down to where the Nile had flowed, hundreds of years ago. We sat for a while, shaded by a reed canopy, hidden from the blistering sun. We gazed at the never-ending expanse of yellow sands, with the odd patches of greenery still growing in what remained of the silt deposits.

Clusters of trees struggled to grasp hold of the water deep beneath the ground. Large boulders were randomly strewn across the landscape, as if they had been thrown by the gods. Sand dunes almost completely covered crumbling walls: the remains of farms that had enjoyed green pastures in centuries past. Beyond that, it was nothing more than a barren place that offered no shelter, water, or signs of life. Father told us that a man could only last three days out there with no water. I remember wondering why anyone would want to even attempt a walk across such a place.

Father went to the cart, to fetch the lens that was tucked away among a collection of timber, rope, and wooden boxes. He sat between us and uncovered it.

"Are you ready to see magic?" he asked with pride.

Both my brother and I nodded excitedly. It was the first time we had ever seen this done. Father stepped out of the shelter and raised the lens into the air. The sun's rays at our backs hit the flat side of the lens, shooting out a narrow beam that hit a small boulder ten feet from where we were sitting. He steadied his hand the best he could, aiming the beam at a single point. Within only a few seconds, the boulder began to emit a small stream of smoke; a little burst of fire erupted, and died down again, where particles of solid rock melted into a small puddle of lava. Father quickly lowered the lens, returning it to the safety of its wrappings. My brother and I raced down the hill to inspect the boulder and sure enough, the beam had made a small indent in the rock, and the lava had begun to cool, leaving behind a smooth obsidian layer.

"But father, isn't there a quicker way?" I asked, thinking of past lives when we used to hammer wedges into fissures to shape the rock. Father returned to the cart and began pulling out the timber and laying it on the floor beside us.

"Give me a hand with this, will you?"

My brother and I grabbed hold of each end of the wooden box and placed it on the floor by the timber.

"Now boys, you have seen what a single lens can do to a rock, but have you seen what all of these can do?" Father swung open the lid of the box, revealing half a dozen finely polished lenses, all wrapped up separately.

With our father's guidance, we constructed a tripod; it held an arm that could be moved freely in a circular motion. The arm had nicks cut into the wood, to hold the lenses still. The first lens was placed in the front of the contraption, and its beam was aimed at a boulder a little further away. It soon began to smoke like the last, just as we expected.

"What if we make that beam even more powerful?" father asked.

He unwrapped another lens and placed it behind the first in an opposite direction, creating a sphere-like structure. Every piece was positioned accordingly, and the beam grew thinner and strengthened in intensity. With a little adjusting, the beam was strong enough to shoot straight through the boulder, and liquify the sands behind. My brother and I stood with our hands on our heads, watching with disbelief, as father cut the boulder in two in only a matter of a few minutes. As the two halves fell to the sides, still glowing, we were both speechless.

"Our great land gives us everything we need. You must only open your eyes to see, and use your intelligent hearts, to discover ways of using what's around you to your best advantage. Khnemu, god of the water, brings fish and feeds our crops; he gives precious water to our animals and indeed to us all. Geb, god of the earth, on which we plant our crops and graze our herds. Ra, our sun god, who lights the darkness and brings life to us all. Our lens here is the same. We used the sand from earth to polish it, fire ignited by the sun to melt the sand, and water to cool the glass. The three are essential and work together to solve all life's problems."

As always, my father was right. Those who claim to have nothing at all have everything, if they possess the three gods working as one, and they were always ready.

It turned out that father had no need for our lens, because he already had a collection to be proud of, made by his father and himself when he was young. The technique had been passed down through five generations, after being first taught by a friend of the family. I have no idea when it was first discovered, I wasn't there to witness it with my father and brother.

Later that evening, my father showed me how to gaze at the stars through a single lens, which was the first time I ever saw the moon closer than my own sight could manage. The lenses could be very dangerous during the day, but were harmless when Ra disappeared below the horizon. I have never witnessed the Milky Way in such a way as I did during that lifetime, and probably never will again. The lens was as big as our faces, so there was no squinting through a tiny tube, with your mouth open, hoping to catch a glimpse of a shooting star. We just held the lens in front of our faces, and tried not to steam up the surface with our breath.

A week rolled by before the time had come to construct the home. Now that we knew the technique, we had the entire structure built in a month. As always, I took time perfecting the skill. I'm pretty sure that my bodged-up slabs still lie somewhere in those sand dunes, where the great Nile once flowed. Mostly, the line ran dead straight, but ended in a zigzag when I became frustrated that I couldn't keep a steady hand.

The heavy granite stones were easily transported and lifted into place, using a contraption that I cannot divulge, in fear of being sought out by the authorities for the umpteenth time. Not even a hair's-width gap was left between the bricks, ensuring a draft-proof, rodent-proof, and snake-proof home for the new family. Heavy beams were placed across the top, and we left the home in the hands of others, who were expert roofers and carpenters, ready to fit the door, gates, and shutters.

My brother and I grew to be well-known in our village and beyond. Work was never far away, and we soon discovered what a hard day's work was really like.

My brother, at the age of around twenty, took on a wife of his own, and I helped to build their home, only a few feet away from the family dwelling. I expect that he found comfort within those walls and preferred not to be too far away.

As we grew older, I decided to visit the priest on a more regular basis. I never took a love of my own, because women, although some were very beautiful, were never an interest I was willing to pursue. The greatest love of my life was a big, hairy lad, whose eyes shone like emeralds. He was so very handsome, with his deep echoing voice and tender touch. He would rest on my lap the entire evening, petting me lovingly with his small furry paws. I am, of course, talking about a cat. He came to me whilst I was quarrying with my brother; a stray who had chosen me as his companion, or slave as it appeared to be, after a while. I called him Anoon, and he loved me as long as I provided him with the best fish I could catch, and a warm bed at night. Anoon and I lived alone in our little house for many years until his time came. It's sad that cats' lives don't last as long as humans. My old friend aged far too quickly for my liking, and left me after only twenty-seven years, which was young for a feline back then. I did what I could to ease his pain, until the night came when he was taken from me. And yes, I did have him mummified and kept in wrappings, until my time came, with instructions that we would be entombed together.

Nowadays, people say 'It's just a cat', but they are so much more, especially when you live a solitary life and feel the pangs of loneliness. Since Anoon, I have always tried to have at least one cat by my side; a stray is preferred, because the choice is theirs.

The day I saved my brother is a story that will bring this chapter to a close. Our great Pharaoh had died unexpectedly. He lived far away from our village, so I knew little about him except that he was named Khaba, and he was a good and fair ruler. By this time, our stonemasonry devices were widespread throughout Egypt. Workers came from all over our land to help finish Khaba's tomb.

The tombs of kings always sat close to a pyramid, because it was believed that the energy would help their souls' final journeys into the afterlife. The pyramids were never built as tombs, but as a partnership between the sun, water, and earth. In effect, they were giant power stations, plucking the free-flowing energy out of the air all around us. Today, we pay a fortune to people who harness that energy and gain overwhelming profit from it. I did try and explain this in a future life but was silenced quickly and threatened with violence.

The new tomb was being built under a hill, which required different tools for the excavating. Our task was to prepare and fit the thick slab for the interior. After us, the craftsmen would be ready to carve and paint the spells written by the scribes. We brought in the lifting device to carry a six-tonne piece of stone into place, but as the first slab lifted it opened up a nest containing two cobras. My brother didn't notice one of the cobras lunge for him. He was lucky that the snake only bit into his clothing.

I didn't think twice, and dived for the snake, grabbing it by the tail and throwing it away from my brother. The other snake had been startled by all the action and plunged its poisonous fangs into my calf muscle. To save my brother and the other workers, I tried to ignore the pain and made a grab for that snake also and tossed it in the direction of its nestmate. My leg pounded, as the pain shot up my leg, and I knew instantly that my fate was sealed. I could feel the venom travelling through my veins, and up my body. I collapsed on the floor and began vomiting; my whole body shook as the venom coursed through me. My head became numbed, and my stomach cramped like it was being twisted in a machine. My brother helped me into a more comfortable position, while he yelled for help. I don't remember too much more after that, only the faint sounds of people, and my brother crying out as he cradled me in his arms.

My brother was a husband, and a father of three amazing children, whom I was very fond of. I knew that if it was a choice between me and him to take the fall, it must always be me. My brother knew of my secret, as he sometimes came along with me when I visited my priest friend. He sat and listened, whilst I told my stories and shared my knowledge, always fascinated by what I had to say. I left that life at the age of around fifty. My father and three mothers were still alive. I had always planned on retiring to my priest's home, but it obviously wasn't meant to be. He outlived me, but I left behind one hundred stories from one hundred lives. I only hope they served him well.

\*

Knowledge is, by far, the one single thing that should be shared for free. Some knowledge must be hidden, but only until humanity is ready. I'd hate to think of anyone injuring themselves, or others, trying to slice rock using the power of the sun and a magnifying glass. For this reason, I must admit that I have left out some significant details about our rock-slicing device. I feel that, in the wrong hands, it could be lethal. I don't want that on my conscience. When humans' lust for war, hate, and power dies, then maybe they will have the time on their hands to discover something new—or old, as it were.

Passing down knowledge is the only way humans will ever progress. While in Egypt, I heard tales of visitors from the stars sharing knowledge with the common people, as well as the rulers. Knowledge these days comes either at great cost or is hidden away if it means that profits will be lost. This is the reason why there is such a divide today. The keepers of knowledge grasp it tightly, like a petulant child screaming 'It's mine', even while others suffer in its absence. Energy is something given freely by the earth, and only needs a net to capture it, but you cannot make money from something that's free. Paying for energy is like paying for air. I'm sure greed will one day tax us to take a breath, and that's when mankind will truly be finished. All we need to support our existence is water, earth, and the sun and of course the air. We already have seeds and the tools to create something to keep the rain off our heads.

Mankind's biggest failure is ownership: owning land and charging people to use it. When will they learn that land is not theirs to give, and never was? We belong to the land, not the other way around. We spend our lives working hard to pay for something that the earth gives us freely. Have you ever wondered why? Why are we the most intelligent species on earth, yet we are the only ones who have to pay to live here? The answer is greed: the selling of products at gross profit, to make more money than can be spent in one lifetime. World hunger could be solved swiftly, with what resides in the bank accounts of one percent of the population. How sad must it be to desire a top branded car, rather than to ease the pain of a billion people.

An enormous collection of knowledge was held within the walls of the Great Library of Alexandria. It held plans of technology that even *I* didn't understand. I visited on a few occasions and was forever in awe of what was hidden in those texts. Devices that were easy to construct and would provide energy for a thousand years. Devices that could pluck water from the air, even in the most arid places. Great machines that took DNA from a species and could replicate it into a clay egg in the event that the species became extinct. It wasn't only texts, but also samples and seeds, and precious metals and crystals that held powerful magic not seen on Earth. Spheres that opened portals, and machines that could give you access to time itself.

Some objects and text were added to the collection from star people, who described their planets of origin. Those other worlds may be a haven for those who feel the need to leave this planet, and they would be welcomed—in exchange for knowledge. There were plans for the construction of ships that could defy gravity and give life-preserving conditions to humans wanting to travel through space. Maps of wormholes, invisible to the naked eye, that would take you to another world simply by stepping through. Plans of great ships, hidden beneath the deserts' sands like arks, which will become active when human beings' struggle to survive, or the planet itself, reaches the end of its time. Most importantly, it held documents explaining the origins of planet Earth itself, and how it came to our sun, travelling through space after the death of its own sun.

Sadly, a man came to Egypt seeking to rule and dominate its people. He was jealous of the power we held, and our enriched lives.

Some of the library's documents were stolen and moved to an undisclosed location, I can only guess where, hidden from the people who they were intended to help. To cover up the theft, what remained in the library was burned. Thousands of ancient scriptures were reduced to cinders, while the perpetrators laughed. Thousands of years of history cataclysmically destroyed in a single night, because of one man's jealousy and lust for power. I only live in hope that what remains is hidden from view until the time comes when mankind can simply look upon them with awe, without the need to use them to gain profit or power. That time will come again, I'm sure of it. But not in this lifetime.

# THE OLD SOUL

I have been wondering if it would be more realistic to give what I call 'the darkness' a name, but after thinking about what aspects it holds, I simply can't. It's nothing. A place between, a dark waiting room, a void in time and space. A place where no light penetrates, and no life exists other than my own. That was, until I was met there by another.

I could not see him or her, but I could feel them. They caught my attention with a gust of air that wafted past my soul. I had that overwhelming feeling of being watched by someone, or stared at by a person awaiting your response to a question you did not hear. I was worried, for a time, that the darkness was all that awaited us when the soul was freed from the shackles of planet Earth. Now I know that there is more, because I have seen it: only through tiny cracks whilst another is welcomed in, but it is definitely there.

The old soul who joined me explained that I was part of something bigger: the only one currently on Earth gifted with my abilities, and for very good reason. Souls are sent to Earth to learn and grow to greater strengths, to experience what it is to live with your feet on the ground, in a body that is built to last only a blip of your existence. In the time you have, if you didn't experience your quota, as it were, then you were thrown back for more: a life reset, just like a video game. Memories remain in what the Buddhists call the 'overself', the 'puppet master' if you like. With me, it was different: I was destined to sit amongst a different kind of soul, and for that privilege I had to learn everything. Every lesson, every sadness, every happiness. I had to learn how it feels to break, and how to repair myself, then break again to become stronger. I had to learn how to conquer fear, and how, sometimes, you must fear to survive.

I had to learn how to succeed, and how to cope when success is out of reach. Pain to the point of death—again and again, until the pain becomes numbed. One thing I could never achieve, no matter how hard I tried to convince myself, was to kill another human being. So many times, that decision ended in my own flame being extinguished and my soul propelling itself into that darkness, but ending my life was better than killing. Who was I to have that sort of power, to end a body, releasing the soul? I am not a god, far from it. Like everyone else on this spinning rock, I'm just trying to get through every one of my lives, the best way I can. This curse is mine, and mine alone. A burden that I do not want, yet it has chased me since what seems like the dawn of time.

The old soul stood beside me and opened a window down to Earth. Through this window, I saw a man with a small moustache and black, slicked-back hair. He stood upright with his head held high, his arms were tucked into his sides, and blood dripped from his fingertips. He was standing on a mound of bodies, surrounded by the screams of death, pain, and suffering. He oozed power like the pus of an open wound, yet he had no compassion, he was an empty vessel sealed shut with his own ego. I saw the bodies of millions of humans, starved and skeletal in appearance, with loose skin and bulging eyes. Babies with bullet holes in the sides of their tiny heads, and women on the brink of death being callously raped by soldiers, their sorrowful cries echoing into the air like poisoned gas, fogging my brain. It was a mountain of sadness, suffering, and unconceivable pain.

"Is this hell?" I asked. "Is this where the evil souls go?"

"This place is Earth. Earth has become hell." The old soul explained, with a solemn voice.

The soul said two more words that cemented themselves into my memories from the exact moment that I arrived in my mother's womb:

"Observe only."

All it needs is one man: place him on a narcissistic pedestal built from the bones of slaves, add a voice so loud that everyone is compelled to hear it, offer a heap of money and some ideas that promise riches for the majority of the listeners, and include a generous helping of fear. These essential ingredients are the recipe for the birth of a tyrant.

I hate war. I hate the fact that revenge can dominate the mind of one man, causing millions of innocent people to perish so wickedly. I have never been able to understand the concept. I can't fathom why or how a man can pull the handle, releasing toxic gas into a room stuffed with innocent men, women, and children. The sounds of their deathly screams permeating through the brickwork, whilst they claw at the walls in their desperation to reach fresh air. One action that extinguishes not only *their* lives, but also those of future generations: scholars, doctors, professors ... who knows what they may have achieved? How can that man sleep at night, surrounded by the ghosts of his victims, without so much as a shudder of regret? I hear what people say: if the soldiers didn't carry out their orders, they would be killed themselves. Surely one death and a clear conscience is better than the death of thousands, but then the job would only be passed to the next, until the task is complete. For every command there is a task, which must always be completed. I wonder how long the man who sent the orders took to contemplate what he was asking. Did he pray to his god for forgiveness? Did he really believe that his actions would hold no consequences for his own soul?

How could soldiers watch, as so many people starved to death? Thousands of living skeletons, walking amongst corpses that had become so weak they still lay rotting where they fell. Treated like litter, as they waited for the next death-pit to be dug, and having their human status stripped away from them, they were solely referred to as 'animals.'

The corpses became such an everyday sight that survivors had to step over them, assuming they had the strength to. They knew that death snapped at their own heels, like a hungry vulture, and they could do nothing to change the fate which awaited them. The only hope worth clinging to was the hope that they might be liberated, or, at least, have a pain-free end. How must it have felt to be a young child— the last survivor of your family? A loving family who made sure you received their share of the rations. Looking around at the bodies of your mother, father, and siblings, wondering where you should lay down once death came looking in your direction. Clinging on to the hope that the rotting corpse of someone familiar would offer comfort in those last moments.

How must it have felt to drag people from where they were hidden concealed in homes, behind shrouded doors? To march them out of their sanctuaries and into the streets for all to see, paraded like criminals whilst others wept for their souls. Knowing that they were destined for a train that would certainly end in death, and the extinction of their family name. Were their consciences clear when they yanked babies from their mothers' arms, knowing that children were used for experiments? To observe while they had their tiny veins pumped with radiation or poison, to see how long they would live, and the pain they'd have to endure in the name of science.

How did they manage to silence the screams that must have been imprinted in their memories forever? How can a man murder a twin, just to see how the other would react, to see if they were spiritually linked? If one would feel the pain of the other suffocating, drowning, or being blasted with electricity.

There are so many atrocities of war that if I listed them all, they would be all this book contained. I would dearly love to list the names of all the people I have known, and the torturous acts that snuffed out their lives, but there are simply too many. Sometimes it is better to let the dead rest in peace.

# SILENT HELL

I was born to a wealthy family, on the outskirts of Berlin. I was a big, burly boy with a head of golden hair and light, icy-blue eyes. A perfect specimen of a German boy, with only one small problem: my ears were incapable of hearing. I was completely deaf, but not from birth; I caught a virus in my first few weeks of life that robbed me of sound. My parents loved me regardless and taught me sign language, which offered a way into the world past a locked door.

When I was around twelve years old, I was sat by the open fire in our living room, reading a book. My parents were listening to the radio so loudly that I could see the speaker vibrate. Out of the corner of my eye, I saw movement that caught my attention. My father was in his usual armchair, smoking his wooden pipe, his right leg crossed over his left, and nodding in agreement to what was being broadcast. My mother seemed different: she looked anxious—more so than I had ever witnessed before. She was always a strong woman, who had no need to worry, but that day something was different. I saw her plead with my father: she stood before him waving her arms around, but he replied with only a few words and ignored her after that. Eventually, she left the room, and slammed the door so hard that I felt the floor shake. My father shook his head, sighed, and drew in the smoke from his pipe. He looked at me and smiled reassuringly, rolled his eyes, and shook his head. I presumed that they had had one of their disagreements.

My home was in the wealthy part of town. It had tall ceilings, high enough that a second floor could easily be built into each room, and still leave plenty of head space. The sash windows housed heavy drapes, which kept the heat in the room when closed. Large antique chandeliers swung from ornate ceiling roses, and huge oil paintings, in decorated golden frames, adorned our walls. Father claimed that the pasty-faced, broad-chested, chubby creatures in those paintings were our ancestors. I remember trying to see a family resemblance, and struggling to do so because we were all well-built, but tall and slim.

We had servants around the home, who did everything from cleaning to serving meals cooked by the chef. We also had a tutor, who visited three times a week, and taught me about the world. He was chosen specifically, because he was familiar with sign language, and he provided me with plenty of books to read. Sometimes he took me out on trips, to see some of the amazing architecture around our city. Mighty buildings, carved with such elegant detail, were so beautiful and unnaturally huge that it did not occur to me that they were lived in by a single family. The Reichstag building was my favourite: with its tall columns and beautifully carved statues, the building reminded me of my time in Rome, so many lifetimes before.

Being deaf gave my parents the opportunity to shelter me from what was happening outside our home, but all too quickly I saw the world change dramatically. I remember asking my teacher why he wore a gold star on his arm, a fashion that I had noticed appearing in abundance around the town. My teacher replied,

"Because I am Jewish."

I asked why Jewish people had to wear the star, but he changed the subject abruptly. I asked a second time, but he glared at me as if to say, 'Shut up, or else'.

The next week my teacher did not appear and was not replaced. Lots of people in my town disappeared. Soon, everyone who I had seen wearing that yellow star vanished from our town, without an explanation. I asked my mother what had happened to them, and she said that they had been taken to live in a camp while people found them a new town, just for them. I didn't understand the concept—what was wrong with them living here? It was their home as well as ours. Mother explained that Jews had a tough time in our country: there were people who didn't like their ways, or their religion. It had been agreed by our government that they were moved, for their own safety.

Father decorated our beautiful home with red flags, with strange-looking crosses. They were on the mantle and beside the front door. My books were replaced with texts that bore the same strange symbol, but my parents said very little, and explained only what they wanted me to know. One evening, a servant fetched me from my room. My father had requested my presence in his office, which was a rare occurrence, as it was my mother who cared for me. Father usually just smiled and ruffled my hair with his fingers. I knocked on the heavy door and waited. A servant on the other side opened the door and led me to my father. He was standing by the window behind his dark oak desk, with his hands together behind his back. He was dressed in a strange uniform, whilst peeking through the net curtains at the street outside. I asked why he was dressed as he was, and he replied using his hands. He had been called upon by our leader: he was to become a general, which he saw as an honourable position. War had broken out, and it was his duty to join the effort and fight the enemy.

Mother was sitting in a chair in the corner of the room, holding her forehead in her hand, pushing up her yellow hair. Her face was bright red, and her eyes were swollen. Her hands shook with a rage that she tried to hide from me, but I felt her pain—I just didn't know why she was hurting. She rose to her feet and grabbed my arm, dragging me from the room. She marched me upstairs to my bedroom and grabbed a suitcase from under my bed. She threw it onto my ottoman and began emptying the contents of my drawers into the case. I sat silently on the chair, not knowing what to say or do. Father appeared and, in a fit of rage that I had never witnessed before, he pinned my mother against the wall by her throat. I began to yell as he brought his face so close to hers that their noses touched. His arm reached out towards my window with a pointed finger, and back at his pouting lips. I was never very good at lip-reading back then, but that day I saw what my father said to my mother:

"Shut your fucking mouth. If they hear you, they will kill us all."

My mother looked terrified and, as father released her throat, she fell to the floor, sobbing. I ran into her arms, and hugged her, whilst she buried her head on my shoulder. I wanted to scream at him to never lay a finger on her again, but 'they will kill us all' did not appear to be just an idle threat. Later on, we placed all my clothes back in the drawers; all except for a change of clothes for both mother and I, two blankets, and some money. A 'just in case bag', she called it.

Father left the following day, in the back of a shiny black car. He did not say goodbye to either of us, he just opened the door and left. Later that day, mother found two notes upon his desk: one for her, and the other one for me. Mother didn't show me her letter. I presume it was something heart-warming, as her smile returned to her lips, and a happy tear fell from her eye while she was reading it. They hadn't been apart since they were young and had spent many happy years together. This war, though, caused them to argue. They were both German, and both Roman Catholic, but my mother's heart accepted all, and did not stand for racism or any prejudice. Father's heart was harder and believed in the ideals of the man who spoke on the radio. My letter read as follows:

*To my dearest Rolf,*

*I have been called away to help with the war efforts, which, as you are well aware, is an honour. I have been asked to help build a better world for you and your mother. Eventually I am to be stationed, to where I do not know yet. Look after your mother and see that she takes good care of you both. I know it is a strange world at the moment, but I assure you that Germany is strong, and we will win this fight. I will always do my utmost to keep you both well-protected.*

*In my desk, in the drawer to the right, is a pair of gold cufflinks that belonged to my grandfather. The stones are real diamonds, and they have been in the family for over one hundred years. Will you take care of them for me? They will be passed down to you one day, anyway.*

*Make sure you keep up with the reading, I have some literature in my office which may interest you. Please feel free to take a look.*

*I will call for you to join me once I have settled at my posting.*

*Papa.*

Mother swiftly dismissed what was left of the servants, and closed the front door, bolting it top and bottom. She tried to hide her unrest, but her expression told no lies. I was instructed not to go near my bedroom window, under any circumstances. I wasn't to open it to let in fresh air, or even peek past the curtains. The house, which I had spent so many years in, became my prison. While I lay on my bed and stared at the ceiling, those words 'observe only' rang out in my mind constantly. How was I supposed to observe when I couldn't even look out of my bedroom window? I had nothing to observe, stuck in this home. So, I went against my mother's wishes and, when she went out shopping for food, I stood by my window, watching silently through my laced net curtains.

The streets were eerily still, like a postcard. The town square, opposite my home, usually full of hustle and bustle, was now completely empty. Children no longer skipped on ropes on the green, ladies no longer took strolls around the pond, throwing bread to the ducks. Even the ducks themselves had disappeared; in fact, there were no birds at all. All that moved was a neat row of ladies, standing silently in a queue by the shop on the corner, wicker baskets hung over their arms. They kept looking back and forth, as if they were waiting for a lion to appear and pounce on them. They didn't speak to each other, and they kept their heads down, with just an awkward smile from time to time while they continued to wait. When each lady appeared from inside the shop, baskets filled with groceries, she wrapped a scarf around her head and dashed home. They did not run, it seemed that they dared not run, but they had all mastered the art of speed-walking.

On every corner stood soldiers, with rifles pointed towards the ground. They chatted and smoked cigarettes, one after the other, flicking the butts wherever they pleased. One of the officers said something to another that made him throw back his head with laughter. I remember thinking that these men must have felt so powerful, with weapons in their hands, all the women cowering at their feet. It was one Saturday morning, at around ten o'clock, that I learned why they feared them so.

Mrs Maya, our old maid, appeared at her window. She lived above the shop next door to the grocery store. She had a little boy of around ten years old, who she'd bring over to our home sometimes to play. I had thought she had moved months ago, but I watched in wonder as she frantically tugged at the window, tears rolling down her distraught face. I looked at the door below for any clues as to why she was so upset. I could just see a pair of black boots through the shop window. They appeared to shuffle around, like they were trying to dislodge something heavy. Mrs Maya bared her teeth as she pulled as hard as she could, finally freeing the swollen wood, pushing it up around five inches. I expected her to crawl out and onto the roof but instead, she grabbed hold of her son, and hugged him lovingly; she held his head still, whilst reeling off her instructions. She kissed him tenderly on the head and lifted him to the open window. The boy pushed his head and shoulders through easily and, with one last push, Mrs Maya flung the rest of his small body out onto the roofing. The boy crawled on top of the roof, as high as he could, and waited for his mother to join him.

As I was watching the scene, movement came from the empty shop below. A bookcase lay face down on the tiled floor, and the boots had disappeared from view. Her son straddled the rooftop, rubbed his eyes, and looked out around him at a view that he had never witnessed before, filling his lungs with the fresh air like he hadn't breathed that well in weeks. A few minutes passed, and those same boots re-appeared. They belonged to one of two soldiers, who now had their arms linked under Mrs Maya's arms, dragging her behind them; her face was unrecognisable. In the short time that those boots were out of sight, their owners had beaten her to near death. Blood spewed from her head and nose, and her front teeth had been smashed from her mouth. They stood together, propping her up, her legs clearly broken, as they hung in an unnatural way.

They waited with her on the street corner, laughing like it was a sport. A van pulled up moments later, and Mrs Maya was tossed into the back like a rag doll. As they did so, Mrs Maya's son peeked over the roof, and screamed loudly for his mother. One of the men looked up, and quickly spotted the young boy. He raised his rifle and, without a second thought, shot the boy in the face. I was deaf, but I could have sworn I heard Mrs Maya screaming, as she watched her beloved son slide from the roof and hit the concrete path with half of his face missing.

My heart was racing, I couldn't believe what I had just witnessed. I expected some of the ladies to give aid to the boy, who was clearly still showing some signs of life—but they did nothing. The poor boy died shortly afterwards, still spluttering blood out of what remained of his mouth. I couldn't help but cry for him. He was alone on that path, without any comforts or company. He was only ten, and a friend of mine. His name was Jonah. He had a passion for astronomy and was a talented violinist; he taught me how to feel for vibrations, as he slid his bow across the strings. His end was agony, an agony he did not deserve.

The ladies who queued by the shops did everything possible to avoid looking at the small boy's corpse, as his blood stained the paving slabs. They pretended not to hear the deathly screams of his mother, who grabbed hold of the end of the soldier's rifle and held it to her head. They didn't appear to care that the woman was once a friend to them, and had helped them all, in one way or another. I think, in truth, they were scared. They walked home in silence, and I expect that, as soon as they were safely inside their homes and away from the eyes of soldiers, they wept for poor Mrs Maya and her young son Jonah. They sobbed until the tears ran dry.

My mother entered the home, and collapsed before she could slide the bottom bolt across. She crawled into the back room and cried until morning. Nothing I could do brought her comfort, and she refused to tell me what had happened. I knew, of course, but I didn't tell her that. Despite her pleas, Mrs Maya lived that day, as I spotted her bloodied face in the back window as the van drove away, but I don't suppose it would have been for long.

It seemed that the soldiers relished a mother's suffering: the harrowing screams met with the satisfied smirks on their heartless faces. For four days Jonah's body lay on that path, rats gnawing on his flesh when the evening came. Eventually the smell became too great, and a grave was dug on the green and the body was laid to rest. No prayer was said by his graveside, no stone was laid or, indeed, any marker. To my knowledge, he still lays there, as the green remains to this day, undisturbed.

With every opportunity I had, I stood by that window and observed the outside world. I watched as men, women, and children were rounded up. One by one, every house was emptied of Jews, who were piled into the back of trucks that drove up the road in the direction of the train station. All of them had the gold star pinned to their clothing. The ones who refused were put to death, on the street, in front of their pleading families. Very quickly, no one refused;

if anything, the stars seemed to be worn like a badge of pride.

Mother never told me about anything she saw in those streets; in fact, she saw my deafness as an advantage, because I couldn't hear the radio. I knew it was on constantly, as I could feel the vibrations while I read. The shelves on the walls in my father's office were littered with stories of war, but I preferred a good adventure story; a way to take myself to a different world.

After a year had gone by, we received a telegram from my father. He had been posted to Amsterdam, and we had three days to pack up our belongings and join him. We were to lock up the house securely and take as little as possible. The driver was expected at our door at 6am to collect us. He had everything we needed, we were only to bring our clothing and a few personal items. I was glad to be leaving that place, as the stench of death had become all too familiar. At the same time, I feared what we were to witness in Amsterdam. I packed up a few of my more favoured books, my father's cufflinks, and his letter, which had become a prized possession after not seeing him for so long.

As I packed my clothing in the case, I wondered to myself ... I wondered if my father knew what had happened in our town. Did anyone know what these soldiers were doing?

Should I be reporting them to anyone? I know that I was only in this life to observe, but I was a human, too, and had seen things that a young boy of nearly fourteen should never witness. They didn't know that the age of my mind outdated any of theirs, so I had to play along.

At five-thirty in the morning, we sat at the kitchen table finishing our breakfast.

"Are you excited?" My mother signed to me.

I shook my head. I was worried—I couldn't hide that. I kept thinking back to the picture I was shown in the darkness: the man standing on the hill of corpses. Could that man be in Amsterdam?

"You will be fine; we are yellow-haired: no one dares harm those with yellow hair. And Rolf, read lips when you can. It's better that we don't tell anyone that you're deaf, okay?"

She smiled at me, but I could see the unease in her expression, and how her hands trembled whilst signing. I could make no sense of what she was trying to say; why would the colour of my hair give me immunity from persecution? Were we not the same as everyone else? What made us so special?

I gazed at my reflection in the mirror. My hair was blond like my mother's, my eyes bright blue, but I was the same as everyone else in every other way. It seemed that everyone in my town only had one aspect about their person that I lacked: the ability to hear.

My memories of previous lives filled in the gaps. Jonah's head hitting the concrete made a sound like a coconut hitting a rock, his blood splattered like the milk inside the shell, bursting through the cracks. The sound of a mother's screams, as she watched her child die, knowing she could do nothing to help. I had witnessed that scream before, in some cases escaping from the depths of my own lungs. They all sound similar, like part of the mother died along with their child—a heart shattering into a thousand pieces, burst open by a sharp punch of sheer sorrow. Anyone who has heard such a cry can never truly describe how harrowing it is. It's the worst sound in the world and it was all around me, yet my ears could not hear. Some might say it was a blessing, but my eyes saw what the ears didn't.

This time I was able to see the pain crease the skin, releasing an invisible fire. Her face reddened and every muscle in her body exploded in spasm. Tears burst out of her eyes and her mouth opened wide, releasing every ounce of happiness and joy that she had stored away, leaving behind a vessel containing nothing. All that remains in her body is a sad soul, and a broken heart, which yearns to follow her child to the afterlife. When a child dies, the heart does not break. It explodes.

The car arrived at ten minutes past six in the morning, but it was a strange man, who looked almost like a caricature, rather than my father, who collected us. He was well-built, yet he had a long, gaunt face, his thinly framed glasses sat on the tip of his long, pinched nose. I could tell he spoke in whispers, or with an accent, as mother kept asking him to repeat his words. We were accompanied by a car to our rear and a truck up front, filled with men with rifles between their legs. My mother noticed my concern and explained that it was a precaution: in case we were attacked by the enemy.

"It's a ten-hour journey, if the roads are clear. We should arrive at tea-time."

My mother conveyed the message to me, keeping her hands just above her lap. She also told me to get some sleep, something that I was not going to do. I would take this opportunity to do as I had been instructed and observe every detail that I could, no matter how grisly the scene.

We came across countless blockades, constructed of brick walls and barbed wire, which looked as though they were put up in a hurry. The scruffily cemented walls were stained with blood and sprayed with bullet holes. Rubble littered the roads from buildings that had been destroyed by fire, and some paths were avoided for reasons I was not informed about. I'm guessing that this was at the request of my mother, due to what was occurring at the time.

As I looked out of my window, my eyes studied all that I saw. Mother tried so hard to protect me from the horrors of the outside world, but she could not forcibly close my eyes from it. She tried several times to distract me, even using her own tears, but I did all I could to see.

At first, the roads were quiet, the town's doors closed, whilst people cowered inside with their curtains pulled shut. The army seemed to outnumber ordinary people, as they gathered in their groups, smoking cigarettes, and pushing civilians around for no apparent reason.

As we drove through Berlin, it became eerily still. It was like everyone was watching a sand-timer and waiting, knowing that at any moment that last grain of sand would drop through the tiny gap of hope. They knew that no matter how hard they prayed to their god, they could not stop that sand falling. Hope kept them alive, but it also kept them prisoners in their own homes, praying that they would not be called upon to take part in the war, or worse.

As we left Berlin, a convoy of cattle trucks waited in a side road for us to pass. In the driver's seat of the first truck, was a man in the familiar khaki uniform and tin helmet. He gave the driver in front of our car a smile and wave.

As we drew closer, I noticed that the truck was not filled with cattle, as it should have been. Cattle would not have been holding on to the enclosed truck with their fingers, peering through the gaps with their reddened eyes. Some were the wrinkled fingers of the elderly; some were smaller digits that held on lower down. For a single split second, a pair of eyes met my own. I remember the sheer anguish in those eyes. They were eyes full of pain and panic, but also a tiny glimmer of hope that maybe they were being rescued. I did not ask my mother any questions on my journey, or become upset, as I knew that it would hinder my mission.

We drove alongside a railway for a time; it was mostly unused, except for a convoy of tanks pulled by a huge engine. Another slowly rolled past us, pulling wooden carriages with the sliding doors sealed shut. I couldn't see what was onboard, until it came to the last carriage. The door was open wide, while a german officer sat on the edge, smoking a cigarette, with his booted feet dangling. Behind him was the sight that first introduced me to the true horrors of this war.

I never thought anything could be as bad as what I saw from my bedroom window— sadly, I was wrong. Behind the man who carelessly drew from his cigarette was a large, brown, hessian blanket tossed indiscriminately over the top of the cargo. The blanket did not hide the horrors that hid beneath, as the pile overwhelmed its small size. I stared, inquisitive, as I tried to make out what the strange, pale, skeletal objects were. I tried to remain emotionless, but when I suddenly realised what the objects were, I couldn't help but cry. I hid my face away, so that I wouldn't be noticed. By now, mother was looking out from the other side of the car into the small village that passed our window. She didn't notice the tears rolling down my screwed-up face.

Under the blanket lay a twisted mountain of what, once, was humanity. Bony arms and legs covered in thin layers of skin, with no flesh or muscle remaining. The bulbous kneecaps protruding from the side of the pile moved up and down, with the motion of the train. Faces, hidden amongst the limbs, stared endlessly into nothingness, their eyes dark wells of despair. Mouths opened wide, showing oversized white teeth, with lips curled back, void of any muscle to keep them closed. Sunken temples showed the outline of their skulls, removing any aspect of a human appearance.

They were all stripped naked, taking away every last ounce of dignity that they had once held. At least two hundred men and women, all dead. Murdered by war, murdered at the order of the man who stood proudly at the very top of the corpse pile in my darkness.

The man on board, the only one I saw who was still able to draw breath, flicked his cigarette onto the rails, took one last gasp of fresh air and slid the door across. His complete lack of empathy for these human beings in his care was plainly evident to me. He hid the macabre scene from the outside world, but it was too late. The picture is one of many that haunt me, even to this day.

It took all the strength I possessed, but I managed to pull my emotions together before they were discovered, and my mother was none the wiser. We continued our journey to Amsterdam along what seemed an endless road through a patchwork of fields. The deserted countryside brought with it a brief respite, whilst the image of all those poor people, whose lives had been so cruelly taken, swam in my mind. Was it just because they were Jewish, like all those people who had disappeared from my town? Was it, in fact, disease that killed them—a secret pandemic that only affected the Jewish community? I had seen with my own eyes the murderous intent towards anyone who wore the yellow star, but I couldn't understand what they had done that was so terrible to be deserving of this torture and genocide. I could not understand what was happening, or why, but I felt that I couldn't ask my mother. I tried to, in the past, only to be side-tracked. Her motherly instincts still tried to protect me from the horrors of the world outside, but now my head was drowning in the reality of this horrifying war.

It wasn't long before the rolling countryside was replaced by small towns, which grew larger the closer we got to our destination. Our cars took a sharp turn and rolled slowly along the narrow road. All that greeted us was an endless expanse of razor sharp, barbed wire fencing that stood fifty foot in height, held in place by tall wooden poles. Despite my mother's efforts, she could not shield me any longer. The sight took her breath away and left her speechless and paralysed.

We saw children playing behind the wire barricades, amongst the remains of what used to be friends, neighbours, and family. It was a sight that they had grown so used to, so much so, that the rotting carcasses were normal. The corpses were strewn across the grass verges, propped up against posts, and piled high. I witnessed one of the uniformed workers carelessly drag a skeletal man across the muddy yard by his arm. He was met by another worker, who took hold of the man's legs, and they effortlessly tossed the victim to the top of the pile of rotting bodies. I assumed this poor soul was dead, until I saw his arm move and his mouth gape.

For a moment, my thoughts transported me to where that man lay: his emaciated body propped up by the remains of what used to be his friends or family. I could only try to imagine what must have been going through his mind. He had been drained of all strength, to the point that he had none left to let out a scream, or even inform the workers that he was still alive. He lay on a pile of at least thirty people, staring up at the cloudy sky, praying that death would come swiftly.

As we turned the corner, I noticed the wood at the base of the pile and a man attempting to light the kindling. As death approached him, I felt that the numbing pain of fire might be a welcome release for that poor soul. I think my mother saw the man too, and she became hysterical, yelling at the officer in the passenger seat and pointing at the poor man.

"He's still alive. Please help him. Look ... look."

Her pleading earned her a stiff yelling from the driver. She sat back and cried silently; she knew that she had no power in this place.

No one wore the yellow star; most were dressed in baggy clothing that had vertical stripes from top to bottom. I learnt later, that amongst the prisoners were local German people, who had opposed the treatment of Jews and hid them away, in secret. The punishment for such an act was to be shot against the wall, along with the Jews they were trying to protect.

Those I saw were the unlucky ones who were sent to the camps, to save on ammunition. Among them were also captured soldiers of many nationalities: French, Argentine, Polish, British, and even some American soldiers mixed freely with Jewish people, who by now were few amongst the many.

    Great pits emerged on the outskirts of the complex, which were being filled by workers who looked so frail that they, themselves, walked in the shadow of the grim reaper. The wire fencing was topped with a lethal amount of barbed wire to prevent their escape. They had been ordered to toss the partially dressed corpses of their friends and relatives into the hole, without anything that even resembled dignity. I had no doubt that the last occupants of those mass graves would be the workers themselves. I'm sure they knew what was to come, but a man will do anything to see a few extra hours on planet Earth.

    It was likely that they had given up on life, the hope that they held onto so fiercely was being tossed into those pits, along with their comrades. Their lives now served only one purpose: to help bury the dead and stop disease spreading to anyone who was still managing to survive. Maybe hope did indeed remain; that tiny flicker still faintly lit at the back of their minds, that the soldier may gain a pinch of humanity and set them free. Or a scenario that they could only dream of: a sudden liberation by invading countries.

Our destination was not as my father had said. The journey came to an end just under six hours after we left Berlin. We had not arrived in Amsterdam, like we were told, but a place called Hanover. Our car pulled up outside a large brick-built house, far larger than the one we had left behind. An overnight snow flurry had covered the roof and gardens in an inch-thick of fresh crisp snow. It was a million miles away from the horrors that lay only a few miles away.

The door was already open, and a man with a cane in his hand waited, ready to greet us. A few people unloaded our cases, and headed upstairs with them, whilst my mother and I were shown into the home.

They led us down the brightly lit hallway, decorated with red banners adorned with the strange black cross. The men wore flat peaked hats, with golden eagles embroidered onto the front, and their shoulders appeared square in their thick, woollen, khaki coats. As we entered the room occupied by my father, the officer threw an arm in the air and bounced on the spot.

I looked at my mother, but she was still suffering from the shock of what she had just witnessed. She looked scared and confused and didn't seem to recognise her own husband sitting behind the oak desk. My father looked pleased to see us and raced over to greet us. He hugged me first and signed that he had missed me. He said that I had become a strong-looking gentleman, and handsome like him. Mother acted differently towards him, frozen to the spot and filled with so much emotion that I was afraid she'd burst. She stared through my father, fixing her gaze on a picture of our family on the wall behind him. Father spoke words to her, which caused her face to redden and her hands to tremble. I could see that a fire inside of her wanted to explode, but she was trying her best to hold back her tears.

Father spoke to the officer at the door, who saluted again and left the room, pulling the door shut behind him. As soon as we were alone, mother could no longer contain her fire, and exploded with a long, drawn-out cry—tears rolling down her cheeks in torrents. She fell into father's arms, then collapsed on the floor. An officer knocked on the door after hearing her cries; father left my mother on the floor and dashed over and spoke to the man outside. Whatever excuse he gave seemed to appease whoever was out there. Father shut the door and knelt down to give aid to my mother.

I stood in the corner of the room, watching without moving. Father was angry but remained calm. I learned from him later that day that our convoy had had strict instructions to use a route that took us far away from the sights that we saw. It was a route that would have protected us from the horrors of the nearby camp. The officers claimed that the desired way was blocked, so they'd had no choice. We were eventually shown to our rooms upstairs, where my mother lay on the bed to rest, still weeping hysterically. I had my own private room, which was filled with toys suitable for a younger boy.

"Sorry. I was meant to ask for all this to be cleared away," father explained, without using his hands. I attempted to answer with sign, but he pushed my hands down.

"Not here, Rolf. Read lips only. I have told the officers that you are a shy, quiet boy. We shouldn't have too many problems."

For only a few minutes, I sat alone with my father. He asked how my life had been back in Berlin. I wanted to tell the truth about all that I had seen, but I was afraid for my mother, so I lied and said that everything was fine. He was called downstairs by another officer soon after.

"Go and see your mother in a while, will you?" he asked. I nodded, and said that I'd go when I had unpacked my case. Father agreed and left me alone in the room.

I sat on the bed, and looked at all the items that adorned the room around me. Small hand-carved animals, two of every kind, all fitted snugly in their painted ark, tin cars and other vehicles, metal planes hanging from the ceiling on thin wire, and a brightly coloured clown that swayed on its base, amongst other items. On the bookshelves were fairy story picture books, and adventure tales fit for a boy of around six or seven. I picked up a copy of *The Three Bears* and opened up the front cover; written on the first page was a note from a family member:

> *To our dearest Freddy,*
> *We hope you enjoy the story.*
> *With love to you as always.*
>
> *Grandfather and Grandmother Abrams 1936*

As I held that book in my hand, the worn-out pages and broken spine looked as if it had been read a million times; a favourite amongst his small collection. I wanted to learn all I could about the young boy whose room I had stolen, so I began rooting through his belongings.

His drawers were filled with his clothing, neatly organised and folded like they were a prized possession. I searched his toy box for any clues as to what Freddy was like: what hobbies he enjoyed or any secret messages to imaginary friends. Mostly, it seemed that cars were his preference, until I stumbled across a small hidden drawer at the base of his wardrobe, which stuck out ever so slightly as I closed the door. In it was a small red notebook, with words scribbled across the cover in different coloured crayons:

*Freddy Abrams. Age seven.*

I gently opened the pages to a world filled with colour. A world seen only through Freddy's eyes. A world adorned with kings and queens, castles and brave knights on noble steeds, princesses in tall towers with hair so long that it fell to the floor below. The picture that stood out to me the most formed that unmistakable lump in my throat: it was a picture of his family. Every figure drawn had a name beneath it: Mummy, Daddy, Eve, David, Samuel, Matya, Alma, who appeared a babe in arms, and Freddy. A small brown dog named Filo completed the family. The picture was of them all on a green hill, with a bright sunshine in the top right-hand corner, which held a smile like those on the faces of the family. Later that day, I took the pad down to my father to inquire as to what had happened to them. His answer was brief:

"They were Jews, Rolf."

He did not offer any form of explanation beyond that, and he snatched the book from my hands and threw it on the fire. I protested, and tried to grab hold of the spine, but father grabbed hold of my shirt before my hand burnt. He pulled me back and slapped me around my cheek. He yelled at me so loud I could feel the vibration in the room, and spit flew from his mouth as his face changed to that of a man I'd never seen before. He had never previously struck me—not once, and I had done a lot worse than ask a simple question.

I spent the next few days in my room, as requested by my father. I sat on the window seat that overlooked the rear garden, watching the snow thaw. My room was being slowly stripped of everything, by my father's officers, until only the bed and furniture remained. I was powerless to do anything. I had hoped that sitting on the window seat might have protected hidden treasures beneath, but, sadly, it had already been emptied. When the officers had finished, the only trace of poor Freddy left was a single glass marble, with a blue and green flash in the centre. The last remaining piece of Freddy Abrams, the boy with a mind filled with all the colours of the rainbow.

In the weeks that passed I learned that my father was the commandant of the local, what he called, 'work camp'. I assumed it was the place we had passed on our journey. Father had changed: he was no longer the loving, caring man that he used to be, now he was a cold-hearted man that others feared. Most of his time was spent at home, behind his desk writing orders and signing letters, and ordering others around and shouting at men.

Mother grew more and more depressed, only appearing at the table in the evening for supper, as ordered by my father. Every day she looked more ill and tired; her eyes were haunted by what she had witnessed. Where I possessed the strength to hold back my emotions until I found myself alone, my mother's eyes constantly wept. She had been taken over by a sadness that she could not escape, or even try to. Her heart was kind, far kinder than a lot of people I had met in this life. I knew, deep down, that she, too, would leave this world. I just hoped that the decision remained her own, rather than it be taken by another.

My fifteenth birthday came far too quickly, and I spent the day at my mother's grave. My predictions came true far sooner than I had expected, because only a month after we arrived, my mother was found hanging from a tree in the woods by the side of our home. The night she left, she slid a note under my door. I was awake at the time and began to read it as her footsteps creaked down the staircase.

*Goodbye my son. I'm sorry that I have brought you into a world that is so cruel. Please keep hold of the compassion that I see in you every day. Don't be afraid to cry when you are alone, as I will be there by your side to comfort you. I am sorry that I must leave you, but my heart cannot bear to beat whilst so many hearts have stopped forever. Be strong my love.*

*I love you forever.*
*Mother.*

I could have run after my mother, and attempted to save her life, but I knew that this war was already killing her mind. Death would only set her free, and freedom was what she deserved. I only hoped that she found peace in the afterlife, and that the darkness swept aside allowing her to enter paradise.

I later discovered that my mother was part of a secret organisation that helped give aid to those in hiding. She provided food and medicines to so many families in our area. She had no idea of the scale of cruelty until she witnessed the death camp with her own eyes, and it was all too much for her to take. She never truly recovered from those scenes, or the fact that her own husband played such a big role in the atrocities. Father, in his anger, had dragged me out to the woods to show me my mother's weakness. He claimed that it would toughen me up and make me a 'cast-iron man'. As she swung from that tree, her emaciated body looked similar to those at the camp. I was happy for her; she was a good person—an angel amongst demons. She was free from this hell on earth, and she died on her own terms: in her own way, and at the time that she chose. Father saw the smile on my face, as I pictured her sitting amongst the wildflowers, memories of this life shed like the seeds of a dandelion. Father saw this as my strength, and a sure sign that I was ready to face my future. A future as a commandant's son, and at the age of fifteen I was signed up to what my father called, 'Hitler's war'.

The day after my birthday, my father suggested we visit the camp that was under his control. It was a trip that I had dreaded since learning of my father's position. I didn't want to go; I had had but a glimpse of what those camps held on the journey here, and that was far more than my nerves could handle. Sleeping with those visions was nearly impossible. All thoughts of my own selfish mental capabilities were pushed to one side, when I remembered *why* I had been sent to this life.

The task, my *job*, in this life is so important that my hearing was stolen in order to achieve my goal. I had little to observe, whilst locked away in this house. With my mother gone, I had no one to stop my father from subjecting me to the horrors that he claimed would make me 'a stronger man'. No longer did I have an overprotective mother, who would have preferred to gouge out my eyes than have me see those sights again.

My first task was to be fitted with an appropriate uniform. A man was brought in to take measurements of my limbs, and the width of my shoulders and chest. His hands shook so violently that he dropped the measuring tape on two occasions. Sweat poured from his brow and when he spoke, I saw his bottom lip flap like the wing of a moth, as he stuttered every word. My father seemed to like the power he had over people, and the man's nervousness caused my father to taunt him cruelly. As he held the tape measure from my hip to my heel, my father took a gun from his belt and opened up the mechanism, just to show this poor man that he had power over him. When the man saw the gun, his nerves only worsened. His face turned crimson, and he looked up at me with panicked eyes, as if he were begging for his life. I wanted to help him but, in truth, my father scared me too.

The measurements were finished before time, and the man shuffled swiftly out of the room with his head bowed. Later that week, a new uniform was neatly piled on my bed, the jacket hung up on the wardrobe door. The appearance of my uniform marked the day I dreaded: my first visit to the camp. I sat next to the uniform for a moment, contemplating what the day would bring, and trying to harden my exterior as I knew that any sign of weakness would come with a price. I felt my floor vibrate, as heavy footsteps approached. I turned to see my father, dressed in his uniform.

"Half an hour, Rolf. We leave in half an hour. Let me know if you need help with the uniform."

He looked cocky, like he was about to show me a shiny new car. In reality, he was about to accompany me into hell. Hell, created by men like the one who had emerged from my, once loving and caring, father. This man I did not recognise as my father. He had become the devil himself. He showed no emotion after my mother's passing, not even arranging a funeral for the woman that he had vowed to love forever. I was not allowed to grieve for her either, because men did not cry; crying was a sign of weakness.

The uniform felt like the mask of a murderer, but to me it held no symbol or status; it was simply a disguise to aid my mission in this life. It was made from the finest material, stitched with care and attention to detail. It fitted perfectly, made by a man who feared for his life should he have so much as wronged a single stitch.

The importance of my father in the area meant that everyone expected me to be as cold and as callous as he was, but, in truth, I was more like my mother. I was strongly built and had the look that some described as 'dominant' and that of a 'leader'. At fifteen I had already reached over six foot in height, and I weighed way over 200 pounds, but it was not fat, just broadness.

    The reality was that I would rather see a spider freed, than lay my boot upon it. Not an inch of me was tough or fierce, only soft, and gentle, kind and compassionate. It killed me to remain silent and not try to help, even in a small way. If I could free one man, one single man. It wouldn't be enough to stop the war, but it would make a difference to that one man. If I had saved one man and we had been caught, it would not only have ended his life prematurely, but mine also, ending my journey before my time had come. I had to stick to the mission at all costs.

    I stood in front of the mirror in Freddy's room and gazed at the monster that I appeared to be. I was literally dressed from head to toe in the most menacing-looking grey on the spectrum. I had gold buttons, and an eagle emblem sewn onto the right side of my chest. I was told that wearing the uniform made me superior amongst men—like I had some special power to control, because of the gold buttons and a shit-coloured uniform. I knew that I was no more special or important than those people who lay dead in the streets. I had thought my deafness to be a curse but, as my eyes struggled to take in the scenes, I realised that, if I also heard the screams of tortured people, the death rattles of the dying, and the crackling of what fat remained on the corpses burning on the pyres, my mind would break and not allow me to continue. My corpse would swing from the same tree that liberated my mother, and I would probably have to begin this whole story again.

My uniform was on, my boots were pulled over my feet, and my hair was oiled and combed back. I was ready to face the day, and surely it couldn't get any worse than what I had already witnessed—famous last words of an ignorant man. I scooped up my hat, took a deep breath, and headed down the stairs and out to the waiting car.

My father was already seated in the back, smoking a cigarette, his left arm stretched across the top of the seats. He looked at his watch as if to tell me to hurry, as if hell could not wait a moment longer. As I climbed into the car, my father offered me a drink from his hip flask. Usually, I would have refused his offer, this time I took the flask, and filled my mouth twice with the burning liquid. It was tough to swallow, but it brought an unusual heat to my stomach, which my father explained helped to prevent me vomiting. He also offered me a cigarette, which I refused; I hate the smell.

The entire journey my father was speaking to me, and I read his lips carefully. He outlined what I was to expect. He called the inmates 'animals' and 'scum,' 'the lower race' that had the 'audacity to bring war to our glorious country', anything to de-humanise the prisoners. The man was clearly delusional; I saw nothing glorious about it during those times.

It was springtime and an unusual spell of warm weather covered our part of the world. The skies were almost completely blue, but for the odd wandering white cloud, and a grey plume of smoke rising from the distance.

Our journey was short, and decorated with a rainbow of spring flowers. It was like the last remnants of heaven before we hit the gates of hell; no flowers grew in hell, not at that time anyway. The fences which surrounded the complex were built to keep the devils inside but, from what I could see, the only devils were the ones who were free to come and go.

As we passed through the gates, a harrowing scene greeted me. Around twenty emaciated men lay in the dirt in a row; thin blankets separated them from sharp stones that would otherwise pierce their delicate skin. I firstly assumed they were all dead, but quickly ascertained that not all of them had passed.

These men, so weak from hunger, did not have the strength to lift an arm in the air, or turn their heads to face the warm sun. The only indications that they still clung to the last glimmers of life were the slight rise and fall of their ribcages, and their eyes. I can never forget their eyes, no matter how hard I try. Whenever I close my own eyes, I can see theirs: their black vacant stares, sunken into their skulls. It's like a recurrent nightmare, a constant reminder that I was there, standing over them. I still feel guilty that I did not offer them comfort in their final moments. The eyes are the one muscle in our bodies that takes the least amount of energy to move. Their eyes followed me, as I walked along the path; their stares taking in the last pictures, the last scenes, imprinted on whatever remained of their shrivelling brains. They did not break the stares, not so much as a blinking, until further movement required that they turn their heads.

    Out of the twenty men that lay in the sun, only two still lived, which dropped to just one by the time my visit had come to an end. There were wooden huts filled with bunks and yet more people. Some had only just arrived and could still walk around freely, so they could offer some care to others. Most of them slept side-by-side, to preserve any warmth, and bring comfort to one another, in their final hours. The only living things that managed to have regular meals in that camp, besides the staff, were the rats. The rodents feasted on the exposed limbs of the living, as well as the bodies of the dead. Big, fat rats, with their snake-like tails, were also the cause of the disease that swept through the prisons.

The other aspect that caught my attention was the smell: I had never smelled anything so horrendous in my entire existence. I have inhaled the odour of bodies burning on a funeral pyre, and even witnessed piles of animal carcasses rotting in the summer sun, but they were perfume compared to the acrid stench that came from this place. It was entirely different, and on another level of vileness: a noxious blend of rotting flesh, excrement, urine, sweat, and vomit. The rats added to the pungency of the smell with their own piss and shit. Just one single inhalation caused the lungs to shut down in protest. I had to cover my nose with my sleeve during my brief, yet heart-breaking, tour of this hell.

My father led me through the camp on what he called 'a tour of my workplace'. It was supposed to help me understand that these people, these human beings, were not people at all, but animals. They had no soul or conscience—they had no right to live here. They were thieves and murderers, rapists, and liars. It was the Gestapo's job to cleanse the land of these animals, so that Germany could rise stronger and more powerful. These 'animals', as he called them, were enemies of Germany and its regimes, and we had to show our strength. Hitler was our leader, and he promised to make our country the most powerful on Earth, filled with riches and technology beyond our imagination. Father continued with his ridiculous monologue, and I pretended to take in every word.

My vision stretched beyond his lies—I saw hundreds of men and some women too, I think. Their gaunt, empty looks made it hard to tell the sexes apart. These were fathers, brothers, sons, husbands, mothers, wives, and daughters. These were people who had lived lives like everyone else. They bravely signed up for war to protect the people they loved, and to fight for a country that swore to protect them; only to be captured and starved to death by men who had power from gold buttons and pistols in their holsters. Some of the men were covered in blotches, which was typhus: a disease spread by lice. It was seen as an asset, because it increased the death toll. My father tried to tell me that it wasn't starvation that killed them, but the symptoms of typhus. However, I was reading the lips of the soldiers who whispered behind him, which made the truth clear.

"They should all be hanged. Free up beds for more of the bastards." said one man. The other answered with, "That would be too quick. Let the fuckers suffer."

I was shown a large shed, away from the prisoners; its doors were pushed ajar by the contents spilling out onto the path in front. As father swung back the door, a thousand rats dashed for cover in all directions. The burrows of the rats were the eye sockets, rib cages, and gnawed shoulders of the dead. The shed was filled with corpses. The shaven-haired remains of hundreds of inmates, all waiting for the pits to be dug. Mass graves were usually dug by the inmates, but at this time there were not enough able-bodied inmates to complete the job. They had been waiting for help to arrive from another camp, but on arrival most of the men had already died, and the rest were far too weak. The staff called them 'bad stock' and complained that they'd have to do it themselves if the pile of bodies grew any bigger.

A trench big enough to accommodate all the corpses piled in the shed, on the grass, and in the sleeping quarters would have to be huge. It was agreed that instead of a trench, a great fire was to be lit to burn the bodies, with the ash and bones tossed into the canal that flowed adjacent to the camp. It was a practice that had been done many times before.

Father was asked into the office by an officer, so he asked me to remain outside. I noticed one man sitting on a wooden bench, just outside the sleeping quarters. He was frail, like the others, but not quite as bad; he still had the strength to walk. He had an American accent and held something in his hand. I stood in front of him, and he looked at me with fear. I smiled a little, so's to not be noticed by anyone else, and pointed to his hand. He timidly opened his fingers and raised the item towards me. It was a lock of hair, tied in a dirtied yellow ribbon.

"It's from my sweetheart," he said, with a look of despondency.

A small brunette lock of hair sat in the palm of his hand. This token told me that, even after all he had suffered, he was still clinging to hope. If the devil existed, then the man who stood on that pile of corpses was Lucifer. His ability to brainwash an entire country was a gift given to him by the purest, most repugnant evil. Despite all the death and disease that surrounded this man, he still clung to that lock of hair. The only item he possessed that gave him the smell, feel, and touch of something that made him happy. A reminder that across the sea, a young lady waited for him and loved him; no matter what happened, she had once shown him love and humanity. He knew love, he could feel love, so how could he be soulless? How could he not deserve to live on this earth? How could he be called 'greedy', when all he possessed was that lock of hair that he cherished? I placed my hand on his thin shoulder and gently folded his fingers over his prize. I placed my hand on my heart and smiled.

I was a German commandant's son; a fifteen-year-old boy who was feared by all in that camp, but this man smiled back at me. That smile was the greatest gift that I could receive that day. No one witnessed it but me and that American man. I wish that I knew his name. I would have loved to trace that woman and tell her that until his last breath, his hand still gripped that lock of hair. He took it with him, wherever he ended up.

I hope beyond all things that a special paradise awaited all of the victims of the holocaust. A place where families could be reunited, and loved ones embrace, without fear or prejudice. A place where they can speak freely, love freely, and live for eternity—freely. I hope that they had all lived lives that ticked the boxes required to move on into paradise. One thing was for certain: the man they named Hitler did not deserve such a place.

I returned many times to the camp, and witnessed first-hand that it was not only disease that killed these poor souls, like my father had said. It was mainly man's cruelty and greed. The food rations that arrived at camp were measly. The officers who ran the site took the first bites, leaving what was left to be thrown on the floor. The prisoners had to scoop up the leftovers before the rats descended. The officers were all well-fed, and some even struggled to fit into their uniforms.

If the population of the camp grew to a size that they deemed 'unacceptable,' they would have a recount. The amount set by them was half of the bed capacity; those who remained, usually the weakest, were left out in the cold. They were taken outside, and left in the dirt, without clothing or dignity. They were too weak to scream for help, too weak to huddle together, or even to shiver. As the temperature plummeted, death came quickly and left no survivors. In the morning, the staff picked up what the wild animals had left behind and tossed it either in the shed, in a pile to be burned, or in the pits.

I never thought I'd ever harden to seeing them, but in the end, I just grew numb. I tried to bring some sort of comfort to some of the victims, even if all I could bring them was kindness in their remaining days. I wanted to sneak in during the night and free them all but, in the state that they were in, how far would they have run? I'd smuggle food occasionally, but this only prolonged their suffering. I was rarely alone in that place, and the staff were painfully loyal to Hitler and his crackpot, narcissistic ideas.

At sixteen I became a fluent lip reader, and no longer needed sign language. With my extensive knowledge of languages foreign words were never an issue, and I became aware, through whispers, that the end of this hell was approaching. I refused to have a gun, although it was standard issue for someone with my privileges. My father begged me to take one, if only for my own protection. I placed the gun in my holster, to appease him, but removed the bullets. I had seen so many horrors that I began to pray for death.

I wanted to see only one more piece of history and witness one more moment: the liberation from persecution and death that so many people yearned for. My life was coming to its end, death was galloping up the road, but I got my wish.

Less than a year later, American soldiers joined the war efforts, making the so-called 'enemy' more powerful than Satan. With almost the whole world fighting against him, our devil leader had finally accepted the fact that he had lost the war and had taken his life in a final act of cowardice. The world was free from him at last, and those who had opposed his regimes, who had had no choice but to remain silent, rejoiced.

My father and I were captured by the American soldiers, along with other top-ranking officers from our area. We were all lined up against the wall to be executed. My father was beside me. He reached for my hand, but I took it away from him, a final "Fuck you" to the monster who was once my loving father.

In our final moments, I saw his face. I looked at the panic in his eyes, the scared expression, and the sheer terror of what was to come. Yet, behind those tears, I did not see an ounce of remorse or regret. He was lucky that the bullet punctured his skull, allowing a quick death, one which he did not deserve. I felt his blood splatter upon my face and watched as his lifeless body fell to the ground, leaving pieces of his shattered skull and brain on the brickwork.

I closed my eyes, and waited for the same gun that killed my father to release the bullet aimed at my head. After a quick jolt of pain, I felt a sense of peace. I had lived that life with only one intention, and although I wished that I could have at least saved a single life, I knew that it wasn't possible.

The last image that appeared in my mind, before that bullet hit me, was that American man's smile as I folded his fingers over his lock of hair. For a split second it brought me comfort.

One man with a big voice, and the ability to persuade, is a dangerous thing, especially whether he holds prejudice and hate disguised as power. I have visited war a fair number of times but have always taken the first bullet because I cannot bring myself to kill. I'd rather save a life by forfeiting my own, like I did in Vietnam. Some say that the children of the sixties, who chanted peace and love, were the incarnations of those victims that I witnessed during Hitler's war. That's a prospect that I admire.

As I live today, in the year 2022, I can see the world changing again. I watch as a generation is born with minds open to sexuality and race. I see a world where it's normal to be gay, normal to dress the way you want.

It's refreshing to see some shed all labels so as to enjoy what it is to *live*, to be free, and be exactly who they want to be. What's sad is, that among those who seek freedom, are those who still like to point the finger and call for persecution.

Those who snigger at the man wearing a dress, at the gay couple holding hands in public, or the mixed-race couple who fall in love. How sad their souls must be, stuck in their jars with labels saying 'normal'. Normal is who you were *born* to be, not how someone *expects* you to be. I hope, in some ways, that I will indeed return to this world in the future, because, so far, I have not gone beyond this point. I'd like to see it when all the jars are broken, when the new generation is born from the ashes of the old.

I did attempt to look for the American man for a short time, if only to put a name to the face. His face was changed, though, from the man caught in any pre-war image, and I knew so little about him before his death. To me, he was named Billy, and he held love tightly until the ashes of that lock of hair joined his own. I wonder if his lady knew how loved she was, and how much hope that lock of brunette hair brought him.

## MINI HARVEY

In this book, I am trying to alternate my stories between good and uplifting, and those which taught me my greatest lessons. After two days of battling my memories for a life filled with love and promise, though, I feel compelled to tell you about another hard life. I apologise for this now, especially after the last story, but this one is just as equally important and deals with the same lesson, but in a different perspective. This time, my job was not to observe, but to live amongst the brutality of mankind—persecuted and demonised for nothing more than the colour of my skin.

I was born a girl in a small village, somewhere in the west of Africa, I couldn't tell you exactly where or when.

Our village consisted of a small gathering of huts, which housed five families that had all broken away from a larger tribe. We were lucky, as a river ran near to where we settled, which provided fresh, clean water for most of the year. If the river ran low during the dry season, we knew where to dig to find water; as always, the Earth provided for us all. We raised goats and some poultry for meat and eggs, and grew crops that fed not only us, but also the animals. We were happy in our own small slice of Africa, surrounded by both green pastures and the dry savannah. For most of my childhood our village was isolated, and I saw no other humans other than those people I already knew. Our village elder said that outsiders brought disease and famine, so we were raised to fear anyone but our own people. I kept the memories of my previous lives to myself and thought of this life as a rest from the pain and hardship that I had suffered in previous lives. I didn't realise at the time how very wrong I was.

My father was the head of the family, and one of the elders in our village. The elders consisted of three brothers, who all represented their own families, their own wives, and offspring, and decided to lead our village together. I was the youngest of four children, and the only girl. I was loved by my mother, but I always found my father to be a little cold towards me.

My oldest brothers were strongly built, and proved themselves to be good hunters, along with my father. Not only did they provide meat regularly, but they also kept predators away.

Over the nine years that I lived in that village, I only ever knew of two fatal animal attacks. One was an elderly woman, who had been dragged into the river by an unknown creature while fetching water, and the other was, unfortunately, a young boy of three. He had woken during the night and wandered outside his home looking for his father. I was told that it was a big cat that took him and tore up his body to feed its young. From a young age, we knew not to exit our hut unless we had an adult tell us it was safe to do so. After hearing some of the stories our elders spoke of, we were all too afraid to anyway.

My other brother was still young, only a year older than me, but he too showed promise as a great hunter, and my family encouraged it. I, on the other hand, was born quite small and weak, and being a girl, I had only one task. When I came of age, I was to marry a boy: the son of another elder, who was, indeed, a cousin of mine. It was expected that we were to have a handful of boys, and the odd girl, to carry the family into the future. It was a task asked of girls all too often in human history.

The boy that I was promised to was my friend, so a future by his side did not upset me. We had grown up together and shared many hours at play. Even though the thought of a union was a little strange, it was better than being married off to someone I wasn't keen on.

It was one night, when the sun had been unforgiving during the day; the heat so intense that the watercolour sunset was a welcome friend. We sat down on the ground outside our hut, enjoying the cool breeze that blew gently from the river. One by one, the stars appeared as we watched the bats dart around in the hazy skies, catching insects. It was a beautiful night, surrounded by my family and friends; music and songs gently drew the day to a close.

From far in the distance, we heard someone yelling. It was my mother who was the first to notice, and she immediately alerted my two oldest brothers and my father. As a precaution, my young brother and I were sent inside the hut, away from any danger. My mama stood guard in the doorway, peering out to catch a glimpse of what had caused the commotion. The most likely scenario would have been an uninvited visit from a neighbouring tribe. This had happened in the past but had not been problematic. The other tribe sought help when their food ran dry; if we had plenty ourselves, they were sent on their way with supplies, if only to avoid conflict.

This time, though, my mama acted very differently. She was nervous and panic-stricken. We began to hear a commotion: yelling and shouting, arguments amongst the men that only grew louder. A gun was fired, which sent an echo through the air, and triggered the jungle to awaken with the screams of monkeys and calls from diurnal birds.

A woman screamed and began to cry uncontrollably. Mama turned to us, her eyes bulging with fear.

"Stay where you are. You hear me? Stay here."

She took one last look at us both and disappeared into the night. As my brother and I huddled together inside, we couldn't help feeling afraid of what was outside our flimsy hut. We could hear the desperate calls of our people, as more men yelled brutally. Another shot was fired, and another scream echoed into the surrounding air. My brother began to cry in terror, letting go of his strong hunter facade to reveal a side that I had never seen. He was petrified, and so was I, but I had to find out what was happening, so I moved to the doorway and slowly peered out into the carnage.

A group of men armed with rifles had come to our village—not to stock up their provisions, but to gather people for the slave ships. Some of our hunters battled with the men, but bravery cannot stop a bullet. My father was one such man—without thinking, he charged at one of the gun-wielding tyrants as he held his rifle to my older brother's head. The man turned and shot my father in the chest, without remorse or thought of the life he had extinguished. On seeing my father's lifeless body, blood pouring from his wound, my mama cried out and rushed back inside the hut. She held me and my brother close to her and began to pray to her god.

I'm not sure how they escaped, but my elder brothers appeared soon after and convinced my mother to hide away in the trees with us. She agreed, but as we exited the hut it was evident that our actions came too late. Our whole village had been surrounded, and we had no chance to escape. Men were waiting by the trees and the river, to the left and to the right; all armed with weapons, and rage in their eyes. I didn't understand what was going on at the time. I held my mother's trembling hand and hid behind her for protection.

A man ran up from the left, and both my young brother and I screamed in terror. My elder brothers fell to their knees and placed their hands behind their heads.

"Please. Let the children go free. They are no use to you." pleaded my mama, attempting to shield us all behind her.

"Shut them up, or I will shoot them both."

He signalled to another man that appeared behind us; he pressed his gun to my temple, embedding the cold metal into my delicate skin. I closed my eyes, waiting for that familiar pain to end my life, but this time it wasn't to be. What happened was worse—much worse than death.

My mama and some other stronger members of our community were tied up, with heavy branches resting on their shoulders and ropes stretched across their throats. Their hands were bound and linked together. We became a chain of prisoners, led by a man with a rifle under his arm. The children, including my young brother and I, had the rope tied loosely around our necks and attached to the end of the chain. My mama pleaded with the captors for aid, fell to her knees and screamed out in pain, bringing down the man attached to her and causing some others to stumble. I wasn't the only person to notice that her dress was soaked in blood; our captors noticed too. The bullet that had killed my father had passed through his body and hit the top of her thigh. Our captors took no pity on her; she was now seen as a hindrance and cut loose from her bindings.

She knelt down on the ground, by the body of my father and placed a hand on his chest.

"Babba, are you alive? Talk to me please." she sobbed.

Her hands trembled as she pressed down on his wound.

One of the captors grinned callously at her pleas, aimed his rifle, and shot her in the head at close range. All of us screamed as her body hit the ground next to my father's. As I looked upon my parents lying in the dirt, blood gushing from their bodies, I noticed that my father still lived. His hand was reaching for my mama, in the hope that she would comfort him, or he could comfort her. He didn't notice the hole in her head until he pulled her face towards his. We marched away from my village to the harrowing screams of my father, as he lay dying, next to the corpse of my dear mama. I'd never thought I'd hear him scream, he had always been a man of strength and courage. His emotions were always well-hidden, especially from his children.

A lot of the people from our village had the sense to run at the first signs of danger. They hid in the trees, too afraid to offer us any help. Seventeen adults and seven children, including me and my three brothers, were marched away from our homes that night, and dragged to the boats that were waiting further upriver. Some of us fell and had to hurry to get up before being struck by a fist. Sometimes we weren't so fortunate and were dragged behind, by the rope around our throats, bloodied and bruised. They did not stop to give us a chance to steady ourselves, we had to be quick otherwise the rope would press on our airways.

When we arrived at the boat, our captors wasted no time. They forced us on board, like cattle, and took us upriver. They barked orders at us to sit with our heads down until the sun peered over the horizon, for fear that others might see us and claim the prize as their own. I found a place next to one of my older brothers and rested my head on his leg, as I silently cried for our parents. A small consolation after such a traumatic and harrowing night. My brother didn't speak or offer me any comfort. His eyes didn't even meet mine: he stared at his feet, frozen in time; his body trembling, as beads of sweat trickled down his face.

I was awoken by one of our captors yelling as loud as his lungs could manage.

"We have seventeen and four here."

I sat up and looked over the side of the wooden boat. The sun was bright, so I had to adjust my eyes. I gazed upon a busy town, built with bricks and mortar. Row upon row of small houses, with grass roofs trimmed in a straight line to match the homes on either side.

Horses and goats were tethered to anything that would hold them. In this life I had never seen so many people going about their daily business. Some of them looked out at the river and watched us arrive. Some looked upon us with sadness, and others saw us as a spectacle. Most people watched us without expression, like it was an everyday sight—nothing out of the ordinary.

Our captors moored the boat at the dock, and we were dragged, one by one, towards an enormous stone building with dome roofs edged by merlons. Neat red tiles sat uniformly on the roofs, hanging precariously over the edges. Heavy cannons sat guarding the walls and pointed out over a vast ocean; none were manned but, nevertheless, the sight of them was still menacing. We were dragged through an archway, into an open cobbled courtyard.

Many white faces stood around with canes, whips, and other weapons; waiting for an opportunity to beat our bare backs and tear the flesh from our bones. They were all dressed the same: black trousers and loose-fitting, white, buttoned shirts. Some looked stifled in military-style overcoats and black hats; they were the men who hollered the orders.

Most of my group had never seen men with white skin and feared them, whispering tales of ghosts and monsters. These men were not ghosts, but their actions were indeed monstrous. The other children cried with fear if one stepped too close, not understanding that these men were like us, but from cooler climates. I tried to calm them but gained a leather whip around my back for my efforts. Thankfully, despite the pain, it left only a welt and did not break the skin. The children were all silent after that.

They led us down some dimly lit stairs into the building's gloomy underbelly. My young brother and I were separated from our other brothers and bundled into a room with scores of children from other villages. We were all frightened and crying, not only from fear, but for the traumatic way we had been separated from those that we knew and loved. Torn from our parents and families, not knowing what we had done wrong, or where our journey was to end. Our only solace was that we were together, and not alone. Fear is easier to cope with when we have company, as it seems to get divided between us all, and this enables us to find comfort in one another. It was dark in that place, with only dimly lit lanterns outside a dungeon-like room, which only allowed us to make out the outlines of each other. The smell was repugnant; the floor was covered in human waste and dead rats. We were all from different tribes and villages, but this was not a time for war or competition—not even friendly chatter or a whispered name. We found comfort where we could and huddled together at the end of the room, in the farthest reaches from the door.

I tried to yell for my older brothers, but they did not answer me. I'm not sure if they ignored my calls or if they couldn't hear me, but I held on to the hope that they were still alive. Eventually, a man from another room bellowed, startling us all.

"Shut your dirty little fucking mouth, or I will come in and shut it for you."

He took out a wooden club and struck the wooden door hard, while peering in through the gaps in the bars. He looked like a bulldog: his face was bright red, and his teeth were bared. He snarled at me as I sat back down with the other children. I did not make another sound.

A fat man with a round pink face appeared outside of our room, accompanied by a black man, and began yelling as loud as he could. The black man translated it into the language of our people:

"All of you are very fortunate, very fortunate indeed. America has asked for aid with their sugar cane farms. They need manpower to help yield their crops, and other tasks will be asked of you as well. As of now, you are all owned by us until you have been sold to the highest bidder. If you try to escape, you will be shot. If you resist, you will be shot. If you try to overpower your captors, you will be hanged publicly as a warning to others. The ship arrives in the morning to take you all to your destination. Do not speak unless you are spoken to. Do not make a fuss, or your provisions will be taken away. Food and drink will be provided shortly."

In English, his statement was very different:

"Right, you filthy scum. What a lucky lot you are. Tomorrow, you set sail for America. They want workers for their farms, and you will work for them for free. As of now, you are all owned by us until we can sell you to the highest bidder. If you try to escape, and we catch you, we will just shoot you. There's plenty more of you out there. If you try to fight, we will shoot or hang you; we don't care as long as you're dead. Ship arrives in the morning. Shut your mouths and don't fight. If you're good, I might bring food. If I don't feel like you deserve it, you will get only water. Up to you."

The two men disappeared up the stairs, leaving the bulldog man as guard. Everything fell silent. We dared not whisper, or even cough. The only sounds to be heard were the weakened sobs in the darkness, from children mourning their loved ones.

With so many bodies, the dungeon was stifling. The air felt thick and lacked any usable oxygen. We were fed meagre amounts of warm water and some kind of broth-like soup: a single ladleful, just enough to keep us from passing out with hunger. Some of us didn't touch a drop, for fear that it might be poisoned, but as others approached their bowls, hunger took over all rational thinking. For the entire day we sat silent, fearing that any sound may lead to our deaths. We slept huddled together because the air cooled to near freezing, as the night drew in. None of us slept much that night; some complained of empty bellies, and others still sobbed quietly for their parents.

News came to us at sunrise that our ship had arrived at port. We were to continue our journey across the vast and treacherous Atlantic Ocean.

Our captors brought out the men first. They were all paired and shackled together with iron chains that rattled across the stone floor. Two by two, they were led out of their dungeon without protest. They looked broken and lost; the fight had left them all long ago. The women were next. They did not fight and were not known for resisting, so their hands were bound with rope and tied together to form a different kind of chain. They too were led out of their dungeon, in the direction that the men were taken. One woman cried loudly for her child, but was quickly silenced by the threat of a beating with an iron chain. Our turn arrived only too quickly. We did exactly as we were asked, too fearful to protest. We had no need for shackles, because there was nowhere to go—even if we tried to run. We kept our heads to the floor, frightened that any wrong move might lead to our deaths.

    We were bundled down a dark corridor into another room, where other men looked us over. My young brother and I, along with the other children, were inspected for any wound that may have festered, or signs of disease. When they were satisfied that we were healthy, they sent us through a small doorway into the open air. Ahead of us was a long stone walkway, stretching out to sea. At the end was, a large wooden galleon, with two masts pointing skywards, waited for us to board. The officers were dressed in white clothing, with different coloured jackets. The man in charge wore a dark blue jacket, decorated with gold buttons, and his tricorn hat sat upon a white wig. He held his thumbs in his buttonholes as he ordered us onboard with his broad English accent.

We climbed the ramp but did not immediately see any of our fellow prisoners. A wooden grate was opened, and we were practically thrown into a pit of bodies, with hardly any room to move, sit comfortably, or even stretch. Piles of people, squeezed in like cattle. Men and women were segregated: the men kept in shackles, and the women free to move, if only they had the space to do so. Us children could do nothing more than lie across the back of someone who lay on another. We had nowhere to relieve ourselves, so we had to empty our bladders and bowels where we lay. Once a day, the women and children were taken, group by group, onto the deck for just enough food and water to keep us alive. They were moments that we began to look forward to: the smell of the ocean, and the feel of the sea breeze on our faces, sea birds flying free above us, and the dolphins that followed alongside the ship, breaching the waters as if they were eager to see the cargo. I remember thinking, what would the dolphins think of us, if they knew what was occurring? Maybe they were trying to help us. I had often heard tales of stranded victims being rescued from the ocean and taken to shore by grasping a dolphin's fin. Maybe they were waiting for us to fall in, so they could take us home. I never had the courage to try. If I'd known what was to come, maybe I would have taken my chances.

The sailors were hard to read; some were kind to us one moment but beat us the next. Some were just evil: yelling orders and opening up the men's flesh with their cat o' nine tail whips if they so much as gagged on the horrible soups. Some tortured the men simply for breathing, and brutally raped the women just because they felt the need for sex. On a few occasions, a prisoner was beaten to death and his torn body thrown callously overboard. Sometimes the whip caught an eye or tore off a nose, deeming the prisoner 'too ugly' to be sold. They too were thrown overboard—still alive. The iron shackles carrying them to the bottom of the ocean, beneath the crushing weight of the water, eliminating any chance of survival.

It felt like we were the only survivors in the entire world. We were told that below the waves, creatures with razor-sharp teeth waited to devour anyone who dared jump overboard. We had cuts and bruises, sores, and welts, from the urine and faeces, and from where our limbs rubbed on the wood as the ship rocked to and fro. Disease always threatened us because we had no means of keeping our surroundings sanitary. In the tangle of bodies, I managed to locate my brothers and we stayed close for our own protection. The sailors often searched our cramped space for prisoners, just to dish out a beating, or to rape them. Some fancied themselves with girls even younger than I was, but it was not only women and girls who were taken for pleasure. Men and boys were also victims—violated by countless crew members and denied the right to yell out with the pain. My small frame made me appear to be a lot younger than my nine years and I was small, so it was easy to hide away.

When the evening arrived, my older brothers took us far away from view and told us not to look at the sailors. This seemed to work, as none of us suffered in the way that many around us did. My brothers covered my ears, but I still heard the grunts of the sailors, and the cheers of the crew when they were done with their victims. Most of the time they came back bleeding and empty of any emotion, staring for hours at a single spot of nothingness. Some did not return at all.

We finally arrived at our destination: the land of America. As swiftly as humanly possible we were bundled off the boats, to where a gathering of black slaves was ready with buckets of water. We were stripped to our bare skin, and the piss and shit scrubbed from our bodies with stiff brushes. Our hair was cut short, and our emaciated bodies were inspected for insects or injuries. They were preparing us to be sold at the slavers' market, for as much profit as possible. That was the day I would be separated from my brothers and have to face the world on my own.

Women did not fetch as much money as the men. They were considered halfwits, and only capable of raising children, cooking, and cleaning. They were seen as the weaker sex, without the brawn needed for manual labour. The truth was, the women worked the crop fields alongside the men in our village, but none of the men made this known to our captors. I'm guessing that they thought this to be an honourable act, but they weren't to know what horrors we might face in other types of labour. Men who had the know-how of crop management fetched the most, as it was the knowledge they held that was worth the money, along with men who were well-built, because they were labelled good labourers. Children were sold to families, to help around the home, or for their potential as future breeders or labourers, depending on their age, gender, and build. I had the wits to claim that I was seven years old, with the idea that at least it would buy some time. I was scrawny, even more so now that the rations we had been given had halved my weight.

I entered the town square with the other children, and one by one we stood, mostly naked, on the podium. Our stances were weak and feeble, bent over through lack of energy, and our malnourished bellies swelled abnormally. We were all shadows of our former selves, but this didn't stop the sale. Wealthy white people in expensive clothing raised their hands, as the seller mumbled prices. The strongest were bid on like animals, buyers fighting over them as if they were prized bulls. We were all animals in the eyes of the law and could be treated as such. In America we had to earn the right to be human and, even then, we weren't fully classed as one. We were not free but owned; we could only earn our freedom at the cost set by our masters, and with their permission.

When my turn arrived, I stood on the podium with only a small piece of cloth around my waist to hide my private parts. I felt intimidated while I was prodded and poked by more white people than I thought existed in such a small area at the time. I remember one woman with a southern accent came to me: she covered her hand with a lace glove and pushed my chin up from my chest to take a look at my face. I kept my eyes to the floor.

"Open your eyes, child."

A man approached her from the left.

"Kitty, darling. They don't speak English. It won't understand you."

I opened my eyes, if only to prove the man wrong.

"See, of course it can understand me. It opened its eyes, didn't it?" said the woman.

The man walked away.

"Stanley, come here. Watch this …"

The man returned and stood gawping at me.

"Won't you smile, child?"

I knew exactly what she said, but I didn't smile. Even if I'd wanted to, my legs were taking up most of the energy I possessed. Besides, it takes a tiny glimmer of happiness to raise a smile and, with my family either dead or gone, it was hard to find any. The woman made a strange little disappointed noise and moved on to the next child.

"How about you?"

Again, the woman was met by silence.

"Are there any goddamn niggers who can understand English?"

We all remained silent.

Stanley placed both of his hands behind his back and puffed out his chest.

"Don't be silly, dear. They are all African. Everyone knows that they are far too uncivilised for an education. Try grunting at them a few times, like an ape." The man looked around, while awkwardly laughing at what he had presumed would be funny. No one laughed back, and they both moved swiftly on.

The bidding began soon after but, despite the calls, no one wanted me. I began to wonder what would happen if I could not be sold, and the thoughts that entered my head were filled with the most gruesome deaths.

I had heard whispers, on the ship, of unwanted people being taken out to deep waters and tossed overboard; or sold for pennies, for the value of our bones; our bodies fed to dogs; and our skin used to make leather for boots. It seemed that we needed to find a place in this society or suffer the consequences. It has been a long time since I have feared death: it's a fate I have faced on countless occasions, but I strongly felt that I had to survive. I had to go on. I felt that this life had a lot of lessons, and I always held on to hope that this would be my last. I couldn't give up hope.

I found some reserve of energy within, and raised my head and gave a small, albeit false, smile. I glanced around at all the faces of the men, with beads of sweat dripping down their red faces. The women fanned their flushed cheeks, whilst their neat hairdos turned to fuzz in the heat of the day. They stared blankly at me: a small, insignificant, black girl, who teetered on the podium with skinny legs. My hair had been cropped to the skin, my knees scabbed over, and my slender frame weakened by the journey to this strange land.

"I speak English." I stated timidly.

A hand in the crowd shot up in the air, holding a folded fan with lace sewn onto the end.

"I'll take her, if no one wants her."

The auctioneer pointed at the woman in the crowd.

"And what will you pay?"

"I'll pay you ten dollars, right here and now, and not a dollar more." The woman held a piece of paper in the air.

The auctioneer looked around the crowd.

"Any better offers for this young girl?"

There was silence.

"Sold to the lovely Mrs Harvey."

The instant the word 'sold' left the lips of the auctioneer, I was officially owned. I even had paperwork as proof of ownership. I had no rights as a human being, my freedom was left far behind, in my slice of heaven, in Africa.

On the journey across the ocean, we were constantly reminded of how lucky we were, to be going to America. It was promised that a better life awaited us, and that we should be thankful. 'Thankful' was a word that I couldn't comprehend. The life we had been ripped from had been the best life anyone could ever want. I was surrounded by my family, had limitless freedom, and felt like I *belonged*—not *owned*. How could they possibly assume that this life was to be more favourable, without even asking us what we classed as a better life? The reality of it all was simple. The day we were dragged away from my home, we had nothing. Our lives had just been sold to the highest bidder, for them to do whatever they wanted with our bodies, our minds, and our spirits.

When the auction had finished and the slaves collected, I waited quietly for my owner to arrive. I watched in numbed silence as my young brother was hauled away in the arms of an older man. The tears tracked stripes down his cheeks, as he reached for me and yelled out my name. As I looked over at him, his new owner silenced him with a hand around the mouth, and then used a horse whip, thrashing him twice around the shoulder blades. He was ten years old, with a small frame like myself. He had yet to grow into a man. It was the last time I ever heard someone speak my true name, or saw any of my family, and the fear stretched across my brother's face haunted me for many years to come.

One by one, the other children were collected: bought and paid for by their new owners. Some were lucky enough to travel as the passenger in a horse and cart, others had to run along behind, with the threat of a beating if they couldn't keep up. Only one other girl and I remained sitting on the wooden bench. She was younger than I was and looked to me for comfort by holding my hand. Her left foot had swollen, a sure sign that infection had set in.

Beads of sweat gathered all over her body, and her breaths were laboured. She was clearly in pain as her hand cradled her belly. Her lips were squeezed tightly, while she curled over, quietly moaning as she tried to hold in her screams.

I wanted to help, but every move we made was watched, and I didn't want to make matters worse for either of us. I held her up when someone came by, but her pain was too great. She collapsed onto my lap, unconscious. I tried to cling to her, but my hunger made me weak. She slid off the bench, hitting the floor like a rag doll. I noticed that the white cloth around her middle was stained with blood, saturated to the point that the material had become overwhelmed. Deep red streaks stained the bench where she had sat and, as her young body lay on the floor, I noticed blood trails down the inside of her leg that had already dried. A man came over, and callously pushed her with his boot.

"Get up and sit back down." he yelled.

The girl did not move, her pained moans were all that indicated that she was still alive. The man lifted the cloth from around her backside,

"Oh lord GOD. Henry. Come here."

He waved his colleague over, from a few yards away. He held a clipboard in his hand and wrote with the stub of a pencil. He was fat, like the rest of the white men, dressed the same in partially buttoned shirts, which bulged at the seams, and braces that hung down over his hips. He came over to join his colleague, and looked down at the young girl who was writhing on the ground in agony. He lifted her bloodied cloth with his fingertips.

"Get rid of it and arrange a refund."

"Urgh, not another one. How many times have we got to remind them? If they're gunna pleasure themselves with the merchandise, at least pick one who can take it."

The man with the clipboard walked away, shaking his head.

The girl was dragged away by her arm and thrown into a barrow. I'm guessing she died shortly after, as I didn't see or hear her again.

"Where the god damn is Mrs Harvey? I need to close this thing down." yelled the fat man.

From across the courtyard, the face of my owner appeared. She was a very ordinary-looking woman of around thirty and, as she came closer, I noticed that a young girl who looked like a doll walked by her side. They were dressed nearly the same, with matching cotton dresses and white parasols that they held up to block out the sun. They had brown hair, tied up off of their necks. They both tip-toed over, like they were walking on air. Their chins were raised, as if they were the most important people in the town.

"Good afternoon, Mrs Harvey." said the fat man.

Mrs Harvey did not reciprocate and strolled straight past him and over to me.

"I'll advise you, Mr Miller, to not ever use the Lord's name in vain before mine again, sir, or I will see to it that my husband pays you a visit."

The fat man bowed his head,

"Please accept my humble apologies, Mrs Harvey. It's the heat: it brings out the devil in me."

The woman held my chin and pushed it upwards. She seemed to be inspecting me for any flaws or imperfections. The young girl stared at me like she had never seen someone with skin as dark as mine.

"Hmmm. I'll feed her up a bit, dress her well, and teach her how to stand correctly. What do you think, Florence? Do you think she will make a good servant for you?" Mrs Harvey asked.

Her little girl walked around me and poked her finger into my left rib. It tickled me, so I sniggered slightly.

She looked at me with her ghostly blue eyes and smiled.

"She will do just fine, Momma. She can sleep in my room."

"Now, let's not be too hasty. We need to break her in first."

I had no clue what they meant by 'breaking me in,' but I presumed it was not good. The promise of food and clothing was a different matter: my belly yearned for sustenance, and I felt vulnerable wearing nothing more than a rag around my waist. The weather was warm but that didn't bother me; I was used to a warm climate. The smell was something I was not used to: America had a smell that was different to my own country. It was like the smell of dust and soot, compared to the scent of fresh grass, bark, and wood fires that I grew up with.

I was ordered to follow Mrs Harvey and her daughter to a carriage, which waited for them in a nearby street. It was a grand white carriage, pulled by two matching chestnut horses. I was told to sit upon the luggage rack at the back, where a case was strapped in place with belts and silver buckles. I did as I was asked, and sat cross-legged, clinging to the sides whilst the carriage shifted back and forth over the dirt roads. Hours went by without even a single sip of water, or the suggestion of stopping for a rest. My mouth was as dry as the Arabian desert, and my head pounded from dehydration. I listened to the conversation that Mrs Harvey and her daughter were having; they didn't seem to realise that I could understand every word they said. It was mostly about the daughter: her temper tantrums upsetting her daddy, her school schedule, and how she was to treat her new pet—meaning me, of course. It was up to the young girl to give me a new name, without even asking me the name I was given at birth. I was to take the surname of my family. Both the mother and daughter suggested names for me; some were silly, but I had no say in the matter.

After a while, they settled on a name: I was to be called 'Mini Harvey'. 'Mini' because it rhymes with skinny: Skinny Mini Harvey. They never asked me any questions; they preferred to be blind to the horrors of the industry that they spent their ten dollars on. They preferred to be ignorant of the pain, torture, and murder that occurred in their country every day. Why would they want it otherwise, when they had the means to buy matching horses, an overpriced carriage, and matching garments? But that was only the tip of the iceberg as far as their wealth was concerned.

We arrived at an enormous white building decorated with white pillars, and pale-yellow shutters on every window. The family already had several slaves working within and without the property. Some lived as family units at the far end of the owners' land, far enough to be out of sight and earshot, and others lived in the attic rooms and cellars. The tall windows looked out over a thousand acres of fields, which grew row upon row of green tobacco plants taller than most men. The land was worked by men with skin as black as my own, also owned by either my Master and Mistress, or their family. The slaves' family homes were cramped, with basic amenities: usually with just enough food and supplies to stay alive and fit enough to work.

  The owner's home itself was like a different world. Its walls were covered with patterned paper, and polished floors that shone like mirrors were strewn with soft rugs from foreign countries. Furniture with carved patterns stood in alcoves that looked like they were built to fit the furniture. Their drawers and cupboards were filled with silver cutlery, crockery, statues, and trinkets. In every room was a black woman, wearing a white dress, bonnet, and apron, busying herself with her assigned chores. A cook in the kitchen, with her assistant, chamber maids, and laundry maids. A nanny who raised Florence as her own and had fed her from her own breast as an infant. Slaves stabled the horses, and tended the ornate gardens, and an old black man served the family as a butler. He had earned his freedom but had chosen to stay with the family for a small monthly wage, simply because he would have no means to live outside the home. Even freed slaves were looked down upon.

I was led into the home through the servants' entrance, where I met two black women dressed in white dresses and white cotton bonnets. They took my arm from the man and pulled me towards them. They threw a stern look at the man, and closed the door in his face before the poor fellow could say a word.

The two broad women stood me by the fireplace and took a step back, their arms crossed over their inflated chests whilst looking me over, shaking their heads in disappointment.

"Where in the world did they find such a skinny piece o' string?"

"I can't tell for shaw, but I'm guessin' this be the first time she steppin' on these lands."

"I do wish they'd stop cuttin' their hair so short.

We can't do nuthin' to make her look good. I mean, wadda we s'posed to do wi' dat?"

Both women picked pieces of debris from what remained of my hair.

"They do it 'cause o' the lice. They prolly crawling wid them on the ships." said the first.

"One thing for shaw, gonna be a task teaching dis young 'un the Lord's English. I'm bettin' she don't even know a single word."

I was prepared to stay silent, but these two women seemed friendly so I decided that it would be beneficial for me to speak up, and in English.

"I know English. My mama taught me."

It was a small lie, but I expected the truth would not be believed.

Both women placed a hand on their chests and sighed with relief.

"Where you from, chile?" one woman asked.

I shrugged my shoulders.

"I lived in a village in Africa, by a river and a forest. Men came and killed my mama and pa. They took me and my brothers and brought us across the sea to here." I explained.

"Oh, chile. Did you come here, to this house, wid yo' brothers?"

I shook my head sadly.

"Sweet chile. I'm sorry for what ya been through. But believe me, we be all the family you's ever gonna need. We is gonna take good care o' you. Ya hear?"

Both women smiled warmly and placed their hands on my shoulders.

The ladies gave me as much water as I could drink without vomiting and helped to clean me up. Then they filled a wooden barrel that had been cut in half with lukewarm water, and turned the water white with soap. My skin was scrubbed with brushes so hard that it felt as though they were trying to scrub the colour from my skin. What remained of my hair was washed with more soap, and a washcloth was used for the hard-to-reach areas. To rinse all the suds from my body they poured cold water over me, which made me yell out. The chill was refreshing and needed, but I would have appreciated a warning, at least. The women laughed, as they pulled me from the tub.

"Now, chile. When you last eat?"

I shrugged my shoulders again.

"Well, we will soon rectify dat one. Get y'self dried off and get y' butt over to the table. I got summat special ready 'n' waitin' for yah." She smiled and left me with the other woman.

"How olda ya, chile?"

"I'm seven, nearly eight I think."

The woman helped to rub down my body with a cloth, and she looked at me with a puzzled expression.

"Girl, I myself have got me a seven-year-old, 'n' I'm damn shaw she don't look like you's do."

She placed her hand on my chest and pressed down in a circular motion.

"No breast buds yet, but I is bettin' they be growin' soon enough. Don't worry yourself, chile. It be better that you is seven than older, so I'll be keep yah secret, but if anyone find out, I don't know. Ya hear?"

She looked at me with bulging eyes. I agreed, gratefully.

"I'm nine really, and my name is ..." I was interrupted before I could speak my name.

"Chile, we don't ever say our African names in dis land. We go by our slave names. I is Mary, and that fine woman cookin' yous a meal is Agnes. What be ya slave name, chile?

"Skinny Mini Harvey, Mam." I said softly.

"Welcome to the house o' Harvey, Mini aged seven nearly eight. Welcome to yaw new family."

I was wrapped in a drying cloth and embraced by Mary. It was the first time I had been shown any affection in *such* a long time. For a moment I felt safe.

Mary helped me dress in a uniform fit for a child of my colour. My dress was grey, with a matching grey cloth hat. I wore an apron as I ate the meal that Agnes had cooked. Scraps of chicken, a whole corn on the cob, and some corn bread. That was my first taste of Agnes' sweet potato pie. My stomach felt as though it would burst after dinner, but it was so delicious I had to finish my meal. Mary said that it was 'soul food'—it was amazing. She took me up three flights of stairs to my room, way up within the roof space of the house. It was a small, white-washed room, with a wooden bed and a mattress, a bedside table with a candle holder, a cupboard with a hanging rail, and a table that held a large bowl and jug of water. Under the bed was a plain white chamber pot. I had a window which overlooked the farmlands—miles and miles of farmlands. As soon as I was left alone, I laid down on the bed and fell asleep, overwhelmed with exhaustion.

I was woken at dawn by Florence's nanny. She was a fierce woman, who barked orders at me like I was an intruder in her territory. It was expected of me to be young Florence's living doll and servant. When she dressed, I'd help her climb into her clothes: fasten buttons and tie up the bows. I had to brush her hair at night and help her to style it in the morning. When Florence wanted to play, I was her companion. I'd have to follow her everywhere, even to the bathroom sometimes. She was almost eight when I first arrived, with the attitude of a spoiled brat and a temper that she took out on me. I received every poke, slap, and kick but remained calm, even when she spat in my face and called me the most horrible names that referred to my colour.

Despite her pleas, Mrs Harvey never allowed me to share a room with her. Just as well, for I think the overwhelming desire to strangle her in her sleep, with her own braids, would have been too much for me. When she went to school, town, or church, I had to stay with my own people, which I didn't mind so much as they were always kind to me. Mary and Agnes became my closest allies.

When Florence misbehaved, and getting into trouble was what she did best, I'd be blamed for all her bad behaviour. It was me who the Harveys punished, and the punishments were brutal. When she realised this to be the case, getting into trouble became fun—if only to satisfy her macabre desire to hear me scream.

The punishments began within a month of my arrival. Every morning I was awoken by the nanny, to get Florence's clothing laid out for the day. This meant going down to the very bottom of the house and fetching her laundered clothing, which had been freshly pressed. I'd sneak into her room and hang everything neatly in her wardrobe. I'd fetch the jug, take it down to the kitchen, and fill it with hot water, then slowly carry it up the long stairway to her room, without spilling a drop. I'd tiptoe in and place it on the washstand.

Florence slept in a huge bed, covered with comfortable silk cushions, and stuffed animals. The four posts almost reached the high ceiling, and from them hung crisp, white, transparent linen to keep out the mosquitos. Once everything was in place, I had to open the drapes and gently rouse her from her dreams. This particular morning, she had already awoken, but pretended otherwise. When I let in the morning sunlight, I saw her eyes were wide open, but she wore a devilish smile on her face and closed them up tight.

I walked over to her bed and gently tapped her shoulder, but she did not stir.

"Come along Miss Florence, we will miss breakfast if we don't dress soon."

Florence remained still in her bed. I tried speaking to her as normal. I knew that she could hear me, but still she pretended to sleep. I stayed with her for half an hour, trying my best to get her up, but still she stubbornly refused to open her eyes. I heard footsteps climbing the stairs towards her room and started to worry.

"Missy please, they are coming. You're gonna get me in trouble."

That devilish smile appeared again, until the door of her room swung open. Her father had returned from his travels. It was the first time I had seen him. He was tall and broad, with a muscular physique, and a domineering demeanour. His face was stern and menacing, with a long, pointed, hooked nose, and raised brows. He wore smart clothing, made from the finest cotton, and a tailored jacket with gold embroidered into his cuffs and collar.

"Nearly six-thirty in the morning and still in bed?"

Florence's eyes sprung open, and she leapt out of bed, and ran into her father's arms.

"Father, you're back."

They hugged for a while, as I stood awkwardly by the bed, hands behind my back and head bowed.

"Who the hell are you?" he asked.

"Oh, she's the silly girl who was supposed to wake me up half an hour ago. She's such a lazy-bones, father. I think she's trying to get me into trouble."

Florence blatantly lied to him. Mr Harvey marched across the room and grabbed my arm.

"We shall see about that."

Mr Harvey squeezed my arm so hard I was afraid the bone would break. He dragged me downstairs and threw me onto the floor in front of Mrs Harvey. I tried to tell them what had happened.

"Hold your tongue. You will be dealt with accordingly." Mr Harvey snapped.

I wasn't allowed to speak or have any opinion. It was decided quickly, by both Mr and Mrs Harvey, that I was to be punished in the hope that I would learn a lesson about respecting my owners. Mr Harvey took me into the hallway and threw me down the staircase into the kitchen, where Mary was finishing breakfast.

"This beast needs fifteen of John's lashings. See to it that it's done," he demanded.

The fall injured my ankle, and I lay at the bottom wincing with the pain.

The cook rushed over to me and looked up the stairs to Mr Harvey.

"I'll see to it, sir. It will be done as soon as he's back with the flour."

Mr Harvey nodded and shut the door with a slam. Mary lifted me onto a stool and held my ankle in her lap.

"What on earth did you do to rattle his cage, chile?" She pressed on my sore ankle, and I moaned in pain.

"I tried to wake her, but she wouldn't listen. She was already awake, cos I saw her. I saw her in the reflection, and her eyes were open, Miss Mary."

I pleaded and pleaded, but the outcome could not be changed. My sentence was set.

John was Mary's husband and had the physique of any man who worked the tobacco fields. He was strong, but a kind man. After Mary had informed him of his duties, he sighed deeply.

"Honey, why he askin' me to beat a chile. A man I can beat, if I must, but sweet Jesus, a chile?" he said, with dismay.

"You gotta John. Better you than old Brutus. Think about it. I'll put in extra paddin' and you use the soft whip."

John wiped his giant hand over his face and sat on the stool next to mine.

"Now see here, lil' girl. I is a good man, who loves his children—all God's children. If I don't do as the boss asks, not only will I get a whippin' m'self, but you'll be getting' worse. My wife here is gonna pad you out good, ya hear?"

I nodded solemnly.

"It's okay, John. I can take it. Don't you worry about me."

John smiled.

"You's a good, brave girl. I'll try not to hurt ya too bad. If I do, I'm sorry. Ya understand?"

I nodded again, as he held my hand.

Mary bound my injured ankle as best as she could and concealed the bandaging under my stockings. She took off my shirt and placed three layers of material across my back to help protect my delicate flesh from the leather whip. I was led out into the yard, where a thick tree stump grew from the ground. On the other side of it, a rope had been nailed into the wood. John leant me over the stump and brought my hands forward to tie them down. As he loosened the rope, a loud voice hollered from the house. Standing at the window that overlooked the yard were Mr and Mrs Harvey and, of course, my tormentor, Florence. They wanted front row seats to my beating.

"We wanna see bare back, John: strip her down."

John said nothing, but the look on his face spoke a thousand words. He pulled me up from the log and turned me around. He gently unbuttoned the back of my dress and slid the sleeves over my shoulders, being sure to cleverly conceal the extra padding by pushing it all around to my front. He did all this, gently whispering how sorry he was, while tears trailed down his cheeks. I remember thinking how cruel they were being to such a gentle giant. It was clear to us all that John hated every second that he held that leather handle.

He leant me back over the stump and tied my hands securely. A moment later I heard the whip rise, displacing the air around it and, as it fell, I heard a loud snap. At first I felt nothing at all, and assumed his whip didn't even touch me. Then, out of nowhere, came a sudden rush of pain like I had just been trapped in the jaws of a crocodile. The burning raced down my legs and turned them to jelly, and up my spine, and made my eyes bulge. Before the pain dispersed, the whip came down again. I couldn't help but scream out and pull on the rope that bound my hands. Again, it thrashed my back; it felt like my spine was in flames and melting through my skin. Again and again, the whip struck me. After a while, my body became numb as the nerves were destroyed. I felt blood dripping down my sides, over my shoulders, and onto the sandy yard. The sand clumped around the blood, forming small red craters in the dirt. He kept lashing my back, opening up my flesh, until I couldn't even hear my own screams. I didn't hear the orders from Mr Harvey, when he called out for more lashes. I was supposed to receive fifteen lashes that day but, in the end, Mr Harvey's blood lust was finally satisfied at twenty-seven. John wiped the sweat from his face, and the tears from his eyes. He threw the bloodied whip to the ground and walked to the shaded doorway, to his wife. The Harveys could not see his anguish as he threw himself in Mary's arms, the pain of his guilt greatly outweighing my own pain, as he wept on her shoulder. My wounds would heal, but his guilt never did.

The instant the Harveys stepped away from the window, many slaves rushed to my aid. I was carried through the kitchen and into the back room, where bandages and Agnes' own healing ointment were waiting to treat my wounds. Even after all of the trauma I have suffered over the years, nothing felt quite like the intense pain of that whip. I expect it was because my skin was still young, and my flesh was tender. John did his best not to break the skin, but I heard him say that the leather went through my skin like a hot knife through butter. It was three days before John could bring himself to face me. I was still sore, but I was glad to receive a great big bear hug from John.

I decided that I had to be clever with Florence. She clearly had a vicious nature, just like her father, and befriending her was not working as successfully as I had hoped. When we were alone, she played nicely, but grew bored easily. For her, me being punished was a form of entertainment, but it also meant two or three days of her having to play alone whilst my wounds scabbed over.

A few weeks later, her wicked side appeared again. Like before, she remained in bed, awake, refusing to acknowledge me. I lost my temper with her, and dragged her out of bed by her ankle, and spoke to her unkindly. I threatened her with African magic and curses if she did not do what she was told. Florence had an active imagination, and I was thankful that there were no witnesses. It worked a treat—she never ignored me again, for fear that I might curse her or her family.

The nanny explained to me that I was the one who had to teach her respect, not her parents. My punishments were not given because *I* had been bad, but because I had not stopped *her* from misbehaving. A strange concept, but it came with a small amount of power and that opened up a doorway for me. Raising children was what I had done countless times, so I set to work and raised her like she was my own child. I took her into the yard and, using insects, taught her how to care for creatures, no matter how tiny they were. I taught her kindness for all things and encouraged her own achievements. She was an extraordinary artist, so I encouraged her abilities, which also made her parents happy. It was a fitting hobby for a young girl of that era.

In the end, I and Florence had a mutual respect for one another. I think she actually came to see me as a friend. She did, however, like to remind me from time to time that she had paler skin and hair that was long and silky, unlike my thick, wiry African hair. She liked to remind me who held the authority, and that I was still just her living black doll. In truth, I think she'd been taught those words by her parents, and by the way things were in that place and time.

Florence and I grew to be young women, receiving our first menstruation only a few months apart. Florence was sent to a school for young ladies, while I remained in the home, without a job or a purpose. I was worried that I might be sold on, taking me away from my new-found friends. I knew that life was about to change dramatically, and I dreaded to think what my life would hold next. However, Mr and Mrs Harvey had plans for me: plans that would secure my place in their property for a very long time.

I was fifteen years of age, without the security of an assigned job in the household. I tried to busy myself the best way I could, if only to appear useful. I helped Mary and Agnes in the kitchens, mucked out the stables, even flitted around the home with the maids. Despite all my efforts, Mr Harvey carried out the preparations for the next part of my slavery journey.

It was late in August when he summoned me to his office. I was outside, assisting one of the groundskeepers to put away his tools. He was an elderly man, with crippled hands, so he appreciated the help. I saw Mr Harvey in the window, with his usual king-like stance. Our eyes met, and he hooked two fingers towards himself: a familiar signal that he required my company. For a split second, I felt as though my stomach dropped a few inches. It had been a while since my last beating, and my wounds were healed nicely. I searched my thoughts as to what I might have done. I was afraid another beating was in order, if only to satisfy his malevolent nature. It was a pain that I never grew accustomed to, but I still had to endure it more than most in that household.

I ran upstairs and stood by the double oak doors with the bronze handles. I took a deep breath and brushed the dirt from my dress in an attempt to look presentable. As I raised my fist to knock on the doors, they swung open before my knuckles made contact.

"Ah, Mini. Come with me."

He marched across the hall and down the stairs, and I followed closely behind. I was nearly as tall as him by now, but I still felt so small in his presence. The front door of the house was opened wide, and outside was a horse and cart. The cart was not the one used by the family, but the one used to transport the tobacco from the fields to the market. In all the time I had spent in that home, not once had I ever had the privilege of using the front entrance. I wasn't sure whether to be happy about it or worried.

"Get in the cart. Do as you are told and, if all goes well, you will be back here by sunset."

Mr Harvey didn't look at me, or even attempt to explain where I was going. As always, I could do nothing more than what I was told. As soon as I jumped onto the back of the splintered cart the wheels began moving, knocking me off my feet. I only just avoided tumbling off the end and landing on Mr Harvey!

My driver was a skinny white man, who wore a dirty grey shirt and a peaked hat. He said nothing to me on the journey. I was merely a package that he was delivering for my owner. We travelled for at least an hour at a horse's walking pace, although it was slower than most, as the horse was one of our old mares. She had swollen knees and a greying mane, but a calm temperament. She plodded along at her own pace, while I took in my surroundings and used that time to sink into my imagination. I pretended for a short while that I was free. I sat upon the stool inside the cart and leant back, with my arms outstretched. I pointed my face towards the sun, and closed my eyes, while inhaling the fresh air. The sound of the horse's hooves hitting the dirt, and the rattle of the wooden wheels, were my music. The gentle wind blowing over my face was like the touch of a friend, telling me everything was going to be okay. I smelt the green grass, and the cotton fields, and the sweet scent of the meadow flowers. I imagined my home back in Africa, my mother and father sat beside each other outside our small home. I imagined my young brother, running around barefoot in the dirt, and my two older brothers, sharpening their weapons with stones and water. In my mind, I could hear the sound of the river as it gently flowed by our village, and the birds that nested in the trees.

"We're here. Wait in the cart to be called."

The cart halted, bringing an abrupt end to my daydream. The driver remained in his seat, whilst he tapped and scraped out the contents of a clay smoking pipe. In front of us was a house that looked a little rundown. Its painted walls had been stripped by the weather, and the bottom step of the porch was missing and replaced by flat stones, and some windows were broken and covered from the inside by odd pieces of wood. A muscular black man stood in the doorway, with his bulging arms folded sternly. He turned his head into the house and, with a voice as deep as the ocean itself, summoned someone from within:

"Nan. It's the girl from the Harveys."

There was a brief pause, and a deathly silence, which made me nervous. The man fixed his gaze upon me, and I couldn't help but stare back at him. A woman appeared in the doorway, and the big man stepped aside for her, like she was royalty. She looked around forty years old, but she was glamorous in her fine, black silk dress, with sparkling jewellery adorning her neck and ears. Her skin was lighter than mine, and she was undeniably beautiful. She smiled at me, and slowly sauntered over to my carriage, like she owned the grass, trees, and sky. To me, she looked like a movie star, with everything she had ever wanted—including her freedom. She stood before me like a goddess and offered me her hand as I stepped off the cart. I stood still, while she walked around me, inspecting my posture, and cupping my breasts and behind. When her face met mine, she addressed me:

"Why, hello chile I hear you is breedin' stock now. Don't you worry girl, I'll fix you up wid a good one. You is a pretty girl, with a good set o' titties and a fine ass; no man is gonna say no t' you."

My heart sank; now I knew the plan that my masters had in store for me. I was to put my body to good use and breed more slaves for him. More people to torture—my own children at that. But, on the other hand, if not this, what else would be done with me? No one likes a freeloading slave; they'd rather put me to death, than waste food rations on me. Despite my young age, in this life puberty had blessed me with a womanly figure. All I could do was what I was told—it was the only way to survive in those times.

"You are in luck, girly. My boys'll be back from the fields at any moment. They is guaranteed to be filled with top-quality baby gravy. How old are you?"

It had been nearly sixteen years since my birth, but this was a secret that I would take to my grave. As it turned out, it was a lie that again went in my favour.

"I'm fourteen, mam, soon to be fifteen" I answered, in a timid voice.

"And what shall I call you, pretty girl?" she asked, placing a reassuring arm around my shoulder.

"Skinny Mini, mam. Only, they just call me Mini."

The woman took my hand and walked me over to the crumbled-down house.

"You can call me Nan: short for Nancy. Have ya had the pleasure of a man's company yet, Mini?"

I shook my head.

"Oh, that's a good thing; my boys much prefer a clean girl. They is good at breaking ya in gently; if you know what I mean."

The large flat stone squelched in the mud when I stepped on it. I walked up the creaking steps, and through the front door. I passed by the big man, who looked at me with a menacing expression, his frightful stare burned into my soul like a thousand knives.

"Now, don't you worry about him. He's m' husband and, despite looking like a big ogre, he be a big old teddy bear. He's here to stop you gettin' hurt, as some men can be filled with anger when they get back from the fields. He will see it all goes well. My boys are his sons, so it shouldn't be something we need worry about."

I looked back at the man and gave him a friendly smile. In return, he gave me something that I still, to this day, find inconceivable. A stare that reached into my body with giant hands, captured the fear that I was trying to hide, and melted it away like a wax candle, to reveal a face that shone with kindness. It was a transformation that I didn't expect, and the shock of it made me question every judgmental glare I'd ever thrown at strangers. It was like an actual teddy bear stood before me, with friendly eyes and a sparkling white row of teeth. His cheeks jutted out of his face, and his nose flattened against his soft skin. His muscular physique was replaced by a rounded belly, and his arms fell to his sides as he showed me into his home. It wasn't a feeling of love that I felt for Nancy's husband, but a feeling that I was in safe hands. I instantly knew that whatever happened to me, he would be there to make sure that it was as pain-free and as non-traumatic as possible. Naturally, he was named 'Bear.'

Nancy and Bear's home was filled with beautiful things: solid wood furniture, and lamps that dripped with crystals, and a comfortable seating area, complete with a small table covered with a lace doily. Fresh lemonade and silver platters, filled with cakes and pastries, sat on the table, willing me to dig into the banquet. I didn't, of course, until Nancy gave me permission. I remained polite, sipping at the lemonade although, in truth, I wanted to swallow it down in one gulp and refill the glass.

"Eat up Mini. You need sustenance if you is gonna grow a baby in that belly."

Nan handed me a pastry that tasted so sweet it made my mouth fill with saliva. It was the best thing that I had eaten in that life. I tried not to think of what was to come: I simply enjoyed the moment and hoped that those men would never come back to the house—not until I had quenched my thirst and eaten my fill, anyway.

While waiting, Nancy spoke freely with me. She was a slave herself, brought from Africa in the belly of her mother. She died giving birth, and Nancy was nourished by a slave woman who had lost her own child. She raised her as her daughter, but always made sure that she knew where she came from. The man who became her husband arrived shortly after, and when Nancy came of age they were paired to produce more slaves for her owners, for free. Nancy had given eighteen healthy children, earning her freedom, and her husband had produced over one hundred children. His potency was renowned in the area but, at the age of forty-seven, his manhood began to fail him. His owner, the brother of Mr Harvey, had granted his freedom on the same day that Nancy was freed.

The house we were stood in was only where they made money; the home they owned and lived in was through the wooden gates on the other side of the road. The couple still had five of their own boys living at home; although they were not free men, they were free to live with their parents until such time as they were paired off for breeding.

I learned quickly that it was Nancy and her husband's intention to add me to their family as a daughter-in-law: a prospect that I felt could be an awful lot worse. So many slave women were impregnated once a year, by a man they did not know—raped time and time again, only to be left alone to raise the child owned by their masters. If I was to spend a life with a husband, then at least life would not be so lonely. If he treated me as well as the teddy bear treated his Nancy, then I was not in a position to complain. It also meant that we'd eventually get to have our own family home at the end of my owners' field, away from the tiny attic room and the main house. It was a basic life, but at least we could be free behind our own front door. It was the best option that I could hope for in that life, and I couldn't help but feel fortunate.

All thirteen of Nancy and her husband's sons were owned by the Harvey family; their five daughters were already married and shipped off to other plantations. Their sons tended to the tobacco fields, along with many other slave men. The field workers were always built like they had lived a hard life, with muscular torsos and wide shoulders. This also made the punches hurt more, if I were unlucky enough to get a bad pairing. On the other hand, I put my trust in Nancy and her husband because they gave me no reason not to.

Half an hour passed by within a blink of an eye. I had drunk my way through five glasses of lemonade and eaten a few fancy sweet pastries. I was feeling ready to face a new chapter in my slave journey.

"Here dey come. Nan, did ya tell 'em we had company? They look a damn mess, if ya ask me." Bear exclaimed.

"Well, what do ya expect? They be workin' hard in this heat. Besides, our boys are still just as handsome, if they been rollin' around in pig shit all day. Jus' like their daddy."

Nancy smiled at her husband, who tried to remain emotionless, but a small smile appeared at the corners of his mouth.

Nancy fetched some cool water and glasses for her sons, while I sat nervously on the chair, my belly bulging from all the drink. I hurriedly brushed any crumbs off my skirt and sat with my back straight and my knees together. One by one, the sons greeted their father and entered the home, and straight away spotted me. I remained seated and smiled at every one of them. All five men were alike: big, muscular, and eager to introduce themselves. Nancy appeared from the other room.

"Now, boys. May I introduce you to our new girl, Mini Harvey."

I stood to greet them but felt awkward, looked upon by five grown men, like I was a prized cow at an auction.

"She a little on the skinny side, momma," said one of the older sons.

"Why, she's still young; she's still growin' into her womanly body. Give her time. I can see the makings of some fine chile-bearing hips under that dress. And just look at those titties. They ain't goin' south any time soon; I tell ya that now."

All of them surrounded me, while Nancy stood me up and spun me on the spot. She knew her boys well, and those disapproving glances softened to those of lust. One man approached me and grabbed hold of my hips. He curled his oversized hands onto my buttocks and pulled me close to his groin.

"I think I love her already. Can I have her, momma? You did say I was ready to take a wife."

Nancy shook her head.

"Now, you know how these things work, son. We have to get you ta put a baby in her before we can even think about getting' ya hitched."

The man grabbed hold of my wrist and pulled me along behind him.

"Jus gimme ten minutes. I got balls fit to burst."

I won't lie to you now; I *did* find the man attractive. He was literally a younger version of his father, mixed with the confidence of his mother. He was medium build, with a smile for days. His eyes looked like they housed a kindness, rather than any ill intentions. Even though I had not been consulted, I was happy to go along with the arrangement. If anything, the feel of something stirring in his lower regions, and pressing against my belly, made me feel quite excited for our union.

He took me into a small room with white paint crumbling from the walls. It had a large bed, with floral covers tucked in tightly around the edges. A blanket had been folded to rest my head against the bare wall.

When the family was out of sight, the son kissed my lips and held me close to him once again. The stirring beast below was now growing and pushed the material of his trousers outwards. He unbuttoned my dress at the back and pulled it off of my shoulders, allowing it to drop to the floor. He kissed my neck, which felt so nice, while he pulled down my panties, leaving me naked in front of him.

He took a step back and looked at me in my flesh, which made me feel a little insecure at first, but his facial expression said that he liked what he saw.

He swiftly pulled his shirt over his head, and dropped his trousers, revealing his prize.

"You ready for what I'm bout ta give yah?" he said, grasping his erect penis.

I smiled and sat down on the bed.

"Ooh, you is ready for the stallion, ain't yah, skinny girl?"

He smiled as he approached, and joined his lips to mine as I slunk back onto the bed with him between my legs. He used his finger inside of me first, to ensure lubrication and gently slipped his penis inside. I thought it would hurt, but I only felt pleasure as he gyrated, pumping his penis up inside of me. It felt so good that, for a second, I forgot that I was a virgin in this life, and grasped hold of his pert buttocks, pulling him upward for a deeper penetration, gyrating my own hips to match his rhythm. He seemed to like what I did, as only moments later his penis exploded, filling me with his juices. I, too, felt the sudden rush of an orgasm, and the feeling of my cervix dipping into his sperm, as endorphins raced around my body. We both let out a series of loud grunts, before he collapsed on the bed beside me. He was sweating beads and gasping for air.

"Jeez, Mini Harvey. I'm gonna marry you. You can do that to me anytime. You a virgin? For shaw?"

I nodded my head, for it was technically true.

"Damn girl. You got some moves. You pleasure me like yous know whatcha doin'."

I was a bit worried for a moment that he might have thought I was lying, but nothing more was said, to my relief. The whole deed was over in a matter of a few short minutes. Back then, a quick mating was more efficient. There was never any heavy petting, foreplay, or love involved, unless a pairing had been established and agreed by both owners.

Shortly after, Nancy entered the room.

"You done already, Ben?"

"Yeah, I sure am. I gone and filled her, real good."

I tried to hide my naked body from Nancy with my hands, but she pulled them away from my vagina and looked up inside of me.

"Hmm. You lay on your back for a good twenny minutes, young Mini. Gotta give 'em a chance to get on up inside ya. You can come back here in a few days, when our Ben here has restocked the merchandise."

Although I secretly enjoyed my meeting with Ben, I felt like the last piece of me had been taken away. My life was sold to the highest bidder, and now my body was being used to increase my value.

At this point, I did not think of what a cruel life I would be bringing a child into. My thoughts were only to survive and learn all that I could from this life. I was to be a breeder, and hopefully a wife, giving birth to as many child slaves as my body could produce. Boys were preferred, as they could work the fields, but at the time I had no idea what would become of any girls that might grow inside of me.

Ben was a nice man who, despite working the field all day, smelled of cut grass and cherries. He was kind and caring, but knew that being the son of a bear, he had the job of impregnating as many slave girls as possible. He would never be exclusively mine, not until the day came that his goods didn't work as they should. I stayed on that bed, with my buttocks elevated by the folded blanket, staring at the cracked paint and old spider webs that hung from the ceiling. I held my legs closed and my hands over my breasts, as all of the other brothers passed by the room. They all glanced in at the freshly mated girl on the bed. I was a woman at only fifteen. A girl who was lucky to have flowered early and grown breasts and body hair in places a woman should, who had only bled twice before, but now needed the bleeding to stop for nine long months.

Nancy walked me down to the cart that had delivered me. The driver was away from his seat, pissing up the trunk of a nearby tree.

"Hey ... Hey you!" Nancy yelled over to the driver, angrily.

"What in God's earth gave you the right to piss up my daddy's tree?"

The driver turned his head to see the feisty woman stomping towards him. He hastily turned to face her, with both hands in the air. His penis was still dangling out of his trousers, leaking urine down his leg and onto the dirt road.

Nancy stopped walking and placed both hands on her hips menacingly.

"Did you just reveal yow tiny pink maggot to me, fella? M'I gonna have to get the bear to come chop that thing off and insert it up yow butt?"

Nancy spun around and walked back towards the house in a threatening manner.

"Bear. This driver is waving his tiny little piss pickle at me."

The driver hurried back to the cart, tucking his penis into his wet clothing. He leaped up onto his seat and threw his whip down on the horse's back. The cart sped off down the road, with me trying desperately to hold on. Nancy waved at me as we left, with Bear by her side. Further up the road, we passed three of Nancy's sons: one being Ben. I looked over to him, and his face ignited with a smile. His brothers began to heckle him.

"Awe, Benny boy is in love."

Ben held a hand in the air to me.

"See ya soon, Miss Mini. I be waitin'."

Ben made me smile; it was the first time since I was torn from my homeland that I had felt wanted. I knew that our pairing would depend on my fertility, so I selfishly hoped that I would fall pregnant because I wanted to be with Ben.

A few days later, the cart appeared again, this time with a different driver. He was old, with a creased face, and dirt covering his clothing. He looked as though he had been digging graves all day, and a pungent smell of smoke permeated the air around him. He wore a broken straw hat, and braces that held up his oversized trousers. I climbed into the back and sat down.

"Get under that there blanket, nigger."

I looked at him, questioning why he wanted me to do such a thing.

"Just get under the goddamn blanket, nigger. Don't want the good folk round here thinking I cart around your kind. Look at ya. Goddamn niggers invading my country."

Everyone in the yard turned to look at me, afraid to say anything.

"Look at this place—looks like a goddamn nigger zoo."

Mr Harvey appeared in the doorway and walked over to the cart. With one swift action, he yanked the old man off the cart and held him up against the side, right where I sat.

"Now listen here, Jacob. This farm produces enough tobacco to fill the lungs of ten thousand folk like you. Every plant is grown, trimmed, cared for, and harvested by these people, and I'm guessing that you, yourself, indulge in our fine tobacco."

The driver nodded.

"Yessir, Mr Harvey."

"Firstly, I have the power to have you hung for addressing my slaves in that manner. Secondly, this land is not yours, because your own parents were of Irish descent, were they not?"

The driver bumbled his words and tried to offer an apology but was spoken over.

"So, before you go bleating like a lamb that you have more rights to this country than any of my coloured slaves, go find a native of America and ask him who this land belongs to.

Now get off my property this instant, you foul-mouthed piece of shit."

Mr Harvey threw the driver through the open gate and stood watching, hands on hips, as he swooped his hat from the floor and ran away. It was the first time we had ever seen Mr Harvey act in such a way to a white man. It shocked everyone in the yard that day, and was spoken about for weeks, if not years.

Mr Harvey addressed the cook.

"Mary, see that John delivers this girl to the Porter's residence; Nancy and Bear are waiting for her. Have him wait for her and return after she has finished."

"Yessir. I'll fetch him now."

Mary went inside the house and returned shortly after with John. Satisfied that the situation had been resolved, Mr Harvey went back into the big house.

The journey was a pleasant ride with my friend John. I sat up front with him, and we sang songs and giggled over times gone by. We had grown close since I arrived, despite the beatings he had to give. I knew he had no choice. We were like family, and for that short journey, we both decided that we were free. Only for a short while, but we felt the freedom denied to us for such a long time. He did ask about how my meeting with my mating partner was going, and he guessed by my smile that I was pleased with the choice. It turned out that

Ben was his nephew—John was Bear's older brother.

"If all goes well, then you truly will be family by blood, young Mini."

When we arrived, Bear and John greeted each other warmly. They took the time to laugh, drink lemonade, and sing old songs. Ben was waiting for me in the other room; I had been longing to see him, and he greeted me with eagerness.

## BLOOD OF THE INNOCENT

For once, things went my way and, although I felt the pain of guilt for bringing a child into this environment, it was a way that I could continue in this family. In only a few months my belly began to swell, and new life inside me was big enough to make itself known. My bleeding stopped, my breasts ached, and for weeks my stomach threw back anything it didn't agree with.

Mrs Harvey was the first to find out, because she saw me knelt down over a bedpan evacuating my breakfast.

She had taken a dislike to me since her daughter had left and made no secret that she wanted me out of the house. This was the perfect opportunity to do just that.

The next day I was called down to the drawing room, where I was met by Mr and Mrs Harvey, and John. John was smiling like a Cheshire cat: his chest puffed out like he was the king of the house.

"Mini, when did you last bleed?" asked Mrs Harvey.

"Last June, mam."

Mr and Mrs Harvey whispered amongst themselves for a moment.

"A residence has become available in the lower field. You will pack up your things and move this afternoon; John will lend a hand. We have decided that young Ben will be partnered with you. My brother is his owner and has allowed him to reside with you on the condition that he will remain his property. Your children will be shared between us, the first birthing being my own. The children will remain under your care until they come of age. Is this clear?"

"Yes sir, Mr Harvey, sir." I said, trying to hold in my smile.

"If you provide twelve children, alive and healthy, you will have earned your freedom. You'll be allowed to either work for us for a small wage or leave this place at your own will. You will still be put to work until your sixth month. That is all. You can gather your things and spend this afternoon settling in. Ben will join you one week from today, as requested by his mother."

As I walked from the room, accompanied by John, I felt overwhelmed with happiness. I was not a free woman, and my children would be born into servitude, but I now had a goal: twelve healthy children. I knew that Ben would have to impregnate many more women: the legacy of the virility of his family tree made his offspring valuable.

Bear and his brother John had all but used up their supplies, but Ben was still young and had a lot to give. I knew that I had to close my jealousy off. John explained to me clearly that there was a difference between sex and love. I had the love—a gift not often given to a slave. I must have done something to impress the Harveys, although I couldn't think what that could have been. My only achievement to that day, was that Florence had grown to be a half-decent human being: a far cry from the heinous child I had first met.

My bag was packed in record time as I owned very little, and John helped me down the stairs and onto the waiting waggon. The home was nearly three miles down the road, nestled against a line of trees. Only those who were trusted not to run from their owners earned the right to live in such a place. As soon as we arrived at our line of small wooden dwellings, I very quickly learned the one and only outcome for an escapee.

Amongst the wooded area was a big sycamore tree. Its trunk was so wide that three people holding hands could only just reach around it. The branches grew thick and strong, adorned with leaves that shone different shades of green in the sunlight. They reached up so high that I had trouble seeing the top through the leaf cover. This tree also had something more sinister hanging from its branches—something that I did not expect. Six corpses, with brown skin, swung from its lower limbs, suspended by hemp rope tied around their necks. Their eyes had been eaten by birds, and the flesh from their cheeks had rotted away, revealing their white skulls beneath. Their feet were cut, despite the thick skin, their shoulders were slumped, and their hands were tied behind them. As John turned the cart around the corner, a breeze blew, causing the bodies to swing gently two and fro.

"They is slaves who fancied freedom, Miss Mini. Poor bastards didn't get further than the river. They set em there as a reminder that we ain't free till they says we free. I would urge you not to look at dem, but if you decide to then it's a sight you'll get used to. When the heads come off, 'n' they fall to the ground, we bury them in the woods. We give 'em a proper, free man's burial. The big man don't know bout that, so keep it to yourself."

The homes were close to one another, and my house was at the far end, the furthest away from 'the swinging tree,' as they called it. I was thankful for that, at least. As I approached the front door, I asked John a question that I quickly wished I had never asked.

"Who lived here before me?"

John placed a hand on my shoulder and sighed.

"The second man on that tree, missy. He tried to escape with his wife and two younglings. They shot the wife in front of him. She took her milk with her so, without means to feed them, they tossed her three-month-old twin baby girls into the river. The boss blamed us for not having a nursing mother to take 'em on. They were the first to be born in a while. That is, until you ... Well, I live right next door; just give me a knock if you need assistance."

John looked as though he was close to tears, so I left him alone with his thoughts and didn't ask any more questions.

The house had two rooms: a living/cooking room, which had bunks for children at the far end, and a back bedroom with a double bed, two cots, and some furniture. The living area had a table and four wooden chairs, a comfortable nursing chair, and a stone fireplace. Outside was a big stone, used for chopping wood, and an axe leant up against the small porch. To the side was a small area where vegetables for my use grew, and an outside shelter to house the chopped wood. The whole structure was built from old timbers. The windows had no glass, but they did have shutters that closed tightly, which helped to keep the heat from the fire inside. On the hearth hung a big iron pot, and the fire was made up ready to burn. Two sets of baby clothing were folded neatly in the chest, along with bedding and a few other provisions.

A small amount of food sat on the worktop, including a pot of rabbit meat covered in a hessian cloth. Jars containing flour, grains, and pulses lined the shelves. The cups and plates meant I had all that was needed to sustain basic living. It was dark and a little dusty, but it was a space that was all mine until Ben arrived. I sat upon the chair where the mother would have nursed her babies and was instantly immersed in the smell of stale mother's milk. I looked at the wide arms, which still had the small indents from where she would have rested her elbows. In my mind I could hear her singing, and the gentle babbles of her twin babies as she sang them to sleep. All she wanted was for her children to be free.

    I sat back in that chair and cried. I cried for hours, rocking back and forth. I cried for those babies, cried for their mother and father. I cried for all of the slaves around the world, who had been snatched from their families and brought to this hell. I cried for my mama and pa, and my brothers who I'd never see again. I cried for that poor little girl at the auction, brutally raped by her captors, who most probably ended her days tossed into the sea while still alive. I cried for my own child who grew inside of me, not knowing that the world outside would be a world of suffering, pain, and hardship. Eventually, I fell asleep in that chair out of exhaustion. After so many years of concealing my emotions, and pretending to be strong, it was a release I so desperately needed.

The next day I had my orders sent down to me: I was to start the day at six each morning, as Mary's new assistant in the kitchens. Agnes had moved to another farm, leaving an opening to work alongside Mary, my adopted mother. She was always kind to me, and taught me many cooking skills, some of which were new to me, despite my memories. Soul food was her speciality, and she claimed that some of the recipes resulted from experiments with the master's left-over foods. They were basic on their own, but when Mary added her touch to them, what she called her 'juju,' the dishes came to life. Her cornbread was my craving throughout my first pregnancy, and she made sure to provide me with enough to sustain both myself and my unborn.

True to his word, a week later I returned to my home to be greeted by Ben. He was waiting for me, completely naked on our bed, a big, satisfied smile etched on his face.

"Didn' I tell you I was gonna marry you? Come over here and do that thing ya did ta me."

Of course, I did 'that thing' to him, and soon treated him to many other 'things'. I'm the first to admit that in this life, I was pretty amorous. Sex was the only pleasure there was, and I was happy to get it whenever Ben hinted—or even when he didn't—because pregnancy had given me an insatiable sex drive.

Ben and I were like two halves of the same person: we enjoyed each other's company and got along tremendously well. We did argue, but always made up with a night of passion. My belly grew, and Ben was sometimes called away to help another slave become pregnant. I knew that he was worried about my feelings, but I reassured him that it was just a job in my eyes and, as long as he also saw it that way, I was fine. Of course, I hated it—even the thought of Ben dipping his penis into someone else hurt like hell at first, but that was the life we were dealt. I felt sorrier for the poor woman who had to be impregnated, by a stranger, against her will. I knew that Ben would be gentle, though; he didn't know how to be any other way.

The pregnancy went as smoothly as it could, with no major complications. My breasts grew to twice their size, which caused Ben's eyes to pop from their sockets. In my sixth month, I was excused from my duties and sent home to rest until the baby arrived. My belly was huge; everyone expected a twin pregnancy, but I wasn't so sure. I guessed that it was only one, but a big one. At the end of the third trimester, I grew so big that just moving around in my bed caused me to cry out, as the pressure on my hips took its toll. Mary was a frequent visitor, as she lived only next door and had delivered babies in the past.

She was the midwife amongst the slaves, and a well-respected member of our community. In my last few weeks, I could hardly move, and my appetite grew wild. Mary tended to my every need: cooking several small meals a day, cleaning the home, and looking after Ben when he returned from the fields. When I thought my belly would split right down the middle, my waters finally burst, filling the bed pan several times. I was blessed with a quick birth, albeit with my ankles up by my ears to help him past my pelvis. Our baby was born only thirty-eight minutes after the first contraction and, sure enough, as predicted, the second made his way out soon after. When the news spread, everyone gathered outside my hut, while my two baby boys screamed with healthy lungs. The pain did not stop for me, though, and thirty minutes later the third baby fell out of me, which shocked everyone. I had been positive that I was carrying just one.

They were big babies, considering they had had to share such a small space, and all very healthy. Ben, who had a very smug grin, was outside with John. A twin pregnancy rarely occurred, and a triplet pregnancy that produced all healthy babies was unheard of. He was literally cock of the walk.

When the news reached Mr and Mrs Harvey, they took a carriage to view the spectacle for themselves. Three healthy baby boys: all with ten fingers, ten toes, and heads full of hair. They all looked like their dad: handsome and butch. I was blessed again that my milk flowed well, and I managed to provide for all three of the babies without too many issues. In return, they gave me plenty of rest and were well-behaved. I loved them all dearly, but always kept it in mind that, despite me birthing them and Ben being the father, they belonged to someone else. It was a thought that broke my heart, but I was powerless to do anything to prevent it, and only prayed that times would change before they came of age.

Life settled down when the triplets turned two and started coming to work with me, playing in the yard outside while I carried out my chores. They were surrounded by our slave family, so there was always someone willing to entertain them. Those boys were loved by us all and had the best childhood we could possibly give them, despite our circumstances.

One afternoon I was called upstairs to repair Mr Harvey's shirt. The children were playing happily outside with the groundkeeper's daughter, so I left them under Mary's supervision. As I opened the door, Mr Harvey was sitting on the edge of the bed, with a shirt on and a blanket over his lap. He looked saddened, as he drew on a cigarette.

"What can I help you with, Mr Harvey?"

He looked up at me.

"Close the door."

I had never been alone with him before. I felt uneasy with the situation, but I did as he asked.

"I have a problem with my penis that I'd like you to look at."

This request was very unusual. I was not a medic nor a nurse—why was he asking me? He looked as though he was worried, so I approached him. He pulled away the blanket, revealing a semi-hard penis. I waited for him to show me what the issue was: I could see nothing unusual.

"What's the problem, Mr Harvey?"

He looked at me, and smirked.

"It wants you to suck it, Mini. It wants you to suck it good and hard."

I'd had a feeling that something like this was about to happen: Mr Harvey had been singing my praises for a while. I was his prized cow: birthing three baby boys in one day had got me a lot of unwanted attention. He was always at that window, watching when I was out in the yard and, despite Mrs Harvey's dislike of me, he refused to find me work away from the house.

"Woman! I said, get on your nigger knees and suck it. Now!"

I knelt down between his legs and put his now-hardened penis in my mouth and sucked on it as hard as I could. The temptation to bite down hard on it, rip it away from his body, and spit it into the corner crossed my mind, but my babies needed a home. The last thing I wanted was for them to see their own mother swinging from that sycamore tree, with her eyes pecked out by crows.

"I feel it's time that you give me what you give your husband. You give me three babies, you hear? Give me three babies, like you gave your husband. I am your master, and you will do as I tell you."

He grabbed hold of my braid and yanked me away from his penis, stood up and threw me down on the bed. He lifted my skirt and pulled down my underwear. I could do nothing to stop him. Without saying another word, he climbed on top and rammed his penis inside me. As he moved on, and in, my body, I closed my eyes and took my mind far away. I went back to my world of freedom in Africa: the smell of the earth and the freshness of the air, and the sound of my family singing together. I imagined my Ben and the boys joining us. As he filled me with his seed, I came back to reality with him groaning like a dying pig in my ear. He collapsed with his head over my shoulder, breathing heavily. I lay still, waiting for him to roll off, but he stayed where he was, his penis still inside me.

His weight became heavy on my chest. He had fallen asleep, and I was pinned underneath him. Mr Harvey was a broad man, and I was not the strongest. I tried to slither out from under him, but he was too heavy. I tried to wake him, but his snores grew only louder. I couldn't move.

For half an hour I was pinned down, with Mr Harvey's now-flaccid penis still loosely inside of my vagina. I managed to manoeuvre myself until it fell out of me. I heard footsteps drawing closer, and the door creaked open. I was hoping that it might be one of the housekeepers, who could help me escape from under him, but it was not to be.

"What in God's name is going on here? Why, may I ask, are you on top of Mini? Are you fucking the goddamn slaves now, Fred?"

Mrs Harvey was standing in the doorway, with her hands on her hips, looking understandably upset. Mr Harvey woke instantly to her voice, and rolled off of me, leaving a puddle of spit on my shoulder and my woman parts exposed. I sat up and pulled my underwear up and my dress down.

"You. Get the fuck out of here. I'll deal with you later."

Mrs Harvey scowled at me, as I hurried past her. I ran down the hallway in tears. The door slammed shut, and I heard the two arguing fiercely.

I headed straight to the kitchen, where Mary was busy preparing lunch.

"Mini girl, where y' been all this time?"

As she looked at me, her expression instantly changed.

"What in jesus' name has he done ta ya this time?"

"I need to wash, Mary. I need to wash him out of me," I cried.

Mary sighed deeply and embraced me while I sobbed.

"These fucking white men are goddamn animals. All of them—I tell ya! Mark my words, the good lord will make 'em pay. Mark my words to be true, young Mini."

She led me out to the washroom, where she had just prepared a large tub of hot water for washing clothes. I stripped down as fast as I could and threw myself in. Mary helped me wash my body. His smell still reeked all over me: his sweat had soaked into my chest and his armpit stench was in my hair. I scrubbed my skin so hard I thought it would leave me with more scars than I already had.

"You must go on living, Mini. For ya babies, if nothing else. Ben will understand. What that monster did to you, it ain't yo fault—don't ever blame yaself, ya hear?"

When I felt clean, Mary helped me to dry and dress in fresh clothing. She grabbed armfuls of the master's clothes and sunk them into my bath water.

"What they don't know won't hurt them. Only we will know that the Missus is wearing rape-water clothing."

Mary gave the tub a mix, and then left all the clothes to soak in my bath scum.

I prayed that, given his wife's reaction, it would never happen again, and for a time it didn't. Mary thought it best that I tell Ben what had occurred, as he would have found out anyway. As expected, he was angry, but not at me. He held me close, as I cried in his arms. He loved me and the boys more than anything.

"What if he made me pregnant, Ben?" I asked.

Ben sighed.

"Then we will deal with it, Mini. Chances are, I already beat him to it."

As fate would have it, my period stopped, and I felt my abdomen begin to swell. I prayed that the baby inside me was Ben's, but I couldn't be sure. I didn't tell Mr Harvey until he called me up to his room again. When I arrived, he was sitting on the bed as before.

"It's fine, Mr Harvey. You already got me pregnant. See."

I stood sideways to show him the small swelling on my belly. He raped me again anyway—he claimed that it was simply for the pleasure of doing so.

This became my life for the next few months: an endless cycle of being a mother and caring for my children, and being raped once, sometimes twice, a week. It always happened while Mrs Harvey was away in town or at a friend's home. As my bump grew bigger, I became less desirable, so the rapes became fewer. I was not granted leave at six months: Mrs Harvey claimed that it was a punishment for seducing her husband. At the end of my ninth month, my waters broke. I was inside the big house and collapsed on the kitchen floor. As I pushed, Mrs Harvey appeared and watched over me from the kitchen table. I was afraid that if the child was born with lighter skin, she would take it away and raise it as her own—a prospect that terrified me. I loved all of my children and even though the conception was horrific, it didn't change the fact that it was my child. Ben was ready to raise it as his own, along with our triplets, regardless of the shade of its skin.

"Push Mini girl. You can do it. Push."

Mary and a few other women were helping me. This time the birth wasn't so easy, as the baby was breech. The feet came out first, and with one last squeeze the baby was born—a daughter, Mary grabbed her feet and held her upside-down, and gave her small pale body a shake. I was worried that she wouldn't make it, but after what seemed like forever, her little lungs opened, and she began to cry.

"Is she okay, Mary?"

Mary looked at me with joy.

"Oh, Mini. She is a beautiful little girl—just beautiful."

Mrs Harvey's voice shattered all of the joy in that room.

"Give her to me. I want to see her."

I pleaded with her to let me hold her first, but she refused. Mary held her up for me to see her sweet little face. She was indeed beautiful. A little miracle. Her face was darker than the rest of her, due to being stuck the wrong way up, but she was okay.

"*Now*, Mary, or I'll have you beaten."

"Just gotta cut the cord, Mrs Harvey."

Mary wrapped the baby in a cloth and took her to the table, placing her in Mrs Harvey's arms. I waited for her to smile at the sight of my new, sweet daughter, but a smile never appeared. She lay my baby on the hard table and undid her covers, exposing her precious new body to the chill of the evening.

"This baby is mixed with a white man."

The room fell silent. Mary looked at me with sorrow. She knew what was about to happen. I didn't have a clue.

"Look away, Mini. You need to look away."

I didn't want to look away. What was she going to do with my child? She wouldn't hurt her, surely? With one swift action, Mrs Harvey yanked open the drawer from under the table and pulled out a freshly sharpened cleaver. Without hesitation, she brought the blade down over my baby's neck, severing her head from her body.

Her tiny head rolled off the table, and fell onto the stone flooring, her eyes twitching behind her eyelids as life drained from her.

I screamed so hard that I felt like my brain would explode and pushed out the afterbirth onto the kitchen floor. If I could have got up, I would have taken that same cleaver and buried it in Mrs Harvey's skull without a second thought.

"That will teach you for sleeping with my husband. Don't let it happen again."

Mrs Harvey pushed her chair back before my baby's blood fell over the side of the table, to save her precious clothing from being stained. She didn't look at me, she didn't look at any of us. She callously exited the room, with her nose in the air, without saying a word.

My sweet girl had not even opened her eyes or taken a feed. She had never felt her mother's embrace, felt the touch of my kiss on her head, or heard me sing her to sleep. I had spent the last few months watching my belly move, as she wiggled around, and twitch as she hiccupped. I heard her cry only once and was denied the first hold. My only comfort was that she was a slave for just a moment, then she was free.

When Mr Harvey found out what she had done, he seemed only angry that I hadn't managed a multiple birth, like he wanted. On the outside he was remorseless, but I could tell by his eyes that he felt deep sorrow. Regardless, I had no pity for him. I hated every ounce of them both—a sort of hatred I had never thought could exist in me.

When Ben found out what had happened, he flew into a rage. His face screwed up in anger—something that I had never seen in him before. We all tried hard to stop him taking revenge, if only for the sake of our surviving children, but we couldn't reason with him. He hugged me and kissed my head.

"Take good care of our children, will ya?"

I pleaded with him, but he left our home and headed for the big house. Word had got to Nancy and Bear, and they arrived right at that moment. Bear grabbed hold of Ben and held him tightly, as he screamed and struggled to escape, but Bear was stronger and walked him back to our home. Nancy threw her arms around me and hugged me so hard that I cried. She didn't let go until my tears ran dry. Bear sat Ben down at the table and talked with him. I couldn't hear what was being said but, whatever it was, it helped to calm the fire inside him.

"Ben, I'm your mother," Said Nancy.

"Do you think I wanna see my son dangling from that tree? Do you want that for yo wife? Crows pecking at yo flesh? Do you want that for your babies? To see their daddy hanging from his neck? Just because you are the prized breeder don't make you immune. You is angry now, and you have every right to be, but you gotta see sense. There be no point punishin' yo wife and kids for what that cruel bitch did, now is there?"

Ben hid his head in his arms and cried inconsolably.

"She was mine, ma. I didn't even get ta look at her. She was my daughter."

"I know dat son. Mary told me that she looked like you in every way. That woman, the devil up there, will be punished, jus' you wait 'n' see. She won't live another year. But we can't jus' go up and murder her. You know what happens to a slave who kills his owner: they will hang yo babies before they hang you, jus' because they can. Now, quit cryin' and come see to yo wife. She needs you now."

Ben looked up at me. His anger had softened, transformed to a screwed-up tearful mess.

"I'm so sorry Mini. I'm so sorry."

I held out my arms to Ben, and we collapsed onto the floor in each other's arms.

Mrs Harvey instructed the slaves to hang my decapitated infant from the sycamore by her foot, as a warning to others, but thankfully Mr Harvey protested. Mixed race or not, he saw the baby as his and didn't want her on show. She was placed in a wooden box and handed to us the next day. We buried her in the woods, far away from the hanging tree. It was under another tree, with branches far too high for a hanging, just outside the borders of the estate. We named her Angela, and she rested in free land, in a grave marked only by that tree and a big white stone that somewhat resembled a heart.

Mr Harvey didn't touch me again; I'm not sure if it was through fear or regret. Fear that I might lose my mind and actually bite down on that dick of his, most probably.

Mrs Harvey died, like Nancy had predicted, eleven months later. A tumour had grown on her stomach, and, despite the efforts of many medics, her life could not be spared. The big house was in mourning, but only Mr Harvey was truly sad. Florence appeared from the city, with her young family and wealthy husband. She greeted me with kindness and introduced me to her two children. She seemed happy to see my triplets but refrained from mentioning what her mother had done. She knew all about it, as she made it obvious by avoiding the subject at all costs.

Mrs Harvey's funeral spared no expense, filling the whole home with the scent of fresh flowers and people that I had never met. Us slaves had to keep a low profile: if we weren't serving guests we had to keep away from the house, which suited us. That evening, in our slave family homes, we rejoiced and danced til the sun blessed us with its warm glow. Mrs Harvey was dead, and this pleased *me* more than anyone else in our small slice of land.

Both Ben and I learned to live with what had happened to our daughter because, no matter what we did, nothing could change it. We went on to raise eight more children, who were all fit and healthy and contributed to the running of the tobacco plantation when they came of age. Mr Harvey never remarried, but in secret he grew close to one of the other slave girls. They both seemed content with the way things were, so we learned to turn a blind eye.

My children played alongside the children with lighter skin than our own, and they became part of our community—the only free black children on the property. The woman in question never knew what had happened that fateful night, or even that I was raped by him. She was happy in his arms and he treated her well, which was fine by us.

After our twelfth baby was born, Mr Harvey was true to his word, and granted mine and Ben's freedom on the same day. I was forty-five and Ben forty-seven, so we still had a lot of life to live. Sadly, those times offered little to people like us. We decided to move into the home belonging to Ben's mother, Nancy, who had been widowed a few years before, and our remaining children were allowed to live with us. Mr Harvey's brother died childless, so he had to take on both plantations. There was plenty of work, and he paid us fairly for our services.

We spent many years in the same routine, but we also made time for ourselves, even if it was just sitting on the porch, watching the sun set. Nancy died peacefully in her sleep at the age of eighty-seven, a fair age for someone with her history. I will admit now that on the day I earned my freedom, I took a stroll up to the cemetery at night. I squeezed through a gap in the gate, and found Mrs Harvey's beautifully carved gravestone. I sat for a while and thought about what she did to my child and how, even though she died shortly after, I still felt that she went unpunished. As the full moon shone down on me, I dropped my underwear and left a big pile of crap right where her head would have been. I have never in my many lives felt so much hate towards one woman. Her behaviour was the one time that thoughts of murder raged through me. She was just lucky that I had been pinned down by my friends, and lucky that Ben was not allowed to confront her, because I'm pretty sure he would have torn the limbs from her body.

    Our lives were taken in the end, along with two of our younger sons. One night when we were in bed, we had a visit from a group of men on horseback. Ben woke up first, as he could smell smoke. He woke me, as well as our two sons. Our home was built of wood, so we needed to escape. When we ran outside, we saw two wooden crosses burning in our front yard and six men, all dressed in white, with strange hoods hiding their faces. Ben tried to protect us, but they shot him in the heart. The bullet passed through him and hit the side of my neck. I collapsed beside Ben and held him until he drew his last breath. I lived just long enough to see the men execute my two sons. They were on their knees, with their hands behind their heads. Their bare backs were ripped apart as the bullets passed through them. I died shortly after.

    I arrived in the darkness alone. I could only presume that my husband and sons had already passed through. Ben and I lived twelve years of freedom and, despite our duties and doing things we wished we hadn't, we loved each other til the day we died. For twelve years, he was all mine exclusively because, despite the past, he didn't stray once. I was a mother to twelve, and he was a father to over sixty infants, which included five sets of twins. Even now I miss his hugs, the way he would envelope me in his big, muscular arms. I felt like nothing could ever harm me—I felt safe and secure and owned by only him.

I revisited that place, in a life that followed on from that one in time, but several lifetimes later. The slaves had all been freed, but society still looked down upon the black community. Hundreds of years had passed, but I still saw men that resembled Ben: built like bears, with mean menacing looks, but smiles that melted hearts, wandering around those streets. I have no doubt that his genes still run strong in those parts and will do so for many years to come, if not forever.

The sycamore tree still stands, but there's no sign or dedication to remind folk of its past. It's just a tree among others, with no particular importance. If you look closely, indentations are evident in the lower branches, where ropes once held the weight of hung slaves who took a chance and ran for freedom. They wanted nothing more than to belong to a community, rather than be owned by a wealthy man. Mounds of earth still mark the graves of those fallen to the ground: hundreds of them throughout the woodland, where wildflowers mark their resting places.

I wandered up to the grave of my child and found that a river had changed its course and ran right through the spot where she lay. The tree had long fallen, leaving not even a trace behind. Along the riverbank was a bench, constructed from logs. I sat on it and contemplated my life as a slave: living with invisible shackles, owned by a pig who thought he also owned the rights to my body. The children we had raised, born into slavery for my own selfish desire for freedom.

I never found out what became of the surviving children. Our three daughters were taken from us when they became women and were only seen again from afar. Others were sold to places far away, and we could only hope that they were living well. No doubt our sons were used for their potency, as well as their working abilities, just like their father and grandfather. We had no say where our children went, and no records were kept. I only knew that they were out there somewhere, surviving like the rest of us.

We all had scars on our bodies that told stories, and we all had stories to tell that left scars far deeper than those on our skin. Some struggled to live lives far, far worse than my own; some took an easier road. All of us had a life which took away what we were all entitled to: our freedom.

Slavery still exists in these times, but we don't hear about it in the news or read about it in the papers. We're only told what the big masters in the grand houses, with all the money, want us to hear. That is the way it has been for hundreds of years, and that is the way it will remain for hundreds of years to come. Many hierarchies, even now, wallow in big mansions bought and paid for by slavery. Each wall was paid for by money earned by those considered undeserving of a wage, working for hours every day with the hot sun burning their backs, fed scraps from the master's table, and denied even the right to raise their children.

Society today closes its eyes to such atrocities because they do not affect them personally. Only when they, themselves, learn the real truth do they stand up. But one voice is silent: it needs a nation of screams to be heard and, even then, the rich masters have the power to shut them up and fight one another with the use of propaganda and lies.

We put our trust in those we see as higher entities but, in fact, they are just using us, controlling our thoughts, and pissing on our struggles. They point and snigger as we grapple to live on the scraps they leave behind. Most of us living now are still slaves, we just call it other names to make it seem less horrific. We must work so many hours, and hand over our entire wage packets to people who promise to make our lives better but give us only illusions in return. Freedom is only a privilege for those who make the rules and crack the whip, for those who hold the wealth and the power.

# SCARLET

This story is from a more recent life. I will tell you now, that although times were hard, it had a happy ending. I feel that this story will end this book. Maybe I will feel the need to write another, as this book contains only a tiny proportion of the stories I feel have to tell. Maybe I'll be content with just this one. I do know something; in this life, the one thing that brings me joy is exactly what I am doing now: writing, pouring my memories onto the pages of a book.

With each story I tell, I feel as though the ghosts of my past are being freed. They are shrinking smaller and fitting into the corners of my mind; they no longer scratch at the walls and demand attention but sit content in their assigned space. A great man told me once that knowledge should be shared, so I will do just that.

I was born into the world a boy, arriving prematurely by about six weeks. Nonetheless, I was strong and needed little help to thrive.

My mother was a God-fearing woman, controlled by her highly strung husband, who was truly set in his old-fashioned ways, and her religious parents. She found her God as a comfort, because her life with my father was turbulent, to say the least.

It was the 1940s and we lived in a picturesque town in New Zealand. Our town was mainly immigrants, and none of us ever mixed with the Māori people. If anything, my parents raised me to believe that they were a lesser race: degenerates, uneducated and Godless. Of course, I had a different view, but I had to fit into the lifestyle, until I reached an age where I could break free from their prehistoric beliefs. Their ideas were etched in stone, so trying to change their minds, and make them believe that the indigenous people were just as human as we were, would only cause ill feelings. Christians believed that they were the dominant species, and that any other religion was blasphemous, and the work of Satan himself. Personally, I found their views disturbing and, at times, ridiculous. They had long forgotten that the words in their bible were stories: lessons designed to teach the reader how to be a better person. The events in the bible didn't necessarily actually happen: most were written by someone with a good imagination. Some were stories, which had been remembered, but had changed over the years, adding a magical element intended to make them more appealing to children at bedtime.

My father was the church fundraiser. It was his job to pass the pot around after a service and to organise gatherings, with the intention of taking more money from the congregation. It was my job to wear a big, blue, oversized gown and sing as loud as I could. The songs always mentioned how good and great God was but, as a child, I couldn't help thinking, 'If God was so good, how come he took three husbands from poor old Mrs Benson? How come Mr and Mrs Smythe lost every child they conceived, when they clearly would be doting parents?' When I asked these questions, the answers were always scripted, 'It was the devil's work.' or 'god works in mysterious ways.' The songs we sang had words that explained that God was the greatest force on earth, so how come the devil defeated him all the time? God can't be that great! If God worked in mysterious ways, how come my father could get away with beating my mother whenever he'd had a few too many drinks? He's supposed to work for God.

Anyway, as far as religion was concerned, I was brought up with the idea that I was to live my life with the teachings of the 'good book' in mind. My brain had been conditioned into thinking that maybe, just maybe, my journey would come to an end if I lived by God's rules and embraced his love. My parents insisted, since I was old enough to speak, that the words spoken by preachers were true. There was one flaw to this plan, one that at a young age I didn't expect. As a young boy, girls were a different species altogether and I only liked *them* as friends. I had a close female friend and preferred the company of girls to boys; they seemed to communicate better. Boys ... well ... I found that they were more reserved, although they loved nothing better than a bit of rough and tumble.

That was not something I felt comfortable with; I'd rather help my girlfriends with their hair and makeup, than kick a ball around a dirty field. As I grew older, all the other boys were getting girlfriends, and talking about big boobs or pretty faces and stealing a kiss behind the gym.

I was looking over the chiselled features of a boy in my year called Charlie. He was an Adonis, with a heavy brow and a smile that melted my heart, even when it wasn't aimed in my direction. He was taller than me, with longer brown hair that parted on the left side and, at times, hid his right eye. He'd bring his muscular arm up and run his hand through his hair, revealing his blue eyes and squared chin. He was the epitome of a male and every one of my girlfriends became a quivering wreck whenever he was around, but none more than me.

Being a Christian, my job was not to stare lovingly at men, but to couple with a woman, get married and have a mountain of Christian babies, and worship God—no matter how miserable that made me feel. Being gay was not an option. If my parents had found out ... I could only imagine their reaction. My father ... well ... he'd probably slide his belt out from his trousers, and beat the gay out of me. My mother would get on her knees, and pray for the devil to leave my body. The bible was very specific:

*'If a man lies with a man as one lies with a woman, both of them have done what is detestable. They must be put to death; their blood will be on their own heads'*

I remember, once, someone made a suggestion that a member of our community had dealings with another man. The fellow in question was a husband, and father of six. They had the wife's brother to stay for a while, as he had fallen upon hard times. Fortunately, both brother and husband had a good relationship; being old school friends, they accompanied each other to town. While at work, the brother confided in the man about his recent trouble. To comfort him, the husband placed an arm on his shoulder. Another man, from across the street, saw the pair from an angle that looked as though they were sharing a kiss. This was absolutely not the case, as the husband's work colleagues clarified, but it was too late. News of the relationship spread around the village like fire spreads through a dry forest in a heatwave. The two were badly beaten on their walk home from work, by a group of young thugs. The children of the family were teased by other pupils at school, causing them great distress and anxiety. The family eventually had to pack up their belongings and move far away, after receiving an anonymous threat to set their home ablaze whilst they slept. This was the era I lived in—not just in New Zealand—but around the globe. Sadly, in some places, this attitude still exists.

So, at the age of 18 it became evident that I was gay, without even the slightest interest in the opposite sex. I thought to myself that it might have been a test, to see how far my loyalty to God could be stretched. Being gay was a sin, punishable by death, so I had to train my brain to like women in a sexual way; a task which nearly broke me. I aimed to enter into a relationship with a good friend of mine. We had been friends for years and I never saw her in a romantic way, but she was a safe bet; at least we got on well. I'd just have to get past the sex part—it's only sex, after all. She was delighted, as she'd had deep feelings for me for a long time.

I broke the news to my parents, who seemed relieved, but reminded me that we should not fornicate until such time as we were married. This condition suited me, but it wasn't what my girlfriend wanted. She claimed that she needed to have sex before we were married, in case either of us didn't like it. I remembered what the bible said and insisted that we held off. I was determined to see this through.

Months went by with little change. I had no problem kissing my girlfriend, as it was something that I didn't see as sexual, and an arm around her shoulder or holding her hand was something we had done many times previously. I occupied myself with work, which consisted of being surrounded on site by well-built men who thought nothing of unbuttoning their shirts when the sun was hot, exposing their muscular torsos and arms. I had become very good at disguising my attraction towards a few of them, but their physiques were very easy on the eye. I have always been keen on a good smile that lifts not only the mouth, but the eyes as well. One man, in particular, was keen to subtly flirt with me. He was a married man, with a baby on the way. His wife was a pretty, dark-haired woman, who doted on him, but he never seemed to appreciate her efforts and always spoke ill of her to the other workers, which I found strange.

After several flirtatious advances towards me, he introduced himself: William; or Billy, as he was better known. We became good friends very quickly, often confiding in one another about our partners. The lack of intimacy was one of Billy's biggest gripes. He and his wife, Rose, had not had sex since she found out she was pregnant. She'd spent all of his wages on what he called 'tatt' and left him with very little for himself.

She was the total opposite to him, offering only praise for her husband and loving him deeply. He was the provider and worked hard for a living. She was infatuated by her husband; so much so, he felt stifled. I felt that Billy never said anything kind about her. Personally, I thought she was a very nice lady. It was sad to see the pain in his wife's face, when he rejected her.

My girlfriend was named Emmeline and, as we had been friends for a number of years, we already felt comfortable in each other's company. As it happened, she and Rose were already well acquainted through their parents, which was perfect. Rose and Billy needed a larger place to live, so rented a property close to ours with the idea that Emmeline would be there for emotional support when the baby arrived. Emmeline loved children and was eager to help.

This particular day promised pleasant weather, so we decided to take a ride in Billy's car to the countryside. We armed ourselves with an ample picnic, a ball and a tennis set, and headed out to find a spot away from the world. We drove for around an hour and found a place by a small river. It was in a meadow that the farmer was resting, so we were there alone in the overgrown green grass. The sun was at its hottest, and the wind gently blew dandelion seeds through the air. Emmeline and Rose undressed and lay in the sunshine in only their underwear. Billy raised a bottle of ale,

"Don't worry, mate. I trust you."

He looked down at his wife, her swollen belly pointing skywards. He knew damn well I had no interest in her sexually. He had realised pretty quickly that I had no interest in women, but thankfully he kept my secret. There was only one person in that field that I desired, and he was passing me a bottle with his beautiful smile etched across his face, while our partners lay in the sun.

We lay topless in the grass, either side of Emmeline and Rose, and spoke about work. Emmeline interrupted abruptly:

"Jonah, I meant to ask; mother wants to know what church you prefer."

"Church?" I asked.

"Yes, Jonah ... church. Our mothers have decided to take on the task of organising our wedding. We should be looking as close as August, depending on what church you want."

I couldn't believe what I was hearing—I hadn't even *proposed* to her, let alone discussed a *wedding*.

Emmeline turned on her side to face me.

"Jonah, we have known each other for fifteen years now, and have been together for two. You are twenty for goodness' sake, and I am soon to be the same. If I wait any longer, I'm afraid my lady parts may shrivel and die."

Emmeline and Rose began to giggle.

"Oh, Emmeline. Trust me, sex is not all it's cracked up to be. It's hard enough just trying to get his Johnson sufficiently stiff to perform. I feel that sometimes he simply doesn't fancy me enough."

Rose glared at Billy; Billy ignored her and swigged his ale.

"Well, it would help if you gave me a chance to," he said, in a sarcastic tone.

Rose gasped and placed both hands on her belly.

"Billy, I have told you before: I'm afraid that you might harm our baby. You don't want your ... *thing* so close to its head. You might cause damage."

Billy rolled his eyes and looked out over the river.

"Well, we are going to leave you ladies to soak up the rays; Jonah and myself are going to take a stroll."

"Yes, whatever. Me and Rose can talk about you both, while you're away." Emmeline said, as she lay back down.

"And we can talk about you!" answered Billy, smugly.

"Only good things, ladies," I said, trying to soften the mood.

"Indeed." Emmeline answered, pursing her lips together.

We left the ladies on the grass and walked downstream. Billy took a hanky from his pocket and wiped it over his moist head. His dark skin rippled over his body. He had a tattoo on his upper arm of a red rose, with thorns protruding from its stem; on each thorn was a bead of blood. Billy noticed me studying the work.

"Ah. I got that a few years back. Rose was touched; what she didn't notice was the blood on the thorns. Rose is literally the thorn in my side. Don't get me wrong: I love her and all that, and I'm excited for the baby, but I just can't seem to *really* enjoy her. Do you know what I mean?"

I knew exactly what he meant, as I felt the same about Emmeline. She was to be my wife and, by the sounds of it, I had no choice in the matter. I struggled to love her the way a husband should love a wife but could only love her like a friend or a sister. She was kind and loving, but I felt that what I was doing was a lie. In those times, it was either marry a woman or spend life alone. There was no other option, and being alone was not a position I wanted to be in.

I was tempted to spill out the truth to Billy, but I was afraid of his response. I could tell that he enjoyed our time together a lot more than he enjoyed time with his wife, though.

"No matter what happens, we will always be friends; if only to have someone to talk to about these things. I'm glad you're my friend Jonah; I really am."

He smiled again and looked deep into my eyes. I felt as though his face was coming closer to mine. Was it just my imagination, or was it actually happening? I froze to the spot, not knowing how to react. His eyes began to close, and my heart raced, as adrenaline burst through my body, but before his lips made contact, I pulled away.

"Best we get back to the ladies, before they report us missing."

I pretended I hadn't noticed his advances and strolled ahead, until he caught up.

"You need to try to find out what's happening with that wedding of yours. And I want to be the best man, ya hear?"

His voice was different: almost like he was in a panic and trying not to cry. I put an arm around his shoulder, for reassurance.

"Who else would I choose, Billy? You are already my best man."

Billy looked relieved. It was unspoken, but he knew his secret was safe with me, and I knew that my secret was safe with him. Both of us were gay, and we were falling in love. I still had the words of the bible rattling through my head: 'Man should never lay with man, mortal sin ... blah blah blah.' Looking back now, I'm wondering how I could have been so foolish. I should have kissed him that day, grabbed his hand, and run. To where, I don't know—but it may have saved us both.

The mothers busied themselves with the preparations for the big day whilst life went on. With our combined wages we managed to purchase a family home, close to our friends on the outskirts of town, and fill it with all of the comforts that a young married couple needed. The house was ready, and the date set, but we remained under the care of our parents until the big day arrived. On the night before the wedding, serious doubts flooded my thoughts. I loved Emmeline, but I was positive that I wasn't *in* love with her. Could I really live my life making babies and playing house with a woman that I didn't feel that way about? I didn't want to one day break her heart but, at the same time, I didn't want to live a life alone. My mind swirled with a dark unforgiving pool of 'what if's. What if I couldn't perform for her? What if my own 'Johnson' wouldn't rise to the occasion? Could I really live a life knowing that my whole marriage was a lie? If this was a test, then I had to be sure.

That evening, I slipped out of the front door and walked over to Billy's home. He was alone for the weekend, as Rose was staying with Emmeline, to help her in the morning. I wanted some advice from a man who had made the choice that I was faced with. As always, I let myself into the home and called out Billy's name.

Billy was sitting in the living room, with a bottle of ale in his hand. He was listening to 'Cathy's Clown' by The Everly Brothers, while smoking a hand rolled cigarette. He held up his hand as if to say, 'Hang on til the song has finished.' I leant against the doorframe, with my arms folded, and watched as he tapped his foot to the song. As the song ended, he raised both hands in the air to the final guitar strum, and paused as the music faded into nothingness. He took a single deep breath and turned to me.

"I was wondering when you'd turn up. Having second thoughts, are you? What a surprise. Grab a drink and come join me."

I strolled into the room, sat on the chair beside him, grabbed a beer, and tipped it down my throat.

"What am I gonna do? I don't love her like that, but I don't want to break her heart."

Billy shuffled his body on his chair to face me.

"Jonah ... Jonah ... Jonah. Are ya still following that God stuff? Do you really think God would thank you for breaking her heart? Do you think God wants you to live a life in an unhappy marriage? Do you think that—in time—you will learn to love her, learn to feel turned on whilst squeezing her breasts, learn how to enjoy puttin' a baby in her? Holding her tight on a cold night, her being the last one you see when you turn out the lights, and the first one you see when you open your eyes—can you live life that way? Til one of you dies?"

I was confused. How did he know all of this? Did he just crawl into my brain and read my mind?

I looked at him and frowned.

"I know this because *I* was *you*. I was you, the day before I married Rose. I was sitting where you are, speaking to a friend of mine, *pleading* with him to tell me not to go through with it. But you know what? I *did* go through with it, and *now* look at me: I'm married to a wonderful woman, who I treat like shit—and our baby is due in only a month—but all I want to do is run."

The room fell silent, as his eyes filled with tears.

"I'm in love with *you*, Jonah and, no matter how hard I try *not* to be, the truth always stares me in the face whenever you walk into the room. If marryin' your girl is what you want, then marry her. Either way, no matter what you do, you will be breaking someone's heart."

Billy downed his ale and set the empty bottle on the table.

"There. I said it. Now, I won't stand in the way of your marriage, and I will always be your friend. Rather your friend, than nothing. I will go on living my life and try to be a good father and a good husband. Maybe one day, I'll learn to love Rose like she deserves."

He was right—no matter what I decided, someone's heart would break—and mine too.

I watched as a tear hovered in the centre of his lower eyelid. It stayed for a while, before finally falling down his stubbled face. He casually wiped it away, turning his face from me. Before I knew what was happening, my feet took over and propelled my body over to him. Our lips collided, and his big arms rose up and enveloped me, bringing me closer to him. I felt the beat of his heart, racing within his chest; it beat furiously as I kissed him. It felt like I had finally found what I had spent my life searching for. For that moment, I forgot about Emmeline, Rose, my parents, God. They were all just dreams that faded into mist; they did not exist in this time, in this place. This moment was *ours*—and *only ours*.

We both stood up from our chairs and, with our lips still attached, pulled frantically at each other's clothing, breaking buttons, and tearing material. Our passion electrified the air around us like a million bolts of lightning. We stood naked in the living room, our erect penises pressed against each other, and it felt like we were the only people alive in the world. That night, we made love in the living room, on the kitchen table, and on the stairs. Despite our best intentions, we never made it to the bedroom. Maybe that was a good thing.

When the night had come to an end, I had made my decision:

"I'm not gonna marry Emmeline. I love you too, Billy, always have."

Billy grabbed both of my hands and looked at me, with sadness in his eyes.

"Marry the girl, Jonah. You *have* to marry her."

I couldn't understand what he was saying. I shook my head.

"Why, Bill?"

"Because it's the only way—don't you remember that poor family who had to move on, just because of a rumour? Folks around here don't like two men together; they think it's unnatural. Marry Emmeline, and we can find time to be together. If your God is as good as you say, he will make sure we find time. *That* way, we can *all* be happy. Don't you see, Jonah?"

"But we can run away—far away—where no one can find us."

Billy kissed me tenderly.

"Jonah, I have a baby on the way, and I can't abandon my child, like my father did. That would make me like him, and I don't want to be like him. If we're careful, no one gets hurt."

What Billy was suggesting blew all my religious beliefs out of the water: adultery, dishonesty, homosexuality. I wanted him so badly that I was willing to take the risk, and run away from everything, but life is never that easy. Only ten hours after Billy and I had made love, I was dressed in my best suit, with a crisp white shirt and a white rose in my buttonhole, listening to the wedding march at the front of our local church. I knew that Emmeline would walk up the aisle behind me, dressed in a fancy dress. I also knew that the man I loved was beside me, willing me that everything was going to be okay. When she arrived at my side, her father passed her hand to mine, and we were married in front of our families and friends. I still felt Billy's kisses on my lips, and his big hand squeezing my buttock, from the night before. I felt like it was all a lie, and it was, of course, a huge lie, but nonetheless, I went through with the circus that was my marriage.

At the after-party, I had a little too much to drink, but Billy was there to prop me up, swapping my drinks with non-alcoholic beverages to sober me up. I forgot for a while that it was expected of me to consummate the marriage that same day. I needed my wits about me to perform, but the thought of sex with a woman felt unnatural. As the evening drew on, Emmeline grabbed hold of my wrist.

"Come along, husband. Time to go home."

'Husband': a word that I had trouble swallowing. I looked at Billy, as if to say, 'god help me.' In response, he raised his glass and wished me luck. It was like he was passing me over to an executioner and, in some ways, I felt a little hurt that he didn't want to fight for us, but at the same time I understood why. He was happy to lose his wife, even happy to deal with the prejudice, but his child was different—his child was worth the misery.

I had some trouble becoming hard, not only because I really didn't want to have sex with a woman but, also, because the night before had exhausted my manhood. No matter how hard we tried, I just couldn't perform. That night Emmeline and I slept in our marital bed, in our new home, facing opposite ways. She was angry with me, and she had every right to be. She blamed my drunken state for my flaccid manhood, and I went along with it.

In the morning, I awoke to Emmeline gyrating on my penis. She had seen her chance and, without even consulting me first, took advantage of me. I grew angry and pushed her off and ran to the toilet. I felt dirty and violated—how dare she just take, without asking first?

After washing, I came out and found Emmeline crying on the bed. My feelings were set aside as I comforted her.

"I feel like you only married me because everyone expected it. I feel like you don't really love me."

I kissed her on the head.

"Of course, I love you; you just surprised me, that's all. I wanted our first time to be special, not you poke yourself with my morning hard-on. I mean, that's not really romantic, is it?"

Emmeline wiped her eyes and wrapped her arms around my neck.

"Will you make love to me now, Jonah?"

I kissed her lips, and laid her down in the bed,

"Let's start fresh, shall we?"

I unbuttoned her nightgown to reveal her breasts and kissed them gently while awkwardly squeezing them. I had never lived as a gay man and made love to a woman. It was strange, because the parts of a woman's body that *should* turn me on just did nothing for me. It was when I closed my eyes, and imagined Billy lying in her place, that I managed to hold an erection long enough to achieve my goal. It was done: marriage consummated, and the worst bit over with.

I couldn't help feeling that everything was a mess. My marriage was a lie. I had sinned with Billy and damned my soul to hell. If my parents were to find out, my father would probably murder me, my mother would shun me, and the entire town would order me from my home or burn it down with me in it. Not to mention what Emmeline and Rose would do. Emmeline, in particular, had a foul temper and a violent streak that had only ever reared its ugly head once.

She was teased at school, because one of her breasts grew faster than the other. One girl noticed and pointed it out to a group of boys. The girl in question ended up with a broken nose and jaw. Emmeline was proud to tell everyone that story—if only so that no one else made the same mistake—no one messed with Emmeline.

A few months later the attention was taken off of our new marriage, when Rose and Billy welcomed their new baby into the world. It was a little girl that they named Emma. She was a cute little thing, but was forever bringing up sick; and she cried whenever I came too close. It was like she knew that I was secretly screwing her daddy.

Billy and I met up regularly every Sunday evening, when our wives had their 'girls only' night. Rather than spend the whole night drinking and listening to the radio, talking about sport and work as usual, we had that one evening where we could be ourselves. Billy and I had one rule: 'the two-drink rule'. Every Sunday evening when Billy came to my place, I would have four bottles of ale waiting: two for him and two for me. Nothing sexual would occur until those bottles were empty. It was just in case the women had forgotten something, or came back to surprise us and, on a few occasions, the two-bottle rule saved us from being discovered.

We always made love in the dining room; it was the back room, so it gave us enough time to dress if we heard the key in the front door. It was tense at times, but we made it work.

For three years we carried on with this life and, by the grace of God, we were never discovered. Billy doted on his daughter, and, after a time, I was the favourite uncle. It seemed that either Emmeline or myself had a fertility issue because she never conceived, despite our efforts.

I began to notice a change in her: she grew more depressed every time she bled. I was powerless to help, and even suggested adoption, but that did not interest her. She wanted a child of her own. She wanted to experience pregnancy and a natural birth. All we could do was try and try again. I felt as though this was the price I had to pay for living such a sordid life, and I hated myself for making her so sad, but my love for Billy only grew stronger. I couldn't let him go.

One fateful night brought an abrupt end to our affair, and it was a night that would change everyone's life forever.

The usual Sunday night approached, and Emmeline yet again had the disappointment of a bleed. She went over to Rose's home with tears in her eyes. Rose always made her feel better, so I was pleased to see her go a few hours earlier than normal. A few moments later Billy arrived, looking exhausted because he had worked overtime that week.

"Been kicked out again. As we're early, better make it three bottles."

"I'd say four, just in case," I suggested.

So, we did our usual thing: we drank, and sang to some old songs on the radio. After drinking three bottles each, we reckoned that we'd be safe.

As we lay together on the dining room floor, naked and kissing passionately, a brick was flung through the back window, covering us with shards of glass. It hit Billy's head and knocked him out cold, leaving blood pouring from his head.

"What the fuck?" I yelled. I stood up and looked through the broken window.

At first, I couldn't see anything, because it was dark: no moon shone that night. I checked that Billy was still breathing, and covered his private parts, then I slipped on some shorts and headed back to the window. I brushed any loose glass from the ledge, and glared out into the night, leaning my bare chest onto the window ledge. As my eyes adjusted, I could just make out the outline of a woman hovering in the darkness—it was Emmeline—and her face was full of fury.

"I *knew* something was happening here. Rose said I was being stupid, but I knew. You don't look at me like you do him, and you prefer *his* company over *mine*. God damn you. I came to you for comfort. Rose is pregnant again, and I can't have a baby coz you're too busy fucking Billy."

I tried hard to find an excuse, to make her think that she was just imagining things.

"Don't try and deny it. I saw you both through the gap in the curtains. *I saw you*! Maybe if you made love to *me* like that, we'd have twenty babies already. I loved you Jonah, now you can go to hell."

Her rage took hold as she quickened her pace and charged at me. I stood back, not knowing what to expect. Emmeline grabbed a length of wood from the garden and threw herself at the back door, shattering the lock like it was balsa wood. I glanced at Billy, in the hope that he might help, but he was still out for the count. I scrambled over the shards of broken glass to escape her, but my feet were bare, and the glass pierced the thick skin. In what seemed like an instant, I felt her behind me. I turned to face her, but she roared at me. She swung the piece of wood back and smashed it into the side of my head. After that, all I remember is a loud screeching in my ears, and my eyesight fading to black.

I had entered the darkness, but something was different. It all felt like it always did, apart from one small detail: a small glimmer, like a tiny spider web, was attached to me, and it pulsated with energy. It floated in the air like it was drifting in the breeze. It stretched out far into the darkness, until it disappeared.

I waited for something to happen: for my next life to begin, for the doors of the space beyond to open up and welcome me in; but I was bound to earth by this small glistening thread. As time went by, I watched the thread expand, slowly at first but, after a while, the silk thread grew to be as thick as yarn. It glowed brighter than before and pulsed like a heartbeat. It grew still; eventually its appearance resembled an ethereal umbilical cord, like that of an astral traveller. I began to follow the cord through the darkness but, as I moved forward, it was like gravity pulled me down. My soul fell faster than the speed of light towards the green fields of my town in New Zealand, and into a large white building where I halted abruptly. I was back in the body that I had left behind. My eyes were glued shut, and I couldn't move my limbs. The taste of plastic filled my mouth, and the smell of chemicals raced up my nostrils. I heard beeping and the whirring of machinery. I had no clue what was happening.

"Doctor ... he just jolted ... I think he's back with us."

The voice didn't sound familiar to me at all.

My eyelid was yanked open, and a bright light waved over my iris.

"Jonah ... Can you hear me?"

As my eyes adjusted, I could see the blurred outline of a man with black hair and dark skin. He had glasses on the end of his nose.

"Jonah ... if you can hear me, look to your left."

I still felt confused, but managed to look to my right, which felt more comfortable than the left.

The man raised his brows.

"Ah ... I see you finally decided to join us, Jonah. You gave everyone quite a scare."

I began to panic—what the hell was going on? Why couldn't I move? I could hear the beeping quicken as my heartbeat raced.

"Jonah, please ... you have to relax now. You won't do yourself any good getting so worked up." He turned to the other person in the room.

"Top his morphine up, will you?"

"Yes, doctor."

The room became dark again, as I fell asleep.

For the next few weeks, I was in and out of consciousness. It was a constant routine of staring at walls, or the back of my eyelids. As time passed, the walls appeared more frequently and a kind nurse set up a radio for me, which I greatly appreciated. I so desperately wanted to get up out of the bed and dance, or even just sing along, but my body felt as though it were made of lead. My movements consisted of rolling my head from left to right, and blinking—everything else took so much effort that I simply didn't have the strength.

A doctor came in, with a group of nurses, and they all hovered around my bed.

"Jonah, we are going to remove the ventilator now, because your lungs seem to be working against it. It's a procedure that you need to be sedated for. Do you understand?"

I nodded my head, and a nurse pushed the medicine into the tube attached to my arm. When I awoke, my lungs felt free. I took a deep breath and felt the pleasure of filling my own lungs with oxygen. It was the best feeling I had felt in a long time. I still had oxygen blowing into me from a small tube under my nose, but I liked the smell of that, and it felt comfortable.

A few days later, the nurses sat me up a little, so I could see out of the window to the world outside. It was a city with tall buildings that I did not recognise. I watched as the birds flew past, and the trees swayed in the breeze. I watched the technicoloured sunset, and the ethereal moon cross the sky. The nurses asked me if they could close the curtains, but I always indicated for them to be left open and they respected my wishes.

As time went by, with help from the staff, I managed to lift my arms. The muscles had all but depleted, so I had to build them up again. It was three months before I could finally use my voice. The first words I muttered were to a young nurse taking blood from my arm. I looked at her to gain her attention and used all of the energy I had to move my lips.

"What happened?"

The nurse placed her hand on my cheek.

"Aw ... sweety. Let me go and get the doctor; he can explain it better than I can."

She left the room, returning shortly with the doctor.

"Jonah, I hear you have been asking questions, but I am wondering if you are strong enough for the answers."

I nodded my head and gave him a reassuring look.

"Ok. Well, a year and three weeks ago you were picked up from your home in Herring Street. When the ambulance found you, you had been beaten so badly that the odds of survival were against you. A large laceration on the side of your head had shattered your skull; you sustained a total of eighteen fractures in your left leg, arms, and ribs; your spine was fractured, and so was your neck. We believe that your wife confessed to the crime a few weeks later. A trial was held in your absence, and she is currently in the local jail awaiting sentence. Jonah, your heart flatlined twice on the way to hospital, but restarted of its own accord. You truly are a medical marvel, sir."

I felt numb. As the doctor began to tell me the procedure that they had carried out to save me, I remembered a name that had somehow slipped my mind.

"Billy?"

I stared at the doctor in anguish; I wanted to know if Billy was alright. The doctor flicked through some paperwork.

"I'm sorry, I have no information on a Billy."

When he had finished uttering medical words I couldn't understand, he left the room.

A nurse came to the side of my bed and wiped the drool from my mouth. She bent down and whispered in my ear.

"I'm so sorry, Jonah. I read your story in the news—Billy hung himself a few days after your wife attacked you. I thought you ought to know."

At that very instant, I felt my heart crumble inside my chest. My Billy was dead, and there was nothing I could do. The nurse rested her hand on my shoulder, as I wept for my Billy. He was my love that never truly belonged to me—except for a small part each Sunday night.

As the weeks rolled by, I fell into a deep depression. I refused to exercise my body, or even speak. I welcomed death but, like before, it never came for me. The nights were the same, the days were the same, and I watched them pass time and time again. Life was not worth living, if this was all it had to offer, but in the back of my mind a question kept repeating itself. What else was to come? I was still only a young man, so I had time on my side.

One morning, a new member of staff bounded into my room. He was a nurse in his late twenties, with barrels of energy and a knack for making people laugh. It seemed that he owned a sadness-radar, and it had found me in my bed, staring out of the window at the passing clouds.

"Hello, Jesus of Nazareth. I hear you are the man who rose again. Should I bow or curtsey?"

His camp demeanour shone like the star on a Christmas tree. He was a joy to behold.

"Sweety, you think your day is bad; try finding out that all your pants are dirty, then trapping your willy into your zipper. I'm telling you, my poor little fellow looks like a lighthouse!"

For the first time in a long time, I opened my mouth and laughed so loudly that I almost passed out from lack of oxygen. He was a breath of fresh air, wafting through my dismal tunnel of despair. Every time he entered the room, he would leave me laughing to myself. Sometimes he wore a male nurse's uniform, and sometimes he would wear female attire and a pink wig.

He lived as he chose to, and everyone loved him for it. He was a favourite amongst the staff, who nicknamed him 'Naughty Nurse Betty' or 'Naughty Nurse Bob,' depending on the gender he chose to be that day. He was average build, with a head that was so bald it looked as though it had been polished. Sometimes he painted it with fancy art, and sometimes it would glitter like a disco ball. His eyes were decorated with the most flamboyant makeup, and lashes that touched his brows. I have lived thousands of lives, but never before met anyone with so much energy, humour, and zest for life as my nurse Betty or Bob. They didn't care about religion or rules: what a man should or should not look like. If someone confronted them about their sexuality, or choice of attire, the comeback was quick and witty, leaving the shallow-minded individual stumped for words. Five days a week Betty or Bob appeared, and those were the days I cherished.

One evening, as Bob did his final rounds of the ward, he leant down to my level and whispered in my ear.

"By the way ... *I know*."

"You know *what*?" I asked.

"I can smell it on you. It's like Chanel Number Five, with an added dollop of naughty."

I looked at him and smiled.

"You are like me: would rather have a willy than a wallet. Yeah, I know your sort. I see one every day, when I look in a mirror. From now on, we are paired for life. I decided this while sucking on my after-dinner mint. Now, I will give you a challenge: I give you six months and a day."

"Go on."

I was always up for a challenge.

"Six months and a day to get your sexy arse off that bed, and walk over to me, where you shall receive a big, fat kiss on the lips. I know you want it. I can see those come-to-bed eyes staring at me, you kinky devil."

Of course, he was right; not only did I fancy him, but I also admired him a great deal. I admired the freedom that he had, and his ability to make the saddest people laugh so hard that they wet the bed.

After work, he'd spend time on the children's ward, painting their faces and being silly. He was a great nurse, winning awards for his efforts. On the weekends, he worked at a club: he had a drag act that pulled in customers from all around the country. From far and wide they came to watch 'Miss Dusty Nylons' perform her comedy show. She sang and danced, and her comedy had her audience in stitches. Other members of staff, who were regular visitors to his club, told me all about it in great detail.

I decided that I would take his challenge on and work hard on my therapy. Every day, I'd set a goal and would not sleep until I had achieved it. At first, it was simple things, like lifting a glass or pointing my toes. Pushing myself too hard could set me back; I had to be patient.

My voice was my first achievement—I worked hard every day, and slowly regained every word I had lost. My voice box had not been used in a long time, so finding those words was a task in itself. Singing was a great recovery tool, as it not only exercised my vocal cords, but also raised my spirits. All day, I sang along to the radio, probably irritating the nursing staff because my singing voice had never been very good. As I began to regain my life, I noticed that I was changing: not only physically, but mentally too. I was no longer the young man who put his faith in God, forfeiting his own happiness. I was no longer afraid to announce my sexuality, and I refused to be a victim of a prejudiced society.

No longer would I hide, like a scared child, from those who looked down on me for being different. Not once did I get a visit from family or friends, and that's how I preferred it. Their absence was better than their prehistoric opinions. If there was indeed a God, he made me the way I am, and no earthling had the right to tell that God that he'd got it wrong. I was fed up with being owned—enslaved by ideas that dated back to the dark ages. I was gay and proud, and by God I would walk again.

After three months of painstaking work, I had regained all movement above the waist, and was able to move my feet and raise a knee. I had yet to tackle the part that was the hardest, but unfortunately everything had to grind to a halt. Emmeline's court case was a week away, and I was deemed well enough to attend. My determination to walk into that building was not to be. Even though she had beaten me to the brink of death, it was hard for me to think ill thoughts about her because I had broken her heart and married her under false pretences. I may not have deserved the punishment she handed me, but I *did* deserve to be punished for my deception.

My nurse wheeled me into the courtroom in a wheelchair that supported my back, with straps that held me upright. Emmeline was sitting in the chair next to her lawyer, with her elbows on the table and her hands under her chin. She wore a white blouse, with a grey blazer. Her hair was shorter, and her face was covered in makeup; she had never worn makeup, she'd hated it. She didn't look at me once, but I couldn't help being a little pleased to see her.

As the case commenced, she tried her hardest to blame me for my adultery, but it seemed that times were changing and being gay was becoming more acceptable, especially in the eyes of the law. New Zealand was one of the first countries to decriminalise homosexuality, only a year before the incident, so being a gay man was no longer seen as a crime. The judge seemed to disagree though, chastising me for my part in the case.

Regardless of the circumstances, beating a man practically to death and leaving him with life-changing injuries was a crime. In the end, the jury found her guilty. The judge was not so sympathetic towards me: he sentenced her to a mere year in prison and, because she had already been incarcerated for a fair amount of time, she was allowed to walk free. In some ways, even after what she had done to me, I was happy for her. She had been one of my best friends, and I had broken her heart when her heart was already cracking. I hope that she found happiness with someone that truly loved her. Emmeline may have had a temper, but deep down she was a good person who deserved to be loved. I try not to hold on to too much resentment and hate; I've learnt that keeping such things in your thoughts poisons you slowly. What's the point in that? People who treat you cruelly are the ones who give you the tools to learn and to grow. No one learns lessons from a life that doesn't bring them trauma, either physically or emotionally. Maybe that's why a lot of the wealthy politicians are clueless to the realities of life and lack the empathy they need to run a country successfully.

Anyway, back to the story at hand. My healing continued and, with the help of my amazing medical team, I strived to hit every goal set for me. I had to endure operations to loosen tendons that had become stiff, and also needed splints to help straighten my feet, which had curled inwards. The term 'if you don't use it, you lose it' was a common phrase amongst my doctors.

When I was not working on my functional skills, I was exercising my mind with books brought to me by my best nurse. They were all classics, with worn spines and folded pages, but I was enthralled by every one of them. Wuthering Heights, Sense and Sensibility, Pride and Prejudice, Little women; stories with love and hate, sadness and overwhelming joy. They took me into a world where this life and its struggles did not exist; they plunged me into an era that felt familiar, and into characters that I could relate to.

The nights that I spent staring out of the window into the darkness were no longer filled with self-pity and sorrow, but with enormous dresses covered with lace and frills, hats covered in feathers, and shoes lined with silk, belonging to strong courageous women. They did not comply with the normality of their time, and they burst through the pages to shine brightly, living a life that they deserved. After finishing the book, a nurse treated me to the film 'Gone with the Wind', which thrilled me further still, bringing the images in my head into real-life technicolour.

I made a decision that would truly change my life: I would be who I yearned to be. I wanted to be free—I wanted to be free to dress how I wanted, live how I wanted, and fuck anyone who stood in my way. This life had suppressed me enough, with tales of false gods and stupid rules that made someone like me miserable. I had hurt people in my life, and had contributed to two young children being fatherless, and two women having to struggle without the help of a partner. No more. I was going to be a new person, and Nurse Betty was delighted to hear me ask for her help. When I explained my plan, she shrieked with joy and clapped with overwhelming excitement.

I wanted to feel what it was like to be Scarlet O'Hara. I wanted just a day, where I could stand in front of a mirror, wearing her burgundy velvet gown with crimson ostrich feathers on the shoulders, a red organza shawl draped across the arms, and heels to die for. I wanted to know how it felt when Scarlet walked into that birthday party and stood in the doorway whilst everyone sang. She must have felt such power when everyone stopped singing and looked her way, like she was the only one in that room. Her elegant glow surrounded her, and her confidence drove her on. Deep down, she didn't care that she was the only one at that party with a plunging neckline and bare shoulders. I think she felt glorious.

The next day, Naughty Nurse Betty appeared with a bag of makeup and, when my physio was over, she set to work. I was concerned that the scars would hinder her efforts.

"Hinder? No, my love. When I finish with you, it will be like, 'Pfft. What scars?'"

I lay on my bed and closed my eyes. Betty talked me through exactly what she was doing. The feeling of her soft brushes on my cheeks felt strange, but also very relaxing. She covered my face in what felt like a mask. At first, I thought that she was giving my skin a treatment, but it was the foundation that covered my scars, making them near invisible. My eyes were a little trickier, because they kept watering every time a brush came near. The mascara was like torture, but she kept telling me to 'take deep breaths and look up', while she waved a thin brush covered with thick, black gunge millimetres from my eye. Even in the lives where I had lived as a woman, I had never indulged in too much makeup, and never had I felt the need to elongate my lashes with thick gunk quite as much as nurse Betty.

After what seemed like hours, Betty blew softly over my face and said those words that I longed to hear:

"Finished."

I opened my eyes to see a face that looked like a proud mother. She held a mirror in front of my new face.

"Well, what do you think?"

She smiled nervously, as I gazed at my reflection. The first thing I looked for was the scars. I could still see them, but only just; from a metre or so, I expected that they would be invisible.

My eyebrows were narrow and neatly sat about half an inch higher than their previous location, and my lips were plumper and covered in crimson lipstick. My eyes were my personal favourite: they had a natural brown look, lined top and bottom, with buckets of mascara. Betty had done wonders. The scruffy man, with a scarred face and sad eyes, was now glamorous, and showed confidence and determination in her eyes. Betty stayed behind after her shift and took a seat next to my bed, and together we re-watched Gone with the Wind; she seemed to know the entire script. It was a night I will never forget.

Despite the doctors all telling me I would never walk again, I worked hard to prove them wrong. After five months, three weeks, and four days I stood by myself. My legs screamed at me, but I refused to listen. Every day, I promised myself that I would take a step further, until I had reached the end of my bed. It frustrated me that I could never quite get the courage to let go and trust my balance. I was determined to meet the task set for me, but I just couldn't get past that last hurdle.

At six months and one day, I sat in the chair reading a book while waiting for Betty or Bob to arrive. I had given up trying: I could stand, but I could only take steps supported, and that wasn't the deal.

From the end of the corridor, I heard tapping: a clip-clop of heels on the concrete flooring. I dismissed it at first; it was visiting time, so it could have been anyone. I carried on reading, only to be disturbed again by the staff, clapping and whooping. I placed my book on the bed and leant forward to see what all the fuss was about. I couldn't quite see, so I pulled myself up on the bed and shuffled to the end. I looked out into the corridor and was confronted by a gathering of nurses, with a plume of black ostrich feathers peeking out from the middle.

I watched in amazement, as the nurses stood aside to reveal the most glamorous woman I had ever seen. She had long legs and curvaceous thighs, and a black, sequined dress that was split right up to the hip. Her long crimson hair and makeup made her look just like Jessica Rabbit. I think that was the first time, in that life, that I had ever fallen in love at first sight with a woman. She was truly stunning.

Her eyes spotted me, peering out of the door of my room in my nightwear. She smiled and placed one hand on her hip, and with her other she gave me a cheeky wave, then blew me a kiss. I was confused. What was happening to me? She began to walk closer, her high sparkling heels tapping on the floor, her hips swaying to and fro. My heart raced furiously, and my breathing quickened. She approached my door and held out both hands:

"Dusty Nylons has come for her man. Come to me, Tiger."

It was my Betty, dressed in drag and my god did she look like a movie star. I clung to the bed and shook my head.

"I can't. I need more time. Give me a week."

Dusty signalled a nurse, who handed her something.

"Maybe this little beauty will persuade you."

She curved her hand around the door, revealing a beautiful, crimson, velvet dress with a plunge neckline and ostrich-feathered shoulders. The dress was almost identical to the Scarlet O'Hara dress that I had dreamed of. Its material was thick and luscious—the quality of the piece was second to none. It was then, in the excitement of the moment, that my body pumped out enough adrenalin for my legs to take it upon themselves to walk over to Dusty; if only to have a feel of that amazing dress.

Dusty hung the dress on the doorframe, and wrapped her arms around my neck and gave me a big, long French-style kiss.

"You are coming home with me lover boy, but first you need to get dressed."

"But what about work?"

I knew that there were certain rules about patient-staff relationships: a line that could never be crossed.

"Sweety, I have been working here for free for the last six months. I quit the day I gave you that challenge. I have been playing a part, just so I could be with you. My daddy died years ago, and with no other siblings, his gay son inherited his fortune. A real kick in the dead ribs for him because he hated what I am. So, I took his hard-earned homophobic cash and did what he would never approve of. I bought myself a bar, where me and my sisters make a lot of money dancing and singing for incredibly rich people."

All at once, my room was filled with six other glamorous women, all looking like movie stars. Each was armed with the equipment necessary to transform me into Scarlet O'Hara. They immediately set to work on me, whilst Dusty organised my release papers. Two hours later, I was standing in front of a full-length mirror, surrounded by my new family, looking like Scarlet herself. I gazed upon the elegant, graceful woman in her beautiful dress, unable to breath because of the tightness of my corset. My sequined red slippers were hidden under the dress, because I had not quite reached the heels stage yet. My wig was made from human hair, and looked as though it was made with me in mind. I have never felt so powerful and free.

As I was wheeled from the hospital in my drag, surrounded by my Dusty and the glamour girls, every nurse came out and clapped and cheered. I felt so amazing, and so very loved, but most of all—free.

From that day on, my life grew from strength to strength, and I enjoyed every day that I lived thereafter. For 23 more years we lived, only to be struck down by a disease that took many gay men in that time.

Freedom meant everything, and we loved each other until the day we left that life. Betty Bob died a week before me; they held my hand and smiled.

"I wouldn't change a damn thing. I'll be seeing you, girl."

We didn't say goodbyes, we said 'See you soon.' I only wish I'd met them in that place beyond. I have no doubt that they earned the right to eternal paradise.

\*

Before the question is raised about my timeline crossover, I'll refer you to the title of this book. 'Illusio Temporis' is Latin for 'Illusion of time.' Time is a concept made by humans to make sense of the world; it exists only to please us. I have had a few brief crossovers, but the thought of greeting one of my past lives is a little strange, so if I know I'm living a life elsewhere I avoid it at all costs. I did collide once, but that was for good reason, and I will save that for the next book. For now, I will end this book's journey with a few last words.

This world is filled with conspiracy, corruption, and deceit. It is filled with bad people who would think nothing of shooting you down just to get to their mountain of gold. Some people lack empathy, some of whom rule our lands. Sometimes these people can make you feel hopeless, and unable to enjoy your existence to the fullest. The only advice I can give you is work on yourself. Your soul is the only one that matters to you. Don't poison it with hate, worry, misery, and sadness.

Your soul is here to learn and, the circumstances in your life, be they good or bad, mould your soul into the best version that it can be. Without sounding like a Disney movie, always be kind. Always face problems head on, as every problem has a solution. Most importantly: embrace the bad times, because those are the ones that help us to grow. The worse a situation is, the bigger the reward in this life or the next. Greatness does not come from money; greatness comes from a place where money does not exist. A homeless beggar probably has a richer soul than a millionaire. Be kind, love life, and enjoy yourself. Most of all, be free to be whoever you want to be—whether that is a drag queen or a nun. It's your show—the world is merely your audience.

## SEEKING JOY

Whenever I think that life is bringing me down—maybe I can't find love, I'm poor, of ill health, I can't land that dream job, or have come to an age where my body will no longer allow me to do the things I love—those bad times remind me of how thankful I need to be that I have lived, rather than be ungrateful that I have lived so many lives.

I've often referred to my situation as a curse, or maybe a punishment for an unforgivable crime, and I have to remind myself that I am also blessed to have been able to grow into such a strong character. I'm sure that one day my rewards will be great. Taking my own life just to push my soul a step closer towards my final destination is a myth: life does not work that way. When I have felt the pangs of heartache or failure, or found myself alone in the world, I do feel the heavy burden of life weighing down on my shoulders, but if I choose to end that life too soon I awaken in a life practically the same—sometimes even worse.

I have learned a trick that helps me deal with my depression: it is to find that one joy in life that is capable of pushing all the difficulties to one side. To focus on what brings you joy drowns the sadness until it floods away, even if only for a while. It could be a joy to sing, to dance, listen to music, paint, walk, run, knit, or read—it could be absolutely anything.

Some doubt their abilities, so turn their backs on that which brings them joy. They bury their thoughts in what makes them sad, feeling that it's the only aspect that governs their life.

The truth is, humans feel comfort in their sadness. They close their minds into tight balls, and wallow in that which surrounds them. Depression is like an addiction at times: it can shout the loudest of all human emotions, to the point where we feel that sadness is our primary emotion, and in the end our only friend. For some it has talons that dig deep into their flesh, and a sharp beak that snaps at any joy that comes near. But sadness is lying to you. It's a great deceiver: a trickster, enticing people away from their hard-earned joy with promises that it will never fulfil. Sadness is not the greatest emotion—not by far—and you cannot allow yourself to listen to it all the time. Always try to find that thing which silences it.

I think of that man at Hanover, who knew that he was going to die. Starved to the point of exhaustion, and surrounded by death, yet one tiny corner of his mind clung to a memory triggered by a lock of hair. The memory that brought him joy: that is precisely why the hair was so very significant—not to you or me—but to him.

I think of Ben: born into slavery, knowing nothing more than servitude and pain, covered with scars that told a story like words in a book. The joy of his children running to greet him when he came back from the fields was magical, even though in the eyes of the law, they were legally owned by our white masters. The way his whole demeanour changed the instant those children collapsed into his arms, they gave him so much joy and the will to continue his journey. He had to survive, he had to go on—not only for his children, but for me and himself, for his mother and father, his friends, and all the other slaves who existed in those times. Why do you think singing was so prominent in the black community, and still is, even to this day? Soul music, jazz, even rock: it all came from the slaves. Those who love music, and find joy in music, have them to thank.

Without realising it, black slavery blessed the entire earth with the joy of song, and with song comes dance, happiness, and a smile; sometimes even laughter. Have you ever heard a sad song and began to cry? That is the power that music has, and sometimes a song can be filled with so much emotion that, whether it's good or bad, it touches people. Some songs can even cause an emotional pandemic, rising to number one in the charts in a single night. They are purchased by those who find joy in the words, the tune, or even the voice. My advice to everyone who navigates this ever-spinning globe, is no matter what comes your way, find that one thing that brings you joy. Don't be afraid to smile. Everything is temporary and comes your way to serve a purpose and take good care of your soul.

Ingram Content Group UK Ltd.
Milton Keynes UK
UKHW020027220723
425569UK00001B/5